THE
EDEN
LEGACY

HAROLD GERSHOWITZ

ISBN: 153347897X
ISBN 13: 9781533478979
Library of Congress Control Number: 2016908708
CreateSpace Independent Publishing Platform
North Charleston, South Carolina

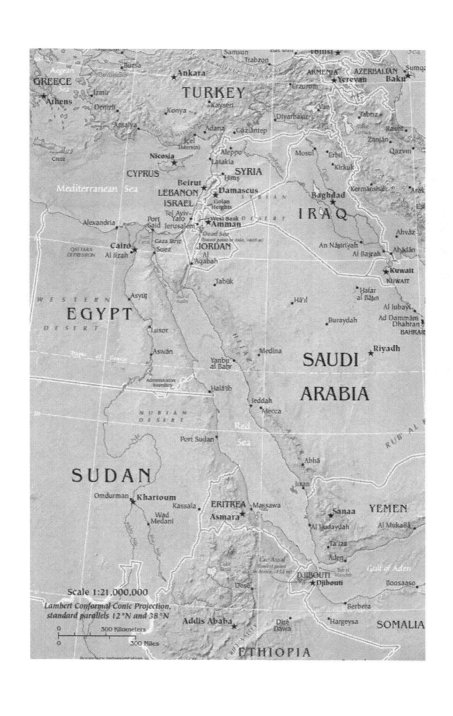

DEDICATION

To Diane, my loving wife of thirty-one years, who has played such an important role in the process of completing each of my novels. Diane's thoughtful suggestions were invaluable in honing the story line of my first novel, *Remember This Dream* (Bantam Books). She was a careful reader of the manuscript for my second novel, *Heirs of Eden* (Amazon CreateSpace independent publishing platform) and this novel, *Eden Legacy* (Amazon CreateSpace independent publishing platform), which is the sequel to *Heirs of Eden*. And, as always, heartfelt tribute to Bayla, my dear late wife, and to our son Steven, both of whom were lost so very young and whose memories I so treasure. And finally, to our children Amy, Michael and Larry, and Danny and Jill.

ACKNOWLEDGMENTS

Heartfelt thanks to my wife, Diane, and to our children—especially Amy Lynn Lask and Larry Kite, who pored over the pages of my manuscript in search of typos, misspellings, and inconsistences. Diane's research many years ago into certain aspects of the Middle East conflict greatly influenced my decision to write *Heirs of Eden*, to which *Eden Legacy* is a sequel.

Special thanks to my good friends and superb readers Gloria Scoby and Terri Ketover. Gloria and Terri carefully read The *Eden Legacy* manuscript and shared with me their comments, edits, and suggestions. The *Eden Legacy* is the beneficiary of the considerable time they devoted to its review.

I would be remiss if I didn't recognize Rema Seddah Manousakis, who as a child fled Jaffa with her family during the fighting in Palestine in 1947. Her journey, which eventually led her to America, closely paralleled that of my fictional character Alexandra Salaman. Rema spent many hours reading the text of *Heirs of Eden*, which preceded *Eden Legacy*, and her recollections and observations greatly enhanced my understanding of the milieu into which I would place my characters.

I express sincere thanks to others who shared with me their unique perspectives on the events that shaped the lives of those in the region who still struggle to find common ground. With heartfelt thanks I recognize Judge Abraham Sofaer, IDF brigadier general (retired) Yitzhak Segev, the late Israeli biographer Amos Alon, the late mayor of Jerusalem, Teddy Kollek, and, finally, the late Arab mayor of Bethlehem, Elias Freij. Mayor Freij gave generously of his time and shared with me his unfulfilled dream of a Holy Land at the center of a prosperous, historic region where peace and goodwill reigned and that would be host to visitors from every corner of the globe. Sadly, his vision remains as elusive today as it was when we met in his office on the West Bank during the first intifada.

Sincere thanks to Robert Habush, one of America's leading trial attorneys, for reviewing the material in The *Eden Legacy* pertaining to litigation and judicial procedure. Jesse Whiting patiently offered an invaluable tutorial on the intricacies of detonation technology and radio frequency jamming alternatives, which was essential to the telling of this story. Special thanks also to Dr. Stephen Prover for his assistance in determining the commercial availability in the United States of pentaerythritol tetranitrate during the period in which this story takes place.

I cannot thank enough those ordinary Israelis and Palestinians who were willing to candidly share with me their stories, their frustrations, and their hopes and dreams for this tortured region they call home. I would be remiss if I didn't pay special tribute to those members of my family, Peninah and Grisha Otiker, now deceased, who, as young pioneers, managed to escape the Nazi rape of Poland nearly eighty years ago and find their way to Kibbutz Yad Mordechai in British Mandate Palestine. They have produced three generations of Sabras—native-born Israelis who have defended their country while seeking peace with their neighbors.

"The truth is rarely pure and never simple."
Oscar Wilde

CHAPTER ONE

JUNE 4, 1967

Thousands of people are about to die, Franklin Markazie thought as he read the morning CIA briefing memorandum for President Lyndon Johnson and shook his head in disbelief. The warm air gently wafting from the small oscillating fan on the corner of his desk caused the document to quiver in his hands.

"Alexandra!" he called out into the *Washington Evening Star*'s cavernous and mostly empty newsroom that hot Sunday afternoon.

"Hi, Frank, what's up?" Alexandra Salaman asked as she walked into the editor's office.

It was just a coincidence that they were both there that Sunday afternoon. It was hot in the building, with the air-conditioning powered off for the weekend. They had only intended to be there for an hour or so. Frank Markazie, the *Star*'s chief editor, had come in to prepare for the Monday-morning staff meeting and to consider assignments for covering the deteriorating situation in the Middle East. Alexandra was simply putting the finishing touches on a story she had written for the Monday-morning edition about the riots in West Berlin. A twenty-six-year-old literature student, Benno Ohnesorg, had been shot and killed two days earlier during a demonstration protesting the visit of the shah of Iran and his wife, the empress Farah.

"I think the Middle East is really going to explode this time. All the saber rattling has the Arabs in a frenzy."

"So what else is new?" Alexandra replied, a touch of sarcasm in her voice.

"I have the CIA memorandum prepared for tomorrow morning's White House briefing."

"Jesus, how did you get that?" she asked.

"Don't ask," he responded, handing her the memorandum. She hesitated for just a moment, glancing at her boss quizzically.

"Go on. Read it," he urged, his eyes riveted to hers.

There were plenty of damn good writers at the *Evening Star*, and most had been around a lot longer than Alexandra, but she was his favorite. A natural—that was what he called her twelve years earlier when he first took her on as a summer intern from McKinley Tech High School. Even then, she could home in on the heart of a story as fast as many of the veterans at the paper. And no one understood the Middle East the way she did. She and her family had fled twenty years earlier from the fighting over in Palestine and wound up in Washington's black inner city living over a tiny corner grocery store purchased for them by a relative who had come to America following the Jaffa riots in 1921. The Salamans, Christian Arabs, were even more alien in LeDroit Park than the Jewish families that seemed to inhabit every other corner grocery store in the city.

Alexandra was an appealing, winsome teenage girl when Markazie first brought her on as a summer intern. Now, a dozen years later, she had matured into an uncommonly striking woman. She had her father Sharif's Arabian olive complexion and her mother Samira's rich deep-brown hair that flowed to her shoulders. It was, no doubt, her mother's lineage—half-Egyptian and half-British—that gave Alexandra her arresting green eyes and delicately sculpted facial features. Slowly, she shifted her gaze to the document he had just handed her. Her eyes narrowed ever so slightly as she began to read.

"The Arabs are sniffing blood. So fast and far does Nasser's bandwagon seem to be rolling that even the Iranian government, long friendly to Israel and bitterly hostile to Nasser, has been compelled to issue a statement mouthing phrases about Muslim solidarity. Tunisian president Bourguiba, the only 'Arab' leader in recent years to suggest publicly some modus vivendi with Israel, has also had his government say that it stands behind Nasser. There can be no assurance that Arab appetites, whetted by unexpected and intoxicating show of unity, will not soon demand further satisfaction."

"The CIA really wrote this?" she asked.

Markazie nodded. "It's in President Johnson's briefing book for tomorrow."

"There's no stopping it now," she murmured, barely above a whisper.

"You think the Egyptians are going to attack?" he asked.

"The Israelis may not wait for the Egyptians to attack," she answered. "Egypt has closed the Gulf of Aqaba and blockaded the Straits of Tiran to all Israeli shipping and, for that matter, any shipping heading to Israel. That's an act of war. Israel is free to fight back."

"So you think the Israelis could strike first."

"Of course they could strike first. These people are deadly serious when they feel threatened, and the surrounding Arab countries and the rest of the world have certainly given them every reason to feel threatened. U Thant has withdrawn the UN peacekeepers from Sinai, and the United States and the Europeans haven't done a damn thing to challenge Nasser's blockade of the straits. What are the Israelis supposed to do? Besides, eighty percent of their army is civilian. They've all been called up, so their economy is at a standstill. How long do you think they're going to stand by and just wait for the Egyptians to strike? Frank, they're going to do something, and I'd bet they're going to do it sooner rather than later."

The editor of Washington's only evening newspaper sat there looking at her, contemplating what she had just said. *She understands this shit better than anyone at the paper,* he thought to himself.

"Yeah, you're living testimony that they know how to strike when they feel threatened," Markazie replied.

"You don't need to remind me," she answered.

"What does your fiancé say about all of this?"

"Not much. The tension over there creates a lot of tension for us here. We mostly avoid talking about it. Deep down, I think Noah assumes my sympathies are with Nasser and the Arabs."

"Aren't they?"

"Frank, Nasser thinks he's winning because he successfully blocked the straits and no one has done a damn thing about it. I think he's bitten off much more than he can chew, and he's probably intoxicated by the hero status he's achieved throughout the region. His fiery rhetoric has created mass hysteria on the streets, and I don't think even he can control it now. Frankly, I think his ego has far outstripped his judgment."

"You think the Israelis can beat back the Egyptians and the Syrians and maybe even the Jordanians, even without French support? Just two days ago, de Gaulle instituted an arms embargo against Israel."

"You don't know these people, Frank. They're smart. I mean they're really smart, and they act very decisively when they have to. They're not just sitting around wondering what will happen next. Nasser has started something the Israelis are probably quite capable of finishing—probably even eager to finish—which is something the Arabs just don't get. Besides, they already have their Mirage jets, so the French embargo is really no big deal. I don't know what the Israelis are going to do, but I suspect Nasser is in for the surprise of his life."

"Do you think the Russians are just going to stand by and watch Egypt square off against Israel? They've armed the Egyptians to the teeth."

Alexandra thought for a moment and then just shrugged. "Who knows? They've been goading the Arabs. Maybe they would like to see Nasser attack."

"I think I agree with you. Whatever happens is going to be quick. I don't see a long-drawn-out fight. Neither Johnson nor Kosygin, nor de Gaulle for that matter, is going to let this escalate into Armageddon."

"No, they all know the Israelis would probably win," Alexandra replied wryly. "Well, whatever happens, the aftermath is going to be awful.

"For whom—Egypt or Israel?"

"For my people, Frank—for the Palestinians who are caught right in the middle. The Israelis and the Egyptians will fight this battle and then go back to their lives as usual. My people will live with the continuing trauma of statelessness."

"Do you still think of yourself as a Palestinian, Alexandra?" Markazie asked.

"I *am* Palestinian, Frank. I may be an American now, but I was born in Jaffa, remember? If you're asking whether I feel for them, the answer is yes. And, for the record, I feel for the Israelis too. Life is going to be endless conflict for both peoples."

"That's not what I'm asking, though."

"I'm an American woman, damn it," she snapped, a touch of ire in her voice, "an Arab American woman who is engaged to marry a Jew, and yes, I come from Palestine…or what used to be Palestine. So, what's the point?"

"My point is that you're pretty much one of a kind, Alexandra. Like I told you years ago when you were just an intern here, you're an Arab girl who became an all-American girl in love with an all-American guy who just happened to be a Jew. Then you go off to college in Beirut, get mixed up with terrorists, and, causing an international incident, get yourself rescued by an Israeli agent. Then you get kidnapped by a terrorist and rescued yet again, this time by the Israeli army. You're a one-woman saga, Alexandra."

"So let me ask again, what's the point?"

"There isn't another newspaper in the country that has anyone like you to cover the conflict over there. You know the people on both sides, and God knows you've lived the conflict from every angle."

"Frank, I'm not a war correspondent, damn it. You want someone to cover the war, go hire Martha Gellhorn away from *Atlantic Monthly*."

"But the war isn't the conflict I had in mind, Alexandra. We both know that, one way or another, the war is going to be over before you could even get there."

"Frank, whatever are you talking about?"

"The peace, the *aftermath* as you just called it, Alexandra. That's going to be the big story. You tell me, who in this entire country can cover that story better than you?"

"You can't be serious."

He looked at her, cocking his head just a bit to one side, his lips slightly curled, almost mischievously.

"Oh my God, you *are* serious," she replied incredulously.

"Alexandra, war is about to break out, and from the stuff I've been reading I think it will be quick. After the bloodletting stops, I believe one of the biggest stories of the century will start unfolding, and we are going to have someone there to cover it. Why don't you chew on that overnight and come back tomorrow and tell me who on our staff can best do that?"

She stood there staring at him. The thought of going back was, just moments ago, out of the question. The thought of someone else going in her place was, she knew, also out of the question.

"Frank, all of the wire services will be sending dispatches to us from their bureaus in Cairo and Tel Aviv," she said, without conviction.

Markazie peered over the rim of his reading glasses. "Is that what you think we should do, Alexandra, pull stories off of AP and UPI Teletype machines?"

"You don't know what you are asking of me, Frank."

"I think I merely asked you to recommend whom we should send to Tel Aviv, or depending on who wins this slugfest, maybe to Cairo, to cover what I think will be the biggest story of the decade."

Alexandra knew she was trapped. The *Evening Star* was going to send a journalist to the Middle East.

"*Shit,*" she murmured under her breath as she turned and stormed from Markazie's office.

"Alexandra!" he yelled after her, tauntingly. "You tell me what reporter we should send to cover this story?"

CHAPTER TWO

Noah Greenspan sat at his desk reviewing plans for the grand opening Monday morning of Potomac Center, the massive urban-development project that had occupied all of his time for the last four years. It seemed that all the i's were dotted and the t's crossed. The property was almost entirely leased, and all the local newspapers and television stations were expected to cover the press conference at the opening. Even the networks were going to be there as well as a number of national magazines. It all seemed too good to be true. And, perhaps, it was. His sanguine mood was soon interrupted by the buzz of his telephone intercom.

"Yeah, Barb," Noah answered.

"It's Ed Scallion. He said it was urgent."

"Hi, Ed, what's so urgent?" Noah asked as he snapped up the phone.

"Noah, I think we have to change the program around a bit tomorrow."

"Why, Ed? We've been over the plans a hundred times."

"So what? If they need changing, we should change them. I'm supposed to be your go-to guy for marketing and promotion."

"You are my go-to guy, Ed, and we wouldn't be where we are without you and *Urban Architect*. Your magazine put us on the map. So what do you want to change tomorrow?" Noah heard Ed take a deep breath before he started to respond.

"I think we should scratch Yusuf Salaman from the program tomorrow," Ed replied.

"Bullshit!" Noah answered, irritably. "Yusuf designed the whole goddamned project, and you think we should scrub him from the program tomorrow?"

"Yeah, I do, Noah. I think he might soon be toxic with all this shit going on over in the Middle East."

"Oh, come on, Ed. Let's not replay that song. You thought he was going to be toxic when we selected him as our architect in the first place. Well, you were wrong then, and I think you're wrong now."

"Jesus Christ, Noah, don't you read the papers? A war is about to break out any minute, and everyone in this country is fed up with all of the Arab saber rattling."

"Yusuf isn't rattling any sabers, and he isn't on the program to talk about the Middle East. He's our architect, for God's sake. We cancel him, and that will become tomorrow's news."

"He gives talks about the plight of the Palestinians all the time, Noah."

"Well, that won't be what he'll be talking about tomorrow. There's no way I'm cutting him out of the program. No fucking way."

"And what about Alexandra, Noah?"

"What about Alexandra?" Noah snapped, sharply.

"Look, Noah, I love that girl as much as you do, and I can't wait to dance at your wedding. Everybody loves Alexandra, but…"

"But what, Ed?" Noah yelled, his knuckles turning white as he tightened his grip on the phone.

"Jesus Christ, Noah, what's wrong with you? Your fiancée is an Arab, your architect is an Arab, and whether you like it or not, you're the Jew who is going to open Potomac Center tomorrow, and you'll probably be sharing the news on TV and in the daily papers with coverage of Arab mobs screaming death to the Jews. Noah, it was barely five years ago that Alexandra was on the front pages over that terrorist shit in Israel."

"She saved a lot of Israeli lives, Ed," Noah replied, calmly.

"Yeah, and that'll be in the news coverage too, Noah. I love Alexandra and Yusuf, but we want the news to be about Potomac

Center, not about the Jewish developer and his Arab connections. I'm telling you, this could be a PR nightmare."

"Go to hell, Ed" Noah replied, his voice now more melancholy than angry.

Ed Scallion knew when it was futile to argue with Noah. "You're going to drive me to drink, Noah."

"If I didn't drive you off the wagon four years ago when we selected Yusuf, I doubt that you'll jump into the sauce now," Noah replied sympathetically. "Ed, Yusuf stays on the program, and let's leave Alexandra out of this."

"OK, have it your way. Just remember that I told you I thought it was a bad idea."

"Fine, Ed. I'll remember. It's etched in my brain."

"OK," Ed replied, drawing out the word to emphasize his disapproval.

"Good-bye, Ed. See you tomorrow…and Ed, I do understand and appreciate your concern—about everything. See you tomorrow."

Noah leaned back and ran his fingers through his hair while he collected his thoughts. He knew Ed had every right to be concerned. The papers and television newscasts were full of hysterical Arab mobs screaming "death to Israel" and endless coverage of anti-Israel street demonstrations throughout the Middle East. Many of the Potomac Center tenants were Jewish. Myron Abrams, senior vice president of Capital City National Bank, his financier, would be there, as would David Wald of Fenner, Wald and Nolan, the Chicago architects who teamed up with Yusuf to design the project. Even his rabbi from Washington Hebrew Congregation would be there as his guest. *Just what I need,* Noah thought, *the closing of the Gulf of Aqaba competing with the opening of Potomac Center.*

CHAPTER THREE

Yusuf Salaman and Associates was located on the top floor of an old renovated five-story warehouse overlooking Baltimore's historic Inner Harbor. The land abutting the port was about to be transformed into one of America's most exciting urban-renewal projects, and Yusuf had been one of the young architects working on the project ever since he graduated from Yale seven years earlier. The Inner Harbor project had monopolized nearly all of his time. But that, of course, changed when Noah Greenspan selected him to be the architect for Potomac Center. Now, he was one of a select group of young architects who were making history as America began the task of remaking its inner cities through a series of massive urban-renewal projects. Yusuf stood, taking in the view through the floor-to-ceiling window behind his desk. He absently sipped the strong black coffee, which he had picked up on his way to work as he did every morning at Jimmy's, a favorite breakfast eatery a few blocks away over on Broadway. He enjoyed starting his workday looking out over the old port and the old McCormick Spice building that towered over the arca, from which the strong suggestion of vanilla drifted across the entire waterfront. Yusuf sometimes quipped that he couldn't start the day without looking at the huge McCormick Spice sign atop the nearby building and deeply inhaling the rich vanilla aroma.

A few moments later, Yusuf sat down at the oversize drawing table he used as a desk and glanced down at the business card his visitor had just handed him. The man had introduced himself as Abu Salma,

managing director of AASLF Ventures. After the briefest of pleasant-
ries, Mr. Salma began describing the project he said he and his associates were developing in Palestine, or as he corrected with a shrug of
his shoulders, Jordan, given the nakbah, or catastrophe, of 1948. It was
almost as though he were describing Potomac Center. Abu Salma explained that the large commercial project, Palestinya Center, would be
in the heart of the Jordan Valley, with Ramallah to the north, Jerusalem
and Bethlehem to the south, and Jericho to the east. "There will be hotels and casinos, but at the core we envision a commercial and residential center very much like your Potomac Center," the Palestinian
explained enthusiastically.

"It's not exactly my commercial center," Yusuf replied. "I'm just the
architect."

"Yes, yes, I understand," Abu Salma replied. "But you designed the
entire project. Isn't that right?"

"Of course—that's what architects are retained to do, but I have no
ownership in the project."

"But of course—we understand that perfectly well. But we could retain you to help us with the architecture we'll need for our project, yes?"

"If I may ask, exactly who are 'we'?" Yusuf replied, glancing down
once again at the man's business card.

"We're a relatively new Middle East investment and development
group. The S is for *Salma*—that's me of course—and the other initials
simply stand for our primary investors, who are all passive, or as you
say in America, silent partners. So, as I was asking, could we retain you
to help us with our project?"

"Yes, me or any other architect. But I have to tell you this project
of yours sounds crazy to me. Poor people populate most of the region.
Why in the world would you select such a place for an expensive project of this magnitude? Where do you ever expect to find a market for
your project?"

"Was Las Vegas such a prosperous area before it became such a
huge tourist attraction?"

"You expect people to flock to Palestine like they do to Las Vegas?" Yusuf asked, incredulously. "You have to be kidding."

"Mr. Salaman," the Palestinian continued, "soon, as you observed, the entire matter of Palestine will be settled. There will be nothing like our project anywhere in the Middle East. Only Beirut will rival what we have planned. We are in the middle of the most historic areas in the world—the Holy Land, as the Christians call it. I'm telling you people will come from all over—from Europe, from the entire Levant, even from America. The Christians will come in droves."

"You're assuming Nasser and the Arabs will win the war that's about to break out."

"Of course Nasser will win, but it doesn't matter if he doesn't. If the Israelis win, even more people will come. Let the Jews come with everyone else. They can stay at the King David Hotel in Jerusalem and visit Rachel's Tomb on the short drive to our new Palestinya Center. Twenty years ago the Jews in this area called themselves Palestinians. I grew up listening to the Palestine Symphony Orchestra. All the musicians were Jews. I remember, as a ten-year-old, when Arturo Toscanini came to conduct the orchestra. I'm telling you whether Nasser or, God forbid, the Jews prevail in the battle that's about to take place, the new Palestinya Center we are planning will be a huge success. This area is going to be a mecca for tourists the world over."

"Well, I wish you well," Yusuf replied after considering his visitor's vision for his Palestinya project. "So, what do you want from me?"

"We would like to purchase your architectural plans for Potomac Center. It could save us precious time and money in planning our project. What would you consider to be an appropriate fee to provide us with the plans for Potomac Center?"

Yusuf sat back in his chair and contemplated the man sitting across from him and what he had come to ask. "They're not my plans to sell. They belong to Potomac Center," Yusuf finally replied. "You should come to Washington with me tomorrow for the opening of Potomac

Center, and I can arrange for you to meet the developer, Noah Greenspan. Maybe he'll sell you the plans, but, frankly, I doubt it."

"I'm afraid I have to leave tomorrow morning. I don't think I can do that."

"That's too bad," Yusuf answered. "You've come this far; you should really let me introduce you to Noah. You could also meet my parents and my sister Alexandra. In fact, Alexandra would love hearing about Palestinya Center. She's a reporter for the *Washington Evening Star* and has covered news involving Palestine pretty extensively. She would probably find your vision for Palestinya Center something she'd want to write about."

"Yes, yes, I'm sure she would," the Palestinian replied, the slightest trace of sarcasm in his voice. "But I'm afraid it will not be possible. Perhaps on my next trip to the area."

"I'm sorry I can't help you. You'll have to talk to Noah Greenspan if you want to use the architectural plans for Potomac Center."

"Maybe you could provide the plans, just temporarily, as a consultant to our project. We wouldn't have to buy them. Perhaps we could study them for just a week or so while we commence with our planning. It could be part of a consulting arrangement."

"I couldn't do that," Yusuf replied. "It would be highly unethical."

"But what if this Mr. Greenspan gave you permission? Surely you could discuss this with him. Couldn't you just ask him?"

"It would be more appropriate for you to meet Noah and ask him yourself. I can give you a copy of the manual of architectural-design criteria, which is available. It's given to every tenant, but if you want anything more detailed than that, you'll have to ask Noah Greenspan."

"Ah yes. This design manual might be very helpful. I would appreciate that very much."

Yusuf excused himself to retrieve a copy of the manual and returned a moment later, handing the generously illustrated document to the Palestinian.

"You might find this helpful," he said. "And anytime you would like to meet Noah, I'll be glad to make the introduction."

"Well, yes, I appreciate that. Perhaps we might do that. It's just that I would prefer working with you. You understand, don't you?"

"You mean because you don't want to ask Noah because he's Jewish?"

"Let's just say we preferred asking you because you're Palestinian and you are passionate about our people."

Yusuf studied the man thoughtfully for a moment before responding. "I'll be glad to introduce you to Mr. Greenspan," Yusuf finally replied. "That's how I can best be of service to you."

"Well, let us consider what you propose," the man replied, as he stood to leave.

"You could also go through some back issues of *Urban Architect*," Yusuf suggested as he accompanied his visitor to the elevator in the reception room. "They covered the project very thoroughly from the very beginning. In fact, they ran a number of schematics of the layout. Of course, they're not nearly as detailed as the architectural drawings, but they would give you a darned good idea of the layout, and they have been in the public record for quite some time now."

"This *Urban Architect* you speak of…It's a magazine?"

"Yes, of course. You're not familiar with *Urban Architect*?" Yusuf asked, somewhat surprised.

"No, I'm not. We've been following the project through stories in the *International Herald Tribune*."

"Ah yes, I've seen those stories," Yusuf replied. "That was just some PR, you know, publicity about the project."

"And this *Urban Architect* magazine…Where can I buy it?" Abu Salma asked.

"I would just call the magazine. It isn't sold at newsstands—only by subscription," Yusuf replied. "It's written for architects."

"Ah, a trade journal."

"Exactly. They're located over in Washington. Call Ed Scallion's office. He's the publisher. Tell him I suggested you call. I'm sure Ed will be glad to help."

"Thank you, Mr. Salaman. This is very helpful."

"Really, you should let me introduce you to Noah. He's a great guy and would probably be willing to help. You never know—maybe he would want to invest in Palestinya Center."

"Yes, one never knows," the Palestinian replied, with a smile.

And with that, the man who called himself Abu Salma shook hands with Yusuf, turned, and departed. He had no intention of going to Washington to see Noah Greenspan and certainly not Yusuf's sister, Alexandra. *I will see her soon enough,* he thought. Yusuf's ethical bearing and his loyalty to Noah presented a wrinkle the Palestinian hadn't anticipated. He had hoped to leave with the drawings for Potomac Center in his hands. He thought he had presented a perfectly plausible reason for wanting the architectural drawings for Potomac Center. But, of course, the story he told Yusuf about plans to develop a project called Palestinya Center was no truer than the name he had taken, Abu Salma, for his meeting with Yusuf. Omar Samir lit a Turkish Murad and inhaled deeply before stepping from the building to hail a cab back to the Hotel Baltimore.

CHAPTER FOUR

Karen Rothschild reached for the phone on her desk before leaving her office high atop Chicago's 35 East Wacker Drive, once the tallest office building outside of New York. She would soon join a few colleagues for cocktails and dinner—just a small celebration among friends on the evening of her twenty-ninth birthday. But first she wanted to make one last call, one she had put off all day. She stood and glanced down at the Chicago River as it ambled slowly west, away from Lake Michigan and past the Wrigley Building twenty stories below. The clock on the South Tower signaled that she had only a moment or two to make her call. She took a deep breath and slowly began to dial the Washington, DC, number. She could feel her heartbeat quicken as the receptionist on the other end answered the phone.

"Potomac Center," the voice said cheerfully. "How can I direct your call?"

"Noah Greenspan," Karen replied, a hint of anxiety in her voice.

"Noah Greenspan's office," a familiar voice announced, a moment later.

"Hi, Barb, it's Karen—Karen Rothschild. I wanted to call and wish you guys well on the opening tomorrow."

"Karen?" Noah's secretary replied excitedly. "Karen, is it really you?"

"It's really me," Karen replied, relieved by the warmth in Barb's voice.

"Karen, let me get Noah for you before he leaves the office. I know he'll be excited to hear from you."

"You think?"

"Yeah, I think...Hold on."

"Greenspan."

"Hi, Noah, it's me. I'm just calling to congratulate you and wish you well tomorrow."

"Karen..." Noah answered, his voice trailing off for a moment.

"I've been following the project in the press," she answered before he could continue. "Ed Scallion has sure pulled out all the stops to promote the opening."

"Karen, I'm...so glad you called...How are you?" he asked, haltingly. It had been nearly four years since they had spoken—since their bitter disagreement over Noah's selection of Yusuf to design Potomac Center and Alexandra's sudden return from the Middle East, and the breakup of their engagement. "It's been so long. I don't know where to begin."

"Look, I don't want to keep you. It sounded like you were about to leave the office. I just wanted you to know that I was thinking about you and that I wish you and the Potomac Center every success."

"You're one in a million, Karen. I can be a little late for my next meeting," he said, not wanting to rush the conversation. "I want to know more about you. What are you up to?"

"I'm good, Noah. I'm the marketing director for Mid-America Ventures. We're a boutique investment-banking firm mostly specializing in promising start-ups," she replied. "How's Alexandra—and your mom and dad?" she quickly added.

"Alexandra is great, and my folks are both well. Thank you for asking. Are you—"

"Still single?" she interrupted, with a slight laugh.

"Well..."

"Yes, I'm still a bachelor girl. It's a long story. Can you imagine? Still single and almost thirty?"

Noah paused, awkwardly.

"Yes, Noah. Today's my birthday," she said teasingly.

"Of course, of course," he replied, clumsily. "Happy birthday, Karen."

"Can you believe it's been almost twelve years since we first met at Stanford?"

Noah sighed into the silence. "God, twelve years—so much has happened," he said, awkwardly.

"I'll let you go, Noah. I know how busy you must be. Good luck tomorrow."

"Karen..."

"Yeah..."

"I...I wish you could be here—for the opening, I mean."

"Good-bye, Noah...Good luck tomorrow," she replied, a sad, faint quiver in her voice.

CHAPTER FIVE

Six thousand miles to the east, Amos Ben-Chaiyim stood on the small dimly lit balcony outside his room at the Eilat Hotel. He stared into the darkness enshrouding the Gulf of Aqaba, contemplating what was about to happen in only a few hours. The night was deathly still but for the sound of waves collapsing on the beach below. He hadn't had a decent night's sleep in days. Shortly, by first light, his country would once again be at war for the third time in two decades. War, either fighting it or preparing for it, had become life's constant for the young Jewish nation. He reread, once again, the intelligence dispatch and breathed a sigh of relief. The gamble he promoted had worked. The Egyptians had taken the bait and moved their navy from the Mediterranean through the Suez Canal and into the Red Sea, far from where the real action would be.

Amos understood just how vulnerable Tel Aviv would be to a naval attack. The fledgling Israeli Navy could not stand up to a Russian-supported Egyptian naval assault, and he knew the Israeli Air Force would be preoccupied and overextended elsewhere. Israel's Mediterranean coastal cities would be terribly vulnerable if the Egyptian gunships could reach them.

The audacious plan for which he had argued had worked after all. His team had convinced the Egyptians that the Jews were going to strike far to the South at Sharm el-Sheikh, where the Gulf of Aqaba and the Gulf of Suez converged into the Red Sea. That was where the Jews had struck in 1956, and he had made a strong case to the high command that Israel had to convince the Egyptians that that was where they would strike again. At first, few senior IDF officers thought it was possible. They questioned whether Israel could spare thousands of men to conspicuously travel south to act as decoys when they would be needed for the battles far to the north in the Sinai at Rafa and Abu Agheila. Amos argued that it wouldn't take a large troop movement but just the appearance of one.

A grand deception might be pulled off, he argued, with only a handful of men. The plan was outrageously simple. Israel had at its disposal several useless old surplus landing craft. Amos wanted to load the landing craft on transporters and send them south in a convoy to Eilat by day and then return them undetected at night. The process could be repeated each day during the week leading up to the actual assault that would be launched into the Sinai well north of Eilat. The ploy worked. The Egyptians detected the constant movement of landing craft to the Israeli port of Eilat and assumed an invasion force was going to be launched from Eilat through the Gulf of Aqaba against Sharm el-Sheikh, far to the south. The Egyptian Navy, having redeployed into the Red Sea, would be of no use to Nasser, and if things went according to plan, the war would be over before the fleet could be redeployed. Not a single shell would be fired at Tel Aviv.

Amos, feeling both elation and a hint of dread, left the hotel to head north. The air rushing over the windshield of his 1957 camouflage-painted Land Rover offered no relief from the heat, even at two o'clock in the morning. Amos sped from Eilat into the Negev toward Beersheba, the headquarters of Israel's Southern Command. There he would join other intelligence officers and follow the progress of the war, which he knew would erupt in a little over five hours. His team had done its work well.

Amos was surprised by Nasser's bellicosity, given the haphazard way his armed forces had been mobilized. So certain were the Egyptians that Israel would not strike first that they sent seven divisions into the Sinai ahead of the most basic provisions. Food and water deliveries lagged behind troop deployments by as much as two days. Israeli agents observed thousands of men, many still wearing civilian peasant clothes, being called up and rushed into the desert. The enemy, it seemed, was rushing into the Sinai long on rhetoric and short on readiness. It had been a tense three weeks. Nasser had recklessly cast the die when he closed the Straits of Tiran. It was a blatant act of war that the world seemed quite willing to tolerate.

President Johnson's call for an international armada to sail through the straits had been roundly ignored. Secretary General U Thant removed all of the UN peacekeeping forces from the Sinai within hours of Nasser's request that they leave. Israel stood alone. Its people, tuning in to Arab broadcasts, listened as Nasser declared, "The battle will be a general one, and our basic objective will be to destroy Israel." Iraqi president Abdul Rahman Arif publicly boasted, "There will be practically no Jewish survivors," and Syria's defense minister, Hafez al-Assad, proclaimed, "The time has come to enter into a battle of annihilation."

And so, once again, the Jewish nation quietly, reluctantly, and resolutely mobilized for war. The entire citizen army of 205,000 men and women, nearly 10 percent of Israel's entire Jewish population, left their jobs and their homes to augment Israel's standing army of 70,000. Amos knew they were ready—even if Israeli prime minister Levi Eshkol wasn't so sure. The entire country knew that war was inevitable when on June 1 news broke that Eshkol had, reluctantly, called Moshe Dayan out of retirement to assume the defense portfolio. It was a pivotal moment. Only days earlier Chief of Staff Yitzhak Rabin had been treated to a tongue-lashing by the old man, Israel's retired first prime minister, David Ben-Gurion. The elderly Ben-Gurion did not believe Nasser intended war even if Nasser was running at the mouth as though he did. Ben-Gurion berated Rabin for mobilizing for what the old man felt was an avoidable war. Ben-Gurion's dressing down had badly shaken Rabin, and there had been a moment of grave indecision, but that ended when Dayan was named minister of defense.

Egypt was going to get the war it was demanding whether it really wanted it or not.

Amos was pleased at how ready Israel was for the coming battle. He had every reason to be. He and his people had provided the military with valuable intelligence. They had operatives everywhere. They knew when the enemy airmen ate and what they ate. The schedules of every important Egyptian commander had been carefully noted day after day, and Amos knew the rank and file would be paralyzed if an attack came when their commanders were not in a position to communicate with them. The Israeli military was ready for war. All they needed was the order to act.

Eshkol, however, dreaded the prospect of war with Egypt, and everyone knew it. Bringing Dayan back signaled to the nation that the prime minister had given up on a peaceful way out. His poorly delivered and confusing radio message to the nation just a few days earlier had been a disaster. Israelis were being treated to nonstop news coverage of Nasser strutting about, flexing his muscles, and claiming that he was about to launch a total war, the objective of which would be the annihilation of Israel. Eshkol, meanwhile, was still pursuing diplomatic solutions, but to no avail. Dayan's return changed all of that. There was no turning back.

Every Israeli understood that if Israel didn't respond to Nasser's reckless blockade of the straits, the deterrence value of its armed forces would evaporate, causing events to spiral out of control very quickly. Amos was certain that Nasser's incessant calls to arms and the nonstop coverage on Egyptian television of street mobs crying "death to Israel" wasn't routine Arab bluster. Nasser had intoxicated the Arab streets with a nasty and hateful brew. The war genie wasn't going to be bottled up again without a lot of blood being shed. Just three days earlier, Amos had received a dispatch from his intelligence sources in Aden that Egypt had quietly begun redeploying three brigades from Yemen to join the huge force Nasser had already sent to Sinai. *Nasser must be crazy,* Amos thought. He knew Nasser had now rushed seven divisions into the nearby Sinai Desert. Nasser no doubt believed that a concentration of at least one hundred thousand Egyptian troops would be an intimidating and fearsome show of strength. Amos, on the other hand, saw it as a disastrous concentration of sitting ducks.

***

Israeli Air Force commander Motti Hod excitedly strode into Chief of Staff Rabin's modest office with the most current intelligence reports in hand. Amos and a phalanx of other intelligence officers had, indeed, done their work well. They had, essentially, won the war in the weeks before the fighting began. The Israeli military was provided the hard intelligence it needed to assure a fast and decisive victory. The Israelis knew everything they needed to know. The Arabs, led by the Egyptians and hell-bent on holy war, knew next to nothing by comparison.

"Yitzhak, my pilots can destroy the enemy's airpower by noon—early afternoon at the latest," Commander Hod reported excitedly. "Nasser's troops will have no air cover in the Sinai."

"The Egyptians have over five hundred fighter planes. You think you can destroy them by noon?" Rabin replied, a touch of skepticism evident in his voice.

"Yes, and all of Jordan's and most of Syria's. Our people have been tracking them night and day for two weeks. They never deviate from their schedules. They take off on their routine patrols at dawn and begin landing an hour later to go to breakfast. By a quarter to eight, every plane is on the ground, and every pilot is having breakfast. That's when we strike."

"I wish we could match them plane for plane," the chief of staff replied.

"Actually, we can," Commander Hod continued. "Yitzhak, we can refuel and rearm our planes in eight minutes. We've practiced doing it over and over again. We can have a plane refueled and rearmed and over its next target an hour after it completes an attack. No other air force in the world can match that. It is, effectively, like having two or three times the number of planes we actually have. It takes the Arabs at least an hour to refuel, rearm, and turn around their fighter aircraft."

"We have to totally neutralize their air capability at the very outset of the war. Otherwise, they'll cut our ground forces to ribbons."

"Yitzhak, you can trust our pilots. They'll do their part. The enemy's air forces will not be a factor in this war. I'm positive."

Shortly before Amos reached Beersheba, at around five that morning, Egyptian pilots began climbing into their Russian-supplied MiG fighters to begin their morning patrols, just as Commander Hod said they would. Their routine was also as predictable as he had said. They returned from their uneventful flights, left their planes, and joined other pilots for breakfast around seven o'clock. Most of those MiGs would never fly again.

As the Egyptian pilots began a leisurely breakfast, the first Israeli airmen lifted off in their Dassault Mirage fighter interceptors and their Super Mystères. The young pilots flew out just a few feet over the Mediterranean, below the gaze of radar, and in groups of four they headed to each of the thirty-two Arab air bases in Egypt, Jordan, and Syria and one in western Iraq. Israel was only minutes away from preempting its foes in its third war in twenty years.

***

Twenty-five miles south of Beersheba, Benjamin Bar-Levy pondered the note that had just been handed to him only moments earlier by Brigadier General Ephraim Meyer. Two unauthorized, non-Israeli, high-altitude jets had briefly flown over the very complex in which they sat.

"Commercial airliners off course?" Bar-Levy asked, knowing full well the preposterousness of his own question.

"Wishful thinking," General Meyer replied. "Too high and too small, and commercial airliners don't fly in pairs."

"Egyptian?"

"Maybe—or, perhaps, Russian."

"Reconnaissance?" Bar-Levy murmured, more a statement than a question.

"The Egyptians know what we're doing here, Benjamin. That we've kept it quiet this long is a miracle. Not even the Americans fully understand what we are doing here."

"Everyone knows this is restricted airspace," Bar-Levy replied. "They would only fly aircraft over this spot if they knew we couldn't reach them in time to stop them."

"Do you think the Egyptians are planning to bomb here?" General Meyer asked.

"I don't know, but it sure looks like they could have been scoping the facilities for a bombing run. They have to know we have more cooling capability than any peaceful purpose would require." Bar-Levy paused, glanced at the note again, and then looked up icily, peering into Meyer's eyes. "Who knows about this?"

"Right now, just you, and that's only because you're here. I've put an urgent call into Eshkol, Dayan, and Rabin. I should have them on the line in a moment or two. You're Mossad, and they'll want you on the call. That's why I've shared this with you."

"All hell will break loose if word of how far we've progressed gets out. We won't have a friend in the world. The Americans will be livid. This makes a mockery of their push for nonproliferation. The Russians might attack and—who knows?—the French might just cheer them on. President de Gaulle is furious over the extent of French involvement in all of this."

"What the hell are we building the damn nuclear weapons for if we're that worried what the world will think when it learns we have them?" Meyer replied.

"Look, fifteen years ago when we started building this doomsday program with the help of the French, we didn't care what the world thought of us. We were still recovering from Europe's orgy of hate. Fuck the world, like the world tried to fuck us, was what we thought. Going nuclear would be our ace in the hole, our never again. That's what we thought then, and that's exactly what we should think now."

"Then why all the hand-wringing?"

Bar-Levy paused and, slowly, thoughtfully, shook his head and sighed. "Maybe it's too soon for everyone to start hating us again."

At that moment the phone rang on General Meyer's desk. The prime minister, the defense minister, and the IDF chief of staff were all on the line. The conversation was brief.

"We think the Russians or maybe the Egyptians flew over Dimona less than an hour ago. We were unable to intercept, so we can't be one hundred percent sure."

"Clearly not one of ours?" the prime minister asked, curtly.

"Clearly," came the equally curt reply. "They were military jets, and we had none in the air in this area."

"If it happens again," the defense minister interrupted, "if there is any new incursion into the area, we'll bring down the intruder immediately, no questions asked. We'll use the mobile interceptor Hawk missiles we got from the Americans. That's exactly what they're there for."

"They've never been used in combat by anyone," General Meyer replied. "The Americans haven't even used them in Vietnam."

"Then we'll be the first. Every Mirage we have will be otherwise engaged," the chief of staff replied. "The Hawks are there to defend Dimona. We'll use them to do just that." The prime minister's silence conveyed his concurrence.

CHAPTER SIX

Alexandra decided to wait until after the Potomac Center opening the following morning before discussing with Noah Markazie's bid to send her to the Middle East. Besides, she reasoned, if all the war bluster turned out to be just that—bluster—there would really be no reason to launch into something so stressful as talk of her possibly accepting an assignment in Israel.

Alexandra and Noah dined on burgers that night at the 823 Rathskeller on Fifteenth Street and then walked around the corner to catch a late showing of *Bonnie and Clyde*. They cabbed back to Alexandra's apartment at Tiber Island, not far from the newly developed Maine Street waterfront. Alexandra wanted their lovemaking to be special that night. She almost desperately wanted it to insulate them from the ever-mounting stress that had, once again, begun to challenge their love for one another. The impending Middle East conflict didn't involve them. Except it did. Once again there would be bloodshed—bloodshed between her people and his people—bloodshed between Palestinians and Israelis, between Arabs and Jews. This deadly struggle from which there seemed to be no escape intruded into their lives yet again, challenging their sense of identity and loyalty. They loved one another fully and passionately, and yet there was always this unbridgeable chasm. The rising turmoil in the Middle East was about to intrude into their lives again, as it had in the past.

And so that night their lovemaking was almost frantic, especially intense, and especially fragile. They held tightly and passionately to one another, their bodies pressed together almost as one. They kissed feverously as he entered her. In rapt rhythm they moved together—desperate to sustain and strengthen their love with every thrust.

And then, afterward, following their lovemaking and the intense heights to which their rapture had carried them, as they lay facing one another exhausted in sublime repose, calm and cloaked in the warmth of blissful tranquility, she reached up and ran the tips of her fingers ever so tenderly across the side of his face.

"I love you," she whispered.

"And I you...so very much," Noah replied, softly.

And then the telephone rang. The splendor of the moment dashed, she looked into his eyes sorrowfully as she reached over to the end table and lifted the receiver from the cradle.

"Alexandra, turn on the radio...WRC...right away."

"Frank, is that you?"

"Yes, of course it's me," he replied without apology. "Turn on the damn radio. News is about to break from the Middle East."

I'm so sorry, she mouthed silently to Noah as she dropped the phone onto the bed and reached over to switch on the clock radio. The illuminated numbers read 1:00 a.m. She immediately recognized the familiar voice of UPI correspondent Bob Musil as it crackled through the static.

"War came to the Middle East today with stunning suddenness. Israel charged that Egypt launched the surprise blitzkrieg with troops, tanks, and planes in the South near Gaza and announced that its own forces were counterattacking. Air-raid alarms sounded in both Egypt and Israel, and Arab radios were reported to be hailing the start of a long-awaited Holy War against this country. This is Robert Musil in Tel Aviv."

"Alexandra!" Markazie's voice barked from the folds of the bedsheet where she had dropped the phone.

"Yeah, Frank, I'm here," Alexandra replied, snatching the phone from the bed, her voice tinged with resignation as she propped herself up on her elbow. Her gaze was fixed on Noah, who looked back at her, his eyes betraying the dread he felt.

"Alexandra, tomorrow I have to announce whom we're sending to the Middle East to cover this story. You're going to have to piss or get off the pot."

"How professional of you, Frank," she replied, making no effort to mask the ire in her voice.

"Alexandra, you have the balance of the night to decide. I'm sorry to put it to you this way, but tomorrow I'll have ten staffers who will want this assignment. It's yours if you want it, and I'll understand if you don't. But I'll have to know first thing in the morning."

"Talk to you in the morning, Frank," she replied.

"Sleep on it."

"Yeah, I'll do that. Good night, Frank," she said, looking into Noah's eyes as she carefully placed the phone back on the cradle.

"Alexandra, Markazie has plenty of reporters he can send to cover this mess," Noah said, anticipating the argument he knew was about to take place.

"I know," she replied, sadly.

"Please, don't do this, Alexandra."

She looked into his eyes through the tears that had begun to blur her vision.

"I have to," she whispered, her voice sad and barely audible.

"No, Alexandra—no, you don't have to do this. Markazie can assign this to any number of your colleagues."

"Yes, he can. He knows that. He even told me that."

"So, then it's settled."

Alexandra lowered her head into her hands—not so much to consider her decision as to consider how to tell Noah what she had already decided. The tension between Noah and Alexandra grew as the war progressed. Noah, like nearly all Americans, identified closely with the Israelis and was thrilled by the courage of the young Jewish nation and the élan of its fighting men and women who were successfully pushing back against Nasser and his Syrian and Jordanian allies. But there was also the angst Yusuf and Alexandra were experiencing. While they were no fans of Nasser, they knew that innocent Palestinians who were not involved in the fighting would, ultimately, bear the brunt of the dreadful aftermath that was sure to follow—the aftermath that Alexandra would soon be covering for the *Evening Star*. She would be leaving as soon as the fighting stopped, and Noah knew that would be very soon. It was a tense time.

***

Commander Hod's young airmen performed almost flawlessly, and their exploits against a much larger and superbly equipped enemy mesmerized the world. By early afternoon on June 5, Israel had destroyed nearly every runway at every Arab air base. The young fighter pilots had destroyed 304 out of 419 Egyptian aircraft, 53 of Syria's 112 planes, and virtually all of Jordan's air force. To add insult to injury, Egyptian field marshal Abdel Hakim Amer was flying to Bir Tamada in the Sinai when the air war began and, fearing he would be shot down by his own air defenses, ordered a shutdown of all air-defense batteries in the region. With the Arabs unable to attack or defend by air, Israeli divisions under the command of General Israel Tal in the north and General Ariel Sharon in the south rolled into the Sinai. At two in the afternoon the following day, Nasser ordered his army back to the Suez Canal, and the war with Egypt was, effectively, over. During the next three days, the Israelis took the Golan Heights from Syria, ending years of Syrian shelling of Israeli villages. By the tenth of June, the Old City of Jerusalem and the landmass all the way through the Jordan Valley to the Jordan River were securely in Israeli hands. The fighting ceased on the sixth day. On the seventh day, the SS *Dolphin*, flying the Israeli flag, passed through the Straits of Tiran and anchored at Eilat. The Six-Day War had passed into history.

All had gone according to plan. Well, almost all. On June 5, the first day of the war, the Dassault MD 450 Ouragan flown by Israeli Air Force captain Yoram Harpaz was hit over Jordan. With his control system crippled, the plane began losing altitude as it headed back into Israel toward the Negev. Then, the unimaginable. It was determined to be descending, out of control, toward Dimona. General Meyer silently wept as the minister of defense gave the order to bring down the plane with one of the American-supplied Hawk missiles. It was the only Hawk missile fired during the fighting. It found its mark. The young Israeli pilot perished, the victim of the first US Hawk missile ever fired in combat.

CHAPTER SEVEN

Dany Haddad sat watching the Egyptian newscast in his small third-floor studio apartment on Rue Harma in Beirut not far from the Armenian-founded Haigazian University where he taught Middle Eastern history. *They never learn,* he thought, as he watched the screaming mobs in Tahrir Square. He was only ten years old when his family, like thousands of other Christian and Muslim families, fled Jaffa twenty years earlier to get away from the fighting between the Jews and the Arabs. Now the cycle was being repeated, and he knew there would soon be tens of thousands of new refugees.

Dany's father, Elias, had been a civil engineer in Jaffa. It was said the founder of the Jaffa Electric Company, the Jew Pinhas Rutenberg himself, had hired the Palestinian the day he graduated from Technion in Haifa. He was offered a job at Rutenberg's electric company in Jaffa or, if he preferred, a job helping Rutenberg plan a new electric company in Haifa that was scheduled to open in 1935. Elias Haddad selected Jaffa and worked at the Jewish-owned Jaffa Electric Company for fifteen years. He made a good wage and provided well for his family. But that all ended abruptly with the violence that erupted in Jaffa in 1947 when the UN approved the partition of Palestine into a state for the Jews and a state for the Arabs. Vicious and deadly fighting broke out between the two groups, and there was carnage everywhere.

Elias Haddad, his wife, Dahlia, and their young son, Dany, fled like so many others. Elias's two brothers and one sister also left with their children. One brother made his way to Kuwait and another to Jordan.

His sister, Helena, took her family to Canada, where her husband's uncle lived. Elias knew the manager of the electric utility in Beirut. They had been classmates at the Technion, so he and his wife and son made their way north along the coast, through Haifa, across the Galilee, and, eventually, on into Lebanon. The once-close-knit Haddad family was now dispersed throughout foreign lands. Occasional letters and rarer telephone calls became their only means of contact.

Dany Haddad had planned to fly to Nicosia, Cyprus, and then on to Tel Aviv on June 7 when he was to join the staff of *Desert Song*, a Christian, Arab-owned weekly newspaper headquartered in Jaffa that published in Arabic, Hebrew, and English. But that would have to wait now. He had received a call that morning from Cyprus Airlines. All flights into Israel from Nicosia were being delayed until the emergency was over.

Desert Song was widely read among university faculty and students, artists, intellectuals, politicians, and even many higher-echelon government officials. Its pages were pregnant with essays and commentary on a wide range of issues unique to the cultural cornucopia that was Israel. Its focus was remarkably apolitical, and it left the nitty-gritty of breaking news to the Jewish-owned dailies. *Desert Song* had been searching, on and off, for three years for someone to replace the young Palestinian American writer Alexandra Salaman. She had left, abruptly, to return home to America following the incident with the terrorist Ali Abdul Shoukri. No one was surprised when she left. She and the Israeli with whom she had been traveling, Amos Ben-Chaiyim, were lucky to have survived.

CHAPTER EIGHT

Noah knew the grand opening of Potomac Center was not going to go well when Rabbi Feldman called first thing in the morning to say he wouldn't be attending. He said it wouldn't be appropriate for Jews to be celebrating the opening of a big commercial project when Jews were fighting and dying for the survival of Israel. It was a party to which few people came. Well, some people showed up. All of the tenants were there, and all of the shops, restaurants, and offices were open for business. But the media were mostly preoccupied with the war. Only WTTG-TV, Channel Five, Washington's independent television station, showed up. The network affiliates were all preoccupied with the war, and their camera crews were diverted to Capitol Hill, the White House, the Pentagon—everywhere, it seemed, except Potomac Center. The three dailies—the *News*, the *Post*, and the *Evening Star*—sent young business reporters to cover the opening, and the *Star* sent a photographer. Shoppers, like everyone else, were mostly at home glued to their television sets.

Noah, Ed Scallion, Yusuf, and Alexandra sat alone at the press table sipping warm coffee from plastic cups emblazoned with the Potomac Center logo. The room was otherwise empty. Prepared remarks were tossed aside. Noah and Yusuf had fielded a few perfunctory questions from the young reporters who showed up but would have rather been covering the war. Unclaimed press releases were strewn about the table. Noah just shrugged as Alexandra explained how the outbreak of fighting reset all of the scheduled news assignments at the paper.

"I guess our project is pretty unimportant in the overall scheme of things," Noah said, as he threw his empty cup over to a wastebasket as though sinking a one-handed jump shot from his seated position. "Man, all of the planning that went into this grand opening down the drain. Everyone, including me, is totally focused on the fighting in the Middle East. What a day to have planned our little celebration."

"The project is huge, Noah. The opening is not that big a deal. Think of all the publicity Potomac Center has already enjoyed in this town," Scallion replied.

"What in the world are we going to do with all these danish?" Noah asked to no one in particular, as he gestured toward the refreshment table. "We could have fed the entire Washington press corps."

"We could freeze it," Yusuf replied, smiling. "There may be an opening for Potomac Center's twin in about two years."

"What are you talking about?" Alexandra asked.

"Yeah, you have my attention too," Noah said.

"Well, it's a Palestinian pipe dream," Yusuf replied. "I had some Palestinian investor in my office yesterday. He's the managing partner of an investment group that's planning a huge project in Palestine, not far from Bethlehem—hotels, casinos, and world-class shopping—and he wants to model the project after Potomac Center."

"You have to be kidding," Noah replied.

"No, I think he's very serious. He calls his project Palestinya Center. He wanted to buy the architecture plans for Potomac Center. That's why he came to see me. I told him the plans weren't mine to sell and urged him to come here this morning so that I could introduce him to you."

"So why isn't he here?" Noah asked, his curiosity increasing.

"He said he had to return to the Middle East today. Frankly, I think he was uncomfortable with the idea of meeting you.

"Because I'm Jewish?"

"Probably. He didn't put it that way. He just said he preferred working with me because I'm Palestinian. I told him you would be glad to talk to him and that you, Alexandra, might be interested in writing about his project, but he said he had to get back."

Ed looked at Yusuf quizzically for a moment. "That doesn't make any sense at all," he finally said. "He came all this way the day before Potomac Center opened to purchase our plans, had an opportunity to meet the developer of the project he admired so much, and then left before you could introduce him to Noah?"

"That's exactly what happened. I know it sounds crazy, but that's what happened."

"What's his name?" Alexandra asked. "I'll run his name through the *Star*'s morgue. Maybe we've run something about him or this investment group of his."

"Here's his card," Yusuf replied, as he reached into the pocket of his blazer and handed the card to his sister. Alexandra glanced at the card for a moment before looking up at Yusuf.

"Abu Salma?" she asked, quizzically. "He said his name was Abu Salma?"

"Yeah, what's so special about his name?" Yusuf replied.

"Yusuf, Abu Salma is a renowned Palestinian poet. It's a nom de guerre. His real name is Abd al-Karim al-Karmi. He's famous, Yusuf. He wrote beautiful poetry about his love for Palestine and his grief over its sad fate. I wrote about Abu Salma frequently when I was in Israel writing for Desert Song."

"Why would my visitor use someone else's name?" Yusuf asked.

"Well, it could just be a pseudonym—you know, the name of someone your visitor admired a great deal."

"You mean like a nom de guerre?"

"Exactly. Noms de guerre are pretty popular with Arabs, especially Palestinians. And if your visitor is a great admirer of Salma, he may have taken his name as a show of admiration and respect."

"Or maybe to show his passion for Palestine?" Yusuf asked.

"Or maybe he just didn't want Yusuf, or any of us for that matter, to know his real name," Noah interrupted.

"That's definitely possible," Alexandra replied. "But I think his se-lection of such a beloved Palestinian poet might just be a sign of great respect."

"Well, the two ain't exactly mutually exclusive," Ed Scallion chimed in. "I don't know about you, Noah, but I like to know whom I'm work-ing with."

"Well," Noah replied, "right now this Salma guy, whoever he is, isn't working with any of us. Yusuf, if he shows up or contacts you again, tell him I'll be glad to talk to him."

"I would be surprised if we didn't hear from him again. He's seri-ous, and he did come a long way to try to purchase our plans."

"Serious enough to travel a long way to try to purchase our plans, but not serious enough to visit the project or meet the develop-er. Something doesn't sound right. It's like a clock striking thirteen. Anyway, the fighting over there might make a mess of his plans, what-ever they are," Noah replied.

"Salma, or whoever he is, didn't seem to think who won mattered," Yusuf said. "He assumed Nasser would win but said even more people would come if the Jews won. He even said the Jews could stay at the King David Hotel in Jerusalem and stop off at Rachel's Tomb on the way to Palestinya Center. He said all the Jews in Palestine, before it became Israel, considered themselves Palestinians. One day they were Palestinians, and the next day they were Israelis."

"Why don't I hold on to his card?" Alexandra suggested. "Maybe I can find out more about him when I'm over there."

"When are you going?" Yusuf asked. "I didn't know it was definite."

"It's definite," Noah replied, before Alexandra could answer. "I'm not very happy about it, but the *Star* wants her over there, so she's go-ing." There was no missing the irritation in his voice.

"Do you plan to meet with Palestinians while you are there or just Israelis?" Yusuf asked, ignoring Noah's interruption.

"Depending on my freedom of movement, I'll go wherever my in-stincts tell me to go," she replied. "I'm going there to take the pulse of the people, and that certainly includes the Palestinians. No one knows what is going to happen following this war. My job will be to identify the various factions on all sides and try to provide an understanding of what can be expected in the months and years ahead."

"Hopefully, we can expect peace," Noah said. "This endless Arab drumbeating and rhetoric calling for death to Israel has to stop."

"Noah, a decade ago Israel tried to grab all of the Sinai and Suez Canal, and if Eisenhower hadn't put his foot down, they would have succeeded with the help of the British and the French. Eight years before that, they ran tens of thousands of Palestinians from their homes. Our family was among those who had to flee, leaving everything we had in the world behind. If Israel advances east toward the Jordan River, they'll have hundreds of thousands of Palestinians on their hands on the West Bank. What then?" Alexandra asked.

"Well, Jordan has had those same Palestinians on their hands since the fighting in 1948," Noah replied. "What exactly is the difference?"

"So when will you leave?" Ed asked, trying to change the subject.

"The paper wants me there as soon as the fighting is over," Alexandra said, "or at least once things have quieted down." Her eyes darted to Noah, pleading for understanding.

"They want you to cover the war, after the war is over?" Ed asked.

"I'm not being sent as a war correspondent," she replied. "As I said, they want me to cover what Frank Markazie calls the aftermath. He thinks there will be months, maybe years, of tension and political maneuvering after the fighting stops. He wants me to define for our readers what the issues are and whom the players will be. He thinks things will be in turmoil, and he wants the *Star* to be recognized as the source of the most up-to-date and authoritative information about the Middle East."

"How long will you be over there?" Yusuf asked.

"Two, maybe three weeks at the most," she replied.

"She doesn't really know," Noah interrupted, testily. "She'll return when Markazie tells her to."

Alexandra looked to Noah, her pained expression begging for understanding. He wasn't sure whether she was hurt or angry. Yusuf and Ed, both sensing the tension, let the matter drop. In less than a week, it was all over. The swiftness and thoroughness of the Israeli rout of three Arab armies was, to most of America, exhilarating. To the Arab world, it was stupefying.

***

Noah, Alexandra, and Yusuf joined the Greenspans at the Salaman home for dinner the night before Alexandra was to depart for Israel. Conversation at dinner was uncharacteristically restrained. Alexandra's father, Sharif, was the first to address the subject everyone seemed to be avoiding.

"So, Alexandra, do you expect to be back before the July Fourth holiday?" he asked.

"I don't really know for sure, Daddy," she replied. "I think so, but we'll have to see."

He nodded.

"What, exactly, will you be reporting on, Alexandra?" Esther Greenspan asked. "The war is over, isn't it?"

"Yes, the fighting is over, but the political wrangling hasn't even begun yet. That's really what I'll be covering."

"Whose politics are you going to be writing about?" Sharif asked.

"Everyone's," she answered. "Think about all of the participants in this war. You have the Egyptians, the Jordanians, the Syrians, and of course the Israelis."

"Not to mention the Palestinians," Yusuf interrupted.

"And, of course, the Palestinians," she added. "All of these actors are in a state of turmoil right now. There's no one person in any of these countries who knows today what their position will be tomorrow. Will the Arab countries end their struggle against Israel? And if they do, would the Israelis consider the dispute over?"

"Well, I'm sure they would," Esther answered. "After all, isn't that what all the endless fighting has been about?"

Alexandra shrugged. "I don't know. I don't think anyone does. On the Arab side, you have the Egyptians, the Syrians, and the Jordanians, not to mention the Palestinians, who are really stateless people. Does anyone think they'll all agree?"

"It's an opportunity of a lifetime," Yusuf said. "I'm telling you there are Palestinians on the West Bank who would jump at the opportunity to reach an understanding with Israel. Just think of how that area, so rich in history, would prosper if there were peace there. It could become one of the greatest tourist attractions in the world."

"But there are also Palestinians who say armed struggle is the only course of action," Alexandra replied. "I don't know how anyone is going to make sense of it. And even if West Bank Palestinians wanted to work something out with the Israelis, would there be consensus in Israel to do that?"

"And what about the Russians and the French and our own government?" Hy Greenspan asked. "The Israeli's destroyed hundreds of Russian planes when they attacked the Arabs. Don't you think Kosygin will have something to say about how all this ends?"

"And there's this mess with the American naval vessel the Israelis attacked," Yusuf said. "What in the hell was that all about?"

"I think it's pretty clear that it was a horrible accident," Noah replied.

"Nothing is pretty clear," Yusuf answered, his tone punctuated with sarcasm.

"Do you actually think the Israelis would have knowingly attacked an American naval vessel?" Noah asked, incredulously.

"Well, the Israeli planes made several runs at the *Liberty*, and the ship was flying an American flag."

"Any ship could fly an American flag if it wanted to confuse an enemy. You wouldn't expect an Egyptian ship spying on Israel during the war to fly an Egyptian flag, would you?"

"No, I wouldn't, but the fact remains that an American ship in international waters and flying an American flag was attacked by Israeli fighter jets."

"And therefore, what?" Noah asked.

"Therefore you can add the United States of America to the list of countries that will have a lot to say about what happens next."

"All of this is the least of my concerns. What I really want to know, Alexandra, is how comfortable you are going back there. Do you really think it's safe?" Samira asked.

"I think it is," Alexandra answered, anxious to reassure her mother. "The fighting is over. The airport in Israel has been receiving commercial flights with no reported problems. Actually, I'll be one of the last journalists to arrive. There are plenty of newspaper people there already. I really do think it's safe."

"I wasn't thinking of the war. I was thinking about the horrible people you got mixed up with when you were there three years ago," her mother replied.

"Those people are either dead or in prison, Mom."

"Alexandra, we don't even know who all of those people are. You ran into a few of them. There may be hundreds, maybe thousands, just like them," Yusuf said.

"Thanks, Yusuf, that's very comforting," Alexandra replied.

"How do you feel about all of this, Noah?" Sharif asked.

Alexandra looked at Noah, hoping he wasn't going to make an issue of her decision to go to Israel in front of their families. He reached over and gently took her hand in his.

"Alexandra is a professional journalist. This is a huge assignment the paper has given her. I'm not thrilled that she's going, but I understand her need to go, and I respect her decision to go," he answered.

Alexandra tightened her grip on his hand. "Thank you," she whispered.

***

There was little conversation as Noah drove Alexandra to Washington National Airport, where she would begin her long journey to Tel Aviv. As he steered his Corvette across the Fourteenth Street Bridge, he reached over and closed his hand over hers.

"We'll keep in touch every day?" he asked softly.

"Yes," she answered in a whisper, "we'll keep in touch. I promise."

They walked in silence from the parking lot to the terminal.

"We can't let *their* conflict become *our* conflict, Alexandra," Noah said as they made their way to the gate.

"I know," she answered, the sadness in her voice a contradiction of her words.

They continued holding hands after reaching the boarding area but had painfully little to say. Then as her flight was called, they hugged one another, each too caught up in the emotion of the moment to speak. Finally, Noah, his voice shaken, whispered, "I love you, Alexandra." She smiled through her tears, nodded anxiously, and hugged him closely once again before turning to board the plane.

Noah stood at the large window and watched as the outsize four-engine Eastern Airlines Lockheed Electra pushed away from the gate. He felt as though everything in the world that mattered to him at that moment was on that plane. A few minutes later, the white and blue turboprop raced down the runway on its way to New York, where Alexandra would connect at JFK to an El Al Boeing 707 for the ten-hour flight to Tel Aviv. He followed the plane as it rose slowly over the Potomac and disappeared moments later into a beautiful puff of billowy white clouds floating effortlessly below a brilliant azure sky. He remained there for several moments, eyes fixed on the cloud into which Alexandra's plane disappeared from view on her journey halfway around the world. He sighed sadly, wondering when and, momentarily, even if she would ever return.

Alexandra glanced out of the window in time to see the Fourteenth Street Bridge pass below, the same bridge over which she and Noah had driven a short time earlier. The Electra groaned on above Georgetown University just as it was enveloped by the same cloud formation to which Noah's eyes were transfixed. She leaned back and closed her eyes. Images of her and Noah parting only minutes earlier flashed through her mind. Then there were images of her and Noah saying good-bye when he went off to Stanford twelve years earlier, when he would return to school after Christmas and summer breaks, and when she left for Beirut a decade earlier. Somehow the images of departures suppressed images of arrivals. *Why are the good-byes so vivid and the returns so faint?* she wondered.

The banner headline on the front page of Washington's only tabloid, the *Daily News*, caught his eye as he made his way through the terminal—"Israel's Rout of the Arabs." He walked over to the newsstand to look more closely. It was all there in the story's lead. The Arab combatants had now fully retreated from the battlefields, leaving behind over twenty thousand dead and, in Israel's hands, 695 square miles of the Golan Heights, 2,178 square miles of the West Bank, and nearly 24,000 square miles of the Sinai Peninsula and Gaza Strip. More than a million Palestinians lived on land now controlled by Israel. It was one of the most astonishing and decisive battles of the twentieth century, and the outcome had been decided in hours.

CHAPTER NINE

Alexandra arrived in Tel Aviv twenty hours later. She was exhausted as she slowly made her way in line toward the passport-control station. She was surprised at how many people were arriving in Israel so soon after the fighting. As the line slowly moved forward, she noticed two female passport-control officers questioning a man who looked to be about her age at the front of the adjacent line. One of the agents was holding his passport. They were not arguing. They just seemed to have a lot of questions, and they were in no hurry to move the line along. The man was patiently responding to whatever they were asking. Finally, she made her way to the front of the line and handed the passport-control officer her passport. He looked up and into her eyes after perusing her passport for a moment.

"You were born in Jaffa?" he asked.

"Yes, Jaffa," she replied.

"When did you leave Israel?"

"Three years ago," she replied, knowing full well he really wanted to know when her family had left Israel.

"You remained here until 1964?"

"No. We *fled* in 1948," she answered, emphasizing the word *fled*. "I returned and graduated from Hebrew University.

"You're Israeli…Jewish?"

"No. I'm Palestinian…Christian," she answered.

The agent paused, surprised by her response. "How long to you plan to remain in Israel?" he finally asked, his eyes fixed on hers.

"I don't know," she replied. "Until my work is done."

"And what is the nature of your work here?" the agent asked, continuing to peer, searchingly, into her eyes.

"I'm a correspondent for the *Washington Evening Star*," she replied. "I'm here to report on the aftermath of the war. I'm here to write about what I see and hear in Israel."

The agent nodded, holding her gaze. "When will your work here begin?" he finally asked.

"Five minutes ago," she replied coolly, her eyes fixed on his.

He slowly nodded, tapping her passport against the palm of his hand. "Have a good stay in our country," he finally said, handing back her passport.

Alexandra retrieved her suitcase and made her way to the taxi line in front of the terminal. The June afternoon air was hot and humid, and she was eager to get to the hotel so that she could shower and sleep. A moment later the man who was being questioned for so long in the passport line came up to wait behind her. She glanced back and nodded pleasantly. He reminded her of Yusuf—very handsome, with the same wavy dark hair and similar deep-brown eyes. He smiled and nodded back.

"Well, you seemed to be having quite a conference in the passport-control line," she said, smiling.

"It was nothing. They seem to be very cautious…a bit jittery so soon after the war—especially when an Arab has just arrived from Beirut by way of Nicosia."

"Ah, you're Lebanese and came through Cyprus"

"Yes…well, no. I'm actually Palestinian, originally from Jaffa."

"Really? You're from Jaffa?" she asked, her interest in the stranger increasing. At that moment a taxi pulled up.

"I'm staying at the Dan Hotel. Do you want to share a taxi into Tel Aviv?" she asked, eager to continue the conversation.

The man smiled. "I'm staying at the Dan too." And with that they both got into the cab.

"We're going to the Dan," Alexandra said to the driver when he returned to the driver's seat after putting their luggage in the trunk.

"I'm Dany Haddad," the man said, extending his hand.

"My name is Alexandra. Alexandra Salaman," she replied, grasping his hand. "I'm from Jaffa too. I'm pleased to meet you."

He looked at her, dumbfounded—speechless for a moment. "You're Alexandra Salaman?" he finally asked. "You're the journalist from America, who once worked at *Desert Song*?" She was as beautiful as he had heard.

"Why…yes," she replied, somewhat cautiously. "Why do you know my name?"

"This is unbelievable," he said. "I mean absolutely unbelievable. I'm here to begin working at *Desert Song*. I'm filling the vacancy you left three years ago. They told me they always wanted to fill the position you left but could never find anyone with your background."

"And you're it?" she asked, equally astonished. "You're their new Alexandra Salaman?"

"Well, I'm their new Jaffa refugee writer who left Palestine twenty years ago." he answered, laughing. "That's what they were looking for—a returned Palestinian journalist."

"You're a journalist?"

"Not really, but I do write a lot about the Middle East. Actually, I'm a historian. I was teaching Middle Eastern history in Beirut at Haigazian University."

"Ah, the Armenian school."

"You've heard of Haigazian?"

"Actually, I have. I attended Phoenicia University in Beirut for two years."

"Oh yes, I remember hearing about that. But you came to Israel and graduated from Hebrew University. There was some incident—"

"Let's not go there," she said, waving him off. "It's too long a story, and I'm much too tired."

"Perhaps at breakfast then. Do you have plans for breakfast in the morning? I've only heard hearsay about Alexandra Salaman and her exploits. I would love to hear the real story from the journalist herself."

Alexandra smiled and extended her hand. "It's a deal. Breakfast at, say, eight thirty tomorrow morning?"

"Unbelievable," he replied, taking her hand. "This is just unbelievable. I'm sitting here sharing a taxi in Israel with Alexandra Salaman, who wrote for *Desert Song*, whom I've heard so much about, and whose family left Jaffa at the very time I left with my family twenty years ago."

Alexandra sat there staring at him, her hand clutching his just a bit longer than she intended. "Unbelievable," she concurred, releasing his hand.

***

Alexandra and Dany met for breakfast in the hotel's coffee shop at half past eight the following morning, as planned. She told him about Ali Abdul Shoukri and the conspiracy to commit mass murder in which she had, unknowingly, become involved. She discussed the role Amos Ben-Chaiyim had played in rescuing her and bringing her to Israel but did not reveal anything about her personal and intimate relationship with Amos. Dany listened intently and sympathetically.

"You are lucky to be alive," he simply said.

"I know," she replied.

"Your editor made you come back here?" Dany asked.

"Not really. He said no one could cover this story as well as I could but that he would understand if I turned down the assignment. He said he was prepared to send someone else."

"Then why are you here?" Dany asked.

Alexandra smiled. "Because I wasn't prepared to have someone else cover this story. I knew Frank Markazie was right."

"In what way?"

"No one at the paper can do this story as well as I can."

They talked for a few more minutes about their similar backgrounds—the way both families had fled from Jaffa twenty years earlier, how neither family had been able to maintain any meaningful contact with their families, and how, yes, he was, as she assumed, Christian. She found him attractive, engaging, and very easy to talk to. He found her to be pleasant, personable, and incredibly beautiful.

"I have to go, Alexandra," he finally said, glancing down at his watch. "They're expecting me at *Desert Song* in Jaffa. Do you want to come with me? I think they would be very excited to see you."

"I will come by, but not this morning. I have some calls to make," she replied.

As they parted at the entrance of the coffee shop, Dany extended his hand to say good-bye. Alexandra instead reached up and kissed him quickly and lightly on the cheek.

"Good luck, Dany Haddad," she said with a smile. It was a friendly and not at all romantic gesture. Alexandra returned to her room and, nervously, reached for the phone and made her first call.

"Ben-Chaiyim," the voice on the other end answered.

"Amos…" she replied softly.

There was, at first, only silence. "Alexandra—Alexandra—is it you?" Amos finally managed to say.

"Shalom, Amos," she answered, her voice faltering ever so slightly. "Yes, it's me."

"You're here? You're in Tel Aviv?"

"Yes, Amos. I'm here. I've been sent to cover the Israeli-Palestinian relationship in the aftermath of the war."

"How long will you be here?"

"I'm not sure. One…two weeks maybe."

"When can I see you?"

"Now. This afternoon. Soon I hope. I'm dying to see you, and, actually, I would like to interview you, too."

"You want to interview me?" he asked.

"Yes," she replied, laughing. "And I want to see you and to catch up on your life, and, yes, I want to give you a big hug too."

"Are you and Noah…"

"Still together? Yes, we're still engaged. He's a bit upset with me for agreeing to come here, but yes, we're still very much together. I hope you get a chance to meet him someday. You would like Noah, very much."

"Yes, I'm sure I would like him. Really, when can I see you, Alexandra?"

"Are you free now?" she replied. "I'm at the Dan."

"I'll rearrange some meetings I have today. I'll be there within an hour. Alexandra, I can't wait to see you."

"And I you, Amos. I'll meet you in the lobby."

Amos never expected to see Alexandra again. He couldn't imagine she would ever come back to Israel—not after the horrible incident that almost cost her her life, and not with the danger that might always be lurking nearby. He thought so often of that moment when he let down his guard—when he was responsible for protecting her—and how close they both came to losing their lives. And, most of all, he couldn't imagine ever loving anyone as much as he had loved her. It took so long before he could fall asleep without thinking of her or wake up without craving her being there sleeping peacefully at his side. And now she was here, in Israel—in Tel Aviv.

Alexandra was as worried as she was eager to see Amos. She loved Noah with all her heart and was determined never to lose him or to hurt him. She knew how disappointed he was about her decision to accept the assignment in Israel. He knew, of course, about Amos, but he provided the space—that zone of privacy she needed about those years in Beirut and Israel. He trusted her so completely, and she was determined never to disturb that trust. But in a few minutes she would be with Amos again. They had shared so much—endured so much and loved so much.

She spied him before he saw her when he walked into the lobby of the Dan. He was as she last remembered him. Her heart quickened. He hadn't changed at all. He was tanned, even weathered, suggesting he had recently spent considerable time outdoors, probably in the Sinai, she guessed. His hair was as dark as ever, slightly unkempt, and, as usual, in need of a trim. She smiled when he spotted her a moment later. He moved to her quickly and hugged her tightly, lifting her briefly off her feet. He held her by her shoulders and looked into her eyes— those green eyes that haunted him night after night after she left Israel.

They moved to a quiet corner of the lobby and sat down opposite one another. He reached out and took her hands into his. "I've missed you, Alexandra. I've missed you every day," he said.

"I've thought about you often too, Amos. We shared so much."

"You are happy in America?" he asked.

She knew he was really asking if things were working out between her and Noah. Alexandra smiled and squeezed his hands gently. "I'm very happy in America," she replied. They spoke for about an hour that first morning at the Dan in Tel Aviv. She told him about Markazie's offer to send her to Israel or to send someone else instead. While she was reluctant to return, the thought of having someone else cover this story was unthinkable. Her job, she explained, was to write about life in Israel and in the Arab-populated territories for which the Jewish nation was now responsible.

"I think you made the right decision, Alexandra. Everything has been turned inside out. Nothing will be the same here. Our Arab neighbors are in a state of despair. Many Palestinians and Israelis see this as a historic opportunity to find a way to live together peacefully. Others have a much darker perspective about what should happen next. Markazie was right. The biggest story of the next generation is about to unfold, and, frankly, I haven't a clue how it will all turn out. No one does."

"What did you do during the war, Amos?" she asked.

"Nothing I would want you writing about," he answered with a smile.

"Off the record?"

"Another time. My war exploits are the last thing I want to talk about now."

"Oh, I do have something I wanted to ask you about," she said, almost as an afterthought. "A man from Jordan, a Palestinian, met with my brother to discuss a major project he and a group of investors are planning somewhere between Jerusalem and Jericho. He wanted the architectural plans for Potomac Center, which Noah just opened. He said he wanted to model his project after Potomac Center. I couldn't find anything about him or his investment group in our files at the *Star*. I thought you might know something about him or his partners." And with that she reached into her shoulder bag and retrieved the business card Yusuf had given her. "Have you ever heard of this group?" she asked, handing Amos the card.

Amos's jaw tightened, and his eyes narrowed as he looked at the card. He just sat there staring at it for a moment or two. Alexandra knew immediately that he recognized the man's name or, possibly, the investment group. He raised his eyes from the card and looked at Alexandra. "These people were in Washington?" he asked, making no effort to mask his concern.

"No, the man who calls himself Salma came to Baltimore to meet with Yusuf. He said he didn't have time to come to Washington to meet with Noah or me. You know them?"

"First, this man's name isn't Abu Salma."

"Yes, yes, I know that. I assumed it was just a pseudonym. Abu Salma, the poet, is so revered. Noms de guerre are common in this part of the world. I didn't think too much of it."

Amos seemed at a loss for words. He tapped the card against his fingers as he collected his thoughts.

"Alexandra, are you telling me this man who calls himself Abu Salma and who says he represents a group called AASLF Partners came to see your brother and tried to obtain the plans for Noah's project?"

"Yes, Amos. That's exactly what happened. What do you know about Mr. Salma and his partners?" she asked, growing alarmed herself. Amos drew a deep breath before responding as he contemplated how to tell Alexandra the identity of the man whose card she had been carrying—the man who had come to Baltimore to meet with Yusuf—the man who wanted the architectural plans for Potomac Center.

"Alexandra, we know a great deal about this man and his partners. Your brother was meeting with Omar Samir."

"What!" Alexandra cried out. Images of Omar Samir, one of the terrorists with whom she had unwittingly become involved in Beirut, flashed through her mind. "What are you telling me?"

"Samir heads a group of terrorists. It's a cell that calls itself AASLF Partners. Alexandra, AASLF stands for Ali Abdul Shoukri Liberation Front," he replied, his eyes fixed on hers. Alexandra began to speak, but there were no words. She just sat there for a moment, speechless.

"Shoukri…" was all she managed to finally say.

Amos reached out and took her hands into his. "Alexandra, they are plotting something at Potomac Center. I don't know what, but I think I can guess. I also think you and Noah are in danger. Your brother may be in danger too."

Alexandra just sat there slowly shaking her head. "I think I'm going to be sick," she finally managed to say. "I have to warn Noah and Yusuf. I should leave Israel," she murmured.

"Don't say anything to anyone just yet, Alexandra. You're safer here right now than anywhere. Samir and his colleagues won't come anywhere near Tel Aviv or, I would guess, anywhere on the West Bank either. It's swarming with IDF and Shin Bet. They are nowhere near ready to strike if they are still trying to get their hands on the architectural plans. We've been trying to figure out what they've been planning, and now we know. Yusuf and Noah will, of course, have to know what is going on, but we have to think through how we'll deal with this information—and how Yusuf and Noah will deal with it too."

"But they have to be warned."

"Of course they have to be warned, but we need to plan carefully what we do with this information. We can't just blurt out what we've learned without a plan. These people may contact Yusuf and Noah again. One way or another, we'll hear from them. We and our counterparts in America have to carefully plan what we—you, Noah, and Yusuf—do next when that contact is made. We have an opportunity to destroy this den of terror before they strike if we plan carefully."

Alexandra lowered her head into her hand. "It's starting all over again," she said.

"Alexandra, when Samir gave that card to Yusuf, it never dawned on him that it would ever wind up here in our hands. That's sheer luck, Alexandra. We can stop this and stop them, permanently, if we don't do anything foolish."

"You mean like calling Noah and Yusuf right now, which is what every bone in my body wants to do."

"Until we have thought this through, that's the last thing you should do. We have very valuable information now, and we need to use it wisely. If we don't—if we tip off what we know, they'll simply alter their plans, but they won't alter their objective."

"What do you think their objective is, Amos?"

"To attack all of you and to bring down Potomac Center. It can't be anything else. It would be their ultimate revenge," he answered.

"Why do they care about Potomac Center or Noah or Yusuf?"

"Half the Arab world believes the United States attacked Egypt, Jordan, and Syria in concert with us. They can't bring themselves to believe their forces were so thoroughly defeated by tiny Israel. So, striking in the heart of America makes sense to them. They consider you a traitor to their cause, and you are engaged to Noah Greenspan, a Jew. Yusuf refused to provide the architectural plans in deference to Noah, his Jewish client. It all makes sense."

"It's all so insane," she replied.

"Not to their way of thinking, Alexandra."

"Well, I guess this is one story I can't write about," she said.

"Alexandra, I don't think you should have your byline on anything that you write here. Not now. Not in light of this."

"Because?"

"Because they don't know you're here, and I think we want to keep it that way for your own safety."

"Markazie will go right through the ceiling," she replied.

"Look, you can write under a different name, and when this is over, the *Star* will have a huge exclusive story about it all. Until then, you should not have your name on anything you write here."

***

Markazie was relieved to hear from Alexandra when she finally called him later that evening. She spoke to him in carefully modulated, brief sentences, cutting off any preliminary conviviality. She wanted to communicate what had to be done without navigating through unnecessary telephone conversation and certain objections from her editor.

"Hello, Frank," she said, as soon as he answered the phone.

"Alexandra, am I glad to hear from you."

"I only have a few minutes, Frank. Please listen carefully. I'm fine and ready to begin working. I will be using the byline Sabirah Najat."

"What?" he replied. "What the hell are you talking about?"

"My byline while I am here will be Sabirah Najat. Everything I write will be under that byline. S-A-B-I-R-A-H-N-A-J-A-T," she spelled the name letter by letter.

"What the hell are—"

"Frank, I have to go. I'm fine, and I'll explain another time." He paused to collect his thoughts before answering. He knew she was communicating something she didn't want to discuss over the telephone.

"Where in the hell did you come up with a name like...what is it again?" he asked.

"Sabirah Najat," she answered coolly and evenly.

"You mind if I ask why you came up with a name like that?" he asked, again.

"Great question," she replied, very clearly. "I have to go. I'll be in touch." And with that she ended the call.

Franklin Markazie sat there staring at the phone for several seconds before yelling for someone in the newsroom to get him an

Arabic-to-English dictionary. Within minutes, he understood. The words jumped out at him, and so did the message Alexandra was trying to communicate. *Sabirah* meant *patience*, and *Najat* translated to *safety*. She was imploring Markazie to simply trust her. He had no idea what was going on, but he trusted Alexandra as he trusted few other writers at the paper. "Sabirah Najat," he whispered to himself. "OK, Sabirah, go to it."

CHAPTER TEN

Omar Samir stretched out, exhausted, at the New Cataract Hotel, on the bank of the Nile in Aswân, Egypt, several hundred miles south of Tel Aviv. The New Cataract was the low-priced wing recently added on to the famed Old Cataract Hotel, which for years had served Europe's aristocracy. It had been a long and tiring trip from Baltimore. He had been delayed for a week in London waiting out the war in a motel not far from Heathrow before continuing on to Cairo. The New Cataract hotel was ideally located for the meetings that would take place between Samir and his cohorts—far enough away to be out of reach of the Israelis, yet close enough to be accessible to the other AASLF members. And it didn't hurt that no one hated the Israelis more than Egypt's Nasser.

He lay there staring at the ceiling fan overhead as it slowly stirred the warm air in the room. Omar Samir was forty years old and he had been at war with the Jews for thirty of those years—ever since the Irgun's Black Sunday retaliatory attacks around Jerusalem in 1937 when he was only ten. There had been violence between Arabs and Jews in Palestine all of his life. To Omar Samir there was no right or wrong—there were only winners and losers. To Omar Samir the recently concluded war was but a skirmish; the battle would go on.

He hadn't gotten everything he had hoped to obtain from the Palestinian American architect, Yusuf Salaman, the brother of the traitor Alexandra Salaman, but he got enough. He needed a good night's sleep before his meeting to plot the action that would introduce AASLF Partners to the world.

They met for breakfast the following morning after the Fajr, the dawn prayer. Three of them were Palestinian. Ismail Sayegh, the stone-cutter from the quarries, and Walid Ghannam, the university student, were from Hebron. Qureshi, the bricklayer, lived in Gaza City. Khaled Kassab, the electrical engineer who worked for the huge civil-engineering firm Questex-Irvine International, was Egyptian and lived in Deshna, less than 150 miles from Aswân.

"So," Omar began, "we have rough schematics of our target in Washington. I wasn't able to get the architectural drawings as we planned, but we have enough."

"Salaman the architect—the Palestinian—wouldn't give you a copy of his plans?"

"Yusuf Salaman is more American than Palestinian. He speaks of our cause but not because he is committed to liberation. He speaks because of the injustice we have suffered. To him justice is equality with the Jews in Palestine, not eradication of the Jews in Palestine," Omar Samir answered.

"So he will not help us," asked Ismail.

"He gave me the manual they give to the tenants of this Potomac Center, but he said only the developer can give us the plans."

"You mean the Jew?"

"Yes, the Jew—Noah Greenspan. He offered to introduce me to him. He even offered to introduce me to his sister."

"The Palestinian traitor?" asked Walid.

"Yes, the traitor, Alexandra Salaman—the Palestinian woman who deceived us, caused Sheikh Shoukri's death, and is now engaged to the Jew."

"Is it true that she was a double agent working for us and for the Israelis?" Walid asked.

"She had a choice to make," Samir replied. "She made the wrong choice. Alexandra Salaman was a journalist for a big newspaper in America while she was a student at Phoenicia University. She was never really a double agent. Our group at Phoenicia University agreed to let her interview us for the articles she wrote. We used the timing of her articles to alert our comrades when we were shipping arms for an operation we were planning in Israel."

"And she betrayed us?"

"The Israelis figured out what we were doing, sent an agent to Beirut, and divulged to the Salaman women how her articles were being used."

"And her sympathies were with them?"

"Worse. She agreed to work with the enemy. She tricked our sheikh, Ali Abdul Shoukri, into divulging our target, and she informed the Israelis and fled with them to Israel."

"She will soon regret her treachery," Khaled said.

"That's why we're here," Samir replied. "The world will soon know that we are not defeated and that we are certainly not gone—that we can strike anywhere, even in the heart of America." Then Omar Samir directed his attention to Khaled. "What have you learned Khaled?" Khaled Kassab looked at each of them, taking his time before answering.

"There is an explosive compound that is ideal for our needs," he finally answered, authoritatively. "It is like putty—like modeling clay. It can be shaped and disguised any way we want to shape and disguise it, and it can be easily and safely shipped anywhere we want to ship it," Khaled replied. "It is perfect."

"Go on," Omar said, eager to hear what Khaled, the most educated of the group, had learned.

"You mean we don't have to ship dynamite or some kind of bomb?" Ismail asked.

"Well, I suppose almost anything that explodes is a bomb. But this is very different. It can be disguised and shaped into almost anything. It could even be inserted in the bottom of a vase like the material florists use to hold flowers in place. In fact, you could make the entire vase out of this material."

"And how do you set it off?" Ismail asked, his interest piquing.

"With this explosive compound, we'll need little more than a radio transmitter to send a signal to a small detonator; even a citizens-band radio would work."

"You could really plant it in a vase?" Walid asked.

"You could plant it in anything and place it almost anywhere. A receiving antenna could even be disguised to appear as a flower stem. A kilo or two would do a lot of damage. Enough devices placed throughout our target would absolutely destroy the place."

"And you are certain we can do this?" Omar asked.

"It will take time, maybe a year, to gather the material we need, but yes, it can be done."

"What if we can't get our hands on the detailed drawings?"

"We may have all the information we need. Mostly, we need to know where every support column is and the exact location of the air-handling plant. I think we can sever enough support columns with a couple of kilos of this compound planted at each column. It's that powerful."

"And we can obtain this new compound you speak of?"

"Yes, I think so. As I said, it will take time to accumulate enough of this material. They call it plastique, because it is so malleable. It's actually a compound known as pentaerythritol tetranitrate, or Petn for short.

"Where can we find this plastique you speak of?" Omar asked.

"I think I've found a source in Czechoslovakia. There is a manufacturer not far from the town of Pardubice," Khaled answered. "They have been supplying the product in Czechoslovakia for about four years. It's used for demolition, mine clearing, and other similar civil-engineering activities. The company that makes the plastique, Demolishia, has also been selling their plastique to North Vietnam to help them fight the Americans. We have a contact that knows people involved in the shipments to North Vietnam. He says they can supply enough for our purpose and they are willing to sell us what we'll need. It won't be cheap, but I believe we can obtain what we need."

"Why are they doing this?"

Khaled smiled, ominously. "Do you think we're the only people who want to blow things up? It appears there's a huge and growing market for turmoil in the world, and these people intend to be suppliers for this market."

"How will we plant these explosive devices in the target and not be detected?" Walid asked.

"Leave that to me," Omar replied. "I think I have a plan that will work."

"You think you have a plan to place this plastique Khaled speaks of throughout the Jew's project, this Potomac Center, and not be detected?" Walid asked again.

"Yes, Walid. I have such a plan," Omar Samir replied, ominously.

CHAPTER ELEVEN

By the middle of June, the crowds of shoppers at Potomac Center were exceeding all projections. Noah stood at the window of his office and looked down at the massive parking lot below. It seemed that every parking place on the west side of Potomac Center was filled, and the new indoor garage was at capacity too. The war, it seemed, had caused but a brief delay in the traffic flowing into the project, and media crews were now on-site day after day covering Noah's successful urban-renewal project.

He would have been euphoric over the immediate success of Potomac Center but for the nagging frustration with Alexandra. She was so far away and so reticent, even a bit distant, during her brief telephone conversations with him. Something was wrong, and while he didn't know exactly what was troubling Alexandra, he knew she had been with Amos that first day in Tel Aviv and that there had been no excitement—nothing positive in her voice since then. She was not sharing much about her conversations with Amos, and that nagged at him. And, he wondered, what was this ridiculous business that Alexandra's stories were going to be written under the pseudonym Sabirah Najat?

Alexandra was, of course, eager to reveal to Noah and Yusuf what she had learned from Amos about Omar Samir and AASLF, but she understood the extreme sensitivity of the information and the danger. Alexandra would proceed cautiously, as Amos insisted. Whatever plan he was now developing with Benjamin Bar-Levy and his colleagues at

Mossad and Shin Bet would determine how and when Noah and Yusuf would learn of the danger they were facing.

Noah was anything but happy. At thirty years of age, he was responsible for one of the most successful land-development projects in the country, but as he stood looking down at the crowds entering Potomac Center, his mind wandered. His thoughts were thousands of miles to the east. What in the world was Alexandra up to? Why was she being so cryptic? Was she safe?

"Noah," Barb's voice crackled through the telephone intercom.

"Yeah," he called from across the office, as he turned back toward his desk.

"Noah, it's Karen Rothschild calling from Chicago," Barb answered. "She said it would only take a moment."

"Karen?" Noah answered, as he picked up the phone.

"Hi, Noah. I won't take but a second—"

"No, no. Take all the time you want. What's up?" he replied.

"Well, I was wondering if you and Alexandra might have time for dinner next week. I'm going to be passing through Washington on the way to Israel."

"You're going to Israel?" Noah replied, puzzled.

"Yes, Jewish Federation has arranged a mission to Israel. You know, to show support following the war. I've signed up to go. We leave through Dulles. I thought I'd come to Washington a day early and visit you guys."

Noah didn't speak for a moment as he absorbed Karen's message.

"Noah...Noah, are you there?"

"Yeah, I'm here," he answered, a touch of irony evident in his voice.

"Look, I'm sorry," she replied. "I realize what a busy time this must be for you. It was just a crazy idea. I thought—"

"No, no," he interrupted. "It's not a crazy idea at all. In fact it's almost funny. Karen, Alexandra is in Israel. The *Star* sent her over there to cover whatever the hell is going on now between the Palestinians and the Israelis."

"Are you serious?"

"Yeah, you'll see her before I do. She's in Tel Aviv. She's at the Dan Hotel."

"We'll be in Jerusalem at the King David for several days, and then we go to Tel Aviv, and we're staying at the Dan too."

"I'll let Alexandra know when you're expected. I don't know what her schedule will be, but right now I know she's at the Dan."

"So...does dinner work for you next Wednesday?" she asked, haltingly.

"Of course dinner works for me. Come as early as you can. I want to show you Potomac Center," he replied, his spirits momentarily lifted.

"Oh, that sounds great. I'm dying to see it."

"You were a major part of Potomac Center, Karen."

"Thank you for saying that, Noah. I really appreciate it. You were right all along though. Yusuf being the architect didn't hurt the project at all."

"You vouching for him and for the integrity of the selection process in court didn't exactly hurt either. I think it saved the whole project," Noah said.

"I'll check into the Hay-Adams Wednesday morning. That's pretty close by."

"I'll pick you up at National Airport, Karen. I'll show you around Potomac Center, and we can have dinner later. How does that sound?"

"That sounds great. Can you take that much time away from work?"

"The place runs fine without me. Don't quote me, but it really does."

"Wednesday morning then? I arrive at eleven forty-five."

"I'll be there," Noah replied, enthusiastically.

CHAPTER TWELVE

Alexandra spent her first full day in Tel Aviv simply observing people going about their business. The city seemed remarkably normal given that Tel Aviv was barely a two-hour drive from where Israeli forces had burst into the Sinai less than two weeks earlier. She observed both pride and joy among the Israelis and, among the Palestinians, gloom and humiliation. She filed her first story that night.

THE SIX-DAY WAR—AND NOW WHAT?
By Sabirah Najat

Tel Aviv, Israel—There is euphoria here following the lightning speed with which Israel brought to an end the threat to its existence promised by Egypt's Nasser, Syria's al-Atassi, and Jordan's king Hussein. That euphoria, however, may soon be eclipsed by the despair of more than one million Palestinian Arabs who, for better or worse, are now part of the fabric of this nation.

The humiliation the Arab world experienced when the United Nations created the State of Israel in 1948 may well be multiplied many times over by the utter defeat of their greatest military forces at the hands of the Israelis. And while Israelis savor the sweet fruit of victory and the place it has earned them in the annals of history, Palestinians, who were not combatants in this war, contemplate the bitter taste of hopelessness and the prospect of being consigned to history's litany of lost causes.

The extent of the Arab defeat is, to most Palestinians, just sinking in. The three mightiest Arab fighting machines now lie in ruin. No one here believes the claims of Nasser and Hussein that the Americans and British were attacking in concert with the Israelis. They were desperate fabrications—lies, and everyone knows it. In fact, everyone here now realizes that Israel faced its enemies alone. France abandoned Israel, and America, too bogged down in Vietnam, did nothing. The call for an international flotilla to break the blockade of the Straits of Tiran fell on deaf ears. The Israelis have emerged as the strongest fighting force in the Middle East. That seismic reality is just sinking in, and with it the realization that Israel is here to stay.

Arabs in this part of the world refer to the creation of the State of Israel as the nakbah, or the catastrophe. The catastrophe to which they refer, however, doesn't seem to be the plight of those who were displaced by the fighting twenty years ago. If that were the case, every Arab nation in the area would have embraced those who were displaced and moved as quickly as possible to end the catastrophe from which people suffered.

When the Jews suffered the catastrophe of the Holocaust, other Jews and many nations moved quickly to ease the burden of the victims and to ease the catastrophic effects of such massive suffering. But this catastrophe, this nakbah, goes on. It is, indeed, perpetuated by those Arab nations that should be most eager to help. Sadly, this catastrophe, this nakbah, about which the

Arabs speak, is not the hardship created by the establish-
ment of Israel. It is, instead, the very existence of Israel. It
is a type of rejectionism, an absolutism that has gone on
for twenty years and, one fears, may go on indefinitely.

Some Israelis and many historians claim there is no
Palestinian people and that there never has been. They
say there have only been Ottoman subjects, Jordanian
subjects, Egyptian subjects, or subjects of the British
Mandate. They believe that when there was no nation-
hood, everyone who lived on this land was Palestinian
whether Muslim, Christian, or Jewish. Ironically, many
if not most institutions that called themselves Palestinian
were, in fact, Jewish institutions.

Well, now there are more than a million men,
women, and children living within Israeli-controlled
territory who are not Israeli and can no longer be
considered subjects of Egypt, Jordan, or Syria, and
the Ottoman Empire has been gone for half a centu-
ry. The Israelis like to say that this recently conclud-
ed war has created new realities on the ground, and
that is true. One of these realties, however, that no one
here seems to want to address is this mass of humanity
that now lives stateless within this state. What shall we
call them? What will they call themselves? What will
they become? They are not Israelis, and they are not
refugees. They have not been banished, nor have they
fled. If, as many Israelis believe, there has never been
a Palestinian people, then the grand irony of this war
might be that Israel has just created them.

***

Noah picked up a copy of the *Evening Star* at the airport newsstand and read Alexandra's first story from Tel Aviv while waiting for
Karen's United flight to arrive from Chicago. He, of course, knew she

was writing under the name Sabirah Najat, but he wasn't exactly sure why—something about security that she didn't want to discuss in any detail over the telephone. Leave it to Alexandra to raise the tough questions, he thought as he finished reading. He recalled her first story, "Heirs of Eden," which she had written twelve years earlier when she was still a high-school intern at the *Star*. That raised some pretty big questions too, he mused, chuckling to himself.

Noah watched as the passengers made their way from the plane into the terminal. And then, there she was, smiling broadly as soon as she spotted him. She was as pretty as when he last saw her, and a lot happier. He knew she had flown first-class, being one of the first passengers off the plane. Karen looked just as he remembered her. She was dressed smartly, casual but stylish, and she had that same peaches-and-cream complexion and silky flaxen hair and those pale blue eyes that he found so enchanting when they first met at the University Deli at Palo Alto twelve years earlier. So much had happened since then, he thought, as she rushed to him and threw her arms around his shoulders.

"Oh, look at you," she said joyfully as she pulled away from him. "You look wonderful."

"You look wonderful yourself," he replied.

"Tell me everything that's happening," she said, excitedly, as she took his arm on the way to the baggage-claim area.

"Well, in about fifteen minutes, I'll show you."

He grabbed both pieces of luggage as soon as she pointed them out, and they continued on toward the parking lot. "I thought we'd go over to Potomac Center. We can have lunch there, and I'll give you a complete tour," he said, squinting against the bright June sun.

"That sounds great," she replied, as they arrived at his Corvette.

"A white Corvette! You devil, you," she exclaimed enthusiastically. "It's beautiful."

"Hop in," he said, opening the door for her. "I'm so happy you called and stopped off in Washington."

"Me too," she replied. "I thought a reunion was way overdue. I would love to see Yusuf and Ed, and I'm truly sorry Alexandra isn't here."

"Alexandra would have enjoyed seeing you too, Karen. She had to rush off pretty quickly as soon as the fighting stopped over there."

"You look wonderful, Noah," she said, changing the subject as they headed onto the George Washington Parkway.

"And you've never looked better, Karen. It was very exciting to see you step into the terminal from the plane," he replied, as he reached over and turned on the radio. They both burst out laughing as the sound of Frankie Valli singing "Can't Take My Eyes Off You" floated softly from the speakers.

Noah took the Fourteenth Street Bridge over the Potomac and headed into the city. Karen grew silent as they passed old familiar landmarks. "It's been a long time," she said, sadly.

Noah reached over and gently squeezed her hand. "I know," he replied.

"The city looks pretty much the same as when I left," she said, lightening the mood a bit.

"Congress finally passed the subway bill last year. This city will be torn up for the next ten years."

Karen looked over at Noah and smiled. "I remember telling you about the subway when I was working for the House Public Works Committee. I could almost see the wheels turning in your head when I first mentioned the plans for the Metro." Noah nodded.

"I remember like it was yesterday. We were going out to see *Death of a Salesman* at the National Theater that night. You know, that conversation changed my life. It revealed an opportunity of a lifetime."

"And you grabbed it and ran with it, Noah."

"I optioned land around future Metro stops and did it all with borrowed money. The land values skyrocketed around those Metro stations."

"As you knew it would once word got out about the location of those stations."

"All because you gave me an advance peek at the study that included the Metro map before anyone else knew about those details."

"So, I sort of made you rich," Karen said, playfully.

"Sort of," Noah replied with a slight grin.

"Ever think about going public?" Karen asked.

"Are you kidding?" he replied, turning to face her.

"Nope."

"Why would I do that?"

"Why not? This won't be your last project, and you've outgrown Capital City National Bank. Why go around scavenging for loans next time when you can have great investors as partners?"

"Like?"

"Like Mid-America Ventures and a few thousand other shareholders," she answered coolly.

"Are you serious?" Noah asked.

Karen peered back at Noah and simply nodded.

"You are serious."

"Something to think about, Noah. We'll talk more when I return from Israel. I don't want to turn today into a business meeting."

He held her gaze for an extra moment. Karen smiled coyly. "You know development, Noah. We know finance. You'll need capital. We know how to raise it."

"I'll be damned," he said, smiling back at her. "I'll be damned."

Karen's eyes widened as they drove into Potomac Center. "Oh, Noah, it's just as Yusuf drew it. It's beautiful," she said, breathlessly.

"It's almost entirely occupied," he replied, enthusiastically. "All of the residential units are either occupied or under contract, and the offices are nearly all leased too. We'll have lunch in the mall. We have a little space we can still lease out, but all the high-traffic space is gone."

"Wow, it's fantastic. I've seen some photos in the press, but they don't do Potomac Center justice. Noah, I'm so proud of you."

He smiled and turned to her as they pulled into his parking space. There were tears in her eyes.

"Are you OK?" he asked, softly.

Karen just nodded, momentarily too emotional to speak.

"You were a part of it, Karen—a damned important part. Potomac Center wouldn't be here if it weren't for you."

Karen nodded her understanding. "Thanks," she finally managed to say.

Noah reveled in showing Karen Potomac Center. They walked through all five floors of the mall and paused for lunch at the Neptune Room, which occupied prime space on the first floor of the Potomac Center. Karen remembered that it was at the Neptune Room downtown on Twelfth Street that she, Noah, and Alexandra had shared what was, for him, a tense lunch during her first trip to Washington, a dozen years earlier. He cringed, playfully, when she reminded him. Later that afternoon, Noah and Karen walked along the pier at the marina that defined the western boundary of Potomac Center at the riverfront.

"How are your folks?" she asked, taking his hand as they strolled along.

"They're really fine," he replied, tightening his grip ever so slightly. She reciprocated and smiled up at him. They walked along, in silence, for several minutes.

"It's been a wonderful afternoon," she finally managed to say.

"The day is still young," he replied.

"And therefore what?" she asked, playfully.

"And therefore…"

"Yes?" she prodded.

"How would you like to go to Griffith Stadium and watch the White Sox play the Senators tonight?"

"The White Sox are playing Washington tonight?" she asked, excitedly.

"Yep," he answered.

"That sounds great. Let's do it," she replied.

As they drove to the stadium through LeDroit Park, Noah pointed out the old For You Market where Karen had first met his parents.

He drove by the vacated Crescent Market two blocks away, where Alexandra's parents, Samira and Sharif, had embraced her on that first trip to Washington during Christmas break when she and Noah were freshmen at Stanford.

It was not quite the evening either of them expected. The game dragged on for twenty-two innings with the Senators finally scoring the winning run at 2:43 a.m. It was 3:30 before Noah dropped Karen off at the Hay-Adams. As the night doorman came over to retrieve her luggage from the trunk of the Corvette, Karen threw her arms around Noah. They hugged one another as he kissed her on the cheek.

"It's been a wonderful day, Karen. I'm sorry we picked what turned out to be the longest game in history."

"I loved it. It gave me more time with you," she replied. "Noah, I'll call when I get back to the States. Meanwhile, think about what I said about going public."

"I will," he answered. "Karen, remember to call Alexandra when you check into the Dan."

She smiled, grabbed him by the front of his shirt, and kissed him, quickly and playfully, on the lips. "You're one of a kind, Greenspan," she said with a smile, and with that she turned and disappeared into the Hay-Adams.

CHAPTER

THIRTEEN

The ringing of the telephone awakened Alexandra from a much-needed, deep, and peaceful sleep.

"Yes," she whispered, only half-awake.

"Alexandra, it's Amos."

"Hi, Amos," she said, groggy but happy to hear it was him. "You're still a nice voice to wake up to."

"Don't tantalize me," he replied.

"Amos, it's seven thirty. Are you going to be my wake-up call every morning?"

"Alexandra, I'm sorry to be calling so early, but we have to talk."

"Is anything wrong?"

"Can you meet me for breakfast in an hour?"

"Something is wrong, isn't it?" she asked.

"In an hour…the dining room."

"OK, Amos. I'll be there," she answered, knowing better than to press him for more information on the phone. Amos was already waiting at a table in a secluded corner of the dining room when she arrived. He rose as soon as he saw her enter the room. Alexandra walked to the table and looked at him, quizzically. Amos smiled, but his expression was serious. He pulled a chair out for her.

"Amos, what is it?" she asked, apprehensively, as she sat down.

"I assume you are Sabirah Najat," he answered.

"Of course I'm Sabirah Najat. You said I had to use a pseudonym. Is there a problem with the name I've chosen?"

"No, Alexandra, there's no problem with the name you've chosen."

"Then what's the problem?"

"The problem is what you...what Sabirah Najat has written."

"What are you talking about?"

"Alexandra, this business about the war creating among Palestinians a new or stronger sense of peoplehood that didn't previously exist—"

"What about it?" she interrupted. "Did I...Did Sabirah Najat write something that isn't true?"

"No, Alexandra, you didn't write anything that isn't true. Actually, it's an interesting point of view."

"Then what's the problem?" she repeated, an impatient edge to her voice.

"Some people may think it's seditious."

"That's ridiculous."

"Alexandra, people here are already talking about the story."

"So, what are they saying?"

"They're asking who Sabirah Najat is and if she is some troublemaker."

"I didn't create any trouble, Amos. I didn't add over a million un-happy Palestinians to what is now Israeli territory."

"Alexandra, have you no idea how tense this situation is? What would you have had us do, Alexandra?" Amos replied, impatiently. "Do you have any idea what would be happening right now if Nasser and his clique of incompetents had prevailed in this war that he so stupidly blundered into? He and his Syrian partner predicted that no Jews would survive."

"But what does that have to do with my article in the *Star*?"

"You write for an influential newspaper in the capital of the one country we can't afford to alienate."

"Amos, I—Sabirah Najat wasn't critical of Israel. But you have one huge problem on your hands now. Maybe before June fifth you could get away with believing that the million Palestinians living on the West Bank under the Jordanians and in Gaza under the Egyptians didn't constitute a Palestinian people, but they don't live in Jordan or Egypt anymore. They live here. What does that make them?"

"A problem," Amos conceded, in a low voice, barely above a whisper.

"Then what is your complaint about what I wrote?"

"Just that you wrote it. You don't know how sensitive this whole subject is. It could anger people here who aren't ready to deal with this and maybe motivate others who are," he said.

"Amos, that's not my problem. If people are angry and if some are, as you say, motivated by what I write, then I'm probably doing my job."

"You doing your job may make me doing my job a lot harder."

"And just what is your job, Amos?"

His eyes fixed on hers. "Stopping bad things from happening... remember?"

"Touché, Amos. You certainly have stopped bad things from happening. I should know. But I'm a professional journalist now. My job is to write what I see, hear, and feel, and what I feel is what is probably most important. That's why they sent me here."

"And what do you feel, Alexandra?"

"Amos, what is Israel going to do with over a million hopeless Palestinians?"

"You're avoiding my question, Alexandra. You're answering my question with another question. I asked you what you feel."

"I feel the war has exposed a festering sore. Israel has absorbed an immense resentful population into its realm. One hundred thirty thousand Arabs live on the Golan, over one hundred thousand live in and around East Jerusalem, over six hundred thousand live on the West Bank, and nearly four hundred thousand live in Gaza. What is Israel going to do with all those people, Amos? Do you think they're just going to accept Israeli rule?"

"They accepted Egyptian rule and Jordanian rule and Syrian rule."

"Those were Arab rulers, Amos," she answered, her voice rising. "Do you think now they're just going to accept Israeli rule?" she asked again, incredulously.

"Alexandra, can I tell you something off the record?" Amos asked, as he looked around to determine if other diners could overhear their conversation.

"Of course," she replied.

"There are those in this government who are prepared to offer all of the Sinai back to Egypt, as well as the Golan Heights back to Syria," he said, his voice lowered to barely above a whisper.

"Really?"

"Really. There are strong voices in this government that want to do that in return for formal peace agreements with Egypt and Syria."

"What about the West Bank? That's where most of the Palestinian population live."

"That's going to be more complicated. Israel will never agree to a border that places Jordanian artillery within nine miles of Tel Aviv and our coast. Somehow the West Bank would have to be demilitarized. So would the Golan Heights. But those are details that we're willing to seriously discuss, Alexandra."

"Amos, you said there are voices within the government that favor taking these steps. I presume there are voices that also oppose taking these steps."

"Of course there are, Alexandra. We're a democracy. But I'm telling you these proposals are on the table."

"And you've also told me that this is all off the record."

"For now, it has to be."

"Why?"

"Because if you start writing about these proposals too soon, those who object to them will become very vocal and very aggressive. These ideas will die a sudden death if they're exposed too early. Remember this is a so-called unity government. There are men in this cabinet, powerful men, followers of Ze'ev Jabotinsky, Zionist revisionists who still feel with every fiber of their being that Israel should consist of all of what was the British mandate. They don't even recognize the legitimacy of Jordan. To them, ancient Judea and Samaria is Israel."

"Is that what you feel, Amos?"

"Look, Alexandra, Ben-Gurion and Chaim Weizman were practical Zionists. They embraced the realm of the possible, and as a result we have the State of Israel today. The Israel Jabotinsky dreamed of is not realistic—not today and not tomorrow. This tiny country that we do have is a miracle. That's the Israel I've devoted my career to safeguarding."

"What do you want of me, Amos?"

"Alexandra, there's a lot at stake here. We need a period of calm so that we have a chance to seriously explore peace with our Arab neighbors."

"Amos, nothing I write is going to interfere with Israel and its neighbors exploring peaceful coexistence."

"Words mean a great deal to people in this part of the world, Alexandra."

"My words will always speak to truth, Amos. Is there anything I have written with which you take issue?"

"I don't think we've created a new Palestinian identity by winning the war, as Sabirah Najat suggests. These people have lived under a succession of different sovereigns."

With that, Alexandra's demeanor suddenly changed. There was now anger in her eyes. "'These people'! How dare you?"

Amos's regret at his choice of words was immediate. "Alexandra, I'm sorry. I didn't mean it that way."

"You didn't mean it what way?" she shot back at him.

"I wasn't talking about people like you—like Yusuf and your parents."

"Of course you were," she snapped. "What is wrong with you?"

"Your family moved from here. It's not the same, Alexandra."

"My family *fled* from here, Amos. We fled," she cried.

Amos lowered his head into his hand, distraught at the turn the conversation had taken. "We're trying to figure out how to hold things together, Alexandra," he finally said, looking up at her, his expression pleading for understanding. "There is going to be a real effort to find a path to peace with our neighbors."

"Which neighbors?" she asked, calmly.

"All of them. Egypt…Jordan…Syria," he answered.

"And the million Palestinians in Gaza, the West Bank, and East Jerusalem? What is the plan for making peace with them?"

"It will take time," he answered, his voice barely above a whisper.

"Do me a favor, Amos. Please don't ever try to influence what I write. No good can come of it." Alexandra paused for a moment to carefully consider her next words. "I have no ax to grind. What I write will reflect what I see, hear, and feel. I have no desire whatsoever to antagonize anyone, least of all you."

Amos nodded his understanding. "We've spoken to your government about Samir and the AASLF," he said, abruptly changing the subject.

"Oh," Alexandra answered, taken aback by the shift in conversation. "What are they going to do?"

"My understanding is that they will send someone from the FBI to talk to Noah. They'll let him know what we know, and they'll assure him they are on top of it. They'll tell him not to receive anyone without an appointment, especially anyone saying he is from AASLF Partners. They'll let him know that they and we are coordinating very closely and that protecting him and Potomac Center are our top priority."

"Can I discuss this with him?"

"No, not from here. The FBI will let him know that you are aware of what is going on and that you've been asked not to discuss any of this on the telephone."

"What a mess," she whispered. "What a goddamned mess."

Amos stood to leave. Alexandra rose and hugged him affectionately. "I'm sorry I lost my temper, Amos. I know your heart is in the right place."

"Can we have dinner in the next few days?" he asked.

"You know my number," she answered, trying to manage a smile.

***

Barb showed the two FBI agents into Noah's office. They had called early that morning and asked to see him that same day. Agent Lawrence Hogan had been vague on the phone, saying it was something about security. Agent Mike Atkins, who accompanied Agent Hogan, seemed the younger of the two. Noah guessed they were both in their midthirties, not much older than he.

Noah greeted the two federal agents and ushered them to the small conference table at the corner of his office. They declined Barb's offer of coffee.

"Beautiful project you have here, Mr. Greenspan," Agent Hogan said as soon as they took their seats. He smiled affably, but the intensity with which his piercing blue eyes fixed on Noah telegraphed the seriousness of the visit.

"We're very proud of it," Noah answered. "Would you like a tour of Potomac Center?"

"Actually, we would," Agent Hogan replied. "In fact, in the next day or two we'd like a team of our people to have a look."

"What's this all about?" Noah asked.

"We don't want to alarm you, Mr. Greenspan, but we have reason to suspect that Potomac Center and perhaps even you may be the target of a terrorist plot."

"What!" Noah responded. "Someone has made a threat against me or against Potomac Center?"

"No," Agent Hogan replied. "Had there been a threat, we'd have more to go on. We're just putting two and two together and concluding that there may be a plot—a conspiracy under way—and that you and this project might be the targets."

"Based on what?" Noah asked.

"Based on this," Agent Hogan replied, handing Noah a photocopy of the business card of the man who called himself Abu Salma.

"Have you seen this before?" Agent Atkins asked.

"Yeah," Noah responded hesitantly as he looked at the photo. "My architect, Yusuf Salaman, showed it to us the day we opened Potomac Center. This Mr. Salma had visited him in Baltimore and said he represented an investment group that wanted to build a project modeled after Potomac Center. They wanted to buy the plans for Potomac Center."

"Did Mr. Salaman make the plans available to these people?"

"No—of course not. He said they would have to discuss that with me."

"The man who visited Mr. Salaman was not who he represented himself to be."

"I know. My fiancée was here when Yusuf showed us the card and said *Abu Salma* had to be a pseudonym—that the real Abu Salma is some kind of a famous poet over in the Middle East. She said pseudonyms or noms de guerre are pretty common over there."

"Your fiancée is Alexandra Salaman?" Agent Hogan asked.

"Yes. Alexandra and I are engaged to be married," he replied, surprised that the agents knew her name. "How did you get a copy of this card?"

"This was photocopied to us from the Mossad, Israel's equivalent to our CIA or, in some respects, our FBI. In fact, it was sent directly to Director Hoover from Meir Amit, the director of Mossad."

"Holy shit," Noah murmured under his breath. "What the hell is going on?"

"We're not exactly sure, Mr. Greenspan, but here's what we do know. The man who called on Yusuf Salaman to acquire your architectural plans, the man who called himself Abu Salma, is a known terrorist, Omar Samir."

"And this investment group, AASLF Partners—does he actually work for them?" Noah asked.

"AASLF Partners is not an investment group, Mr. Greenspan. AASLF stands for Ali Abdul Shoukri Liberation Front. They're some kind of Palestinian terrorist cell," Agent Hogan replied.

Noah sat there for a moment, dumbfounded. "I know all about Ali Abdul Shoukri," he finally said in a low voice. "He almost killed my fiancée." Then, as though suddenly startled, Noah reached out to Agent Hogan's arm. "Is she…Is Alexandra all right?"

"As far as we know, she's perfectly safe right now in Israel."

"Does she know about all of this?"

"Yes, we're told she's been thoroughly briefed. In fact, all of this came to light because she gave this card to someone in Israel who works for Mossad."

"Oh, now it all makes sense," Noah said, punching his fist into the palm of his hand. "She must have given the card to Amos Ben-Chaiyim, an Israeli friend. He has some kind of job with Israeli intelligence. She said she was going to inquire about the man who calls himself Abu Salma when she got to Israel. This is why she's writing under a pseudonym, *Sabirah Najat*. They don't want Samir or his cronies to know she's in Israel."

"Right now we assume Alexandra is safe in Israel. We're pretty sure Samir and his cohorts have no reason to think she is anywhere near them. Frankly, we're more concerned about you, Mister Greenspan."

"Why me? Why in the world would they care about me or Potomac Center?"

"We're not sure, but we can guess," Agent Atkins replied.

"Please, go on."

"Mr. Greenspan, you're Jewish…is that right?"

"Yes, I'm Jewish."

"And you're engaged to Miss Salaman, who is Palestinian."

"Yes…she's Christian."

"And Miss Salaman was involved with this Ali Abdul Shoukri when she was a student in Beirut a few years ago."

"Well, she wasn't exactly involved with him. He had duped her."

"Yes, yes, we understand that, but we don't think that matters too much. She divulged Shoukri's scheme to the Israelis and fled to Israel with this Amos Ben-Chaiyim person. As we understand the case,

Shoukri was killed when the Israelis rescued Miss Salaman following Shoukri's attempt to kidnap her."

"Actually, he did kidnap her. Ben-Chaiyim almost got killed when Shoukri took Alexandra."

"So she eventually left Israel and returned here to marry you, a Jewish businessman."

"We've known each other since we were kids," Noah said, softly.

"And you have now developed a very high-profile real-estate project in our nation's capital and, we might add, a project that has been publicized abroad."

"Why would these terrorists want to pick a fight with America?"

"They think America was allied with Israel in the war that just ended. They think it was America that destroyed the combined air forces of Egypt, Jordan, and Syria. So, attacking a major high-profile project in the United States would make sense to this group."

"Whew—you paint a pretty frightening picture," Noah said. "So you think they're going to come here and shoot up the place and, maybe, try to kill me?" Agent Atkins looked to his colleague. Agent Hogan carefully considered his response.

"Mr. Greenspan, these people don't need architecture plans to shoot up the place—or, frankly, to try to kill you."

"What are you saying?"

"Look, there's a lot we don't know, so we try to think of what is most logical based on what we do know."

"So?"

Agent Hogan drew a deep breath before responding, "Mr. Greenspan, we're concerned that they plan to blow up Potomac Center and probably try to kill you and, I would guess, your fiancée at the same time."

Silence filled the room as Noah absorbed what the FBI agent said. Both agents sat there silently looking at him as they waited for his response.

"Does Yusuf Salaman know what is going on?

"No, not yet," Agent Atkins replied. "We're driving over to Baltimore from here. "It would be best if you didn't say anything to him until after we talked to him."

"Would you ask him to call me after you have spoken with him?"

"Certainly," Agent Hogan replied, sympathetically.

"So, what should I do?"

"Nothing right now," Agent Hogan replied. "We're hoping they will contact you or Mr. Salaman again. When that call comes, we'll want your secretary, or his, to tell the caller that you'll have to call back. We'll set up a communications system here and in Mr. Salaman's office that will allow us to listen to the call and, hopefully, to be able to trace the call as well."

"What if they don't call? What then?"

"We're pursuing other lines of inquiry. We'll try to identify unusual shipments or thefts of explosives," Agent Atkins answered.

"That doesn't sound very promising," Noah replied. "How in the world can they hope to bring down the entire Potomac Center mall?"

"It would certainly be a very audacious, plan, but that would probably appeal to them. We think it's far-fetched, but there's some very powerful stuff on the market today. It's doable."

"I feel like we're just sitting and waiting for the big bang."

"No, we're not going to just sit. We think we can pick up signs that someone is accumulating this quantity of explosive material. We're assuming they would plan to use C-4 or an explosive called Semtex."

"That's Greek to me," Noah replied.

"It's a puttylike explosive used extensively in demolition, especially in some European countries like Czechoslovakia. It can be easily transported and easily disguised. They'll probably make mistakes in procuring the material. They have no idea we're onto this. With a little luck, we should be able to stop it."

"Why do I not feel reassured?" Noah said, a touch of sarcasm in his voice.

"If we all stay alert, we'll stop them in their tracks. Remember, the Israelis are making this a top priority too. We'll work closely with them, and they're very sharp. They've made tracking these people down a top priority," Agent Hogan said.

"Can I discuss this with Alexandra?"

"Not on the phone. She knows we're talking to you, and she understands the importance of not discussing this on the phone or with anyone other than Israeli intelligence."

"So she knows that I know."

"She knows we're talking to you," Agent Hogan replied.

"Will you keep me posted?"

"We'll brief you from time to time," Agent Hogan answered. "Needless to say, you should keep all of this to yourself. The fewer people who know about this, the better. You should also keep this meeting very confidential. The last thing we would want these terrorists to know is that we're even aware that their cell exists or that they have focused on Potomac Center or any American target, for that matter. We don't want them to know that the FBI is involved. That's an important edge that we have right now."

"Believe me, it's the last thing I want anyone talking about. Is there anything I should do in the meantime?"

Agent Hogan shook his head. "No. Not really. Just go about your business as you normally would. We don't think anything will happen for quite a while, if ever. Just be alert to anyone who is inquiring about details on the construction of Potomac Center. Of course, you shouldn't provide your architectural drawings to anyone without talking to us first. For now, that's about all you can do."

Noah thanked the agents and walked them to the elevator opposite the entrance to the Potomac Center offices. *Shitty way to start the day,* Noah thought as he walked back to his office.

CHAPTER

FOURTEEN

"Alexandra, is that you?" Karen's voice cried out as Alexandra made her way to the elevator from the concierge desk, where she had stopped to inquire about any messages. Alexandra turned and saw the attractive American woman waving, hesitantly, toward her. It had been at least twelve years since Alexandra had last seen Karen Rothschild. It was in Washington during Christmas break, when Karen was a freshman with Noah at Stanford and Alexandra was still a senior in high school. She had come to visit Noah during a brief stop on her way to Williamsburg with her parents.

"Karen…Karen Rothschild, is that you?" Karen hurried over to Alexandra, and the two women embraced after a moment's hesitation.

"What in the world are you doing here?" Alexandra asked, surprised but genuinely happy to see Karen.

"I'm on a Federation mission from Chicago. Noah told me you were here."

"You spoke to Noah?"

"Yes…actually, I stopped off in Washington and met him. He showed me around Potomac Center, and we even went to watch the Senators and White Sox play at Griffith Stadium. He drove me by your parents' old store and the For You Market, too."

"Wow! I'm jealous," Alexandra replied, smiling. Karen returned the gesture. *My God, she's even more beautiful than when I last saw her,* Karen thought.

"Are you just checking in?" Alexandra asked. "You must be exhausted."

"I am. I'm dying to kick off my shoes and just lie back and close my eyes. I know you're here working, Alexandra, but could we possibly meet for dinner sometime? I would love to catch up and just talk with an old friend."

Alexandra hesitated for just a moment to consider having dinner with Karen. After all, this was the woman Noah fell for at Stanford following Alexandra's decision to go off to Beirut for college. This was Noah's former fiancée.

"If you're busy, I absolutely understand…"

"No…no, I would love to have dinner with you. I'm meeting an old friend tonight for dinner. Why don't you plan to join us?"

"Are you sure?"

"Positive," Alexandra replied. "You'll enjoy meeting Amos Ben-Chaiyim. I've known him since I was a student in Beirut."

"Amos Ben-Chaiyim went to school in Beirut?" Karen asked, recognizing the name as Hebrew.

"No, it's a very long story. Much too long to bore a weary traveler with."

"Oh," Karen murmured, nodding ever so slightly. "I remember that name."

"Get some sleep, and we'll meet at seven," Alexandra replied, ignoring Karen's faint recollection of whatever she had heard about Amos. The two women hugged, pleased they had run into one another.

Amos arranged for a car to drive Alexandra to Jerusalem, where an Israeli guide, Baruch Samuels, would join her. They met at the Zion Gate, the same entrance through which a brigade of Israeli paratroopers had liberated the Old City a few days earlier. In just three days, the city would be officially opened to the public and to Jews to come en masse as they pleased for the first time in two thousand years. Baruch Samuels knew Alexandra was a Christian Arab from Jaffa whose family had fled to America during the fighting in 1948. He also knew she wrote for an important American newspaper and assumed that she had some special relationship with Amos.

Alexandra guessed, correctly, that Baruch Samuels was about her age, and he was quite handsome, she thought. He looked more European than Middle Eastern, his brown hair faintly striated with lighter, almost blond tinges from recent exposure to the Sinai sun. He was soft-spoken but quietly rugged like so many of the soldiers she saw on the streets and, she assumed, probably still on active duty.

He made no effort as they walked to temper his joy over Israel's capture of the Old City, which he explained was built by King David a thousand years before the birth of Jesus. Baruch Samuels pointed out the sites where the Jordanians had trashed treasured old synagogues. They stopped at the burned-out hulk of the Hurva Synagogue, the old Great Synagogue built in the sixteenth century, which the Jordanians for no apparent reason had all but destroyed. All that was left of the original structure was a huge arch stretching, pleadingly, skyward. The young Israeli explained how Jordan barred Jews from the Old City in violation of the 1949 armistice.

As they neared the Western Wall, she could hear the rumble of bulldozers crunching through the poorly constructed structures of the old Moroccan Quarter, which over the years had been built to within a dozen feet of the Western Wall. The area was run-down, and the smell of garbage, or worse, permeated the quarter.

"Who lived here?" she asked.

"One hundred and six families," he answered factually and, she thought, coldly.

"How many people?"

"Between six and seven hundred," he replied.

"That's a lot of people to expel overnight," she said evenly and without rancor.

"Yes," he replied, also without rancor. "It's about half the number the Jordanians expelled when they captured the Jewish Quarter in 1948. They never allowed another Jew to visit here. Miss Salaman, this is the holiest place in Judaism," he continued. "These structures are being cleared to provide a plaza that will be open to all people of all faiths—here in front of one of the greatest historical and religious landmarks on earth."

Alexandra nodded without responding.

"Israel will bar no one from coming here as long as he or she comes in peace."

"It must have been a very emotional moment when Israeli soldiers arrived at this place," she said. He turned and faced her.

"It was the most emotional day of my life," he replied.

"You were here?"

"I was here," he answered. "I wasn't ten feet from Commander Motta Gur, our brigade commander, when we liberated this spot. Can you imagine how moving it was to hear the sound of the shofar being blown by General Goren, our chief chaplain, signaling the liberation of this place?"

Alexandra nodded, urging him to continue. "Do you mind if I take some notes while we talk?"

"No, why should I mind?"

"What was it like? What did you feel?"

"I felt—we all felt that we, a small group of paratroopers, had returned a sacred place forbidden to Jews for so long to our people, to whom it belonged. Do you understand, Miss Salaman—"

"Please call me Alexandra," she interrupted.

"Do you understand, Alexandra, that this place is the heart of our eternal capital—that Jews, as a people, had been forbidden from calling this place home for two thousand years, until we came a few days ago? I stood here with my helmet in my hand and looked up at this wall in awe. We cried, Alexandra. We literally wanted to embrace this ancient wall. We felt we were returning here for every Jew who had been denied the right to return here for so long."

"Yes, Baruch, I understand banishment," she said, sadly.

They continued through the ancient streets, walking along the Via Dolorosa as Jesus did carrying the cross on the day of his crucifixion. They stopped for a few moments by the Church of the Holy Sepulcher where Jesus, according to Christian tradition, was entombed and, three days later, resurrected. They made their way through passageways and backstreets, every step a walk through history. Baruch Samuels spoke with reverence as he explained the historical significance of each landmark, and with a hard edge to his voice when he pointed out the dozens of synagogues that had been destroyed by the Jordanians. He pointed to the Mount of Olives, where Jesus delivered sermons, and where Jews had been buried for thousands of years, and where their graves had been systematically desecrated since 1948. "The Jordanians used Jewish tombstones from the Mount of Olives as paving stones for their army camps and even for a hotel," he said, sadly.

As the sun began to set, reflecting brightly off of the Dome of the Rock atop the Western Wall, they began, silent and tired, to make their way back to the Zion Gate where they had met hours earlier.

When they arrived where her car was waiting, Alexandra turned, extended her hand, and clasped his. "I hope you know only peace, Baruch Samuels," she said, warmly.

"May our people live in peace," he replied, managing a faint smile in return.

***

Amos was surprised and, momentarily, disappointed when Alexandra appeared at the hotel dining room with a guest.

"Amos, this is Karen Rothschild, an old friend and a classmate of Noah's when they were students at Stanford," Alexandra said, as she greeted him. "We ran into one another earlier today here at the Dan, and I asked her to join us for dinner. "Karen, say hello to Amos Ben-Chaiyim."

"Hello, Karen. It is good to meet a friend of Alexandra's from America," Amos said, extending his hand to her.

Karen, rarely lost for words, held his gaze for a moment and took his hand, smiling broadly. *So this is the Israeli who saved Alexandra's life in Beirut and with whom she lived in Israel before returning to the States.* Noah had told Karen about Amos Ben-Chaiyim long before Alexandra returned home from Israel.

They dined on traditional Israeli favorites, including tahini, sabih, and shawarma, served with pita and generous portions of hummus and falafel. The three of them got along well. The evening was relaxed and unrushed, and the cabernet from Zichron Ya'akov's oldest winery at the southern end of the Mount Carmel mountain range, south of Haifa, promoted a pleasantly relaxed and convivial evening.

It was during a lapse in banter at the end of the meal that the conversation turned more somber.

"Baruch Samuels was a satisfactory guide?" Amos asked Alexandra, as he poured a second goblet of cabernet for the women.

"He was quite special, Amos," Alexandra replied. "You knew, of course, that he was with the paratroopers that first reached the wall?"

"Yes," Amos answered, nodding. "They were all very moved when they reached the wall."

"You know him?"

"Barely," Amos replied. "I met him at his brother's funeral."

"Oh, I didn't know," she said. "When did his brother die?"

"June fifth. Baruch's brother was killed in the Sinai on the first day of the war. He was among the first of the nearly eight hundred young Israelis who died last week."

Alexandra lowered her eyes and shook her head almost imperceptibly. "It's all so sad," she whispered.

"He lost his brother last week and is conducting tours this week?" Karen asked, puzzled.

"Yes," Amos answered. "He's not religious. He insisted on going back to fight as soon as his brother was buried. He's very passionate about Jewish history here in Jerusalem. That's why I asked him to accompany Alexandra through the Old City today."

"Eight hundred Israelis died fighting last week?" Karen asked.

"Yes, nearly eight hundred," he replied. "We expected many more deaths. We estimated four thousand might die, and we prepared ten thousand graves to be ready for the worst."

"Do you know how many people Nasser sent to their deaths on the other side?" Alexandra asked.

Amos nodded. "It looks like about twenty thousand Arabs died in the fighting last week."

"My God," Karen whispered.

"God willing, we'll all find a way to live together in peace after this," Amos said, soberly.

"Do you believe that, Amos?" Karen asked.

He shook his head and turned to her. "Do I believe it's possible, or do I believe it will happen?"

"Tell us what you think is possible and what you think is probable," Alexandra interrupted.

"Yes, it's possible. We could have peace."

"If the Arabs really wanted it?" Karen asked.

"If both sides really wanted it, Karen. There are Israelis, and there are Arabs, especially among the Palestinians, who would make peace."

"That's encouraging to hear," she replied.

"But…" Alexandra interrupted, urging him on. He shifted his gaze to her and smiled, sadly. "As Alexandra knows only too well, there are also those here in Israel, and certainly those on the other side, who have other plans."

"Meaning?" Karen asked.

"Meaning that the very existence of our tiny nation is absolute anathema to many Arabs, and…" He paused momentarily to consider his words carefully.

"And?" Karen urged him on. Alexandra looked at him intently, as he hesitated.

"And there are those on our side," he continued slowly and deliberately, "who believe that this is our golden opportunity to realize their dream of a Greater Israel—an Israel as it existed in the Old Testament— an Israel consisting of ancient Judea and Samaria."

"And who do you think will prevail?" Karen asked.

Amos smiled, his expression more forlorn than hopeful.

"Anything can happen, Karen," he said with a sigh.

Alexandra reached over and squeezed his hand.

"So, Alexandra, how long do you plan to remain in Israel?" Karen asked, trying to maneuver the conversation away from the somber turn it had taken.

"I don't know. Noah wants me to return as soon as I can, but my boss, Frank Markazie, thinks I should stay through the summer. He believes, as do I, that a new reality is emerging here. As Amos says, things could go either way, and the *Evening Star* wants someone on the ground here to report as it happens."

"Markazie is right," Amos said. "I believe the next ninety days or so will tell the tale. Things will move in one direction or the other, toward peace or toward God only knows what." They sat for a while longer contemplating the evening's conversation before, reluctantly, calling it a night. Amos walked Alexandra and Karen to the elevator and embraced each of the women as they said good night.

"I'll phone you in the morning," he called out to Alexandra, as the door to the elevator closed.

Alexandra and Karen were silent during the brief ascent of the elevator. Alexandra, arriving at her floor first, hugged Karen and asked her to stay in touch while she was in the city. Karen held on to her for a moment and kissed her affectionately on the cheek. "I'm so glad we had this time together," she said.

Alexandra nodded and smiled. "Let's try to get together again before you get too busy with your touring."

***

Alexandra wasted no time moving to the small desk in her room and quickly rolling a sheet of paper onto the carriage of her portable Smith Corona. She sat there thinking about what Baruch Samuels had said in Jerusalem that afternoon and what Amos had said at dinner. Then she began to type.

ISRAEL AND THE ARABS: THE EDEN LEGACY
By Sabirah Najat

Tel Aviv, Israel—It is fervently believed by many here in Israel that 3,270 years ago God gave the law, the Torah, to their ancient forbears at Mount Sinai. Jews commemorate that event on the holiday they call Shavuot. In two days, on Shavuot 1967, or 5727 on the Jewish calendar, Israel will open the liberated Old City of Jerusalem for a mass pilgrimage of Jews for the first time in over two thousand years.

Hundreds of thousands are expected to stream through the Zion Gate into Jerusalem's old Jewish Quarter and on to the Western Wall, the most sacred place in Judaism. This is also a place sacred to Christians and to Muslims. Millions the world over will celebrate this historic occasion. Millions of others will not.

This is a pivotal moment in the history of the Middle East, an historic crunch time. Crucial debates are taking place behind closed doors here in Israel and in every Arab nation. While we do not know who will prevail in these debates, we do know what they are debating. Elected politicians in Israel and their counterparts in neighboring countries—presidents, kings, and emirs—are all debating the same topic. Will there be peace or perpetual conflict? Just what will be the Eden legacy?

Where in this region, rational people might ask, are there leaders who would prefer conflict to peace? Sadly, everywhere. Here in Israel there seem to be two camps. One, which we'll call the Ben-Gurion faction, may be prepared to return all of the recently captured Sinai and Golan Heights in exchange for formal peace. Others, whom we'll call the Jabotinsky faction, believe that today's Jewish state should have the same borders as the Jewish nation of the bible, what they call Judea and Samaria. While neither Ben-Gurion (retired) nor Jabotinsky (deceased) has a say or a vote in this debate, their views have become the deeply held beliefs of present-day politicians in Israel.

Israel's first prime minister, David Ben-Gurion, was a pragmatist. He accepted a smaller legally recognized Israel and would probably urge a return of the Sinai and Golan Heights for peace with Egypt and Syria. Ze'ev Jabotinsky was a militant Zionist revisionist. He believed that Israel should not only include the West Bank (which is now in Israel's hands) but should also encompass the land on both sides of the Jordan River. The Jabotinsky faction in the present government may not, today, have designs on the East Bank of the Jordan River, but it is hard to imagine them agreeing to ever surrendering the Israeli-controlled West Bank.

If peace with Egypt and Syria was conditioned on relinquishing the West Bank to Jordan and returning to the borders that more or less predate the recently concluded war, many believe the Jabotinsky faction would bolt from the government.

On the Arab side, few seem interested in recognizing the Jewish state, and there is little likelihood of any face-to-face talks between the two sides. So thorough and devastating was the defeat of the threatening Arab armies at the hands of the Israelis that it is doubtful that any Arab government could survive face-to-face meetings with the Jewish nation.

So what does all this mean? It means we are, in this region, fast approaching another critical time, a critical period when pressure to resolve this issue is intense and failure to do so may be catastrophic. More than twenty thousand men have been buried here in this region in the past two weeks, more than 95 percent on the Arab side. It was an utter and unnecessary waste of humankind. That's what can happen when nations in conflict ignore an opportunity to resolve their differences peacefully. This war resolved nothing between Israel and its Arab neighbors, other than determining who has the superior armed forces.

The summer of 1967 has just begun. By the time of the fall equinox, the world will know whether this region is drifting toward war or peace. Wars tend to get nastier and deadlier with the passage of time. The conflict that just passed cost nearly twenty-one thousand lives. A new opportunity for resolution is approaching. Nations debate, and the world waits.

CHAPTER FIFTEEN

"We have a problem," Khaled Kassab said as he sat down at breakfast with Omar Samir in Aswân.

"Problems are made to be solved. So what is this problem you speak of?"

"The plastique."

"I thought you found a contact in Czechoslovakia, someone who would sell us this material."

"I have. Our problem isn't finding a supplier. Our problem is finding a receiver, an address to which it can be shipped."

"Why is that a problem, Khaled?"

"Our contact says it is too dangerous to ship plastique anywhere in the Middle East. It would raise eyebrows, he said."

"We can't have it shipped to us here in Egypt?"

Khaled shook his head. "No. My contact won't do it. He says he won't ship anywhere near here. It's too dangerous."

"Where will they ship?"

"Wherever there is no threat of war."

"There are tensions everywhere, Khaled. There is conflict in Southeast Asia, in Africa, the Middle East, the Arabian Peninsula. Wherever we have contacts, there is conflict."

"I think I know a way," Khaled replied. "I have an idea."

"What is your idea?"

"It will be expensive."

"Money is available, Khaled. We have brethren, very wealthy brethren, who are seething at the way the Israelis have humiliated the Arab nation—the entire *ummah*. Money won't be a problem. What is your idea for getting this contact you have to send us this plastique?"

"They don't send it to us. They don't send it here."

"Where would you have them send it?"

Khaled smiled, his expression sinister. "We have them send it directly to Washington," Khaled answered.

Samir looked at Khaled, confused. "I don't understand."

"Omar, last year the American congress approved construction of a huge subway system for the Washington metropolitan area. It will probably be a year or two before actual construction begins, but I think there is an opportunity for us."

How could a subway construction project in America help us?" Samir asked.

"Omar, I think we could establish what would appear to be a legitimate company in Washington. Perhaps an engineering company that claimed its specialty was testing materials for major construction projects. Then we would apply to be placed on the American government's lists of suppliers."

"There is such a list?"

"There is. Twenty years ago the American government created what they call the GSA. It stands for the General Services Administration. This is the agency that buys products and services for the government. The American company I work for here in Egypt does business with this agency. Companies can apply to be included on the list of companies from which the American government buys. This list is called the GSA Contract Schedule."

"You are suggesting we do business with the American government?"

"No, no, of course not. I am just suggesting that the company I am proposing simply apply to be on this GSA list of companies that can bid on contracts with the American government. Then we can say we are on the American GSA list of contractors."

"Go on," Samir urged, his interest rising.

"We'd have an address right in Washington. For all appearances we're a legitimate company. We print on our stationery that we are a GSA-approved contractor. In time, we write to our supplier of plastique and request supplies for testing purposes."

"They would send it?" Samir asked, warming up to the idea.

"Look, the people I'm dealing with are not angels. They can get this plastique to us, but they need cover. They need a plausible reason to send the material. They need to be able to say they were duped if an investigation eventually leads to them. By then we'll be long gone, and Potomac Center will be rubble."

"It's an outrageous idea," Samir responded.

"You don't like it, Omar?"

Samir looked into Khaled's eyes for several moments, and then he grinned ominously. "To the contrary, I do like your idea. I like your idea very much."

"Omar, I think I can get the plastique. You have to figure out how to plant it."

Omar Samir smiled again. "I have a plan, Khaled. You get this plastique to Washington. I'll do the rest."

CHAPTER SIXTEEN

Alexandra's articles quickly became a topic of conversation among many of the *Evening Star*'s readers in Washington, including many influential people in government and the capital's chattering classes. Franklin Markazie was pleased and a bit amused by the growing popularity of the mysterious Sabirah Najat.

Evening Star readers were not, however, the only people reading Alexandra's columns. A number of other publications, including newsletters published by special-interest groups, routinely lifted material of interest to their members from major newspapers and magazines and repackaged and circulated the same news to their subscribers and members.

One such special-interest group that was not pleased with what Sabirah Najat was writing was the Trans-Arab Alliance. The Alliance, as it was known by its members, was, officially, committed to fighting Western cultural influence by promoting Arab culture wherever Arabic was, or had ever been, the predominant language. Unofficially, the Alliance promoted the boycott of all Israeli products, all conferences in which Israelis were participants, and the products of any companies that operated in Israel or whose products were sold in Israel. The Alliance was simply a proxy for those governments and individuals who had no intention of ever recognizing or even tolerating the Jewish state. Its newsletter, *Cultural Jihad*, was published monthly. It ran a handful of Middle East news items invariably copied from other publications and a list of companies and institutions doing business with, or in, Israel. The membership of the Alliance was small, consisting of several hundred officials and royals in a half-dozen oil-rich fiefdoms and several hundred individuals who lived and worked mostly in the United Arab Emirates. Various companies doing business in the Middle East also held a handful of subscriptions. Among its subscribers was the electrical engineer Khaled Kassab.

Khaled generally just skimmed the warmed-over news items in *Cultural Jihad*. He rarely saw anything in them he hadn't already read elsewhere. He was, however, perturbed at the recently reprinted columns written by an Arab woman, Sabirah Najat. Why would an Arab journalist, and a woman no less, write about the utter defeat of mighty Arab armies at the hands of the Jews and dismiss as propaganda the reports of American and British treachery? And then there she was, again, writing about Arab presidents, kings, and emirs debating whether to make peace with Israel. Just who was this traitor Sabirah Najat?

***

It was barely dawn when Alexandra's call from Tel Aviv awakened Noah.

"Noah, it's me," Alexandra said, as soon as she heard his voice. "I'm so sorry to be calling so early there."

"You can call me anytime," Noah replied, still half-asleep. "I had to get up early today anyway. I'm being interviewed on the *Today* show."

"Really! You're being interviewed by Barbara Walters?"

"I'm not sure who will be doing the interview," Noah answered. "All I know is that it will be early. I was told the big story will be Jackie Kennedy's visit to Ireland, so I think they're using me as early filler."

"Noah, that's great!"

"Yeah, Potomac Center has been getting great publicity. Everybody here is talking about Potomac Center—and. of course, Sibarah Najat," he added.

"Very funny."

"Actually, your columns really are getting a lot of attention. I've heard people discussing what you write more than once, Alexandra."

"What are they saying?"

"I think people are curious about—probably fascinated with—the Arab woman the *Evening Star* has reporting from Israel. It's all pretty positive. It's too bad nobody knows it's you."

"Well, I am Arab," Alexandra replied with a chuckle.

"Yes, but Sabirah Najat is getting all the publicity."

"I know, but I think it's just as well that these articles are coming from Sabirah Najat and not Alexandra Salaman."

"Are you worried?"

"No, but I trust Amos's judgment. He thinks it's wise not to publicize my being here. You know what I'm referring to."

"Yes, I had a visit from the FBI, remember?"

"There are some very interesting discussions taking place here. I can't really talk about it on the telephone, but I think big news might be in the making. It's a journalist's dream story."

"Are you about to drop some big news on me, Alexandra?"

"Noah..."

"I'm listening."

"Noah, I can't leave now. I think the major story to come out of this war is simmering right now."

"Alexandra, there will always be big news simmering in the Middle East. If you stay to cover big news in the Middle East, you'll never come home."

Alexandra was silent. She knew, of course, that Noah was right. But this was different. This was the aftermath she was sent to cover."

"Alexandra, you said one week, two at the most. What is it going to be? A month? Two months? The rest of the year?"

"Noah, please try to understand—please," she pleaded. "Maybe a month, maybe two. This is my story, Noah. I can't just walk away from it. I can't call Markazie and say I want to come home because I told you I would only be gone a week or two at the most."

"What's going on here right now with Potomac Center is *my* story, Alexandra. I'd like you to be here sharing it with me."

"Oh, Noah, I'm so proud of you. What you've accomplished is amazing—all of the news coverage, the *Today* show. There is no place I would rather be. You know that."

"But?"

"But I can't leave here until my work is done—until all of this plays out."

"Alexandra, it might take the rest of our lives for this to 'play out,' as you say."

"Noah, there's talk of a meeting of all the Arab countries. It could be historic."

"When is this meeting supposed to take place?"

"It's just speculation, Noah. Nothing has been determined as far as I know, but the Arab world is going to have to take a unified position—either peace or perpetual conflict. No one knows what is going to happen, but everyone here knows something is brewing."

"It's the Middle East, Alexandra. Things can brew for a very long time. I don't have to tell you that. You and I were kids when this conflict was brewing. It's still brewing."

"What do you want me to do, Noah?" Alexandra snapped, exasperated.

"I think it's time for you to come home," he replied. "Neither you nor anyone else knows how long things are going to brew, as you say. You've been there for the entire month of June. Enough already. I think you and I have to get on with our lives."

"Goddammit, Noah! I'm a journalist covering one of the biggest stories of our time, and I'm not running home because you're impatient with the time this is taking," she replied, her voice angrier than she intended.

"Fine! Let me know when the story is through brewing."

"Noah, please. Be reasonable."

"Be reasonable? Alexandra, first of all, I question whether you should be there at all. For God's sake, you're writing under an alias because it's too dangerous for you to use your real name. Who the hell knows what is going to happen over there…or when? You're six thousand miles away, anything can happen, you have no idea when you're coming home, and you're asking me to be reasonable."

Alexandra knew it was futile to argue any further. "I didn't call to argue, Noah."

"I wish you were here, Alexandra. You've done your job. You dropped everything to cover this story, just as Markazie asked."

"I'm still covering the story, Noah. I can't leave," she said, sadly but firmly.

"Yeah, I know," he replied irritably, but resigned to her decision. "Take care of yourself, Alexandra. Be careful. I have to get moving. They want me over at WRC an hour before show time, and the traffic on Massachusetts Avenue heading up to Ward Circle will be heavy."

"Noah, I love you very much."

"I love you too, Alexandra," he replied, too hurriedly. "Gotta run. Talk to you soon."

Alexandra showered, quickly applied a touch of makeup, and slipped into jeans and a blouse. She couldn't shake the conversation with Noah from her mind. He was, understandably, impatient with her indeterminate absence. And as much as she dreaded upsetting him, she knew she wasn't leaving Israel or its newly acquired territories anytime soon.

The telephone rang just as Alexandra reached the door to go down to breakfast. She hoped it was Noah calling her back, maybe to apologize, maybe to tell her he understood, maybe to end their conversation on a happier note.

"Alexandra, it's Dany…Dany Haddad."

"Hi, Dany. How's it going?" she replied, unenthusiastically.

"Things are going well, Alexandra. The people at *Desert Song* are terrific. They're very friendly and very smart."

"Yes, I enjoyed working there too."

"Alexandra, are you free for breakfast or lunch today? I have something I'd like to discuss with you." She paused before answering. She had been looking forward to a quiet breakfast. "If you're busy, I under-stand," he said.

"No, no, it's fine," she replied. "Can you meet me here in half an hour for breakfast? I have plans to be in Bethlehem, later today."

"I'll be there," he answered. "I'm leaving now."

Alexandra found a corner table, ordered coffee, and began skim-ming the *Jerusalem Post*, which she had picked up in the lobby on her way into the dining room. She smiled as she looked at the masthead. When she and her family left in 1948, the same Jewish paper was named the *Palestine Post*. Days earlier, on June 27, the Israeli parliament had, effectively, annexed all of Jerusalem, including Arab East Jerusalem. It was a momentous, but audacious, act, and it dominated the news. For the first time in nearly twenty-five hundred years, Jerusalem was entirely in Jewish hands. Entirely, she thought, except for the tens of thousands of Arabs in East Jerusalem.

She looked up from the paper after a moment or two and listened to the din resounding in the room. She studied those sitting nearby. Everyone was either engaged in animated conversation about the news of the day or had his or her head buried in any one of the many news-papers that circulated in Tel Aviv. Israel had to be the most news-ob-sessed country in the world, she thought.

"Hi, Alexandra," Dany said, greeting her as he approached the ta-ble. Alexandra stood, smiled, and extended her hand to him. Dany grasped it firmly, leaned in, and kissed her briefly on the cheek. They made small talk until the waiter came, poured them both a cup of cof-fee, and took their breakfast orders. Dany ordered *shakshuka*, eggs poached in a tomato and vegetable sauce. Alexandra asked for salmon and cream cheese on squares of toast.

"Lots to write about, eh, Dany?" she said.

"This has got to be the epicenter of the news world right now," Dany replied. "Could there be a more exciting place for journalists to be?"

"Yes, I feel the same way, Dany. History is unfolding so fast in this region."

They spoke for a while about the implications of the annexation of East Jerusalem, but Alexandra knew that that was not why Dany wanted to meet with her.

"So what's keeping you busy, Alexandra?" he finally asked.

"Everything. It's hard to know what to write about first."

"What have you written about?" he asked.

"So, is that why you wanted to meet me—to pick my brain?" she replied, grinning.

"No. Not exactly," he answered cryptically, returning her smile.

Alexandra grew more serious. "So...?"

"So, why are you writing under the name Sabirah Najat?" he asked, his eyes fixed on hers.

"What—what do you mean? Why are you asking me that?" she replied.

"We get a copy of the *Evening Star* about three days after it's published in Washington. There has been nothing in the *Star* under your byline Alexandra. I have, however, been reading some really good stuff by Sabirah Najat reporting from Tel Aviv," he said, not taking his eyes off of her.

"Is this why you asked to meet this morning—to learn about Sabirah Najat?"

"I'd really like to get to know her."

"If I run into her, I'll let her know."

"How would you feel about *Desert Song* rerunning her material here in Israel?" he asked.

"You don't want to do that, Dany."

"Tell me why."

"It could put her in danger," Alexandra replied.

"How...Why would it put her in danger?"

Alexandra, momentarily lost for words, reached across the table and gently clasped his hand. "I can't tell you that," she answered, as tears welled up in her eyes. "But we don't want people too curious about Sabirah Najat here in Israel."

Dany placed his free hand over hers, squeezing it gently. "Are you in danger, Alexandra?"

"No, I don't think so, but there's been a development. Something we…I learned after I arrived here. We think it's not wise to have too much attention focused on me right now."

"Who is 'we'?" he asked, his hand still gently grasping hers.

"I can't discuss it, Dany. I can't," she answered, her voice betraying a hint of fear.

He nodded, sympathetically, and took her hand in both of his. She made no effort to remove her hand from his firm grasp. Alexandra found the warmth of his touch and the compassion in his eyes comforting. She looked at him and smiled, appreciatively.

"Is this development you speak of the reason you haven't been to the *Desert Song* offices to visit old friends?" he asked.

Alexandra nodded. "I don't want other journalists writing about my presence here. It's not that we're keeping it a big secret. I'm moving about freely, and I'm registered here at the hotel in my own name. We just think it's best not to have my name splashed in the press advertising that I'm here."

"My understanding is that the fanatics who were after you a few years ago were killed when the Israelis rescued you from that Shoukri madman. I can only assume that my understanding isn't correct or that other followers of his are still around and active. Is that right, Alexandra?"

"Dany, there are things I simply can't discuss with you. I wish I could. I really do, but I can't."

"I won't press you, Alexandra. I can add two and two like anyone else."

"Please don't go anywhere near this at *Desert Song*, Dany."

"Alexandra, is that what you think? That my interest is as a journalist?" he asked, firmly holding her hand.

"I don't know what to think," she replied.

"Alexandra, you are probably the most admired journalist who ever worked at *Desert Song*. You're a bit of a legend there. That I met you on the day we both arrived, even before we drove out of the air-port, is—"

"What?" she interrupted, her hand closing around his.

"Fate, Alexandra. I believe it was fate that we met when we did."

She peered softly into his eyes and smiled. "Perhaps it was, Dany. Perhaps it was," she said.

At that moment a hotel bellman walked through the dining room ringing a chime attached to a small blackboard. Her name was printed across the slate.

"My driver is here, Dany. I'm meeting with some local communi-ty leaders in Bethlehem a little later. There are some peace advocates among them. I have to go."

He held on to her hand a moment longer and then released his grasp. As they stood, she leaned over and quickly bussed his cheek. "Thank you, Dany, for understanding, and for caring," she said as she turned and left the table. He remained standing, keeping his eyes on her as she made her way through the dining room.

"I would walk through fire for her," he whispered under his breath as she disappeared into the lobby.

CHAPTER

SEVENTEEN

Avi Ben-Topaz, a career IDF small-arms instructor, was recruited by Amos to escort Alexandra to Bethlehem. Amos wouldn't hear of Alexandra traveling onto the West Bank without Israeli security, especially since learning that AASLF Partners was targeting Potomac Center and, most probably, Noah and Alexandra as well. It took them a little over an hour to reach Jerusalem. Along the way Alexandra observed rusted and abandoned hulks of military vehicles left by the side of the road by the Israelis as a reminder of the fierce fighting that took place there in 1948. Upon reaching the outskirts of Jerusalem, they headed south across the Valley of Cedars, on to French Hill, and through the Judean Mountains. It took less than fifteen minutes to make their way to Bethlehem from Jerusalem. There were few other civilian vehicles on the road, and the only landmark that caught her eye was the small and, she thought, sad and drab edifice of Rachel's Tomb.

Manger Square, at the center of Bethlehem, was nearly deserted when she arrived just before noon. There were a few dozen locals milling about and an equal number of uniformed Israeli troops strolling through the area. There was no sign of tension or, for that matter, cordiality between the Israelis and the local Arabs, many of whom Alexandra presumed to be Christian. She had some time to spare before her appointment with a local Palestinian Christian, Elias

Khourdri, with whom Amos had urged her to meet. Amos described him as a moderate who was not affiliated with the militant Palestine Liberation Organization. The PLO had been established three years earlier and was known to be active in the area. Amos told her that there were other moderate voices, but they were wary of talking to Israelis so soon after the fighting.

Alexandra, with her military escort trailing a few steps behind, strolled through the narrow streets of Bethlehem. Jesus and, a thousand years earlier, David had both been born in this ancient town. She had learned from the Gospels of Matthew and Luke that David was a forebear of Jesus. No two people in this part of the world should be closer, she thought, than the Christians and the Jews. But history, she knew, was little more than a catalog of conflict, and conflict was the most enduring of all human endeavors.

Alexandra arrived a few minutes early for her meeting with Elias Khourdri. The city's administrative center, where they were to meet, was a rather nondescript old structure on the town square, across from the Church of the Nativity. Mr. Khourdri had arranged for a small meeting room on the second floor. The open staircase was crowded with locals lined up to discuss problems or issues with municipal personnel. As Alexandra and her Israeli army escort made their way up the staircase, the crowd hesitantly parted to let them pass. There were curious but neither friendly nor unfriendly stares as they made their way to the second floor.

Elias Khourdri was a gregarious man and greeted both her and her escort much more warmly than she had expected. She guessed his age to be about fifty. He was somewhat overweight but, she thought, a handsome man nonetheless. He had dark, graying hair, and a droopy puffiness punctuated the circles under his eyes. His mustache was well trimmed and his smile sincere. He was no taller than Alexandra and, she thought, maybe the only man in Bethlehem wearing a suit and tie. He ushered them into a comfortable meeting room, furnished with a small conference table and chairs on one side and a sofa with facing club chairs on the opposite side. A long window ran along one side of the room, providing ample midday light.

"Please make yourself comfortable," he said, directing Alexandra and her escort to the couch as he took a seat opposite them.

"Would you like some fruit or, perhaps, some water?" he asked, pointing to a bowl on the coffee table between them. It was overflowing with grapes, figs, apples, and oranges. Several glasses of water had also been placed on the table.

"I am thirsty," Alexandra replied, reaching for a water glass. "Thank you."

"And you?" Mr. Khourdri politely asked the army escort.

Alexandra's escort held up his hand and shook his head. "No, no, thank you," he replied.

"So how can I help you, Miss Salaman?"

"First, let me thank you for agreeing to meet with us," she began.

"You know, I've known Amos Ben-Chaiyim for many years. I knew his father too. If Amos asked me to meet with you, I am only too happy to do that," Mr. Khourdri responded.

"I didn't know that you knew Amos," Alexandra replied.

"Oh, I've known him since he was a boy. His father was a scholar. Amos came here frequently with his father when the Dead Sea Scrolls were first discovered. You know they were discovered not far from here at the caves at Qumran. The Bedouins who first found them brought them here to Bethlehem to Khalil Iskandar, an antiquities dealer. Khalil is from Bethlehem. He is known here by his nickname, Khalil Kando.

"Ah, I saw an antiquities shop with that name when I was walking through Bethlehem before our meeting."

"Yes, Samir Kando's shop; that's Khalil's son."

"So, you know Amos because of his father's interest in the Dead Sea Scrolls?" she asked.

"Yes, you could say that," Mr. Khourdri replied.

"And you are friends?"

"Does that surprise you, Alexandra?"

"I guess it does. Things are so tense now between the Jews and the Arabs," she answered.

"Alexandra, these tensions will pass someday. It is insane. This region—Bethlehem, Jerusalem, Jericho—it could be the hub of the greatest tourist region in the world if it weren't for all this friction and nonsense."

"Millions of people say this land is all Islamic land."

"Yes, and some people say the entire Iberian Peninsula is all Islamic land, simply because it was for a couple hundred years, but it's all radical nonsense."

"Many Jews feel the same way. They don't call this the West Bank. They call it Judea and Samaria," she said.

"It will all be Armageddon if this nonsense doesn't stop. The history of this land isn't much of a mystery, Alexandra. The oldest recorded documents, the Dead Sea Scrolls, make it clear that Jews were here from the beginning of recorded history. Then, nearly two thousand years ago, many Jews became followers of Christ, who, of course, was a Jew—a Nazarene. But Christianity was born here. Then, six hundred years later, Islam came. So to whom does the land belong? All of us, except no one wants to share. It's disgusting."

"So what do you think will happen now, Mr. Khourdri?"

"I don't know. I fear the Israelis will create the region's second great catastrophe of this century."

"The second great catastrophe? What was the first great catastrophe?"

"We Palestinians were offered a state of our own by the United Nations, except we didn't have a say in the matter. We didn't have a vote at the UN. The Arab nations unanimously rejected the partition of the Holy Land into a state for Jews and a state for us. That was the first great catastrophe. It was the Arab catastrophe. The Jews accepted the partition plan, and Israel became a fact of history, and there has been nothing but violence and war ever since."

"And what do you consider to be the second catastrophe that Israel is about to commit?"

"You're a journalist. You know as well as I do that the Israelis are debating what to do with all of this land they captured and all of us who live here. There are voices, powerful voices, that are demanding the rebirth of the ancient Land of Israel—what they call Judea and Samaria. It would include everything west of the Jordan River. It would include this very spot where we are sitting right now."

"If they did that, their Judea and Samaria would be all Arab. What sense would that make?" she asked.

Elias Khourdri sat back and smiled at her. "Are you that naive, Alexandra? They would send thousands of their people here. They would settle all over their Judea and Samaria."

"And you believe that if that happened, it would be the second great catastrophe in this region in this century?"

He nodded, sadly. "Yes, I fear that would be the second great catastrophe—the Israeli catastrophe. If it happens, we will all spend the rest of our lives fighting over it."

Alexandra looked to her Israeli driver, who sat silently but was listening attentively. "What do you have to say about all of this, Avi?" she asked.

"I'm not here to offer opinions, Miss Salaman. I'm only here to escort you."

"Please, I would like to hear your views, young man," Elias Khourdri said.

Avi Ben-Topaz thought for a moment, trying to decide whether or not to join the conversation.

"I would like to hear what you have to say too, Avi," Alexandra said, urging him to participate. "Please, share your thoughts with us."

Avi Ben-Topaz looked from Alexandra to Elias Khourdri as he considered his response. "Miss Salaman…Mr. Khourdri…we drove to Bethlehem along an old established route. It is known as the Route of the Patriarchs."

Elias Khourdri nodded his understanding. "Yes, Alexandra, what your young driver says is true."

Avi Ben-Topaz paused, hesitant to continue.

"Please, Avi...please go on," Alexandra urged.

The young Israeli soldier's eyes darted from Alexandra to Elias Khourdri before he continued. "The Bible tells us that on this very road God said to Abraham, 'Look to the north, the south, the east and the west. It is to wherever you see I will give you the land. Wherever your feet step, I will give you this land.' We passed by Rachel's Tomb on this very road. In Anatot, right on this road, God told Jeremiah, 'Buy a piece of land and bury the deed in a clay pot as a sign the Jewish people would return to their land one day.' Abraham, Isaac, Jacob, and their wives are all buried farther south on this road in Hebron. My grandparents lived in Hebron, and so did their parents. My grandmother was killed in the 1929 anti-Jewish riots there. The Jordanians forced out every Jew from the ancient Jewish Quarter of Jerusalem after the war in 1948 in violation of the armistice agreement. Nearly all our history is here on what you call the West Bank—what we call Judea and Samaria. Many Muslims tell us that all the land ever conquered by Islam is an eternal Islamic endowment, never to be abandoned. Well, we're here now, and I understand why there are many people who say we should never abandon this land again."

Elias Khourdri looked to Alexandra and shrugged.

"You see, we have a dilemma."

Alexandra simply nodded. "We appreciate your sharing your thoughts with us, Avi," she said, softly.

Alexandra spent most of the time driving back to Tel Aviv rapidly scribbling notes of the meeting with Elias Khourdri. Avi Ben-Topaz didn't want to interrupt her. He hoped he hadn't offended the Christian Palestinian with whom they met. They asked for his opinion, and he provided it. He found even the thought of abandoning the West Bank to be disgusting. What other nation in our place and with our history would be expected to do that? As they pulled up to the Dan, Avi Ben-Topaz got out of the car and opened the rear passenger door for Alexandra. She thanked him as he took her hand to help her from the car.

"I hope I didn't speak out of turn back in Bethlehem," he said.

"No, you didn't. Not at all," she replied.

Avi Ben-Topaz smiled, sadly. "My family, or at least those who survived the massacre, was run out of Hebron. Can you understand why I resent that we were forced from that place—that I can't return to our family home?"

Alexandra sighed. "Yes, Avi, I understand—I grew up in Jaffa where my parents and grandparents before them lived. We were forced from our home too, in 1948." She paused for a moment and then continued, "There's plenty of frustration to go around, Avi." She turned and walked into the Dan. The concierge spotted Alexandra as soon as she entered the hotel.

"Miss Salaman," he called out to her. "I have a message for you," he said, as she approached his desk.

"Thank you," she replied as she opened the folded note.

"Can you meet me at Café Batia in Jaffa for dinner tonight at seven? I'll be there either way. No business talk. Just great food—Dany."

Alexandra knew the restaurant. It was an old kosher café that she remembered as a child in Jaffa, and, years later, she had even dined there from time to time with Amos when she worked at *Desert Song*. She glanced at her watch. It was only eleven o'clock in the morning in Washington. She could try to reach Noah and still meet Dany by seven.

Alexandra hurried to her room, freshened up, applied a touch of makeup, and tried calling Noah. The hotel operator informed her that the lines to America were tied up and suggested she try again later. It would be early in Washington when she was ready to turn in after returning from dinner, but she was unnerved nonetheless. Alexandra was eager to talk to Noah—to take a measure of his mood. Their conversation earlier that morning had left her unsettled. It was going to be a long summer—the longest they would be apart since she returned from Israel four years earlier. It would be unbearable, she thought, if he remained upset for weeks on end. Was she putting everything at risk with her determination to stay longer? Alexandra knew how much

Noah loved her, but this was her work. This mattered too. It was an assignment of a lifetime.

The taxi dropped her off a few minutes before seven. Café Batia was just as she remembered it—perhaps a little more tired. She spied Dany as soon as she entered the restaurant. He stood, smiling warmly as she made her way to the table. Dany greeted her with a casual embrace and brushed her cheek with a light kiss.

"Your day went well?" he asked, as they took their seats.

"Tiring, but yes, it went well," she replied.

"Yours?"

"I like what I'm doing. I focus almost entirely on the less known aspects of Jaffa's history."

"I have fond memories of my time at *Desert Song*," she said. "I enjoyed working there very much."

"They think very highly of you, Alexandra."

The conversation flowed easily, with Dany avoiding any discussion of Sabirah Najat, or whatever danger Alexandra had alluded to at breakfast.

"So how do you like kosher food?" he asked, as they dined.

"It's very good," she answered. "Noah's mother prepares some of the same dishes."

"Noah?"

"My fiancé."

"You're engaged?" he asked, trying to mask his disappointment.

She nodded, smiling.

"To a Jewish fellow?" he asked.

She nodded again, raising her eyebrows playfully.

Momentarily lost for words, Dany nodded back. "You had a close Jewish friend when you were in Israel four years ago too, didn't you?"

Alexandra drew in a deep breath and nodded.

Dany smiled. "Interesting," he said.

"Amos, Amos Ben-Chaiyim—that's his name," she responded. "I mentioned him to you when we had breakfast. He's the one who saved my life."

Dany smiled, awkwardly. "He was with Mossad or something, right?" he asked.

She nodded. "Shin Bet then, actually," she replied.

Dany realized immediately that Amos Ben-Chaiyim had to be the "we" whom Alexandra had spoken of at breakfast earlier that morning—the one who alerted her to some danger. He was the reason she was writing under the name Sabirah Najat.

"If I were your fiancé in America, I would have never let you come back after what you experienced here just a few years ago," Dany said.

"He wasn't—isn't very happy about my being here. But he respects me enough, and loves me enough, to know better than to tell me what I can and can't do. We're Americans, Dany. Women don't have to do what their men tell them to do. Being here at this time is my job—my profession. I take it very seriously, and Noah understands that," she said, with more certainty than she actually felt.

"You are one interesting woman, Alexandra," he finally replied.

"Right now, more interesting than I want to be."

"You're unquestionably the most interesting woman I've ever met," Dany said.

"Probably the most complicated, too."

"And certainly the most beautiful," he replied.

She smiled appreciatively and looked up at him. He smiled back, his eyes fixed on Alexandra's sea-green eyes that so complimented the dark hair that framed her face, and her radiant Mediterranean complexion.

"Thank you, Dany. That's the nicest thing anyone has said to me all day."

"Look, I know you're engaged, but I would still like to call you from time to time for breakfast or lunch, or maybe dinner. You're really the only person I know here other than my colleagues at work. I thoroughly enjoy being with you."

"Of course you can call me," she said. "I don't know that many people here either, and I enjoy talking with you too."

As Alexandra was about to get into her taxi to go back to the hotel, Dany reached out, and they hugged one another. She lingered a moment longer as the good-night hug subtly transformed into an embrace. "I really have to go," she whispered, gently pushing away from him.

"I'll call soon," he said as she closed the door of the taxi.

Alexandra nodded back at him. "Yes, call," she answered, as the taxi pulled away.

The lobby of the Dan was almost deserted as Alexandra made her way to the elevator. She had enjoyed her dinner with Dany, but their final good-night embrace bothered her. She wasn't unnerved because they had embraced but, rather, because she had so welcomed it.

Alexandra, eager to call Noah, waited impatiently for the elevator. When the elevator door finally opened, Alexandra was startled to see Amos step out.

"Amos…" she said.

"Alexandra, this is a pleasant surprise."

"I should say," she replied, puzzled.

"I was just saying good night to Karen. We had dinner this evening. She's going back to the States tomorrow, you know."

"Oh, that's right," Alexandra replied, unnerved by Amos's sudden appearance at the elevator. "I guess I lost track of that."

"So, do you have time for a nightcap?"

"Uh…no. I wish I could, but I want to call Noah and try to catch him before he leaves for dinner in Washington."

"We should talk soon," he said.

"Are you free for dinner tomorrow night?" she asked.

"No. Dinner won't work. I'm driving Karen to the airport."

Alexandra looked at Amos for a moment and just nodded. "Sure," she said, her smile somewhat forced. "Call me whenever you get a chance." With that brief exchange, she stepped into the elevator and pushed the button to her floor. She smiled at Amos again as the elevator door glided shut.

Alexandra waited until she was in bed before trying to reach Noah. The call went through right away, but to her dismay Barb told her that she had just missed him. He had left the office early to drive to Baltimore, where he was meeting Yusuf for dinner. Alexandra lay there staring at the ceiling contemplating all that had happened that day: the telephone conversation with Noah that morning that had left her so disheartened, the breakfast with Dany, her day in Bethlehem and her conversations with Elias Khourdri and Avi Ben-Topez, her dinner with Dany that evening, and that unsettling but pleasant embrace when they parted. And then there was that brief encounter with Amos at the elevator after he had just spent an evening with Karen. *What in the world was that all about?* she thought. It took a long time for the procession of activities to recede from her consciousness, allowing her to finally drift off to a night of restless sleep.

CHAPTER
EIGHTEEN

"It's done, Omar! The US government approves of us," Khaled Kassab said, excitedly, as he rushed into the empty coffee shop at the New Cataract in Aswân, where Omar Samir was waiting for him.

"What are you saying, Khaled? This scheme of yours worked?"

"Yes, yes, just as I said it would," Khaled responded, as he embraced Omar Samir.

"How did you do this?" Omar asked, as the two men sat down at a table along the back wall of the dimly lit shop. Khaled looked around to make sure they were alone. He lowered his voice. "Omar, we are now on the approved list of bidders for US government contracts. The agency that approves contractors for this list, the US General Services Administration in Washington, has approved us. It is known as the GSA in America. They publish a list called the Schedule of Contractors."

"And we're on that list?"

"Yes, we've been accepted to be on the government's list of approved contractors. They think we're really a subsidiary of Questex-Irvine International."

"How did you do this, Khaled?"

"I doctored stationery and used publicly available financial information from Questex-Irvine, where I work, and created a fake subsidiary, Questex-Irvine Materials Testing. I applied to bid for work in what this GSA calls BPA section eight hundred seventy-one."

"What is this BPA eight hundred seventy-one? I don't understand."

"*BPA* stands for *Blanket Purchase Agreements*, and *eight hundred seventy-one* refers to *professional engineering services*. Questex-Irvine is already on the list and has been for years. Now Questex-Irvine Materials Testing, our little fake company, is on the list to bid on materials-testing contracts."

"Won't Questex-Irvine see this new company on the list and complain that there is no such company as Questex-Irvine Materials Testing?"

"No, I don't think so. Questex-Irvine International has been on this Schedule of Contractors since the American government created the list. They have no reason to even look at the list today. Besides, Questex-Irvine is so large that even if someone at the company headquarters in California did see the list, they would probably assume we're a small subsidiary located in Washington."

Omar Samir stared into the empty coffee shop for a moment contemplating what Khaled Kassab had just told him. "This is big, Khaled. You are a genius," he finally said, slapping the tabletop with his hand. "You are a genius."

"Of course, we're not ever going to bid on anything. But I think we will be able to purchase our plastique by showing that we are an approved engineering contractor of the American government."

"And the Americans won't investigate?"

"What is there to investigate? We're never going to bid on anything. We'll simply be able to give our contact in Czechoslovakia the cover he needs to have some plastique shipped to us to be tested. By the time anyone discovers anything, assuming they ever discover anything, our contacts will be gone, and we'll have our plastique safely and secretly stored until we're ready to use it. The address we use for Questex-Irvine Materials Testing will be a legitimate business address, and we'll store the plastique there until we're ready to use it. The plastique won't be traceable to anyone in Czechoslovakia, and neither will we. No one would guess in a million years that the Jew's shopping center, this Potomac Center, would be the target of the plastique."

"You are sure about this contact you have?"

"I think he is reliable. He has accomplices in the company who are sympathetic to our cause. They will approve the shipment as long as the company gets paid for the plastique and the shipment goes to Questex-Irvine Materials Testing, a bidder approved by the US government," Khaled said, grinning widely. "The company that makes the plastique will be paid, and our contacts will pocket the difference between what we pay and what the company receives. I think our plan will work if these oil-rich brethren you spoke of will support our cause as you say they will."

"You are a genius," Khaled repeated again. "Ali Abdul Shoukri, our sheikh—our martyr—must be smiling down upon us from paradise at this very moment."

ROUTE 60: ROAD TO PEACE OR ROAD TO PERDITION
By Sabirah Najat

Israel and the West Bank (Judea and Samaria)— There is probably no more storied thoroughfare in the entire world than Route 60, which runs 160 miles from Beersheba in the south to Nazareth in the north. Almost everything in between rambles through the area Israel recently captured in the Six-Day War—the area the Arabs call the West Bank and the area the Jews call Judea and Samaria. It is an area that has been drenched in history for as long as history has been recorded. It is the land of David and Jesus, of Solomon and Paul, of Rachel and

Mary. According to the Bible, it is also on this ancient road that God gave this land to the ancient Jews. It has been and will probably remain the most contested land in the world.

At about the midpoint of Route 60 lies ancient and historic Jerusalem, the major urban center venerated by Jews, Christians, and Arabs. It stands tall in the histories of Judaism, Christianity, and Islam. It is where the Jews built their sacred temple, which housed the holy of holies, the Ark of the Covenant. It is where Jesus preached and where he was crucified and resurrected. It is the birthplace of Christianity, and it is where the prophet Muhammad ascended to heaven. The name Jerusalem *literally means* Foundation of Peace. *But, sadly, there is no place on earth where peace has been more elusive.*

In many respects, one can travel through ancient Jewish history simply by driving from Beersheba, the southern terminus, to Nazareth, a mostly Israeli-Arab city, which constitutes the northern terminus. Beersheba is where Abraham dug wells and where Jacob dreamed of the stairway to heaven. Saul, Israel's first king, built a fort at Beersheba, and Elijah hid in Beersheba when Jezebel demanded his head.

Hebron is where Abraham purchased burial plots, known today as the Cave of the Patriarchs. It is where Jews believe Abraham, Sarah, Isaac, Rebecca, Jacob, and Leah are buried.

Bethlehem is the city where both David and Jesus were born. It is little more than a stone's throw from the Qumran Caves, where the Dead Sea Scrolls were discovered—those incredible parchments that so thoroughly document the Jewish presence on this land from the beginning of biblical history.

Jericho was the site of the first battle the Israelites waged against the Canaanites. It is where the Maccabees revolted against the Seleucids, who were, perhaps, the first to forbid the practice of Judaism. And, later, it was the site that King Herod leased from Cleopatra.

All of this geographic history describes what the Jews call Judea and Samaria, the land forbidden to them by one conqueror after another—by Rome and then Islam. And now, for the first time in over two thousand years the Jews once again occupy this land as a result of the recent war during which Jordanian forces shelled Jewish sections of Jerusalem and, in retaliation, Israel took the so-called West Bank—their Judea and Samira.

The Jews long absent from the land have, however, been replaced almost entirely by others—Muslims who have settled here for hundreds of years. We are at a crossroad on Route 60. There are those among the Palestinians and among the Israelis who yearn for peaceful and neighborly coexistence. And there are those among the Palestinians and among the Israelis for whom such yearnings are anathema. No one here knows whether the area is on the verge of reconciliation or on the verge of renewed and perpetual conflict—whether the people of this area are on the road to peace or the road to perdition.

CHAPTER
NINETEEN

Alexandra finally reached Noah shortly after sending off her latest column to Markazie. He grabbed the phone, happy they had finally connected.

"Alexandra, I'm so glad you called," he said as soon as he heard her voice. "I was beside myself when I learned I had just missed your call yesterday."

"I tried reaching you yesterday, but I either couldn't get through or I missed you when I did."

"I know," he replied. "Barb told me you called."

"Noah, I was so upset after our last call. I just hate when we finish a call that way."

"I'm sorry, Alexandra. I felt terrible. I worry about you every day, and I've been counting the days until you return. And when I realized that neither of us knows for sure exactly when you're returning, I really became unnerved. I'm still unnerved, but I don't want there to be tension between us. I'm proud of you, and I'm proud of what you're doing. I just want to know you're safe."

"I'm being very careful, Noah. Amos won't let me go anywhere on the West Bank without an Israeli escort."

"I'm glad to hear that. Are you seeing a lot of Amos? I mean is he looking after you?"

"Actually, I've only met with him a couple of times so far. I think he's spending more time with Karen," she replied, laughing.

"You're kidding," he said.

"No, I'm not," she answered. "I ran into Karen in the lobby when she arrived and invited her to have dinner with me and Amos that night. Then I learned she had dinner with him again last night, and he's driving her to the airport tonight."

"How do you feel about that?" Noah asked.

"Look, they'll probably never see one another again. But he's a wonderful man, and Karen has to be very special too. After all, she almost bagged the greatest guy on earth."

"I hope she doesn't get hurt," Noah replied.

"How are things going there, Noah? Tell me about the NBC interview."

"Potomac Center couldn't be doing better. We're surpassing all of our early projections, and the *Today* show interview was fine. I don't think it lasted a full minute."

"Did you meet Barbara Walters?"

"No," he answered, laughing. "I don't think she knows I exist. Potomac Center was early filler. They showed some great shots of the center—aerial views and crowd shots. They asked me if I was pleased. I answered that we were thrilled. Then they asked if we had other Potomac Center–type plans for any other parts of the country, and I said we're always looking."

"Really, are we…you…looking for other locations?"

"Not really—certainly not at the moment—but I think it might be a good idea for people, especially potential investors, to think we are."

"Are you looking for investors?" Alexandra asked, surprised by his answer.

"No. Not right now, but Karen got me thinking."

"Karen got you thinking? I don't understand."

"She's with some sort of investment-banking firm, Mid-America Ventures, and she thinks we should go public. She thinks I should get rid of all the debt we're carrying and replace it with equity from investors."

"Why would you do that? What would that accomplish?" Alexandra asked, curiously.

"Well, it's just a thought, but Karen says we could fund future projects and probably increase my net worth by tens of millions of dollars at the same time."

"That's a wonderful tribute to you," she said.

"It's really more of a tribute to Yusuf. He designed the project, and he was exactly right. People love it for all the reasons he said they would."

"How is he with all this FBI business about Omar Samir and this insane plot he's apparently trying to hatch?"

"We're both less concerned than we were when we first heard about it. Yusuf and I both think it's far-fetched that this Samir character would really try anything here or that he would succeed if he did."

"Don't underestimate these people, Noah. They're crazy. And they did come all the way to Baltimore to meet with Yusuf."

"I'm much more concerned about you over there than I am about me or Yusuf here."

"I'm pretty sure that I'm not in any danger here. I don't think anyone other than those with whom I'm meeting even know I'm here. My job is simply to observe, listen, probe a little, and write about what I see and hear. I don't think anyone really cares about me, or, I should say, Sabirah Najat."

"You can't be too careful, Alexandra. I understand why this assignment is so important to you. I really do, but if anything ever happened to you…"

"Nothing is going to happen, Noah. Honestly, I think I'm quite safe here."

"I'm sure you are, Alexandra, but promise me that if anything happened to make you feel otherwise—if for any reason you felt less safe—you would come home. Just promise me that."

"Nothing is going to happen, Noah."

"Then you should be fine promising me that if something, any-thing, makes you feel threatened, you'll come home right away."

"I love you. I love that you are so concerned about me, and, yes, I promise that if anything happens to make me feel less safe, I'll come home."

"I love you too, Alexandra, and you just made me happier than you can imagine."

"And you can't imagine how happy that makes me feel, Noah. Look, I should let you go. I'll try calling you later tonight."

"I'll be here," he replied.

"Bye, Noah. I love you," she said.

"I love you too, Alexandra—more than you can imagine," Noah added, before hanging up the phone.

***

Over on Virginia Avenue, barely a mile away from Potomac Center, pressmen at the *Evening Star* were busily preparing the Sunday edition of the paper. Frank Markazie had approved Alexandra's latest dispatch from Tel Aviv along with a number of other items for the editorial page before leaving for his summer place at Ocean City, Maryland, across the Chesapeake Bay. Down in the composing room, a radio loudly blasted the Senators-Twins game. Dan Daniels, the voice of the Washington Senators on WTOP, was announcing the play-by-play of the contest. The Senators were about to lose again—in a shutout no less.

"Senators ain't worth shit," Gus Monahan mumbled under his breath as he prepared to lock up the editorial page. That's when he noticed that some idiot had left about twelve to fifteen picas of white space under Sabirah Najat's column for the Sunday edition.

"Hey, Charlie!" he yelled over to one of the pressmen. "Look at what some layout jerk did. Look at all this white space hanging off the bottom of this column."

"Fuckin' amateur day," his colleague said, looking at the page lock-up. "Markazie's gonna really be pissed. Call upstairs to Markazie's office and see if they got any excess copy they cut out of the column they might want to use to fill the space."

"Good idea," Monahan replied.

"Frank Markazie's office," a woman's voice answered.

"Hey, this is Gus Monahan down in the pressroom. Frank Markazie there?"

"He ain't here," the voice replied. "He's gone for the weekend. This is Gladys Murkin. I come in and answer a few of the phones on weekend afternoons when nobody's here."

"Well, he's gonna really be pissed. There's gonna be a lot of white space, at least twelve picas, maybe fifteen, hanging off of one of the columns on Sunday's editorial page. It's right next to the gutter above the fold and really looks lousy. Somebody in composition really didn't pay attention to what they were doin'."

"Whose column is it?" she asked.

"Hold on…It's a piece by…It says 'Sabirah Najat,'" Gus replied.

"Oh, that's Alexandra Salaman's column. She's been usin' a pen name, but it's Alexandra Salaman."

"I don't give a rat's ass who wrote it," Gus said. "I just know Markazie's gonna be pissed when he sees this lousy layout."

"Well, why don't you just throw in a thumbnail picture of Alexandra Salaman? We've run plenty of her stuff with a thumbnail."

"You sure she's Sabirah Najat?"

"Oh yeah, Alexandra's Sabirah Najat all right. She's just usin' a pen name while she's over in the Middle East—probably because it sounds Middle Eastern—probably just bein' artsy fartsy."

"You sure she warrants a picture?"

"We been usin' Alexandra Salaman's picture with her stuff for years. That's what I would do."

And so, thirty minutes later, 240,000 copies of the Sunday *Evening Star* began rolling through the paper's web presses at fifty thousand impressions an hour with Alexandra Salaman's photograph over Sabirah Najat's byline.

It was one in the morning when Frank Markazie's call awakened Alexandra at the Dan.

"Frank? What's wrong? What is it?" she asked, her heart racing.

"Alexandra, you'd better sit down," Markazie said.

"Frank, I'm lying down, for God's sake; it's one o'clock in the morning here. What's happened?"

"There's been a real screw-up at the paper, Alexandra."

"What do you mean a screw-up? What the hell has happened?"

"Alexandra, we've run your picture with the column in this morning's paper."

"You ran my name and picture?"

"No. Just the picture."

"Over Sabirah Najat?"

"Yes," he answered, after a brief pause. "We ran your picture with the name Sabirah Najat."

"What the hell did we do that for? I mean why did we do that? How did that happen?" she asked, making no effort to hide the alarm in her voice.

"It was a royal fuckup, Alexandra. I had left for the weekend, and someone down in the pressroom noticed that a bunch of white space had been left hanging at the bottom of your column."

"So?"

"So someone had the bright idea of adding your photo at the top to take up the slack."

Alexandra was, momentarily, speechless. "Didn't they realize the column was bylined by Sabirah Najat and not Alexandra Salaman?" she finally asked.

"Yeah, they did, but they were told you were just using a pen name and that the picture would be perfectly appropriate because Sabirah Najat was—well, you."

"Didn't it occur to anyone why I was using an assumed name?"

"They thought you just wanted to sound Middle Eastern, but it didn't occur to anyone down there that we were hiding your identity."

"Damn!" she yelled. "Damn, damn, damn."

"What do you want to do, Alexandra? You can come home on the next flight out."

"Actually, that's not why I'm so upset. Frankly, I don't think any of the people we're worried about are reading the *Washington Evening Star*. No offense, but the only Washington paper I ever see around here is the *Washington Post*. Frank, Noah will become unglued when he sees this, and Amos will be furious when he hears about it. I promised Noah earlier today that if I learned of any reason that I should be concerned, I would come home right away. He's not happy about my being here anyway, and I promised him that if anything happened that made me feel less safe, I would come home right away. And Amos might literally send me home. He is so security conscious. He'll think we're incompetent."

"Frankly, right now, I think we are too," Markazie answered. "I never thought to brief our people on why we were using a pen name with your material. I just told them you would be writing under the name Sabirah Najat while you were in the Middle East. They probably thought we were just being creative. I never discussed security issues with them."

"Noah is probably trying to reach me right now. He'll be off the wall when he sees this. He looks for my stuff every Sunday morning."

"Well, maybe you ought to come home," Markazie replied.

"Oh, I don't know, Frank. I've got to think. I'm doing the most important writing I've ever done. I hate the thought of leaving. I really doubt that I'm in any more danger now than I was yesterday. Really, Omar Samir and his cronies aren't sitting around reading the *Washington Evening Star*, and besides, it's just this one issue. Even if they came across the *Evening Star*, what are the odds that it would be this issue?"

"Are you talking yourself into something, Alexandra? I'm depending on your judgment. I'm very uneasy about this. I feel responsible for your safety. Maybe we should run a correction and tell our readers that

Alexandra Salaman's picture was mistakenly used instead of Sabirah Najat's. We could run a different picture with her byline."

"Uh…Frank, she doesn't have a picture. I made her up—remember?"

"We could run some stock photo."

"I think that's a bad idea, Frank. It would only attract more attention to the column. Let's not make a hasty judgment. Tomorrow, today's edition will be old news. If none of the bad guys see it today, odds are they never will," she said. "I'm more worried about Noah and Amos than I am about Omar Samir right now. I doubt Samir will see the column. I know Noah and Amos will. Amos could have my visa revoked and send me home, and Noah is going to go right through the ceiling. Just hours ago, I promised him that I would be home on the next flight if I felt I was in danger."

"Perhaps you should, Alexandra." There were several clicks on the line, and then the hotel operator interrupted.

"Miss Salaman, there's a call from Washington trying to get through, and the gentlemen asked that I interrupt your call."

"That's got to be Noah. Talk to you later, Frank."

"I'm really sorry about this, Alexandra. I'll call Noah a little later and apologize to him." Alexandra took a deep breath as Noah's call clicked in.

"Hi, Noah."

"Alexandra, were you just talking to Markazie?"

"Yeah, he's beside himself over what happened," she replied, calmly.

"Well, what the hell did happen? What is wrong with those people at the *Star*?" he answered, angrily.

"It's a long story, Noah. It was a horrible mistake that was made at the last minute when someone in the pressroom noticed that there was too much white space at the end of my column and decided to throw in my picture to absorb the blank space."

"Didn't they know you were writing under the name of Sabirah Najat for a reason?" Noah asked, utterly exasperated.

"Actually, other than Markazie, and maybe the publisher, I don't think anyone else did know why I was writing as Sabirah Najat."

"That's crazy," Noah responded.

"Well, not so crazy, Noah. Bringing unnecessary attention to the reason I was using Sabirah Najat as my byline from Israel wasn't in my best interest either."

"Anyway, I'm sorry you have to return under these circumstances, Alexandra. I really am," he said.

"Well, let's not rush into anything," she replied.

"Alexandra, I've booked you on El Al's flight to JFK in New York tomorrow night. You'll arrive early the next morning. Eastern has an hourly shuttle from LaGuardia directly to National Airport. Call me when you get to New York, and I'll meet the shuttle when it arrives at National," he answered.

"You what!" she responded, incredulously.

"I've booked your return flight. We agreed that if anything like this happened, you would return right away," Noah said. "I wanted to save you the aggravation of making flight arrangements. I called Barb and had her take care of everything as soon as I saw the paper this morning. I thought you would be thanking me."

"Noah, I said I would come home if I felt my safety had been jeopardized."

"And you don't think this jeopardizes your safety. Are you serious, Alexandra?"

"You booked a flight back to the States without even asking me?"

"Of course I did," he yelled into the phone.

"Well, you can go and unbook it now," she responded, angrily.

"Alexandra, what is the matter with you? You shouldn't be in Israel writing about the Jews and the Palestinians with your picture plastered on the editorial page of the *Evening Star* over a phony Arab byline where everyone can see it and know that it's you."

"Everyone! What is wrong with you, Noah? Everyone doesn't read the *Washington Evening Star* here in Israel. As far as we know, no one does," she retorted.

"Alexandra, you're not thinking straight. Maybe it's too early in the morning in Tel Aviv. You thought of the phony name for the byline.

It was your idea because you didn't think it was safe for that Samir character or any of the other terrorists you used to hang around with to know you were there."

"Terrorists that I used to hang around with! Is that what you just said?"

"You know what I mean, Alexandra."

"Cancel the flight, Noah. I'm not coming home tomorrow."

"Goddammit, Alexandra, what's wrong with you?" he yelled into the phone. "Your fucking picture is in a major newspaper over the phony byline of an Arab journalist who doesn't exist, writing about the Jews' right to live in the territory they've just captured from the Arabs, and we know there are Arab terrorists plotting something against all of us. Have you lost every semblance of judgment?"

"That's not what the column says," she replied.

"Alexandra, what's gotten into you? Your friend Amos, who has spent his life fighting terrorists, said you shouldn't be published under your own name while you're in Israel. He said it would be dangerous in light of this Omar Samir character showing up here in the United States trying to get the plans for Potomac Center. Well, your cover has now been blown, and you should come home. Why are you fighting me on this?"

"Let me discuss this with Amos and with Dany. They'll have a better feel—a more realistic assessment of what, if any, danger this screw-up has created."

"Who the hell is Dany? Dany who?" Noah retorted.

"Dany Haddad. I must have told you about Dany," she replied.

"No, you didn't tell me about Dany. Who the hell is Dany Haddad?"

"He's a friend—I mean a journalist whom I met at the airport when I arrived in Tel Aviv. He actually has my old job at *Desert Song*. He knows about Sabirah Najat. I mean, they get the *Evening Star* at *Desert Song*, and he put two and two together and realized that I had to be Sabirah Najat. He's a very bright guy, and I would really value his opinion," she said, cringing at how she knew her explanation must have sounded.

"Are you hearing yourself, Alexandra? Your new friend—what's his name?—Dany Haddad put two and two together in about two seconds, I would guess, and figured out that you were Sabirah Najat when he saw your column in the *Star*, which you told me two minutes ago no one sees in Israel."

Alexandra sat there, eyes closed, pinching the bridge of her nose, trying to clear her head, trying not to say anything else that would further upset Noah.

"He must have called you as soon as he saw your first column in the *Star* with that ridiculous byline," Noah said.

"He figured it out pretty quickly," she agreed, reluctantly. "He called and said he wanted to meet to discuss something, and Sabirah Najat was it. He knew it was me."

"He called to tell you that?"

"Yes, we had breakfast, and that was what he wanted to discuss."

"Because he was worried," Noah said,

"Yeah, I guess so," she answered.

"I don't know why I let you talk me into agreeing with you about accepting this assignment in Israel."

"Funny, Dany said the same thing."

"What do you mean?" Noah asked.

"He said that if he were you, he would never have let me come here now."

"What does he know about me?"

"He knows you're my fiancé. We were having a kosher dinner at a café in Jaffa, and I mentioned that my fiancé's mother prepared some of the same dishes."

"You were having a kosher dinner in Jaffa? I thought you said you met him for breakfast."

"I did. You came up in a separate discussion."

"At dinner?"

It was almost two o'clock in the morning, and Alexandra was exhausted. She also felt the conversation was turning into an interrogation.

"Noah, I'm exhausted. It's almost two o'clock in the morning here."

"So you've been seeing…meeting…this Dany Haddad fellow at meals and—"

"Noah, please, let's talk tomorrow," she interrupted. "I can't think straight, and I'm so tired I'm getting a headache. I need to sleep."

"You're not coming home tomorrow, are you?"

"We'll talk tomorrow, after I've spoken with Amos."

"And Dany?" he asked, a touch of acerbity in his voice.

"Oh God, Noah, don't do this," she cried, as she broke down in tears.

"Call me tomorrow when you feel rested," he replied. "I don't want to argue with you in the middle of the night. You're not being rational about this, and I want to understand why. Call me after you've discussed this with Amos, and I guess with Dany Haddad."

"Good night, Noah," she replied, her voice both sad and exasperated.

"Yeah, Alexandra. Try to get some sleep."

As Alexandra tried, unsuccessfully, to salvage whatever sleep she could, a photo transmission from the Israeli embassy in Washington was being received at Benjamin Bar-Levy's Mossad office only a few blocks from the Dan Hotel. A brief note accompanied the transmission: "For your information—*Washington Evening Star* columnist Alexandra Salaman, currently reporting from Tel Aviv as Sabirah Najat. We have extensive file on Alexandra Salaman from Shoukri affair."

Amos received Bar-Levy's call hours later, just as he was about to leave his apartment to meet Alexandra for breakfast. She had called earlier and asked him to come to the hotel. It was urgent, she had said.

"Amos—Benjamin here."

"Good morning, Benjamin. What has Mossad calling so early in the morning?"

"The Salaman girl from America. Did you know she is here?"

"Sure, I've met her a couple of times. What's the problem?"

"Why is she writing under this assumed name, Sabirah Najat?"

"That was my idea, Benjamin—not the Sabirah Najat name but the use of a pseudonym. The ASSLF group has been snooping around her fiancé's project in Washington. I told her not to write under her own name while she was here. She came up with Sabirah Najat. Why are you asking? What's the problem?"

"Why wasn't I told she was here?"

"I guess I didn't think it was necessary," Amos replied. "She's just reporting on what she calls the aftermath of the war. I didn't think it was a big deal. I urged that she use a pseudonym as a precaution."

"Then why in the hell did they run her picture with the name Sabirah Najat?"

"What!"

"Salaman's column, or Sabirah Najat's column, in the Sunday *Star* has the Salaman woman's picture."

"Shit. That must be why she called and asked to meet me this morning. Someone at the paper must have really screwed up," Amos replied.

"Get her out of here, Amos. The last thing we need is another incident involving this woman."

"We can't expel her, Benjamin. That wouldn't be wise, and I don't think it's necessary either. That could become an incident all by itself. The *Star* is hardly read here anyway, and I'm sure they've caught the error and it's not likely to ever happen again."

"As I recall, Amos, you had a relationship with the Salaman woman."

"You know damn well we had a relationship, Benjamin, but that's long been over. She's engaged to a man in Washington. I'm just trying to keep her safe while she's here."

"How can you keep her safe?"

"I've had someone accompany her whenever she travels into the territories. She's a fine writer, Benjamin."

"She's trouble, Amos. I've had copies of everything she's written transmitted to me from Washington. She says we're creating a Palestinian people."

"Yes, I've read all of her columns. She's been evenhanded. She writes from both points of view."

"Just what we need, Amos. Someone in America writing about— how did you say it?—yes, both points of view."

"She's a journalist, Benjamin. What would you have me do?"

"We don't need a repeat of her last escapades here, Amos."

"You mean when she was responsible for helping us avoid a massacre?" Amos replied, angrily.

"No, Amos," Bar-Levy replied testily. "I was referring to the kidnapping. She came within a hair's breadth of getting killed, and as I remember, so did you."

"I have a meeting with her in half an hour. Let me take care of this."

"We'll leave her in your hands, Amos. Just don't let her get killed while she's here."

***

"My God, you look awful," Amos said, as Alexandra approached his table at the Dan dining room.

"I've been up since one o'clock," she said. "It's been an awful night."

"Nice picture of you in the *Star* though," Amos replied.

"You know about that?" she asked, incredulously.

Amos smiled and nodded.

"You saw it already?"

"No, not exactly. I got a call from Mossad…Bar-Levy," he answered.

"Mossad has seen it already. I haven't even seen it."

"Our embassy sent a photo transmission."

"Why would they do that? Why would they care what I wrote?"

"They didn't care what you wrote, Alexandra. They just knew the picture wasn't of someone named Sabirah Najat. Someone at the embassy recognized your picture, recalled the Shoukri incident, and sent it on to Mossad."

"Is it going to be a problem?"

"They don't want an incident involving you while you're here—not after what happened when you were last here."

"What are they going to do?"

"They're going to leave it up to me. They're holding me responsible for your safety."

"What are you going to do?"

"Why are you staying? Your presence here is now somewhat public information."

"To whom?"

"Well, we don't know, do we?"

"Noah wants me to come home. He's actually booked a flight to New York for me tonight."

"Do you intend to be on it?"

Alexandra lowered her head into her hand and closed her eyes. "I don't know what to do," she said, barely above a whisper. Amos didn't respond. He just looked at her, recalling an agonizingly similar conversation only a few years ago when they knew Shoukri was coming after her. Alexandra looked up at him, tears in her eyes. "No, I don't want to leave," she finally said. "I'm doing the most important writing I've ever done, and we have no reason to believe Omar Samir or any of his followers have even seen the *Evening Star*. In fact, we have every reason to believe they probably haven't and probably won't see it."

"I happen to agree with you, Alexandra. I doubt that this edition of the *Star*, or any edition, for that matter, would come to their attention. But security is all about anticipating the least likely event, not just the most likely."

"Noah is going to be furious if I don't return home tonight."

"I would be too, Alexandra. This isn't child's play. These people are killers. They hate us, and they hate you even more."

She sat there silently, slowly shaking her head. "What a royal screw-up," she finally said. "What do you think I should do?"

"Well, we'll assume you moving in with me again isn't an option," he replied, trying to lighten the conversation.

"Yeah," she laughed. "How did that work out?"

"All in all, pretty well," he replied.

"You know I can't do that."

"Can't blame a guy for trying," he said lightheartedly.

"What do you think I should do?"

"Look, we know that, whatever mischief they are planning, they are planning to do it in Washington, probably at Potomac Center. More than likely, assuming they haven't seen the column, you're safer here right now than in Washington."

She nodded. "Yes, I hadn't looked at it that way, but you're right."

"However, Alexandra, I'm responsible for your safety while you're here. So here's what I need you to agree to. We have an escort with you whenever you leave the hotel. You give us your itinerary twenty-four hours ahead of time. If you have to leave the hotel for any unscheduled reason, you call me, and my office will arrange an escort."

"You mean even if I'm moving around in Tel Aviv or some other place in Israel proper."

"Yes, that's exactly what I mean. Anything less would be irresponsible."

"I'd have almost no privacy."

"Small price to pay," he replied, quite seriously.

She thought for a moment before responding. "OK," she finally said, nodding her approval. "That might put Noah's mind at ease too. Thanks, Amos. I love you for doing this."

"And I love you, Alexandra," he said, his eyes focused intently on hers. "I've never stopped loving you, not for a single day." She looked at him, stunned by what he said and knowing how much he meant it. Alexandra smiled, sadly, as she reached across the table and squeezed his hand, affectionately. Amos returned the smile and lifted her hand to his lips. "Had we only known one another in a different time," he said.

"And maybe a different place," she answered. Moments later, Alexandra and Amos hugged one another as they parted in the hotel lobby.

She returned to her room, too tired and too emotionally drained to venture out. Alexandra hung the Do Not Disturb sign on the door and kicked off her shoes. She glanced at the telephone on the end table next to her bed and thought of calling Noah. It would only be three o'clock in the morning in Washington, too early to call. Besides, she really didn't want to talk to him—not then, anyway. She knew it would only lead to another argument, and she was tired of arguing, tired of justifying her determination to stay in Israel a little longer. Alexandra lay down, fully clothed, across her still-unmade bed. She closed her eyes, desperate to sleep, but Noah's angry voice intruded into her fading consciousness. "Goddammit, Alexandra, what's wrong with you? Your fucking picture is in a major newspaper over the phony byline of an Arab journalist who doesn't exist," he had said. She wrapped her arms around herself, comforted by her own embrace. *The Arab journalist does exist, Noah. Only the name doesn't,* Alexandra thought as she finally drifted off to sleep.

CHAPTER TWENTY

Karen Rothschild was too busy working to sleep on the long overnight flight back to the States. Her trip to Israel had been everything she had hoped it would be. The Israelis had done the impossible. They had vanquished three threatening Arab armies and destroyed all of their enemy's air forces and were walking onto the pages of history with a sense of pride that the Jewish people hadn't known for two thousand years. And then there was Amos Ben-Chaiyim, whom she was determined to see again. She hadn't felt this excited about a man since she and Noah had called it quits four years earlier. Funny, she thought, how Alexandra, a Palestinian Arab woman, had been so intimately connected to the only two men to whom she had ever felt such a strong attraction. But she had more important things to do than reminisce about her travels in Israel. She was convinced that 1967 was going to wind up being a banner year for the stock market and that this was her opportunity to land her first IPO for Mid-America Ventures. She was already earning a great salary, but landing an IPO would mean a bonus and maybe even a corner office. It might also earn her a vice presidency and a company membership in the prestigious Mid-America Club. Karen was certain that Noah, with his Potomac Center success story, was the perfect candidate. As she sipped her Dom Pérignon along with the other first-class passengers, Karen began taking notes.

Points to make with Noah:

The Dow dropped from 863 just before the Six-Day War to 848 when the war began on June 5. Twenty-four hours later the Dow was back at 862.

The market will almost certainly see a billion-share day this year, maybe even two billion-share days before the year is out.

Participation in the market by both large and small investors is greater than ever.

Most major investment advisers are predicting that 1968 will be even stronger.

Specialty stocks have outperformed blue chips, a good sign for an IPO for Noah's company.

Federal Reserve chairman McChesney Martin is worried about increased speculation in the market. This suggests a rising market in the short term.

The prices of steel and other commodities have been rising, which may result in a move to stocks as a hedge against inflation.

The market, she concluded, was restive, which would probably translate to a robust Dow in the months ahead. Karen glanced at her watch. It would be another ten hours before the Boeing 707 reached New York. She made up her mind. She would call Noah and beg him to clear his calendar and see her. She would take a cab to LaGuardia and catch the first Eastern Shuttle she could to Washington National and be there before lunchtime. Karen reclined her aisle seat, closed her eyes, and smiled. *Noah Greenspan, I'm not through with you yet,* she thought.

Hours later, the phone rang on Noah's desk. It was Karen calling from JFK.

"Karen, you're back!" Noah said as soon as he heard her voice. "Welcome home!"

"Noah, I'm in New York, and I want to fly down to Washington to see you. We've got to talk."

"Now? Today?"

"Yes, I can be in your office in two and a half hours."

"Karen, I'd love to see you, but I have a really full day scheduled," he answered.

"Then how about dinner tonight?"

"Karen, is everything all right?"

"Everything is great, Noah. Look, I've been running some numbers, and we have to talk about an IPO for your company."

"Karen, is that what this is about? Listen, I think it's an interesting idea, but I'm nowhere near ready to contemplate going public. I'll be glad to discuss this with you, but there's no need for you to rush to Washington after flying all night from the Middle East. Why don't you head back to Chicago and we'll set something up later during the summer?"

"Nope!" she replied sharply. "Noah, trust me; we have to strike while the iron is hot, and now is the time to get the ball rolling. I'm telling you, we're at the front end of a great market, and you and Potomac Center are an IPO dream waiting to happen. I think Mid-America Ventures can do for you what ARD did for Digital."

"What is ARD?" he asked, puzzled.

"ARD is the father of venture capital in America. They're Boston based. *ARD* stands for *American Research and Development Corporation*. They were the ones who initially bankrolled Digital ten years ago," she replied.

"You mean the computer people, Digital Equipment Corporation?"

"Exactly," Karen answered.

"Oh, we know them. We're using their PDP-8 microcomputer instead of one of those humongous IBM mainframes. It cost us eighteen thousand dollars, and it's been worth every penny."

"Noah, Digital came out at twenty-two dollars a share last year, and the stock is now selling at around eighty. I'd be willing to bet the stock is positioned to damn near double its current price before the year is out."

"So how does this relate to Potomac Center?"

"Noah, when I left three years ago, you were estimating somewhere around fifty to sixty million to build Potomac Center, almost all debt as I recall—all of it held by Capital City National Bank."

"Your memory is good, Karen. Go on."

"The mall and offices and residences leased like hotcakes, so I'm assuming you paid off a chunk of the debt with the down payments by the time Potomac Center opened."

"You're right. I'll make it easy for you, Karen. We're down to about twenty-seven million dollars at Capital City. We've got great cash flow, we're covering operations, and I'm living pretty well too."

"OK, that means you have at least twenty-three million in assets on your balance sheet. Maybe more—maybe down to fifty-fifty debt to equity."

"You're pretty damn good," Noah said, laughing.

"Noah, you're nearly completely leased. You've had unbelievable press all over the country. You've been on the *Today* show. Potomac Center has a solid balance sheet—"

"Therefore what?" Noah asked.

"Noah, you come out and say Potomac Center is researching future locations around the country, and I think you could have an IPO that would go right through the roof. You could fund your next project with at least fifty percent equity and increase your net worth, I bet by seventy or eighty million dollars."

"There's only one problem," Noah replied. "I'm not sure I want to build another Potomac Center."

"Don't be ridiculous, Noah. If you don't build another Potomac Center somewhere, someone else will. They'll pretty much copy what you've done here and make a fortune."

"You think so?"

"The country loves this sort of thing, Noah. Look at the new mall the Segerstroms just opened last March in Orange County, California, or the new King of Prussia Mall outside of Philadelphia. I'd say there's a big appetite for these kinds of projects, and you're the developer of the moment, Noah. Potomac Center is hot, and nothing sells stocks like something investors consider hot."

"OK, you've got my attention. So how much of my company would I have to give up to do what you're suggesting?" he asked, turning serious.

"Noah, I'm standing here feeding quarters into a telephone booth to talk to you. Will you clear your calendar? I can be there for lunch."

There was a moment of silence, as Noah considered his response. "Karen, call me when you get to LaGuardia," he finally said. "I'll meet your flight at the Eastern Terminal at National…and, Karen, thanks."

"I'm on my way," she answered.

CHAPTER
TWENTY-ONE

Khaled Kassab, Omar Samir, and Ahmed Hebraddi, a colleague of Khaled at Questex-Irvine International, sat hunched over the small dimly lit table in Omar Samir's hotel room at Aswân. They were studying the layout of the mall at Potomac Center, which Ahmed had drawn from the tenants' manual Yusuf had unwittingly provided a month earlier. Ahmed Hebraddi was a young civil engineer. His specialty at Questex-Irvine was explosion technology, and he was part of the team working on the High Dam at Aswân. His group was responsible for blasting from the hardscrabble landscape alongside the Nile up to three thousand tons an hour of metamorphic rock, granite, and sandstone, which had hardened over the ages to steel-hard quartzite.

The young engineer had no particular passion for the Palestinian cause but had harbored a deep resentment of Israel ever since the war eleven years earlier, during which the Israelis along with the French and British briefly seized the Suez Canal. His loathing of Israel had nothing to do with the nakbah and everything to do with the Jewish state's humiliating achievements on and off the battlefield. The young Jewish state was simply running circles around all of its Arab neighbors in virtually every field. Following Israel's rout of Egypt, Syria, and Jordan in the recently concluded Six-Day War, his resentment had turned to rage—rage against the Israelis and their Jewish benefactors in America.

"Ahmed says Potomac Center can be brought down," Khaled said.

"Are you sure?" Omar asked, turning to Ahmed.

The thirty-year-old Egyptian slowly nodded. "It can be done," he said.

"You are certain?"

"If these plans are accurate, we can level the shopping mall."

"All of it?"

"All of it," he answered, with absolute certainty.

"Convince me."

"Look here," the engineer said, pointing with his pen to the center of the floor plan. "Here, on the center of each floor, there are escalators to take shoppers to any of the four higher floors of the mall. You see, here, on each side and running parallel to the escalators are six steel support beams, twelve altogether. They used exposed steel beams, to give their mall an industrial look, I suppose. That actually serves our purpose quite well."

"Yes, I see the beams," Omar replied.

"These twelve beams are your main support columns. Nearly all of the air-conditioning and air-handling systems are situated directly above the bank of escalators on the roof. That's where most of the weight on the roof is concentrated."

"Go on," Omar urged.

"That's also why these twelve steel beams are positioned so close together. They support tremendous weight. Now, here you see these other columns, much farther apart, running on a vertical and horizontal axis away from the escalators and toward the four exterior walls. They are also steel but probably not as thick as these center support beams."

"I see," Omar said, slowly nodding his head.

"The exterior walls are also load bearing, and that actually helps us too."

"I don't understand."

"Well, if we detonate from the center where most of the weight is and along the beams on the vertical and horizontal axis up to, perhaps, the second beams from the perimeter walls, the building will implode inward toward the center. The weight on the roof over the escalators will, literally, pull down the entire structure as it all plunges through the building toward the ground. You see, the explosives just initiate the demolition. Gravity does all of the work. Gravity is what brings the building down."

"Incredible," Omar whispered.

"The outer walls may reflect some of the blast inward before they collapse, but that will simply serve to briefly concentrate everything, even the debris and dust—everything in that mall will be flying like projectiles in all directions. All of the doors and these windows will, of course, be blown out instantly. I doubt that anyone within those walls would survive."

"And we can knock down all those support beams?"

"Actually, the blast doesn't literally knock them down. It cuts through them."

Omar looked at the civil engineer, his expression betraying his puzzlement. "The blast cuts through the steel?"

"Yes, and, of course, severs the beam in the process. You see, the plastique, when detonated, causes an unbelievably rapid chemical reaction that produces highly compressed gas, which bursts into a tremendous shock wave that moves supersonically fast, nearly twenty-seven thousand feet per second. This shock wave far exceeds the tensile strength of these steel beams. If we were able to place our plastique on opposite sides of each steel beam, directly across from one another, these two shock waves would actually collide as they pass through the steel. As the initial shock wave rushes away from the point of detonation, destroying everything in its path, it creates a momentary vacuum, which instantly sucks air back toward the point of detonation, creating a secondary shock wave following the initial blast wave. That causes a tremendous wind effect back toward the center. The destructive consequence of these two opposing waves, which occur in the tiniest fractions of a second, will be absolutely incredible."

"And this shock wave you speak of will slice through the steel support beams?" Omar asked, eagerly.

"Like a knife through butter," Ahmed replied. "I'll determine the thickness and shape of the plastique charge after I've had more opportunity to study the schematics we have from the tenants' manual. We'll have to overcompensate a bit if we can't get the actual architectural drawings, but we can accomplish the destruction of the target, assuming you have a plan to position the charges on these beams. Of that I can assure you."

"This is good. This is very good," Omar said, absently picking at the stubble on his chin.

CHAPTER
TWENTY-TWO

Alexandra decided to try Noah one last time before leaving the hotel for dinner. It was midnight back in Washington, but she knew he wouldn't be asleep because he hadn't answered her earlier calls.

"Hi, Alexandra," he said as soon as he picked up the phone.

"Ah, you were so sure it was me," she replied, trying to sound as cheerful as possible.

"No one else would be calling at this hour. Were you able to get some sleep after we talked last night?"

"No, not a bit. I met Amos for breakfast to talk about the screw-up at the *Star* and then came back to the room and slept until around two o'clock."

"Good, I'm glad you were able to get some sleep. So what did Amos have to say about your picture running with your column over Sabirah Najat's byline?"

"He had already seen the editorial page. I haven't seen it yet, but Amos had already seen it."

"How in the hell did he see it so fast?"

"Mossad. Someone at the Israeli embassy in Washington recognized me from their files on the Shoukri affair and thought it was curious that my picture was being run with Sabirah Najat's byline. The embassy sent a copy of the article on to Mossad in Tel Aviv. I think it was sent with a note to let them know I was in Tel Aviv and writing under a pseudonym."

"Any repercussions?"

"Mossad—well, actually Benjamin Bar-Levy—called Amos."

"And?"

"And he was pretty upset that I was here and that he hadn't been informed. He and Amos are pretty close. Bar-Levy actually ran the operation that extracted me from Beirut during the Shoukri affair."

"What did Amos have to say about all of this?"

"He's OK with my remaining here a little longer, but he's insisted that I have an Israeli security escort with me anytime I leave the hotel. In fact, it's a condition of my remaining here."

"So you're staying?"

"For a little while, Noah. I have to."

"What do you mean you have to?" he replied—a bit sarcastically, she thought.

"Noah, please be reasonable," she pleaded.

"You're asking me to be reasonable. Markazie is perfectly willing to have you return; the goddamned Mossad doesn't like having you there; Amos won't let you leave the hotel without an escort; you really have no idea when you're going to return, and you're asking me to be reasonable. There's something very wrong with this picture, Alexandra."

"Amos says I'm probably safer here than in Washington."

"That makes no sense whatsoever."

"Actually it does—sort of. You see, Amos thinks Samir's focus is on Potomac Center and probably you and me and maybe even Yusuf."

"You're saying that because these creeps are planning to attack us in Washington, it's actually safer to be in Tel Aviv."

"Assuming they haven't seen, and won't see, Sunday's *Star*, then yes, that's what I'm saying—or I should say, that's what Amos is saying."

"So you're going to stay there and continue to write under Sabirah Najat's byline?"

"I would like to for the time being, yes," she answered, her voice strong and more confident than she actually felt.

"I can't believe I'm hearing this, Alexandra," he said, making no effort to hide his anger. "All of this rationalizing about the likelihood that no one saw the column is just that, Alexandra: rationalizing. This Omar Samir and who knows who else are killers, Alexandra. They despise you and I guess me too, and they would come after you in a heartbeat if they knew you were within reach. If you ask me, your insistence on staying is stupid."

"Ouch!" she replied.

"I'm sorry. I didn't mean to suggest that *you* were stupid."

"I think you just did, Noah."

"Look, I'm tired of arguing over this. You are going to do what you want to do, and all I'm doing is getting us both even more upset. There's a lot going on here, Alexandra, and I wish you were here with me. I have some major decisions to make."

"Is anything wrong at Potomac Center?" she asked.

"Things are going very well here, but there are major decisions to be made anyway."

"Such as?"

"Karen has made a really strong case that I should move quickly to take Potomac Center public."

"Yes, you told me she had that conversation with you when you saw her before she left for Israel. Has anything made it more urgent since then?"

"Yeah, we had dinner tonight, and she really laid out a compelling case. I mean a *really* compelling case."

"What? You had dinner tonight with Karen? How is that even possible? She was here last night."

"She landed this morning at JFK and called me. She said we had to talk about an IPO, and she took the shuttle from LaGuardia to Washington."

"And I couldn't reach you all evening because you were out with Karen Rothschild?" she asked, incredulously.

"Yes, we've spent the entire day talking about an IPO for Potomac Center. I think she's really onto something."

Alexandra felt like a cold rock had fallen into her belly. "You were with Karen Rothschild all day and evening?"

"For Christ's sake, Alexandra, we weren't on a date," he snapped. "She spent her entire flight back to the States analyzing why this was an ideal time to think about going public. She didn't get any more sleep than you did last night, and then she altered her flight plans to come here and discuss this IPO idea with me all day."

"And all night too, it seems," she retorted, regretting the snide remark as soon as she said it.

"Oh, for God's sake, Alexandra, don't go there. That's just not called for. We were discussing a very serious business opportunity. I'm grateful that she's given this IPO idea so much thought, and I happen to greatly appreciate that she's gone so far out of her way to present her thinking to me."

"Where is she spending the night?"

He paused a moment before responding to her question. *She thinks she's sleeping here,* he thought. "I booked her a room at the Statler," he finally answered, irritably.

"Does she have a morning flight out?" Alexandra asked.

"Yes…Why is this conversation suddenly about Karen?" he asked.

"You brought her up, Noah."

"I brought up the IPO. Karen was incidental. She just presented the idea to me."

"She came to see you after flying all night, and you call that incidental?"

"I don't want to talk about Karen Rothschild, Alexandra. I was explaining that I have to make a decision very soon about an IPO for Potomac Center. It's a huge decision, and it could be huge—for both of us."

"You know, Noah, I have a lot on my mind too. I'm doing the most important work of my career, and, frankly, I think you couldn't care less. I'm happy that you have this IPO idea that Karen brought to you to think about. I'm sure the two of you will make the right decision about it."

"Alexandra, that was uncalled for. I wouldn't make this decision without you being a part of it."

"It sounds like you're doing just fine, Noah."

"Alexandra, do you think I have any interest in Karen, other than this IPO? Is that what you're sitting there stewing about?"

"I'm stewing about a lot, Noah. I'm not dismissing the photo incident just because I want to stay. I'm not happy about having to be joined at the hip by some Israeli security guy, and I'm not sanguine about the danger an Omar Samir and others like him represent. I'm trying to make an intelligent decision about my work and about the risks of staying here to do it. More than anything, I need your support right now, and I'm not getting it. I understand your concern, and I appreciate it, but you're literally ridiculing my judgment."

"You're right, Alexandra," he replied after pausing to consider what she had said. "I didn't intend to ridicule you. I would never do that, and I'm sorry."

"Actually, I have to run; I have a dinner meeting with Dany Haddad tonight. I want to tell him about the *Evening Star* piece before he sees it in another day or two when they get the Sunday *Star* at *Desert Song*."

"You're having dinner with Haddad?"

"With Dany—yes. To alert him to the *Star* photo before he sees it himself."

"Why not just call him?"

"It takes a lot of explaining, and, besides, I want to see if he thinks it represents a danger to me. He knows all about the Shoukri matter from *Desert Song*."

"Oh," he said.

"Talk to you tomorrow?" she asked.

"Yeah, sure. Let's plan to talk tomorrow," he replied.

Alexandra felt numb as she walked from her room to the elevator. Nothing seemed right. For the first time since she had arrived in Israel, she felt no enthusiasm for her work, and she dreaded her next conversation with Noah. The Sunday *Star* running her picture over Sabirah Najat's byline had made a shambles of the shaky understanding she and Noah had about her assignment in Israel. He had never been happy about her decision to come to Israel, and now he was beside himself over her decision to remain. While they might talk every day, what was there really to talk about now? What was there to look forward to in having these conversations? Talk about her work in Israel or Noah's enthusiasm for Potomac Center going public was, she knew, fraught with the likelihood of tension. She had no interest in discussing her work with Noah, and his newfound interest in taking Potomac Center public was, at the moment, of little interest to her. And now there was the matter of Karen Rothschild's reemergence in Noah's life. How, she wondered, did so much go wrong so quickly? Alexandra was eager for time to pass, the faster the better. Only the passage of time might diminish the danger to which the Sunday *Star*'s error had exposed her. After all, there was nothing so old as yesterday's news. At least that was what she thought as she stepped into the elevator on her way to meet Dany Haddad for dinner.

Alexandra was surprised but pleased to see Avi Ben-Topaz standing opposite the elevators waiting for her. He was in uniform and, she noticed, wearing a sidearm.

"Ah, you're my protector," she said as he walked over to greet her.

"At your service," Avi replied with a slight grin, half bowing in jest.

"I hope I'm not causing you to work overtime."

"I volunteered for the assignment, so there's no need to apologize."

"People must think I'm very important, with such an impressive bodyguard," she said, as they made their way to the hotel driveway where Avi's government vehicle was parked.

"Well, I presume you are very important."

"I'm just a journalist, Avi. I think this is all much ado about nothing."

"When Mossad requests an escort for someone, it's never much ado about nothing," he said, as he opened the rear door of the automobile.

"Do you mind if I sit in the front with you, Avi? I'll feel less like I'm being chauffeured."

"As you like," he said as he turned and opened the front passenger door.

"How come Mossad doesn't use its own personnel to babysit visitors?"

"Amos Ben-Chaiyim requested me, so I'm your babysitter," he answered as he paused to light a Lucky Strike.

"I'm going to Café Jaffa on the waterfront. I'm meeting a colleague."

"May I ask whom you are meeting?" he asked as he exhaled the acrid smoke. "I'll have to record where I've taken you and with whom you're meeting. I'm sorry. It's a pretty basic security requirement."

"I guess I had better get used to it," she replied. "I'm having dinner with Dany Haddad. He's a journalist with *Desert Song*."

"Haddad? He's Palestinian?" Dany asked.

"Yes, he's Palestinian…just like me," she answered.

He turned and looked at her as he drove. "I doubt that there are any Palestinians just like you," he replied, smiling.

"There are many exactly like me, Avi. They may not be journalists writing for American newspapers, but they are like me. This land was once home to them just as it was once home to me and to my family. In fact, we once lived not three miles from where you're driving me to have dinner, and the journalist I'm having dinner with also is from Jaffa, and his family also fled in 1948."

Avi simply nodded his understanding. "It should never have come to this," he said.

"There is plenty of injustice to go around," Alexandra replied. "People resort to violence at the drop of a hat. Then the victims seek revenge and, it seems, a never-ending cycle takes hold."

"You know, it's really not about evil people," Avi responded. "People who never planned to go to war fight most wars. What you and I call evil is committed by people who never planned to do evil."

"So let me ask you, Avi—Hebron, where your family once lived, is now in Israel's hands. Would you want to go back there?"

"Are you looking for a quote for your newspaper, Miss Salaman?"

"No, I'm just trying to understand how Israelis feel is all," she replied.

"I can only tell you how I feel, Miss Salaman. Israel is a very complicated country. You'll have to talk to many more Israelis than me to understand the Israeli mentality."

"OK, let's just say I want to know how you feel."

"If there is peace, my fiancée and I would definitely make our home in Hebron. We would move there right away."

"And if there is no peace? If the people who are there now don't want you and your fiancée to return, what will happen then?"

Avi drew a long drag on his cigarette and turned again to face Alexandra. He slowly exhaled, and as he looked at her, his expression turned deadly serious. "Then, Miss Salaman, it will take a little longer."

"And you would make your home among the Palestinians?" she asked.

"Yes, I would, and so would tens of thousands of others if they had a chance to."

"Do you think they will have that chance?"

Avi shrugged. "The politicians will have to decide."

"And just what is there to decide?" she asked.

"Miss Salaman, there is no place in this land that should be more revered by Jews than Hebron. What right does anyone have to say that no Jews should be allowed anywhere in Judea and Samaria? It is the very heart of our history. It is undeniably Jewish by history."

"But not by population, Avi," Alexandra replied. "There are mostly Arabs there now."

"And once there were mostly Jews in Hebron. Did history stop evolving when the last Jews were driven out in 1929? I don't think so."

They pulled up to the Jaffa Café, and Avi parked the car. "I'll come in with you just to look around and make sure I think it's safe. Then, I'll return to the car and wait for you," he said.

"You're welcome to join us for dinner," she answered.

"Thanks, but no, thanks. Word will get back that I was meeting with two Arabs in a Jaffa café, and my superiors might think I'm plotting a coup," he joked.

***

Dany's heart quickened when Alexandra entered the café. He barely noticed the soldier who walked in with her. She stood for a moment and looked around the room until she spotted him. She said something to Avi, and he nodded to her, looked around the room himself before he turned, and left the café.

I've never known a more beautiful woman, Dany thought as their eyes met and she began to make her way toward him. Her smile was somewhat strained—a bit more sad than happy. He got up from the table and embraced her, not romantically but rather as one greets a close friend. "I'm so glad you called," he said.

Alexandra, momentarily taken aback, found herself lingering an extra moment in his arms. "I was eager to talk to you," she said, gently pushing herself away.

"You seem so serious. Is everything all right?" he asked, as he held a chair for her.

"Yes, I think so, but there is something I wanted to tell you before you discovered it yourself," she said as she sat down. "Dany, when the Sunday *Star* arrives at your office, you'll see they have run my photograph over Sabirah Najat's byline. It's the result of a huge screw-up at the paper"

"I'm sure Sabirah Najat has never looked better," he said, trying to mask his concern. "Is it really a problem, Alexandra?"

"We don't know for sure. It could be, or it may be nothing to be concerned about."

"Are you going to tell me what all the mystery is about?"

"There's some concern that I may be in danger here in Israel."

"Then why in the world are you remaining here?" he asked.

She paused for a moment before answering. "You sound like Noah," she replied, staring down at the table.

"Your fiancé?"

"The last time I checked," she answered, with a forced smile. "He's very upset with me."

"What's this all about, Alexandra?" he asked, reaching across the table and taking her hand. "Are you really in serious danger?"

"I think it may be overblown, but, yes, I could be."

"Is that why that IDF soldier came in with you?"

She nodded. "Yeah, the government has made an armed escort a condition of my remaining here."

Dany and Alexandra picked at their food, too engrossed in the conversation to be bothered with dining. "Is this about that incident you were involved in a few years ago with that Shoukri character?" Dany asked,

She nodded again.

"I thought he was dead."

"He is, but some of his followers are very much alive."

"And they are threatening you?"

"Actually, all we know for sure is that they may be planning to attack Noah's business in Washington. Noah has developed a huge urban project in Washington, and we know some of Shoukri's former colleagues have been trying to get their hands on the architectural drawings of Potomac Center—that's the name of Noah's project. The Mossad and the FBI back in the States take it very seriously."

"And they think you may be a target?"

"I'm the only reason they would go after Potomac Center or Noah," she answered.

"Because of your relationship with Noah?"

"Because they hold me responsible for Ali Abdul Shoukri's death and because I cooperated with the Israelis to stop a bloodbath Shoukri was planning. Hurting Noah would just be a token of their revenge. I'm their real target."

"So you were using this pseudonym, Sabirah Najat, to keep them from learning you were here."

"That was the idea."

"And you're worried that they will see your picture in the *Star* and realize that you're here and, maybe, within their grasp?"

"I'm not as worried as Noah or as some of the people here are," she replied. "I think the odds of any of them even seeing the *Star* are really pretty remote."

"But Noah thinks you should return to Washington."

"He's very upset with me. We've never had such friction between us since I returned from Israel four years ago. He absolutely can't understand why I'm so determined to stay here and see this assignment through. He thinks my determination to stay here a little longer is stupid."

"He said that? He called you stupid?"

She nodded. "Sort of. He said my determination to stay was the stupidest thing he ever heard."

"I'm not sure I can blame him," Dany replied.

"I guess I can't blame him either. It's just that he's so adamant. He dismisses every reason I have for wanting to continue covering what's going on here. He doesn't even try to understand."

"It seems the Israelis are pretty worried too. That armed guard they have watching over you is pretty impressive. Maybe they, and Noah, have a better grasp of the danger you might be in than you do, Alexandra."

"Not you too, Dany," she replied, reaching over and taking his hand. "You're a journalist. You must understand how I feel about all of this. This may be the biggest story I'll ever cover."

"I doubt it," he replied, holding on to her hand. "Alexandra..."

"Yes?" she answered.

"Alexandra, the last thing I would ever want to do is intrude where I'm not wanted. I don't mean to be out of line, and I don't want you to misunderstand my intentions. I just want you to know that you can call on me anytime—to have someone who will listen to you."

She didn't take her eyes off of him as they sat there, hands clasped.

"I mean it, Alexandra. I want to be here for you, for whatever reason you need someone to be with you."

She smiled appreciatively. "Thank you, Dany. You can't imagine how much I needed someone, anyone, to tell me that right now." Her expression softened. "We do have a lot in common, don't we?"

"As I said the last time we were together, I think it was fate that we met when we did and the way we did."

"I don't know whether or not it was fate, but I think it was very good—for me," she said.

"And for me, Alexandra," he replied.

She smiled, warmly, and squeezed his hand ever so slightly before slipping hers from his grasp.

"Promise me you'll call if you need someone to talk to, someone who understands," he said, as he quickly scrawled his apartment telephone number on the back of his *Desert Song* business card.

She looked at the card for a moment and reached up and kissed him on the cheek.

"Thank you, Dany," she said, hugging him, briefly.

Avi Ben-Topaz was leaning back against the side of his car when Alexandra and Dany exited the café. He threw down his cigarette, grinding it out under his boot, and opened the door for her.

"Can we offer you a lift?" she asked as they approached the car.

"No, thanks," Dany replied. "I live nearby, and I'll enjoy the walk." They embraced briefly, and as they separated, he gently took hold of her shoulders. "Remember, Alexandra, call me if you ever need someone to talk to. Call anytime, day or night. I'll be there for you."

She smiled, and there were tears in her eyes. "Thank you, Dany," she whispered.

Alexandra watched Dany as the car pulled away. He stood there and waved before turning to walk back to his apartment.

***

The more Karen thought about the prospect of taking Potomac Center public, the more excited she became. Senior management at Mid-America Ventures concurred and was now routinely referring to their new client as PCPA, the planned ticker symbol for Potomac Center Properties of America. Noah, too, was now fully on board and prepared to sell 49 percent of his company to the public while holding 51 percent himself.

Mid-America Ventures and Noah's public-accounting firm, Forsythe and Adams, concurred that Potomac Center's projected 1967 bottom-line earnings would be no less than $10 million. Mid-America's analysts estimated the initial public offering of approximately two and half million PCPA shares, representing one-half of the company's stock, would yield about $80 million. They assumed that the stock would sell for about $32 a share, at a price-to-earnings ratio of sixteen, which was the average PE ratio stocks were commanding that summer. The public offering would infuse the company with cash of $53 million after liquidating the remaining $27 million of National Capital City Bank debt. The icing on the cake, of course, was the $80 million valuation of Noah's remaining 51 percent ownership of Potomac Center.

Karen and Noah were speaking daily about the anticipated IPO. She and her colleagues at Mid-America wanted to strike while the market was hot, and that meant a road show immediately after Labor Day, with the offering hitting the market a month later. Karen was convinced the market was ready for a major upward thrust. Investors, growing wary of the old-line blue-chip firms that were so vulnerable to the vagaries of general market conditions, were on the hunt for smaller up-and-coming specialty firms for which they were willing to pay handsome premiums. Karen was keenly focused on the dramatic rise in American personal income, which had increased by $2.3 billion in May. Automobile sales during the first ten days of June were ten thousand cars ahead of the total number of cars sold during the entire month in 1966, and, finally, Karen was fixated on bank reserves, which were at the highest level in four years and, she thought, just waiting to be loaned to an eager consuming public. Retail sales, she noted, were already 7 percent higher than at the same point in 1966.

Mid-America Ventures wanted to go to market with the Potomac Center IPO as soon after Labor Day as possible, and so did Noah. He also wanted Alexandra back in Washington well before the public offering. He was growing increasingly impatient with Alexandra traipsing around Israel and the West Bank while so much was taking place at home. It was, he thought, time to insist that she return.

Meanwhile, Alexandra was accumulating bits and pieces of information about fierce debates taking place within the Arab world and in Israel that could affect the stability of the region for years to come. In the absence of any discernible danger, she was not going to run back to America anytime soon. Besides, Noah was going to be tied up with all of this IPO business anyway. It was, she thought, an ideal time for her to own this assignment. No one outside of Israeli intelligence had even seen the Sunday *Star* or her column and picture with Sabirah Najat's byline. At least, that was the way it seemed.

***

Cultural Jihad, the newsletter of the Trans-Arab Alliance, was, as might be expected, still focusing on the ramifications of the Six-Day War and the continuation of the oil embargo the Arab states had imposed during the fighting. It wasn't until, and unless, the reader got to the back of the eight-page newsletter that anyone would have noticed the piece lifted from the Washington Sunday *Star*, and they might have skipped it altogether if the columnist, Sabirah Najat, weren't so enticingly beautiful.

"Mark my words," Khaled Kassab said to Omar, "the greedy, rich Arab states are going to start selling oil to Israel's allies in the West again. American money is more important to them than Arab solidarity with the Palestinians."

"What are you talking about, Khaled?" Omar asked.

"This newsletter the Alliance publishes—it says some of our rich cousins in the Gulf are talking about suspending the embargo. They say selling oil gives us the resources to support the Palestinian cause. They really mean selling oil to the Americans gives them the resources to live in beautiful villas, drive Mercedes, and visit whores when they go to Amsterdam and London. It's disgusting," he said, tossing the newsletter down on the coffee table in Omar's room.

Omar, who was engrossed in the current issue of *Al-Ahram*, largely ignored Khaled's annoyance with the Alliance and its newsletter. He continued reading the government-owned newspaper for several minutes before tossing it down next to the Alliance. He glanced down at the newsletter for a moment before picking it up to peruse its contents. Omar Samir began reading the front-page article about the possible suspension of the oil embargo. He had read enough and started to toss the newsletter back down on the table but decided to read a bit further. He turned the newsletter over to the back page, to read the continuation of the embargo story, and quickly skimmed the page before continuing. Then he froze. His eyes quickly darted back to the picture of the journalist who called herself Sabirah Najat.

"My God, she's here," he said in a low, contemptuous voice. "She's with the Zionists in Tel Aviv."

"What are you talking about?" Khaled asked, startled by the anger in Omar's voice.

"This!" he answered, holding up the newsletter and pointing to Alexandra's picture. "This is Alexandra Salaman!"

"Sabirah Najat?" Khaled replied.

"I'm telling you this is Alexandra Salaman. She must be using the name Sabirah Najat to hide her identity."

"To hide her identity from whom, Omar?"

Omar Samir looked at Khaled, making no effort to hide his rage. "From me!" he hissed.

"You are sure this is the Salaman woman?"

"Oh, I am sure all right. Who could forget that face?"

"Is she really that beautiful?" Khaled asked, looking down at the picture of Alexandra.

"You see beauty. I see treachery. The last time I saw this face was in Gaza the night the Zionists came to rescue her and to kill Sheikh Shoukri. Do you think I could ever forget her?"

"Well, if our plan works, you'll have your revenge in Washington within the year."

"She had the gall to come back," Omar said in disbelief. "She came to gloat over the Zionists' slaughter of Arabs in the Sinai."

"Her writing sometimes seems sympathetic to our cause, Omar," Khaled replied.

"You've seen her writing before?"

"Yes, the Alliance frequently includes her writing."

"I have to think," Omar said.

"About what?"

"About how to make sure she never leaves the Middle East alive."

"Omar, our job is to destroy this Potomac Center and, God willing, this woman and her Jewish lover at the same time. She'll die soon enough."

"We can't be sure she'll die in the Potomac Center attack," Omar replied. "She's here now, in Arab land, and I want her to die here."

"Don't let this distract you, Omar. We have a complicated plan for attacking Potomac Center in Washington. We can't be distracted because this Salaman woman is in Israel."

"She's almost in our grasp, Khaled. I have no intention of letting her leave alive."

"What do you suggest, Omar? The Israelis just defeated three Arab armies at the same time. They killed twenty thousand of our soldiers, and you think you can just go to Israel and kill this woman?"

"I have to think," he repeated. "She must not leave this area alive."

"I didn't join up with you to kill women in Palestine," Khaled replied.

"Shut up, Khaled. I have to think."

CHAPTER
TWENTY-THREE

Karen and Fred Emmons, chairman of Mid-America Ventures, sat across from Noah in his Potomac Center office. After introducing Noah to him, Karen sat back and let her boss do most of the talking. Noah decided, within minutes, that he liked Fred Emmons. He guessed him to be no more than fifty years old, and he was reputed to be one of the sharpest investment bankers in the Midwest. Fred Emmons was equally impressed with Noah. He had always made it a point to personally meet with the management of any firm with whom Mid-America did business. Karen hadn't exaggerated. Noah Greenspan was one of the most impressive young entrepreneurs he had ever met. He marveled at what Noah had accomplished in barely a decade out of school.

They went over everything that would have to be done over the next sixty days in order to have an offering ready by the third week in September. Once the Securities and Exchange Commission had reviewed the Potomac Center prospectus and had no further comments, the company would be allowed to conduct a road show to discuss the business with analysts and prospective investors within the limits of the material presented in the prospectus. Mid-America was shooting to have the road show ready by Labor Day. Noah would have to spend about two weeks traveling to a dozen cities to discuss his company with institutional analysts and other prospective investors and answer questions about Potomac Center's operations and any expansion plans that had been publicly disclosed in the prospectus. Fred Emmons concluded his presentation by explaining that someone from Mid-America Ventures would, of course, travel with him for the road show, and, with his approval, that would probably be Karen.

Noah glanced over to her. She was watching him closely, looking for any sign of hesitancy about the two of them traveling together throughout the country for two weeks. Noah, of course, could just imagine Alexandra's reaction to this aspect of taking Potomac Center public. Then again, she didn't seem too concerned about his reaction to her traveling around Israel with an old lover and this new fellow, Dany Haddad.

"Sure, that's fine," Noah said. An almost indiscernible smile briefly crossed Karen's face as she breathed a sigh of relief.

"One other thing," Fred Emmons said. "I would like to review your list of candidates for the public company's board of directors. I would suggest a seven-man board, and I would expect to be one of those directors. You'll need a compensation committee and an audit committee. I would propose being appointed chairman of the compensation committee, and your banker would be a good choice for chairman of the audit committee."

By the end of the day, Noah and Fred Emmons had concurred that he would ask Elliott Abington, chairman of Capital City National Bank, to join his board along with Cornell Kaufman, CEO of Kaufman Construction, the firm that built Potomac Center, and Yusuf Salaman, his best friend and the center's architect. He also asked William Gerson, who headed the local marketing research firm that Noah had commissioned to do work for Potomac Center, and his own chief financial officer, Marshall Flynn, to join the board. He and Fred Emmons had, in a few minutes, put together a first-class board of directors for Potomac Center.

As the daylong meeting drew to a close, Karen handed Noah an itinerary for the road show on which she and he would soon embark. "Mid-America will make all of the flight and hotel arrangements," she said. "The main sessions will take place in hotel meeting rooms, although there will be some one-on-one meetings with major prospective investors."

"Noah, our analysts will work with you in preparing the slide presentation for the road show," Fred Emmons added as they shook hands. "We've been using those new Kodak carousel projectors. They've only been out for a year or so, but they're very reliable and perfect for these presentations."

"I'm all for trying new things," Noah said with a smile.

Noah decided to try to reach Alexandra in Tel Aviv as soon as Karen and Fred Emmons departed. It was late evening in Tel Aviv, and with a little luck he thought he might catch her before she turned in for the night.

He was relieved when he heard her voice.

"I hope I didn't wake you," he said.

"No, no. This is a perfect time. It's only ten o'clock here."

"How are you?" he asked.

"A little tired but quite exhilarated, Noah. I think I'm onto something."

"Like a flight home?" he replied, without rancor.

"Let's not start this conversation with an argument, Noah," she replied, also without rancor.

"So tell me, what has you so excited?"

"From what I've been able to piece together, there's discussion in the government here about trading back the Sinai and Gaza for peace with Egypt and even the Golan Heights for an understanding with Syria."

"That sounds encouraging," he replied.

"It's a mirage, Noah. There seems to be no interest in Israel about relinquishing any of the West Bank, especially East Jerusalem. They don't even refer to it as the West Bank. It's simply referred to as Judea and Samaria, the land of the ancient Jews. There's been some talk about giving local Palestinian municipalities some degree of autonomy, but

I can't find any indication that Israel is considering returning the West Bank or any part of Jerusalem to Jordan."

"Well, two out of three isn't so bad, is it?"

"It will never fly, Noah. There are nearly a million Palestinians on the West Bank and in East Jerusalem. No Arab government will take that offer seriously."

Noah didn't really care what was playing out in the Middle East, other than that it was keeping Alexandra there. Nonetheless, he feigned interest in the conversation. "So, what do you think will happen next?" he asked.

"Well, here's where it gets interesting," she replied. "There is a rumor floating around that the Arab League is arranging a meeting—a summit of its member countries to decide on an all-Arab unified position to take with Israel. They know they're not going to defeat Israel militarily, so they need to come up with a strategy that they all will abide by."

"Is that good?"

"Who knows?" she replied. "Maybe they'll agree to negotiate as a group with the Israelis, or maybe they'll agree to never agree."

"So when would you guess this meeting will take place?" Noah asked.

"Probably later this summer, but that's only a guess."

"Alexandra, we're taking Potomac Center public as soon after Labor Day as we can," Noah said, abruptly changing the subject. "Mid-America Ventures is preparing a prospectus for SEC review, and as soon as the commission has finished commenting on the prospectus, we're going to do a national road show. We'll probably go to about two dozen cities in as many days. I want you to accompany me on the road show, Alexandra. It should be very exciting, and I think Frank Markazie would agree that you've earned some time off."

"Noah, I want to remain here in the Middle East until this Arab summit I just mentioned takes place. I can report from here much more effectively than from Washington. I have great sources here that can keep me really well informed about the meeting and the ramifications of any decisions the Arabs make. I've asked Frank to keep me here until after the Arab summit."

"But you don't even know for sure that such a summit is going to take place. You even referred to it as a rumor, and you certainly don't know when it might take place."

"If it doesn't happen, I'll head home, Noah. But I want to see what evolves here before I make plans to return to the States. This could be an opportunity of a lifetime. If this summit takes place, it will be historic, and I have an opportunity to be here in the Middle East reporting for a major American newspaper."

"Well, here's what we do know for sure, Alexandra. The Potomac Center public offering is going to happen, and it's an opportunity of a lifetime for us. It puts us on the map, and, Alexandra, the share of Potomac Center that we'll still own will be worth an estimated eighty million dollars the day we go public. What could be more important than that?" he asked, a touch of impatience in his voice.

"Noah, nothing is more important, but this isn't about competing levels of importance."

"Then what is it about?"

"It's about my work, Noah. It's about an assignment that could establish me as a major American correspondent."

"Alexandra, are you telling me that you're going to remain in the Middle East while I take Potomac Center public—that you would skip the Potomac Center road show to report on what the damn Arabs might or might not do?"

"Noah, I would love to be with you while you do this public-offering business, and maybe I'll be able to."

"But?"

"But I can't leave this assignment right when it's building to a conclusion. I just can't do that. I won't do that. This job is as important to me right now as this public offering is to you."

"I want you to be with us when we introduce Potomac Center to the investing public, Alexandra. I want you to be with us on this damn road show."

"Who is going on this road show?"

"From Potomac Center, just me."

"But you said us."

"Of course. Mid-America Ventures will have its representative on the road show too."

Alexandra's attention immediately shifted to Noah's reference to "us" being someone from Mid-America Ventures. A twinge of queasiness swept through her.

"Do you know whom they will have accompany you?" she asked, dreading the answer she feared was coming.

"Yes, it will be Karen," he said.

"You're going to travel through the United States for two weeks with Karen Rothschild?"

"Yes, and, I hope, with you?" he answered.

Alexandra, momentarily lost for words, lowered her head into her hand and tried to compose herself. She felt her heart racing as tears filled her eyes. She felt trapped. She would have no reason to be concerned about Noah traveling with Karen, if she was traveling with him. He was urging her to accompany him and Karen on the road show. She could say yes, she would return to be with Noah for the public offering, or she could stay in the Middle East and do her job—be where history was being made and distinguish herself professionally by seizing an opportunity that might never present itself again.

"Alexandra?" Noah's voice called from the phone.

"Yes, Noah," she replied, almost in a whisper.

"Alexandra, Potomac Center Properties of America—that will be the name of the company when we go public—is for us. It's our future, Alexandra. This isn't just about me. This is as much for us as it is for me."

"Why is Mid-America Ventures sending Karen on the road show?" she asked, ignoring what he had just said.

"Why does that even matter, Alexandra? Did you even hear what I just said about what this represents for us?"

"Yes, I heard," she answered.

"Alexandra, taking Potomac Center public was Karen's idea, and it was a brilliant idea, and her analysis of the market was also brilliant. She knows Potomac Center better than anyone at her company. Alexandra, it will make us wealthy, and it will make a bundle of money for Mid-America too. Why wouldn't they have her be their representative on the road show?"

"I'd like to be part of the team too, Noah, but I'll have to see what develops here. This is no time for me to leave."

"You've already been there for over a month, Alexandra. This is an important time for us, and it's here in America where Potomac Center is about to be introduced to Wall Street and to investors and to major institutions all over the country. How could you not want to be here?"

"Of course I would like to be there. I miss you terribly, Noah, but right now my work is here. Incredible history is unfolding here, and I'm one of a handful of people from the Western world who are here to interpret it and write about it. How can I walk away from that? Noah, over twenty thousand men died here in a couple of days last month. This region is in utter turmoil. I can't leave now, while all of this is sorting itself out."

"There's a lot to sort out here too, Alexandra," Noah replied, impatiently.

"What is that supposed to mean?" Alexandra asked, her heart quickening again.

"Our future, all of the security and stability we could ever hope for, may be taking shape in the next few weeks, and I'm asking you to be here with me while *this* history, *our* future, is being determined, Alexandra."

"Noah, please don't make this a question of which is more important—what is happening here or what is happening there."

"Why not?" he asked, angrily. "You're totally focused on events that you have no control over, that don't affect you personally, that people will read about in the *Star* tomorrow afternoon and then turn on *The Smothers Brothers Comedy Hour* tomorrow night to have a good laugh." Noah immediately regretted the sarcasm, but his words had found their mark. They were irretrievable.

"How dare you, Noah!" Alexandra shouted. "That was uncalled for, the most mean-spirited thing I've ever heard you utter. You've just belittled my work—me!" she screamed into the phone.

"Look, I'm sorry. I didn't mean—"

"Of course you did!" she shouted, cutting him off. "You've been against my being here from day one. You think what I am doing is so damned unimportant."

"I never said that," he retorted.

"I think you just did. In so many words, that's exactly what you were saying."

"Alexandra, I called to urge you to come with me on our road show. I didn't call to fight with you."

"Potomac Center doesn't need me for its road show. The *Evening Star* does need me for its coverage of the Middle East."

"For God's sake, Alexandra, a short time ago, Frank Markazie, your fucking boss, was urging you to return home. Now I'm urging you to return home. What the hell…who the hell is keeping you there?" he yelled, his voice rising in anger.

"Go to hell, Noah!" she screamed as she slammed down the phone.

It was the worst of conversations, and it ended in the worst possible way. They were both more consumed with anger than with regret. Noah sat in his town house in Washington staring at the phone in disbelief. Alexandra had hung up on him in anger. He had called to urge her to travel through America with him—to be with him during a time of wonderful recognition and achievement—and, in minutes, the conversation had ended in bitterness and acrimony. He was dumbfounded that everything had gone so wrong.

Alexandra, seven thousand miles away, was also angry—angrier than she had ever been—and worse, she was deeply offended and hurt by Noah's cavalier disregard for her work. How could he really love her and so belittle her at the same time? She just sat there for several minutes staring at the desktop, her head cradled in her hands. The emptiness and stillness of the room accentuated the loneliness into which she had so quickly descended. When she slammed down the receiver, it was as though she had been disconnected from Noah, not just his telephone call. Her sadness bordered on grief. She felt both separated and, worse, severed from the most dependable person in her life. Then her eyes drifted to the business card Dany had given her, the one on the back of which he had written his personal telephone number. "Call me anytime you need to talk," he had said.

Alexandra picked up the card and just stared at it for several seconds. Then she began dialing the number Dany had written.

"Haddad," he answered.

"Dany?"

"Alexandra?"

"I'm sorry. I shouldn't have called," she said, as she began to cry.

"Alexandra, has something happened? Are you all right?"

"I've just had a horrible fight—with Noah," she replied, through gasps of emotion. "He's furious because I won't come home. He wants me to accompany him on a business tour, and…" Her voice trailed off, as she tried to regain her composure. "He ridiculed my work. He was ridiculing me," she finally continued, her voice distressed. Dany could hear Alexandra struggling to suppress her tears.

"Alexandra, I'm coming to the hotel. What is your room number?"

"I shouldn't have called," she sobbed. "I just had to talk to someone."

"And you did the right thing. You need to continue to talk, Alexandra. I want to be with you, to be there for you so you can spill your guts out if you want to. I told you I would be a shoulder to cry on if you needed one. I think you need one now. Let me be that shoulder. You can cry or scream or just contemplate whatever you need to contemplate; just don't do it alone."

Several moments of silence followed. And then, finally, sorrowfully, "Eight thirty—I'm in room eight thirty."

"Stay where you are, Alexandra. I'm on my way."

"OK," she whispered, hesitantly, into the phone.

She regretted calling Dany almost as soon as she hung up, but she didn't call him back to stop him from coming. Alexandra sat on the edge of her bed for fifteen or twenty minutes trying to compose herself, trying to make sense of what had happened and what was happening. She finally stood and walked into the bathroom to splash water on her face. The reflection looking back at her from the mirror was pathetically sad, her eyes swollen, her hair slightly out of place.

Then came the knock on the door. She took one last look at herself in the mirror. Her heart was racing, more out of apprehension than anticipation. She tried to smile as she opened the door for Dany. Tears had reddened her eyes.

"Thank you for coming," she said, reaching up to greet him with a brief hug. Dany held her in his arms as the door closed behind him. Finding his embrace comforting, she lingered a moment longer in his arms. He reciprocated, tightening his grasp ever so slightly. He then took her gently by the shoulders and arched back just enough to look into her eyes. He leaned down and softly kissed her eyelids. Alexandra laid her head on his shoulder, and, for the first time since taking Noah's call, she felt comforted.

She led him to the small couch in the room, opposite the bed, and they sat down. Alexandra leaned against Dany's side and laid her head on his shoulder.

"I don't ever remember feeling lonelier, or sadder," she said softly. "Everything has gone so wrong. I just want to do my job, to do what I came here to do. Noah is reveling in his well-deserved success but seems oblivious to my work, to my success."

"Maybe he just misses you, Alexandra," Dany said.

"He ridiculed me," she said, angrily. "Noah ridiculed me," she repeated, shaking her head as she wept.

Dany tightened his embrace and gently pulled her closer. He simply wanted to comfort her at that moment. Her weeping diminished to an intermittent sad and sorrowful pant. They sat there motionlessly for several minutes, her breathing measured, her hand resting against his chest. Dany tightened his arm around her shoulder and continued to hold her. He gently brushed back a few strands of hair, which had fallen across her forehead. Alexandra sighed and closed her eyes. She could feel his heart beating through his shirt against the palm of her hand. As Dany moved to embrace her more firmly, more securely, his hand accidentally brushed against her breast. He paused for a moment and then very gently cupped his hand around the firmness beneath her blouse. The touch of her breast briefly sent his senses reeling.

"Don't," she whispered, softly. "Just hold me, Dany. Please, just hold me."

He moved his hand from her breast and tightened his embrace.

They sat there hardly speaking at all for nearly an hour. She kept running the conversation with Noah through her mind, over and over again. She remembered that first time they had made love in Washington before he left for Stanford. Then images of Amos flashed through her mind—their lovemaking and their parting. They, too, had shared such incredible intimacy. She recalled her reunion with Noah after being apart all those years and how wonderful their life had become. It all seemed so fleeting, so tentative. And as her mind wandered and remembered, she was consumed with sadness. There was no longer anger at that moment—just profound sorrow. And then she thought of Karen, who was about to travel throughout the United States with Noah. Karen Rothschild, his former lover and fiancée, had suddenly reemerged out of nowhere and become the person responsible for Noah's newest achievement. Alexandra wondered if he had asked her to return to the States knowing she couldn't…wouldn't. The thought of Noah and Karen traveling from city to city, staying at the best hotels, reveling in their mutual accomplishment, was crushing. *Where do I belong?* Noah, Alexandra was certain, was not in Washington thinking about the work she was doing in the Middle East. He had to be anticipating the work he and Karen would be doing together. She felt, at that moment, abandoned, unloved, certainly misunderstood. Then she looked up at Dany, who was smiling tenderly and holding on to her so firmly. She closed her eyes, sadly resigned to a sense of loss, and then, after a moment's hesitation, she slowly moved his hand back to her breast. Alexandra, tears in her eyes, reached up and kissed Dany.

"Are you sure you..."

She placed her fingers over his lips to silence him and then pulled him down, to kiss him hungrily, and then eagerly. Alexandra rose from the couch and from his embrace and unbuttoned her blouse. Her tears blurred her vision as she disrobed in front of him. He watched her, his heart pounding. Dany hesitated a moment and then stood and removed his clothing. She took his hand and led him to the bed. No words were spoken as they lay down next to one another. He tenderly kissed her, first on her lips and then her neck, and then, slowly, patiently, he moved his lips to her breasts. He rose up just enough to slip one arm around her shoulders and cradled her head with his free hand, and then as she guided him, he entered her. She moved her arms around his neck as they slowly, and then feverously, began to thrust against one another. And at the climax of their lovemaking, when every taut sinew of their bodies convulsed in a simultaneous and sudden release of tension, Alexandra cried out and began to weep.

Dany eased himself onto his side and tried to embrace her as they lay there, body-to-body, face-to-face. Alexandra's mind wandered, and her eyes stared through him, focused on nothing. Dany understood that her thoughts were not of him at that moment. And so they lay there next to one another for what seemed an eternity, both exhausted and burdened by what had just happened—Alexandra lonely and diminished by the fleeting and empty solace she had sought in Dany and Dany troubled by his understanding that her thoughts were somewhere else. Lying there in the stillness of her room, their measured breathing the only sound, they contemplated the moment—both lost in their own thoughts.

"Would you like me to stay with you for the night?" he finally asked.

She shifted her gaze to him and laid her hand on his arm, squeezing it affectionately.

"No, you should go," she said. "I'll be all right."

"I don't like leaving you like this," he replied. "I'm worried about you."

"I was shaken and feeing very sorry for myself when I called, Dany. It was unfair of me…unfair to you. I'm sorry. I really am."

"I'm glad you called, Alexandra. I said I would be a shoulder for you to cry on."

"You got more than you bargained for," she replied, smiling for the first time since he entered her room.

"What are you going to do?" he asked.

"Wait for Noah to call," she answered, honestly.

"Do you want him to call?"

"We have some serious talking to do, Dany. If he doesn't call me, I'll call him, in the morning."

"That's not what I asked," Dany said.

"I don't know what is going to happen between Noah and me, Dany. I love him. I really do. But we are going off in different directions right now. I'm not going to leave here to join him while he takes his company public, not with what I think is unfolding here in the Middle East. And Noah will soon be totally preoccupied with his public offering and with—with an old acquaintance who is responsible for this huge opportunity he has."

"An old acquaintance?"

"An old girlfriend from college. Actually, she was his fiancée, before I returned from Israel after the last time I was here," she finally answered.

"So you two have had this huge argument just as he is about to embark on this business tour?"

"Yes," she replied.

"With his former fiancée?"

"Yes."

"With his single former fiancée?"

"Yes."

Dany got up from the bed and began dressing. "You two have a lot to sort out," he said.

Alexandra nodded. "It was unfair of me to call you when I did. I was beside myself."

"You needed a shoulder to cry on. I'm glad I was here."

"You're not upset with me?"

"Frankly, Alexandra, I don't know how any man could be upset with you. I don't know what I would do in your place, but if I were Noah, I'd be on the next plane here." With that he leaned down and kissed her on the forehead. "Try to get some sleep," he said, as he turned and left the room.

Alexandra watched as the door closed behind Dany. *What in the world have I done?* she asked herself.

***

Noah reached for the phone several times following his disastrous telephone conversation with Alexandra. Each time he hesitated, deciding instead to give Alexandra more time to think. After all, he had not interfered with her going to Israel, nor had he objected as one week followed another while she pursued story after story for the *Evening Star*. He couldn't understand why, after so many weeks, she wasn't eager to return home unless, perhaps, just perhaps, she felt she was home and that Washington was the real distraction. Noah respected Alexandra's commitment to her work, and he knew she was a damn fine journalist. But important news was certain to flow out of the Middle East for years, maybe even generations. When would her need to be there ever end? What did covering the aftermath of the June war even mean? It could well be an assignment without end. Surely, he thought, Potomac Center becoming a publicly owned, national enterprise was important enough for her to return, at least long enough to be next to him for the bell ringing on the day the Potomac Center IPO went active. The looming public offering would demand an ever-increasing commitment of time, and Noah decided he would have to leave the timing of Alexandra's return to her. And so he didn't call that night or the next day. She needed time to think about their future together, and so did he.

Alexandra, not wanting to miss Noah's call, took meals in her room the following day. She waited until midnight before, anxiously, placing the call to his office.

"Hi," he answered as soon as Barb buzzed his intercom and announced that Alexandra was on the line.

"Hi, Noah. Look, I'm sorry I hung up on you," she began after a brief pause. "I was beside myself, and I'm really sorry. That was a terrible thing to do."

"It's OK. I'm over it. My snide remark was uncalled for. I owe you the apology."

"We're OK, then?" she asked, a slight tremor in her voice.

Noah paused before answering. "Yeah, I guess so. I'm not going to pretend I'm happy, Alexandra, but I don't want to do any more long-distance damage."

"Neither do I, Noah. I want to finish here when this job is done and not find my life in shambles when I come home."

"Which will be when, Alexandra?"

"I'll make it as soon as I can, Noah. Please believe me that I'm as eager to return home as you are to have me return."

"I doubt that, but let's not quibble over words. You do what you have to do over there. I certainly have plenty to keep me busy over here."

"How's the public offering shaping up?" she asked.

"I think things are going well. There's a huge amount of planning going on, and Mid-America is working hard with our people on the prospectus and the road show."

"Do you know where you'll be going yet?"

"Yeah, we think so. It looks like we'll start in New York, head up to Stanford and Hartford to meet with some institutions, and then go on to Boston. We'll do Chicago, of course, Milwaukee, and Minneapolis–Saint Paul, head down to Houston and Dallas, and then fly on to Los Angeles and then up to San Francisco, Portland, and Seattle. We'll end up back here in Washington and do a final presentation for individual investors and a handful of institutions here in the Washington-Baltimore area."

"That's quite a schedule. How long do you think all of that will take?"

"Well, Mid-America wants to get it done by the end of September. They want the offering to be a major fourth-quarter event."

"Is Barb making all of the travel arrangements?"

"No. That's Karen's job. They do this sort of thing all the time. She knows which hotels have the best catering, the best staffs, and the best meeting rooms."

And the best bedrooms too, Alexandra thought to herself. "It sounds as though it's all being very professionally handled," she said.

"Yeah, I think it will go well. We have a good story to tell, and Karen has made a convincing case that market conditions will look very promising."

"Noah, you know, I would love to be there with you."

"Well, you have a job to do. Who knows? Maybe things will move along in the Middle East fast enough for you to be able to join us."

"I hope so, Noah. I really do."

"Alexandra, I have a meeting that I have to get to. Take care of yourself. We'll talk tomorrow."

"OK," she replied.

The conversation left Alexandra unnerved. She was thankful it wasn't contentious or argumentative, but she thought Noah seemed distant and markedly unconcerned about whether she would or wouldn't be able to accompany him and Karen on the Potomac Center IPO tour.

CHAPTER TWENTY-FOUR

Benjamin Bar-Levy asked Amos to meet him for breakfast, as he did from time to time, in the dining room of the King David Hotel. These meetings were always at Bar-Levy's suggestion, and there was always an agenda.

"I understand your friend from America is still here," Bar-Levy said, as he casually spread his favorite apricot jam on a wedge of toast.

"You mean Alexandra Salaman?"

"Is that the name she's using now?"

"I think she's still publishing under the name Sabirah Najat. She doubts that anyone of interest here in Israel would have seen the Sunday *Star* with her photograph."

"I wouldn't be so sure of that."

"Well, that's her decision, isn't it?"

"I understand she's been meeting with Palestinians here and on the West Bank. She's met with Palestinian politicians and even a Palestinian journalist."

"And Israelis, too," Amos replied. "That's her job, Benjamin."

"She should go home."

"Why? Do you know something I don't know?"

"I think things may get very unpleasant here."

"You think she's in danger?"

"That isn't what I was referring to."

"I don't understand."

"Amos, there have been some interesting back-channel discussions through private intermediaries—nothing official." Bar-Levy paused and then shook his head, as he poured himself and Amos a cup of tea. "My *kishki* tells me it isn't going to end well."

"I've never known your gut to be wrong, but what does that have to do with Alexandra?"

"We're spending resources protecting her with an escort wherever she goes, and I'm concerned that she's probably going to sniff out what's happening before anyone else does."

"So what? That's her job."

"If she winds up being critical of us, we're going to look pretty stupid."

"Alexandra isn't here to grind an ax, Benjamin. She's remarkably evenhanded, given her family's history, and don't forget, if she's in danger, it's because she helped us when she discovered what the terrorist Shoukri was up to. Alexandra saved dozens, maybe hundreds, of Israeli lives, Benjamin."

"All the more reason to make sure she doesn't get hurt while she's here."

"What is it that you're worried about?"

"We have reason to believe that Jordan and Egypt are prepared to end their state of belligerency with Israel. Jordan wants the West Bank back but would guarantee us unrestricted access to the Western Wall, and Egypt would reopen the Straits of Tiran."

"But?"

"But there would be no recognition, and none of our ships going through the straits would be able fly the Israeli flag."

"I wouldn't think that would go over so well here."

"It could be a start—a first step."

"Not likely," Amos replied. "Our unity government would fall apart if we accepted those terms."

"You can imagine how that would play in the press," Benjamin said. "Right now everyone in the West loves us. We're David, and we just slew Goliath."

"You're worried that Alexandra Salaman is going to discover all of this and write that we walked away from a real opening to change the course of history in this region?"

"What I'm worried about is that we'll look like fools if she does write about these off-the-record discussions and the hard-liners in the cabinet find out that we've been squiring her around at our expense with an armed army escort while she's here."

"So what do you want me to do?"

"Well, as I recall, you have, or had, a very special relationship with her."

"I won't try to influence what Alexandra writes, and she wouldn't listen to me if I did. Besides, the relationship, as you call it, ended a long time ago."

"Maybe she's right, Amos. Maybe she's really not in any danger and doesn't need an escort."

"She's going to have an escort as long as she's here, Benjamin. It's a small price for us to pay, given what she did for us."

"We might wind up looking like fools, Amos."

"That's also a small price to pay, Benjamin."

"Do you think the escort is really necessary?"

"It's a crapshoot, as our American friends would say. If the Shoukri cell knew she was Sabirah Najat and writing in Tel Aviv, I think they would go after her. We know they're contemplating targeting her fiancé's real-estate project in the States."

"All the more reason why we should have her return home."

"What are we supposed to do? Revoke her visa? We can't do that."

"We can't guard her indefinitely either. She's an unbudgeted expense."

"Then budget it."

"If she sandbags us and word gets out that we've been ushering her around with an armed escort at government expense, we'll have a scandal on our hands."

"We've had worse."

"What's keeping her here, anyway? The war has been over for more than a month."

"I suspect she's already picked up rumors about these back-channel discussions. Everyone is expecting an Arab summit sometime this summer. If I know Alexandra, she'll want to be here at least until that happens."

"It could be dangerous for her."

"She knows that."

"Well, maybe much ado about nothing," Benjamin said. "But I'll be happy when she's safely back home in Washington before any remnants of the Shoukri crowd discover that she's here."

***

"Alexandra Salaman is staying at the Dan Hotel in Tel Aviv," Omar Samir said as he sat down with Ahmed Hebraddi and Khaled Kassab.

"We're not here to talk about the Salaman woman," Khaled replied.

"Who is Alexandra Salaman?" Ahmed asked.

"She's the Palestinian woman who betrayed Sheikh Shoukri and who caused his martyrdom. She's engaged to Greenspan, the Jew who owns Potomac Center."

"I'm here to help you destroy Potomac Center. I do not want to get involved in whatever revenge you might be planning for this Salaman woman," Ahmed Hebraddi replied.

"I haven't asked either of you to get involved in avenging Sheikh Shoukri's death."

"Don't do anything foolish, Omar. We have too much at stake with our project to be distracted by this Salaman woman," Khaled said.

"Leave her to me," Omar said. "Today we're here to discuss our special project. Tell me what progress we've made."

"Our contact with Demolishia, the company in Czechoslovakia, will supply the plastique to Questex-Irvine Materials Testing."

"Fantastic!" Omar responded. "But what about the politics?" he asked. "Things are changing very rapidly in Czechoslovakia. Alexander

Dubcek says he wants to recognize Israel. Are you concerned that he might interfere with our plans to buy plastique from Demolishia?"

"The Dubcek government will never know of our little arrangement with our friends at Demolishia. Besides, getting our dummy company, Questex-Irvine Materials Testing, on the US GSA Scheduled Contractors list did the trick. It was just the cover our friends needed. Why should Dubcek care if Demolishia is selling to one of the world's best-known engineering companies?"

"Unbelievable," Omar said. "Khaled, you are a genius."

"We'll have to acquire an address in Washington sometime soon. I don't dare use the Questex-Irvine address in Aswân again. It's a small office, and I was able to monitor the incoming mail and intercept the mail from our contact at Demolishia. But it's much too risky to continue to have mail sent directly to me at Aswân."

"I have an address in mind," Omar replied. "We'll have someone in Washington to accept deliveries."

"Good," Khaled responded. "The next step will be to order material for our little materials-testing company," he responded, sarcastically. "Ahmed, have you determined how much plastique we'll need?"

"Yes, Kahled, I have," Ahmed answered. "I can bring down Potomac Center with one hundred and forty kilos of pentaerythritol tetranitrate, or, as you call it, plastique."

"Tell me," Omar insisted. "How did you determine that so precisely?"

Ahmed took the schematic he copied from the Potomac Center tenants' manual from his pocket. "I'll show you how we do it," he answered.

"Yes, please explain," Omar replied, urging on the young explosives expert.

"You remember I showed you these twelve support beams, six on each side of the escalators?"

"Yes, of course."

"They're at the center of the mall and bear most of the weight on the roof. You'll recall that that is where all of the mechanical systems and air-conditioning equipment, including the cooling towers, are located. We'll need to place two and a half kilos of plastique at the same level on opposite sides of each beam, as I've drawn here," Ahmed explained, pointing with his pen to the places on the beams where the plastique was to be placed. "Severing these twelve beams could possibly bring down the entire building," he continued. "As the center of the roof collapses, it should pull down the rest of the roof as all this weight plunges down through the center of the building. Now, you see there are these support beams running on an axis north and south away from the center and these support beams running on an axis east and west away from the center. They almost look like crosshairs in a gunsight."

"Yes, I see," Omar said.

"So to be absolutely sure, I've also specified an equal amount of plastique to be placed in the same manner on each of the first four beams running east and west away from the center and each of the first four beams running north and south away from the center, toward the perimeter walls of Potomac Center. So we use a total of sixty kilos on the twelve center support beams around the escalators and a total of eighty kilos on these sixteen beams radiating out from the center."

"Ah, I see," Khaled said. "You're using two and half kilos on opposing sides of each beam, or a total of five kilos on each beam."

"Exactly," Ahmed replied.

"And that will bring down Potomac Center?" Omar asked.

"Yes, and probably blow a few hundred cars off of the parking lot as well," Ahmed replied, laughing. "It will be quite a sight. Once the plastique and simple electric detonators are in place at each beam, someone nearby transmitting a radio signal at the right frequency can detonate it all. It's really quite simple."

"We'll have to send payment when we submit the order," Khaled said.

"Money will be no problem," Omar replied. "How do you plan to place all of this plastique?" Ahmed asked.

Omar simply smiled. "I have a plan," he said.

***

Ahmed Hebraddi was not a violent man, yet he loved the ferocity that was the hallmark of his work. He would often stand at a safe distance and, with sensual expectation, anticipate the awesome energy that would be released with every explosion he engineered at Aswân. At one spot or another, just north of the border with Sudan, Ahmed would stare with reverence at the terrain his work soon would, in a nanosecond, forever violently alter. Incongruously, he spent most of his free time quietly reading the great Egyptian authors. Since beginning his work on the High Dam at Aswân, he had begun reading ʿAbbās Maḥmūd al-ʿAqqād—probably because the great poet was born, nearly a century earlier, right there in Aswân. By day, Ahmed Hebraddi was stimulated by the earth-altering violence of his work, and by night, he was soothed by the beautiful poetry of ʿAbbās Maḥmūd al-ʿAqqād.

Omar Samir jumped at the chance to observe, firsthand, Ahmed Hebraddi's handiwork. Ahmed invited Omar to be on location on a day when three thousand tons an hour of granite and other igneous rock would be blasted and transported for use in the construction of the High Dam at Aswân. Omar watched as one blast after another reduced to rubble tons of hard granite, quartzite, and tough dolerite that, eons ago, were a slurry of molten rock that eventually cooled and solidified into the landscape of the Nile River Valley.

"As you can see, my friend, reducing this project you call Potomac Center to rubble will be child's play compared with what we have the capability to do," Ahmed said. "We are making history here. We are taming the Nile. For millennia the Nile flooded this valley, sometimes nourishing the soil, sometimes destroying everything in its path. The Nile supports all of Egypt. It always has. Nearly everyone in Egypt lives within the reach of the Nile. They depend on the Nile, and they always have. Wherever the Nile reaches, the land is fertile. All else in this land is desert. Some years the Nile is good to the people, and some years it is brutal. But tomorrow, because of what we are doing here today, we'll be able to control when and how much water the Nile will release to the adjacent land. Think of it. Because of us, nature will never indiscriminately flood this area again. What you are observing here today is a miracle, my friend. The High Dam at Aswân will be Nasser's legacy, not his foolish military adventures in Yemen or Sinai. This dam will be one of the engineering wonders of the world, rising nearly four hundred feet into the air and stretching over two miles in length. We are creating a reservoir behind the dam that will stretch for nearly three hundred and fifty miles and extend over twenty miles in width. And what contains it all? The rock we bring to the dam site every day. Think of it, Omar: we are now blasting and transporting three thousand tons of rock every hour. It's awesome. This dam, comprised of these rocks, is what will control the annual floods that have inundated so much of the Nile Valley. Now, man and not nature will release the Nile's water."

"I've never seen such destructive power," Omar said. "The precision with which you are carving out the earth is awesome. Frankly, I expected the explosions to be much greater considering how much rock you're extracting every hour."

"What we are doing is very controlled, my friend. We're not bombing cities here; we're reducing and extracting rock from huge geologic formations. When we set off a charge within the rock formation, we produce an immense shock wave that stresses, then compresses, and finally crushes the rock, all in fractions of a second. The instantaneous stress the shock wave produces is greater than the strength of the rock, so the rock fractures and crumbles."

"The same way you explained how the shock waves will sever the steel beams at Potomac Center."

"Exactly the same principle. Here we drill holes and insert the explosive material into the rock formation. At Potomac Center, we'll place the plastique on the surface of each beam we want to sever. The result will be the same. The shock wave we produce will be stronger than the tensile strength of the steel that holds up Potomac Center," Ahmed replied.

"You are mightier than Mother Nature herself, Ahmed."

"Nature carves out the earth too, my friend. But what nature takes millions of years to do, we can do like that!" he said, snapping his fingers. "This is a wonderful time to be an engineer. This river is the longest in the world. If you laid it out beginning in New York and had it flow west, it would traverse the entire United States and flow on halfway to Hawaii, and we, here on this spot, from now on, will control the Nile."

"You love this job, don't you?"

"There are nearly thirty-five thousand people working on this project, and I think I have the very best job of them all."

"You love the river too, don't you?"

"Ah, my friend, there are no rivers like the Nile—none. The river's headwaters are far from us, way to the south. Two tributaries, the White Nile and the Blue Nile, come together nearly six hundred miles south of here at Khartoum in Sudan and form this magnificent river that flows north through Nubia and Egypt all the way to the Mediterranean Sea."

Omar smiled, admiring Ahmed's enthusiasm. "We are fortunate to have you working for our cause."

"Your cause is not my cause, Omar. Avenging Egypt's humiliation is my cause. I hate the Americans and the British and the French and most of all the Israelis. The Israelis tried to steal our Suez Canal. Then, the Americans and the British reneged on their promise to provide financial support for building the dam here at Aswân. They forced us to accept aid from the Russians, whom I trust even less. I am helping you because Khaled Kassab is my friend. He tells me the Salaman woman is a Palestinian who joined ranks with the Americans and the Israelis and that she betrayed her countrymen."

"That is correct, Ahmed. She cost Sheikh Shoukri his life, and now she is engaged to the American Jew who built this Potomac Center."

"And therefore I will help you, Omar. We make mighty walls of granite crumble here, my friend. Making this Potomac Center crumble will be child's play."

CHAPTER
TWENTY-FIVE

Noah's phone started ringing as soon as Mid-America Ventures released the news that Potomac Center Properties of America planned an initial public offering. Noah carefully read the wire story before taking his first call.

IPO PLANNED FOR POTOMAC CENTER PROPERTIES OF AMERICA

Washington, DC—Potomac Center Properties of America today announced that it has filed a registration statement with the Securities and Exchange Commission (SEC) for a proposed initial public offering of 2.5 million common shares representing 49 percent of the company based in Washington, DC. The remaining registered shares are owned by Noah Greenspan, the developer of Potomac Center, a multifaceted urban-development project consisting of a large shopping mall, an office complex, residential housing, and a marina for approximately one hundred boats.

> *Mid-America Ventures, a Chicago-based invest-*
> *ment-banking firm, is managing the offering. A prelim-*
> *inary prospectus has been filed with the SEC containing*
> *important information about the company, and there*
> *will not be any sale or any acceptance of an offer to buy*
> *shares until the company has issued a final prospectus*
> *following final review by the SEC.*
>
> *The offering will be made by means of a prospec-*
> *tus, which may be obtained when available from Mid-*
> *America Ventures—attention Prospectus Department,*
> *35 E. Wacker Drive, Chicago, Illinois.*

Well, that's straightforward enough, Noah thought, as he picked up the phone and placed a call to Karen.

"Well, it's official now," Karen said as soon as she heard Noah's voice.

"My phone has already started to ring," Noah said. "What do I need to know?"

"You, personally, shouldn't discuss the offering or the company with anyone right now. We'd like to keep you out of the limelight until the road show."

"Yeah, I understand we're now in a quiet period while the SEC reviews our registration statement, but what if people call just to ask very basic questions like what Potomac Center does?"

"Have Barb refer them to me," Karen answered. "The fewer calls you personally take pertaining to the offering, the better."

"Really? You mean I can't talk at all to anyone who calls about the offering? Is that what the rules say?"

"No, that isn't what the rules say, but you're new at this, and the most innocuous comments can get the offering into hot water. It's just not worth the risk of you saying something that someone misquotes and us winding up with a delay while we explain things to the SEC. Noah, you need to be coached about the dos and don'ts before you start talking to anyone on the Street or from the press. We really want to get this offering off early in October, and we don't want any unnecessary delays. The best way to avoid that is not to talk to anyone right now. Right after Labor Day, we'll be on the road with this offering, and the less said before then, the better."

"OK, you're the boss."

Karen smiled. "I like the sound of that."

"You've been great, Karen. I'm very excited about going public, and I couldn't be more impressed with the job you've done. I hope there's a big bonus in it for you."

"It's great to be working with you again, Noah, and that's a bonus I never dreamed I would see again. We'll start working on the road-show presentation here at Mid-America, and you and I should plan to get together in a week or so to go over it. We'll fine-tune the presentation once we know what your third quarter looks like, and we should plan to rehearse the week of August twenty-eighth. Labor Day is September fourth, and we should plan to be on the road that week. I'll make all of the arrangements and send them to you to review."

"Karen, thanks for all you've done. I'm also looking forward to working with you again—very much," he added.

"Bye, Noah. I'll talk to you next week, and we'll firm up plans to get together."

Noah slowly pushed back against his chair, tilting it enough for him to comfortably prop his feet up on the contemporary oversize maple and steel-trimmed desk. He would often do that when he simply wanted to think. He glanced around the smartly appointed office, and his thoughts wandered as he recalled how much his life had changed. He thought of his enduring love for Alexandra from the time they were children growing up in Washington's LeDroit Park neighborhood, the children of inner-city corner grocers. Then came the conflicts when he went off to Stanford and met Karen and Alexandra went off to college in Beirut. There was that awful episode with the Palestinian students who were plotting a massacre in Israel and Alexandra's dash to Israel with the Israeli agent Amos Ben-Chaiyim, with whom she fell in love. Karen, meanwhile, had become Noah's constant companion in college and his colleague after graduation and then, later, his fiancée. He remembered their falling out when a blind competition determined that Alexandra's brother Yusuf had produced the best of nearly one hundred architectural submissions for Potomac Center. Then, in the midst of all the controversy over the architecture, Alexandra returned to the United States after five years in the Middle East, and everything so quickly deteriorated between him and Karen. He remembered the day Karen left him and Potomac Center and returned home to Chicago. And now he and Karen, after being apart for four years, were about to spend three weeks together traveling throughout the United States. Four years after she left, brokenhearted, Karen had now reemerged as a key strategist in taking Potomac Center public and, once again, as a conflict between him and Alexandra.

"Barb," he called into the intercom, "refer all calls pertaining to the public offering to Karen Rothschild at Mid-America Ventures in Chicago."

VICTOR AND VANQUISHED STRUGGLE TO FIND COMMON GROUND
By Sabirah Najat

Tel Aviv, Israel—The next month may well set the course for the next generation in this tortured part of the world. Rumors abound, and it seems no one can speak with confidence about what is likely to happen next as events continue to unfold here. We can report with certainty that there are those on both sides of the conflict who want to seek an end to the endless hostility, and we can also report that there are those on both sides who insist that the struggle has only just begun.

In what passes for an extended olive branch in this part of the world, Israel has announced that it is extending "indefinitely" the previously set August 31 deadline to admit Arab refugees, who fled to the East Bank during the fighting and now want to return to their homes, onto the West Bank area of the Jordan River. The announcement was made after a conference between Israeli foreign minister Abba Eban and United States ambassador to Israel Walworth Barbour. The extension, however, will only apply to the admission of those refugees still on the East Bank whose reentry had already been approved by Israel. The Israeli authorities, fearful of saboteurs and terrorists seeking entry, have been poring over the applications of ten thousand Palestinians.

Israel is under pressure from both the United States and the United Nations, through Secretary of State Dean Rusk and Secretary-General U Thant, to lift the August 31 deadline. Israel had originally set August 10 as the cutoff date and then stretched the application period to August 31. Just this week, Israel turned over to the International Red Cross, for transmission to Jordan, one thousand more approved permits. The flow of returnees has been extremely slow, which Israel blames on Jordan for creating unnecessary bottlenecks in the process of distributing the permits. Yesterday, only 679 refugees crossed over, although Israel was expecting about 3,000.

Meanwhile, Israel's military authorities in the occupied Arab areas have employed about 16,200 Palestinians. We've learned that 10,000 have been given jobs on the West Bank, nearly 6,000 in the Gaza Strip, and 200 in the occupied Syrian areas. The Israeli Ministries of Labor and Development claim they are prepared to employ thousands more by promoting tourism and by developing locally produced products for sale abroad.

Rumors are flying that the Arab nations are planning a fourth summit meeting, perhaps to be held in Cairo, Alexandria, or Casablanca, where prior summits have been held, or as far away as Khartoum, Sudan. While it is not certain when, or even if, such a meeting might occur, people are actively discussing what might be on the agenda if such a meeting were to take place.

Certainly, Arab rulers are determined to eliminate the consequences of Israel's victory in last month's Six-Day War, and some in the Arab camp are discussing the possibility of an indefinite oil embargo against the United States, Britain, and other nations they insist support Israel.

On a more hopeful note, usually reliable sources report that Jordan's king Hussein is prepared to demilitarize the West Bank, give Israel a corridor to the Western Wall, and end its state of belligerence against Israel. It is even rumored that the king is prepared to recommend dropping, as a condition, the repatriation of Arab refugees into Israel, which has been a bedrock position of the Arab nations.

Among the panoply of rumors rampant in the area is the tantalizing report that Yugoslavia's president Tito has proposed to Egypt's Nasser that he accept international guarantees for Israel's freedom of shipping through the Straits of Tiran and permit cargoes destined for Israel to pass through the Suez Canal as long as they are not flying the Israeli flag, as well as that he end the state of belligerence against Israel. Reliable sources in Israel say there will be no comment from the government in response to what is, today, only a rumor about Egypt's intentions. Reliable sources also report that President Habib Bourguiba of Tunisia is prepared to call for Arab recognition of Israel, as is King Hassan II of Morocco.

One can find in this whirlwind of rumors either hope or despair. What is uncertain is whether hope or despair will define the future.

***

Benjamin Bar-Levy was livid. Alexandra's latest column represented just the kind of speculation the government did not want to see promoted while things were still in such a state of flux. It could only limit Israel's options and possibly create unrealistic expectations in world capitals. Without diplomatic recognition from its Arab neighbors, Israel was in no mood to compromise.

"We can't keep providing armed escorts and transportation while the Salaman woman writes whatever she chooses," Bar-Levy insisted to Amos.

"What do you propose? That we ask her to write what we choose?" Amos answered, sarcastically.

"Urge her to go home, Amos. You've made her your responsibility, so if she's a problem for us, she's a problem for you."

"I don't think she's a problem. She doing what journalists do, Benjamin. And maybe, just maybe, having these different alternatives aired in public is good."

"Maybe it is, and maybe it isn't. I don't know, and neither do you. What she is doing may be what journalists do, as you say, Amos, but providing an armed security detail for a single journalist among hundreds is certainly not what governments do. If certain members of the cabinet knew we were providing this level of support to one journalist whose writing they didn't particularly like, heads could roll—especially mine."

"Therefore what?"

"Therefore, I want to terminate this special treatment we're giving her. If she wants to traipse around Israel and the West Bank talking to anyone she pleases, writing anything she pleases, she'll have to do it on her own. We can't keep squiring her around indefinitely."

"And if anything happens to her?"

"Amos, we can't let that fear dictate this special treatment we're providing every time she comes to Israel."

"The hell we can't," Amos replied, making no effort to hide his anger. "Look, I doubt that she'll ever come back once this assignment is over, but when she's here, we watch out for her."

"Which will be when, Amos? When will this damn assignment of hers ever be over?"

"I don't know. I would guess she'll return to the States in the next month or two, but that shouldn't matter."

"Sixty days, Amos. We'll continue to provide security for another sixty days, and then she's on her own."

"You're not worried about the security detail we're providing; you're worried about what she might write," Amos replied, angrily.

"You're damn right I'm worried about what she writes. Where in the hell did she get that information about Tito's proposal to Nasser?"

"I have no idea, Benjamin. I learned about it from reading her column. Is it true?"

"Yes, it's true. It's a feeler. It's a baby step, but we have reason to think Nasser is interested. We believe Nasser wants to de-escalate tension. We know he's given the nod to King Hussein to try to work out something with us, probably some mutual understanding about Israeli access to certain West Bank sites like the Western Wall. And if we were able to take a few steps toward peace with Jordan, Nasser might follow suit. The state of endless belligerence could begin to recede."

"I'd call that progress, wouldn't you?"

"Amos, don't be naive. It's a germ of an idea that has to incubate, and maybe, just maybe, left alone it could take hold and maybe, just maybe, develop into a broader understanding—maybe even peace."

"So?"

"So, this damned speculation about it in the press, thanks to your friend, has a good chance of rallying the opposition on both sides against compromise. She'll wind up energizing the rejectionists everywhere."

"Don't you think you're exaggerating Alexandra's influence a bit?"

"Look, Tito's proposal to Nasser has real potential, and we know Hussein wants to disengage and end the state of belligerency between Jordan and Israel. Meanwhile, this damned PLO organization that was formed three years ago will agitate against any accommodation between our neighbors and us. The last thing we need is Alexandra Salaman tossing this information about willy-nilly as the latest rumors from the Middle East."

"I don't understand why you are so concerned about what she speculates on in her columns."

"We're not of one mind here, and the Arabs are certainly not of one mind on the other side of the Sinai or the Golan or the Jordan River. I'm telling you, too much speculation in the press about these feelers, and they'll be reduced to flotsam, debris to be swept away by the next wave of violence."

"So what's the point, Benjamin?"

"Frankly, I don't think she's in any danger. Nobody subscribes to the *Washington Evening Star* in this part of the world, and I seriously doubt that anyone connected to the Shoukri cell has a clue that she's anywhere near here. But, Amos, she's smart as hell, and she's tenacious, and she moves comfortably among Israelis and Palestinians. So yes, I'm worried that she'll ferret out what's being planned on our side and on the Arab side before anyone else does. We don't need her writing about anyone's position before we've had a chance to determine what our position is."

"She's a friend, Benjamin, and she's a responsible journalist. Even we might learn something by following what she writes. We do agree on one thing though. She's probably not in danger, but better to be safe than sorry."

Alexandra, of course, wouldn't have been in any danger if the Trans-Arab Alliance hadn't been reproducing every *Evening Star* column she wrote in its weekly newsletter, *Cultural Jihad.* Alexandra, unfortunately, now had no more consistent reader than Omar Samir.

CHAPTER
TWENTY-SIX

Karen strode smartly into Noah's office for their first IPO planning session. She exuded confidence as he walked from behind his desk to greet her. "Well, you certainly don't look like you just stepped from a hot taxi following a two-hour flight from Chicago," he said, as he grasped her hand and kissed her on the cheek. Once again, the image flashed through his mind of Karen just as she looked when, as freshmen, they first met at the University Deli in Palo Alto. Now she was his investment banker, sophisticated, poised, and stylishly dressed.

Karen handed Noah the itinerary for the IPO road show as she sat down opposite him at the small circular conference table in the corner of his office. She glanced out through the tinted floor-to-ceiling window at the parking lot, which seemed nearly filled to capacity.

"Pretty busy, I'd say."

"Yeah, when the outdoor lots are this busy, it usually means there aren't many spaces left in the garage either. Monument Parking—they're the contractor that manages our lot and garage—has started providing valet service, and they're parking our overflow at a nearby location they operate. Honestly, Karen, we're pulling our hair out trying to handle the crowds."

"Not a bad problem to have. I think we should include a shot in the slide presentation of the parking lot from this angle. It speaks volumes.

By the way, we're getting a great response to the IPO, Noah. We'll have a nice turnout everywhere, and most of the major institutions will be in attendance in just about every city."

"I'm really impressed," he replied as he glanced through the lineup of cities and the list of expected attendees. "Someone has done a lot of work."

"I'll take that as a compliment," she answered.

"And a well-deserved compliment it is, Karen. You're very good at what you do."

"Are you just discovering that?" she asked, with feigned coyness.

"Nah, I was impressed with you from the time we were both eighteen-year-old freshmen at Stanford."

"Best not to go there, Noah," she said, smiling.

"Yeah," he sighed. "Back to work."

"I've done road shows in virtually all of these cities, so I've picked the hotels that have the best catering and the best function rooms. Wherever I could, I booked two-bedroom suites. You and Alexandra, of course, in one room and me in an adjacent room, separated from your room by a common living room. It won't be unusual for us to work into the night from time to time to adjust the presentation based on questions we get or ideas that occur to us as we move from presentation to presentation."

Noah was briefly taken aback that Karen had booked two-room suites but let it pass. He assumed the room arrangements made sense given Karen's rationale regarding the need to sometimes work into the night. Besides, Karen was assuming that Alexandra would be accompanying them, and maybe she would be if events moved along between the Israelis and the Arabs.

"So, whom are we expecting to show up?" he asked, dismissing his concern about room arrangements.

"Interest is really running high, Noah. So far, in New York, we know Kidder Peabody, Manny Hanny, Merrill Lynch, White Weld, Wellington Fund, E. F. Hutton, Morgan Stanley, and Chase Manhattan.

Nearly every institution we would want will be there. I'm guessing we'll have at least one hundred analysts in New York."

"Manny Hanny?"

"Manufacturers Hanover Trust—Street lingo," she replied.

"Anything else I should know?"

"Actually, yes. Deutschland Trust's George Markanos will be there. He's a notorious short seller. If Potomac Center is selling at a sixteen multiple at the closing bell on opening day, or about thirty-two dollars a share, he'll look for any weakness he can find to justify selling Potomac Center short. If he can make a case that the multiple is too high and knock it down to, say, a ten or twelve multiple, he can make a lot of money very fast going short in the stock."

"That could be pretty risky for Deutschland Trust," Noah replied. "If we meet expectations and the share price rises, his exposure to loss on a short sale could be pretty significant."

"That's true, and, of course, he knows that, so if he takes a short position, he'll promote the hell out of his reason for going short."

"Sure. He'll do whatever he legally can to drive down the price of the stock. Once he goes short, that's the only way he can make money."

"Right. So we look at the George Markanoses of the world as the angels of death. They come from the dark side looking for weaknesses they can exploit. That's how they make money in the market. On the other hand, those analysts who have recommended the stock will come to our defense. Anyway, it's nothing we need to worry about. It's all part of the rough-and-tumble of Wall Street."

"Well, I don't think he'll find anything to criticize. We're essentially leased out at terrific rates, and we have a waiting list for premium space. Our numbers are solid."

"We know they are, Noah. Just don't get rattled if he asks questions that seem overly negative. He invariably gravitates to the negative. If he thinks he can knock down the price of the stock, he will."

"One of the risks of going public, I guess."

"Don't worry about it. Just tend to your business. Anyway, we're booked at the Hilton in Hartford. We're getting a strong response there too. We'll have Aetna, MetLife, and a number of other major buy-side institutions. It looks like around thirty attendees in the Stamford-Hartford area."

"Who knew Potomac Center would be the focus of so much attention?" he mused.

"Boston is also showing strong interest. Fidelity, Putnam, State Street, John Hancock, Harvard Management—they're all coming. We'll have at least fifty in Boston, maybe more."

"Harvard University might invest in Potomac Center?"

"I suspect they will," Karen replied.

"Do they know I went to Stanford?" he joked.

"As long as you didn't go to Yale or Dartmouth, I think we'll be OK."

And so they continued throughout the day, breaking only briefly for lunch and dinner. Karen methodically discussed each institution and what she knew about the analysts in the various cities who had indicated an intention to attend. They finished around nine o'clock that evening and made plans to begin again at breakfast the following morning.

"Are you up for a nightcap?" she asked, as Noah pulled into the driveway at the Statler to drop her off for the night.

"Sure, why not?" he replied. "Let's go over to the Gaslight Club. It's right across the street."

"Sounds great."

He turned his Corvette over to the Statler parking attendant, and as he and Karen strolled across Sixteenth Street, she casually took hold of his arm. "You've come a long way, Noah," she said. "I never doubted for a minute that you'd be a big success."

"Thanks, Karen. I think I've been incredibly lucky."

"Incredible luck and a brilliant mind are a pretty cool combination," she said, tightening her grip on his arm.

He looked into her eyes and smiled but didn't reply. Noah inserted the brass gaslight key into the slot on the door, and a moment later they entered the Gay Nineties lookalike. The club was moderately crowded and the ambience very upbeat. A riot of Tiffany lamps hung from the ceiling, and an energetic pianist wearing a straw hat and a red and white pin-striped shirt was banging out "Alexander's Ragtime Band."

"Hey, Noah, long time no see," one of the long-legged, scantily clad waitresses called out as they entered the club.

"Hi, Maddie, say hello to Karen Rothschild," Noah yelled as they made their way to a table along the wood-paneled sidewall.

"You a friend of the tycoon's?" the attractive waitress asked, playfully.

"An old friend," Karen answered. "We go all the way back to our college days."

"Not so old," the waitress answered. "What do you hear from Alexandra, Noah?"

"She's hard at work still reporting from Israel," he answered.

"What'll you have?" she asked, as they took their seats.

"Hedges & Butler on the rocks for me, and…" He paused, looking to Karen.

"I'll have the same," she replied.

"Comin' up," Maddie called over her shoulder as she made her way toward the bar.

"Well, you guys must be regulars here," Karen said.

"Not really. We used to bring people here a lot before Potomac Center opened, but we haven't had much time for this sort of thing for the past couple of months."

"We have a Gaslight Club in Chicago over on Huron Street," Karen replied. "The guys at Mid-America take clients there a lot, but I've only been a couple times. It's almost identical to this one."

"And I thought I was going to take you somewhere for a nightcap you hadn't been before."

"Not this time," she answered.

"I'm really looking forward to the road show," Noah said, following a brief but awkward lull in the conversation.

"So, you guys OK? You and Alexandra, I mean."

"Sure," Noah answered, a bit too quickly. "I mean, this assignment of hers in Israel has dragged on much longer than either of us had anticipated. It's been kind of stressful, I guess."

"She's quite the professional journalist. I was really impressed with her when we met up at the Dan in Tel Aviv."

"I understand you met her friend, Amos," Noah said.

"Yeah, I did. We all had dinner together in Tel Aviv. He's quite a guy, Noah."

"Yeah, I know," he replied. "There was a time when I never expected her to come back."

"Two Hedges & Butler—rocks," Maddie interrupted, as she set down the drinks and placed a bowl of pretzels on the table.

"Thanks, Maddie," Noah said.

"So, when is Alexandra coming back?" Karen asked, as soon as Maddie left the table.

"Frankly, I haven't the slightest idea," he answered. "She says things are coming to a head politically over there, and she intends to stay and report until something is resolved one way or the other."

"That could be a long time, Noah."

"Don't I know it," he replied with a sigh.

Karen reached over and took his hand. "Noah, I know I'm here in Washington with you on business, but, in spite of all that has happened between us, I'm still a friend too. Don't get me wrong. I'm not suggesting anything other than that if you ever need an old friend to commiserate with, I'm here."

He nodded appreciatively and closed his hand around hers. They looked into each other's eyes, and he briefly squeezed her hand, affectionately. "I appreciate that, Karen," he said, softly.

"You know, I was intimidated when I first met Alexandra. Do you remember? You and I were freshmen at Stanford, and Alexandra was still a senior in high school."

"Oh, I remember all right," he answered. "I can still recall my sense of panic when you called to tell me you were in Washington. You and your parents were on the way to Williamsburg, Virginia, during Christmas break, and you stopped off in Washington."

"Yes, and you and I met Alexandra downtown, and we had lunch together and knocked around all afternoon. We went to some pizza place for dinner."

"Yeah, it was Mickey Grasso's Italian Grotto. I'll never forget that day. I was miserable while my two girlfriends were getting to know one another."

"Noah, she was the most impressive girl I had ever met. I remember seeing her from a distance as you and I were walking to meet her and thinking, God, don't let that be her. I mean she was so beautiful, and by the way, she still is."

"You're not so bad looking yourself, you know."

"I'll tell you something, Noah," Karen continued, ignoring his compliment. "She's still intimidating. She's alluringly beautiful, she's smart as hell, and you just know she's on the way to the top of her field. You two are going to become the power couple of Washington."

Noah stared off into the room for a moment before responding. "You know, we were kids when we first met. Alexandra was only eleven years old. I mostly ignored her at first. Her brother, Yusuf, was really my friend. We were best friends."

"And when did all that change? I mean, when did you start paying attention to her?"

Noah smiled. "Believe it or not, it was at my bar mitzvah. I remember it like it was yesterday. I had taken my seat on the bema after reciting my Torah portion, and I glanced up into the balcony, and Alexandra was sitting there between my mother and her mother. For the first time, I saw this beautiful girl in Alexandra. Our eyes met, we smiled at each other, and the rest is history."

"I guess there was no way I ever could have competed with that," she responded, wistfully.

Noah took her hand again. "It was never a matter of competition, Karen."

"It was for me, Noah. I felt pretty secure in my relationship with you as long as Alexandra was far away. When we were at Stanford, she was on the other side of the country, and when we were first together in Washington after graduation, she was on the other side of the world. She was a distant threat then, but when she returned from Israel, she became a very close and overwhelming threat. All of my confidence in us evaporated, and with that our engagement did too."

"Yet here we are teamed up planning the biggest step of my career. You were responsible for my first major success in business when you told me about the Metro when it was first being planned, and now you're responsible for Potomac Center going public."

"I could tell you I saw the IPO as a huge business opportunity for me, and that would certainly be true."

"But?"

"But probably not entirely honest."

"What do you mean?"

"Don't get me wrong. It certainly is a huge business opportunity for me," she said. "Maybe the biggest opportunity I'll ever have. But I'd be less than honest if I didn't admit that working with you again was—well, a tantalizing prospect."

"Well, then, we can both be honest with one another. There isn't a chance in the world that I'd be taking Potomac Center public if anyone other than you had proposed it to me."

"Because…"

"Because what tantalized you obviously tantalized me as well. We really were a great team in college, later as business colleagues, and, well, as a couple too."

"And, as you say, here we are," Karen replied, gently squeezing his hand again.

Noah smiled and returned the gesture. There was little conversation for the next hour as they sat back, sipped their scotches, and enjoyed the soft, sleepy jazz being skillfully teased from the piano by the musician in the straw hat.

As they walked back across Sixteenth Street to the Statler, Noah casually draped his arm over Karen's shoulder.

"I'm glad we had time to just relax," he said.

"It reminded me of another time," she answered wistfully, as she reached up and took his hand. She turned to say good night at the entrance of the hotel, hesitating for a moment.

"I'll see you to your room," he said.

"Thanks, I would appreciate that," she answered.

They didn't speak in the elevator as it rose to the eighth floor, and they walked in silence as they made their way to her room at the end of the long dimly lit corridor.

"I'll come by and pick you up at eight thirty. We can grab breakfast here before heading over to my office," he said as she handed him her key to the room. He opened the door for her and handed back the key. Karen turned and smiled. "It was a great day, Noah."

He leaned forward, awkwardly, to kiss her good night. Karen placed her hands on his arms as he softly kissed her cheek. Noah lingered for a moment and then took her firmly in his arms. Karen reciprocated, her body trembling ever so slightly in his tight grasp. They didn't speak as they held on to one another for several moments. The familiar contours of her body pressed against his, and the light, pleasant fragrance of her cologne stirred thoughts of another time and another place.

"Go," she whispered, pulling away from him. He saw that there were tears in her eyes.

He nodded. "See you in the morning," he finally whispered, briefly hugging her again before turning to leave. Noah started back down the corridor toward the elevator. He heard the door to her room quietly close and the lock snap into place. As he waited for the elevator, he looked back in the direction of her room—the feel of her body encircled in his arms still fresh in his mind. Noah's heart was still pounding in anticipation of what might have been, as he stepped into the empty elevator.

***

The phone was ringing as Noah opened his town-house door. He hurried over to the bar and picked up the receiver.

"Hi," Alexandra's voice greeted him.

"Hey, how are you?" he replied.

"I'm OK. I just thought I would try calling before I left for a breakfast meeting this morning. I called earlier, so I knew I wouldn't be waking you."

Noah glanced at his watch. It was one o'clock in the morning. "Sorry I missed you; we've been working on the IPO nonstop," he replied, cringing at the half-truth. "How are things going over there?"

"Noah, I really think I'm onto something. Dany Haddad called to meet me for breakfast. He said he wanted to discuss my last column. He said everyone at *Desert Song* is talking about it. I think I've hit a raw nerve."

"You think it has to do with the rumor about Tito talking to Nasser?"

"I'm not sure. I know there are Israelis in high places that would jump at the opportunity to engage the Arabs diplomatically, and there are those who are only focused on reclaiming ancient Judea and Samaria."

Noah was relieved that the conversation was about Alexandra's work and not about his whereabouts so late in the evening. "Any movement on the Arab side?" he asked.

"Who knows?" she replied. "I don't think we'll hear much until the Arab summit takes place. There are rumors that Egypt and Jordan might want to reach some kind of understanding with Israel, but it's very complicated, and it might not even be up to them."

"Why wouldn't it be? Who else really matters?"

"Well, how about the Palestinians? One group that was formed three years ago, the Palestine Liberation Organization, is insisting that every inch of what used to be British Mandate Palestine has to be recognized as a Palestinian homeland. To them, armed struggle is the only course of action. There's also another group called al-Fatah. An Egyptian, Yasser Arafat, heads that organization, and they also insist on armed resistance against Israel. Arafat was head of the Union of Palestinian Students in Cairo when I was a student in Beirut. Shoukri used to give me their literature to read."

"In other words, Israel must be destroyed."

"Well, they would say it simply has to be Palestinian. Ahmad Shukeiri, the PLO chairman, has a pretty impressive background, but people doubt he'll hold on to the position much longer, given the magnitude of the Israeli victory last month. He's lost a lot of credibility. And if this guy Arafat takes over, I think things are going to get very dicey. His group isn't interested in diplomacy. I have trouble imagining any olive branches being extended anytime soon. Anyway, I have to run in a minute. Do you have firm dates for the IPO yet?"

"Assuming no delays by the SEC, and assuming I don't screw up on the road show, we're planning to go active Monday, October second."

"I really want to be there with you, Noah. I hope I'll be able to do that—I really do."

"Well, we have a room reserved for the two of us in every city, Alexandra," he said, omitting any mention of the fact that they would be sharing a two-bedroom suite with Karen.

"It will be very exciting for you, Noah, and I'll do everything I can to be there with you."

"I think the real issue will be whether Prime Minister Eshkol, President Nasser, and King Hussein will do everything they can to get you home."

"Gotta go. Talk to you soon, Noah. Love you," Alexandra said hurriedly, ending the call.

"Talk to you soon. Stay in touch," he replied, as he hung up the phone.

Alexandra hurried to the lobby to meet Dany. She hadn't seen him since the night they had been together in her hotel room, and she really wasn't sure what he wanted to discuss. As she made her way to the elevator, she wondered if she had rushed Noah off the phone too quickly. Was he still upset with her? Just how much time was he spending with Karen, and, besides, what was there about planning for an IPO that was still weeks away that kept Noah out until one o'clock in the morning?

CHAPTER TWENTY-SEVEN

Dany was already seated when Alexandra arrived for breakfast. He put down the *International Herald Tribune* he had been reading and rose to greet her.

"Hi, Dany," she said, hugging him, perfunctorily, as she reached the table.

"You OK?" he asked.

She smiled, unconvincingly, and nodded.

"Have you been able to reach Noah?" he asked.

"Yes, we've spoken a couple of times."

"And?"

"And…we didn't argue. He talked mostly about the IPO and his hope that I would be able to join him."

"And?"

"I told him I would try to be there but that it depended on how events moved along here."

"Is he OK with that?"

"Frankly, I'm not sure he cares that much anymore. He said there's a room reserved for the two of us in every city on the tour, but he didn't insist on my being there, and he didn't seem very upset when I said it would depend on developments here."

"That should please you—that he wasn't upset when you didn't give him a definite answer."

"Actually, it left me unsettled. It didn't seem that my presence was as important to him as it had been the last time he and I spoke. I know I'm doing the right thing by staying here while events are unfolding. After all, this is my career, and I may never have another opportunity to cover anything this important again."

"It's a conflict between your personal life and your professional life, Alexandra. This is probably not the last time something like this is going to happen."

"What you really mean is that it's a conflict between the importance to me of my work and the importance to me of Noah."

"Isn't it?" Dany asked.

"I don't think that's a fair way to look at it," she replied.

"I bet Noah thinks it's a fair way to look at it."

"Why do you say that?" she asked.

"You've been here nearly two months, Alexandra. You were originally thinking you would be here for a week or two. You're telling Noah that you're not sure when you're returning home. He's about to embark on something really big and wants you to be with him, and you're telling him maybe, maybe not. To make matters worse, he has to be perplexed that you're OK with him doing this tour with his former fiancée, who happens to be very attractive and very single."

"You're making quite the case for me to return to the States. I bet you'll be glad to get rid of me."

"Nothing could be further from the truth, Alexandra. The fact is I can't get you out of my mind. I've never been attracted to any woman the way I'm attracted to you. I've barely slept since we were together the other night, and if you weren't already committed to someone else, I'd move heaven and earth to be with you."

"Dany, I'm so sorry about the other night," she said, reaching out and taking his hand. "It shouldn't have happened. I was distraught, and I desperately wanted to be with someone—to not be alone."

"I understand, Alexandra, and I'm glad I was there for you at that moment. I didn't want you to be alone either. I don't think you should ever be alone, and if it were up to me, you wouldn't ever be alone," he said, gently squeezing her hand. "But you should return to the States, Alexandra."

"Of course I'm going to return to the States. I just want to see this assignment through," she replied, withdrawing her hand from his.

"You should return now...tomorrow."

"You do want to get rid of me, don't you?

"Getting rid of you is the last thing I want," he replied.

Alexandra, suddenly sensing there was more to Dany's conversation than she had assumed, paused a moment before responding. "Dany, something has happened, hasn't it? Do you have reason to think I'm in some kind of danger?"

He looked into her eyes before responding and then nodded. "I think you may be, Alexandra. More people may know you are here and writing as Sabirah Najat than you think."

"Whatever are you talking about?" she asked, her expression evidencing concern for the first time.

"This," he replied, pulling a document from his pocket. He smoothed it out as he laid it down on the table in front of her.

Alexandra stared down at the copy of *Cultural Jihad* Dany had placed on the table.

"What's this?" she asked.

"Turn it over," he answered.

She picked up the newsletter and, after glancing hesitantly at the front, turned it over to the back page. "Oh my God," she murmured as she looked at a reproduction of the Sunday *Star* column that carried her photograph over the name Sabirah Najat. "What is this?" she asked.

"It's a newsletter published by a group that calls itself the Trans-Arab Alliance. They're out of Tripoli. We get it at *Desert Song*. It's been lying around for a while. I just happened to pick it up this morning and begin thumbing through it and other copies we have on file. They've carried every one of your columns, Alexandra."

"To whom does it go?"

"As far as I can tell, it has a pretty small readership. I'm guessing a few hundred, maybe a few thousand. But from its content, you can tell it's vehemently anti-Israel. There is always something in the newsletter about companies that do business with Israel."

"Do you think Mossad knows about it?"

"I would think so, but no low-level Mossad staffer cataloging anti-Israel Arab publications would make the connection between you and Sabirah Najat. From the quality of the printing and news content, I would guess it wouldn't be considered a very significant publication. I suspect they would just file it away."

"Why do you think it places me in any danger?" she asked, handing the newsletter back to Dany.

"If any of Ali Abdul Shoukri's old friends are still around, they might recognize you," he answered.

Alexandra's pulse quickened. She knew Omar Samir and his cohorts in the Ali Abdul Shoukri Liberation Front were probably somewhere in the area and, of course, scheming to attack Potomac Center because of her. If they came across the newsletter and recognized her, she could, indeed, be in danger.

"Dany, could you contact the Trans-Arab Alliance and ask for their circulation figures for *Cultural Jihad* by country? You could tell them you're a writer for *Desert Song* and working on a story about Arab special-interest groups or make up some other reason for wanting to know."

"Sure, I could do that, but why take any chances, Alexandra? You could return to Washington tomorrow, and the *Star* would still be thrilled with the job you've done for them."

"Look, Dany, I'm not eager to stay here any longer than I have to. God knows I'd like to go home. But I'd also like to cover the Arab summit that everyone thinks will take place in the next few weeks. That would be the capstone of my reporting on the aftermath of the Six-Day War. I'm not going to do anything heroic—or stupid. But if we can determine that this newsletter has no readership in this area, then there may be no reason to run home."

Dany paused to consider what she had said. She was probably right, he thought. The Alliance might not have a single member outside of Tripoli and, maybe, the nearby North African states, and *Cultural Jihad* might not have a subscriber within five hundred miles of Tel Aviv.

"You're one in a million, Alexandra. I think you and I should move to Cyprus, get married, and live happily ever after."

"Dany, I'm serious. I appreciate the proposal, but do you think you can find out anything about the readership of this newsletter?"

"I'll see what I can do. All I can do is ask. Let me snoop around and get back to you."

"Thanks, Dany. It could be really important."

"Moving to Cyprus and living happily ever after or checking up on the readership of *Cultural Jihad*?" Alexandra, of course, understood that there was a message in Dany's humor. He was letting her know that he really cared for her, and, she admitted, she cared for him too.

"Let's stick to the readership of *Cultural Jihad* for now," she answered.

It took Dany only a few minutes on the phone with the editor of *Cultural Jihad* to confirm what he had already assumed. The publication's readership was almost entirely confined to Libya, Algeria, Tunisia, and the Emirates with a few dozen readers in Saudi Arabia and a sprinkling of subscribers in Egypt. Dany was told they had a half-dozen subscribers in Cairo and one in the Aswân office of Questex-Irvine. All in all, it appeared there was little about which Alexandra had to be concerned.

Alexandra decided not to discuss with anyone that the Trans-Arab Alliance was reproducing her columns in its newsletter. All it would do was upset Amos and drive Noah to distraction. And besides, she rationalized, her reporting on the aftermath of the Six-Day War might soon be completed. With a little luck, Alexandra could probably make it back to the States before October, and she and Noah could be together for the IPO after all. She could be home and standing with Noah at the stock exchange for the opening bell when Potomac Center officially became a publicly traded company.

But, then again, this was the Middle East where events rarely conspired to produce predictable, let alone fanciful, endings. Alexandra knew perfectly well that returning to the States in time for the IPO was wishful thinking. She had learned enough from talking to local Arabs to know that Nasser, Hussein, and al-Atassi of Syria probably couldn't survive politically, and perhaps even physically, if even the suggestion that they might entertain some kind of accommodation with Israel were leaked. And then there was the Sturm und Drang within the Israeli body politic.

While Alexandra had no access to key Israeli cabinet members, who were generally avoiding the press, she found plenty of Israelis who were in one minister's camp or another. As she cultivated and talked with these contacts, strong patterns began to emerge that she believed represented the points of view that were being debated within the Israeli government. She even believed she could guess what position each cabinet member was probably taking based on arguments she heard among those identified with the various Israeli political factions.

Alexandra knew it would be an abuse of her relationship with Amos to ask him to comment on what she was learning. After all, she reasoned, she was there to form her own opinions and to write about them. And so she did.

Israel Considers Its Options: Many Alternatives, No Consensus.
By Sabirah Najat

The days turn into weeks, and people throughout this region await the political resolution of the so-called

Six-Day War. The resolution on the battlefield was swift and unequivocal. Israel utterly crushed the threatening Arab armed forces in relatively few hours. Israel has emerged twice its size and with twice its population in terms of the territory and the people it now controls. Israel, or at least the Israel Defense Forces, sits on the west bank of the Suez Canal, the West Bank of the Jordan River, and Syria's Golan Heights. To Israelis David has, once again, defeated Goliath. To Arabs, the West (not merely Israel) has once again humiliated their sense of honor and trampled upon their sense of dignity.

We expect great battles to resolve great conflicts. That's why Texas, Nevada, California, New Mexico, most of Arizona and Colorado, and parts of Oklahoma, Kansas, and Wyoming are part of the United States of America and not Mexico. It is also why Parisians speak French and not German. The Arabs, following the recently concluded war with Israel, have formally ceded nothing. The two sides do not officially talk. Nothing has been resolved.

There is, however, plenty of talk within the countries representing the two sides—plenty of talk but no consensus. We cannot, at this time, know what positions the key members of the Israeli cabinet are taking. We can, however, adduce what their political supporters in the Israeli body politic are saying, and that may represent a pretty good indication of what is going on within the Israeli cabinet.

Arguably, the most important voice within the cabinet is that of Israeli defense minister Moshe Dayan. If talking to his political supporters is any indication, we can assume he is arguing that Israel should keep the West Bank and offer those who live there some degree of autonomy but certainly not citizenship. Dayan is probably arguing that all matters of security and foreign affairs should be solely within Israel's control. We detect little support among Arabs on the West Bank for such a resolution.

Another strong voice in the cabinet is that of Labor Minister Yigal Allon. His supporters are also urging that at least parts of the West Bank be incorporated into Israel and that some areas be designated for settlement by Israelis.

Our guess would be that Israeli justice minister Shimshon Shapira is the most cautious among the ministers. He is most likely to view the positions about which we have speculated (we'll call them the probable Dayan and Allon positions) as tantamount to colonizing the West Bank and, therefore, anathema to Israel's Democratic allies.

We have reported in recent columns that Israel would probably gladly turn back Sinai and even the Golan Heights to Egypt and Syria in return for recognition and an end to the state of belligerency between Israel and these two countries. That seems, to us, to be a nonstarter at this time. We see no indication that Israel has included the West Bank in these overtures. The West Bank, which seems to be the unsolvable crux of the matter, is the landmass that most clearly threatens Israel's geographical integrity as well as the area that is so steeped in Jewish history—the area the Jews call Judea and Samaria.

There seems to be consensus that Israel and Jordan could work something out, as rumors abound everywhere that King Hussein would welcome an honorable peace settlement. The problem, however, is that we can find no one who purports to speak for the West Bank

Palestinians, and Israel has taken no steps to encourage a single West Bank polity. There is no uniform voice on the West Bank, and, from where we sit, the Israelis seem to like it that way. Israelis say they're prepared to give back Sinai and the Golan in return for peace, recognition, and normalization of relations with Egypt and Syria— all seemingly reasonable conditions that no Egyptian or Syrian leader could meet and still survive. It is a seemingly reasonable but meaningless offer for which there will be no takers.

Also adding confusion to the dynamic in the region is the recent emergence of very strident Arab groups that are not affiliated with any government. They act as free agents, evolve their own positions, pursue their own agendas, and reserve the right to take their own action. They include the Palestine Liberation Organization, al-Fatah, the Popular Front for the Liberation of Palestine, and no doubt others about whom we've yet to hear. Given the loss of credibility of the Arab nations that were so recently vanquished by the Jewish state, these freewheeling private groups that owe no allegiance to any government will grow in importance as the region struggles to find its footing.

Meanwhile, we await word that a much-anticipated Arab summit is soon to take place. Exactly when or where such a meeting will occur is unknown. What does seem certain, however, is that this widely anticipated summit is not apt to produce momentum toward peace when and if it does take place.

***

Amos could see that Benjamin Bar-Levy was not happy even before he reached the table to join his Mossad counterpart for breakfast at the King David.

"The shit has hit the fan," Bar-Levy said as Amos pulled out a chair to sit down.

"What now?" Amos asked.

"Have you seen your friend's latest column?"

"Actually, no. I haven't," Amos answered. "What has she done now?"

"Here, read it," Bar-Levy said, tossing a reprint of Alexandra's most recent column down on the table.

Bar-Levy watched Amos as he picked up the column and began to read. "Dayan called me himself, Amos. He asked me, 'Who in the hell is Sabirah Najat?'"

"She must be touching a raw nerve, eh?" Amos said as he continued to read.

"Amos, what she wrote identifies exactly the positions these ministers took at the last cabinet meeting."

"I told you she was good," Amos replied, sliding the paper back across the table to Bar-Levy. "What's the big deal?"

"How does she know this, Amos?"

"She's a journalist, and a damn smart one. She's here talking to people on both sides all the time. I imagine she knows who supports whom. You probably don't have to talk to too many Dayan people to get an idea of what Dayan is thinking."

"And Allon and Shapira too?"

"I would think so. She's pleasantly tenacious. My guess is that anyone who kept taking the pulse of people here would begin to see a pattern develop. She knows when she's talking to Dayan supporters or Allon supporters. Did anything in this column she wrote surprise you?"

"Only that she got it so right. She may as well have been sitting in the last cabinet meeting."

"Do you really think it's such a big deal?"

"Amos, we have a lot of sorting out to do here in this tiny land of ours. Today, we enjoy the sympathy of the world—at least the Western world. We were viciously and loudly threatened, and we stood tall and beat back the barbarians. That's the way the world sees us."

"Not exactly an inaccurate picture," Amos replied.

"No, it isn't. But it's not only the Arabs who threaten the future of this Jewish democracy we have here. We have our own homegrown headaches. There are people here who no more want to pursue peace right now than our Arab neighbors do. That's a sad reality that few people understand, and we'd like to keep it that way."

"And Alexandra Salaman is making that difficult?"

"Look, our cabinet meetings are not necessarily models of decorum."

"No one expects them to be."

"Shapira is right, Amos. We don't want to be seen as colonialists, and what the Salaman woman is describing are high officials who are advocating what many would see as colonialism."

"That's ridiculous, Benjamin. My ancestors have been here for over two hundred years. Arabs and Jews have settled this land for centuries. The Ottomans allowed Jews and non-Jews alike to come. Arabs and Jews both purchased land and settled land here. There is nothing colonialist about that."

"Well, Arabs far outnumbered Jews in 1948."

"And the Arabs turned down a plan that would have created a nation for the Arabs and a nation for the Jews."

"You don't have to lecture to me, Amos, but we don't have to advertise to the world that returning the West Bank to the Arabs would be a political nightmare right here in Israel right now."

"Alexandra Salaman isn't creating the nightmare, Benjamin. She may be reporting it, but she isn't creating it."

"Amos, up to now no one at the ministerial level even knows Alexandra Salaman is here writing for a major American newspaper. She should want to keep it that way, and so should you. They're not happy about this Sabirah Najat writer describing what each of them is advocating in cabinet meetings."

"Benjamin, she's listening to what people on the street are telling her and drawing her own conclusions. Nothing she's writing would surprise anyone here."

"No, but what she is writing might surprise a lot of people in America, Amos."

"What might surprise a lot of people in America, Benjamin, is that we have people in high places who would not be willing to trade Judea and Samaria for peace with Arab countries who were intent on annihilating us a few short weeks ago."

"Defense Minister Dayan doesn't appreciate having what he says at cabinet meetings reported to the international community."

"Alexandra didn't report what was discussed at cabinet meetings. She reported on what Israelis are speculating is being discussed at cabinet meetings."

"I wish she would go home."

"She'll return home after this Arab summit everyone is waiting for takes place."

"That won't be for another month."

"You know when this summit is going to take place?" Amos asked, incredulously. "Even Arab newspapers are still speculating when and where the summit might be held."

"We don't get our information from Arab newspapers."

"So when will they meet?"

Benjamin smiled. "In a month, Amos—August twenty-ninth to be exact."

"Where? In Cairo…Alexandria?"

Benjamin shook his head. "No, Amos. They're going to meet in Khartoum."

***

Khartoum was, Alexandra thought, a surprising choice. She had assumed that Cairo or Alexandria, perhaps Casablanca, or maybe even Amman or Riyadh would be where the Arab League would meet to discuss a unified position following the Six-Day War. The entire world would be watching, and the Arab League decided to showcase Sudan, the least unified of Arab states, the largest country in Africa, and a land torn by perpetual civil war between the largely Christian South and the Islamist North. And to the west in the Darfur region of Sudan, there was the recent emergence of Ahmad Ibrahim Diraige and his National Development Front, also challenging Khartoum's absolute authority.

Alexandra understood the strategic significance of Khartoum, the very spot on the planet where the Nile River sprang to life. The Blue Nile roared down from the highlands of Ethiopia and the powerful White, or Mountain, Nile from Lake Victoria, through Uganda, and north through Sudan. The two watercourses converged at Khartoum and continued on as the mighty Nile, over the cataracts leading to Aswân, and on through the entire length of Egypt before emptying into the Mediterranean Sea. Alexandra knew she had no hope of reporting directly from Khartoum. Sudan, like Egypt, had broken off diplomatic relations with the United States during the Six-Day War to demonstrate its ire over America's supposed support of Israel. She also knew that a female journalist would not be welcome—let alone an American Christian Arab woman engaged to a Jew—and she certainly could not risk writing from Khartoum as the fictitious Sabirah Najat. And then she received a call from Dany Haddad that changed everything.

"Alexandra, I'm going to Khartoum to cover the summit for *Desert Song*."

"How can that be?" she asked, dumbfounded.

"Meet me. I'll explain over coffee," he replied, excitedly.

As soon as they were seated in the Dan dining room, he explained, "We applied to Sudan for press credentials, and I was approved."

"How can that be?" she asked again.

"Alexandra, I carry a Lebanese passport. It still has my address in Beirut. My place of birth is listed as Jaffa, and they probably see me as a refugee journalist. As a courtesy, the Israelis didn't affix my visa directly to my passport. They make that accommodation, when requested, for people who they know will have to travel back to Arab countries. I'll attend as a freelance journalist, and *Desert Song* won't be publishing my work until I'm back in Israel."

"Unbelievable," she answered.

"I thought the odds of getting approval from the Sudanese were one in a million, an absolute pipe dream," he said. He noticed that she wasn't listening any longer. Her mind had suddenly focused somewhere else.

"Alexandra?"

"Take me with you," she said, more a demand than a request.

"Are you crazy?" he asked, a nervous edge to his question. "There's not a chance in the world of you getting approved to cover the conference."

"Dany, I wouldn't go as a correspondent. I would go as your assistant, Sabirah Najat. No one in Sudan has ever heard of Sabirah Najat. I wouldn't publish anything until I was safely back in Israel or back in Washington," she answered. "I don't think there would be any risk at all."

"I don't believe you're thinking very clearly, Alexandra. It's nothing but risk."

"No, it really isn't," she insisted. "Besides, all they could do is refuse to let me into the country."

"Alexandra, you have an American passport. What is wrong with you?"

"What if I could secure acceptable travel documents that Sudan would accept?"

"You can't."

"But what if I could?"

"I won't respond to something so hypothetical."

"What if it wasn't hypothetical?"

"Ask me when it isn't hypothetical," he replied.

"I'd love to stay and chat, Dany, but I have to see a man about a problem," she said, rising from her chair.

"What kind of problem?"

"I'm afraid it's hypothetical for the moment," Alexandra replied as she hurried from the dining room. Alexandra found Avi Ben-Topaz leaning against the side of his car waiting for her in the hotel driveway, as usual.

"Take me to Bethlehem," she said, as she rushed to the car.

***

Elias Khourdri listened carefully as Alexandra explained what she wanted to do. He didn't like what he was hearing. "Why in the world would you want to go to that hellhole?" he asked. "Civil war has been the national pastime in Sudan."

"I would be the only American there," she answered. "It's an opportunity of a lifetime for a journalist like me. Besides, things are quiet there now."

"I don't think it's wise," he answered.

"Look, I don't want to do anything foolish. All I want to know is whether or not there is a plausible way for me to get official travel documents. I'm not looking to go to Sudan with forged documents. I would only go if there was a way for me to obtain official documents."

Elias Khourdri sat at his desk gazing at Alexandra as he tapped the desktop with his fingertips. "It is a very foolish thing you want to do, Alexandra. If anything went wrong, you would be totally at the mercy of the Sudanese. I wouldn't wish that on anyone. You could just disappear off the face of the earth. No one would be able to intercede on your behalf. The United States is, for the time being, persona non grata. Israel certainly couldn't help you, and I'm not sure any Arab country would lift a finger for you."

"So, there is a way, isn't there?"

"It's extremely unlikely to work, but there is a process that might produce legitimate travel documents for you. Not likely but remotely possible."

"What's the process?"

"I'm not sure I even want to discuss it with you. It's a terrible idea, and I don't want to be complicit in something I consider to be terrible."

"The summit meetings will barely last three days. I'll be in and out. I won't be writing anything until I'm gone from the country, and besides, nothing I write should offend the Sudanese. I'm not going to make trouble for anyone."

"Except, possibly, yourself," he answered.

"My job is to report. It's my profession. You've seen everything I've written from the Middle East. Is there anything I've written with which you take issue?"

"No, Alexandra. You're a beautiful writer, and I wish the whole world could see what you write."

"Please, Elias, tell me about this process," she pleaded.

"It's very unlikely to work, and it usually takes weeks when it does."

"Can this process you speak of be expedited?"

"Sometimes," he answered.

"Will you tell me about it?"

He paused and sighed, shaking his head. "I'm not saying I'm willing to help."

"I understand, but please go on."

"Well, in 1949 the United Nations created an agency called UNRWA. It stands for United Nations Relief and Works Agency for Palestine Refugees. Interestingly, it defines a Palestinian refugee as any person who lived in Palestine between 1946 and May fifteenth, 1948, and who lost his or her home and livelihood as a result of the conflict."

"Which my family did," she interjected.

"Don't get carried away, Alexandra. UNRWA wasn't created for a family like yours that is thriving in America. A dozen years ago, the Arab League's Permanent Committee on Palestine began to issue travel documents for Palestinians who were refugees under the UNRWA definition. This was to allow refugees to travel freely to countries that are members of the league."

"Like Sudan?"

"Like Sudan," he acknowledged, hesitantly.

"So, using their definition of a refugee, I could apply to enter Sudan to assist another Palestinian? One who now holds a Lebanese passport and who is properly credentialed to cover the summit?"

"Theoretically, yes. Holders of these travel documents are supposed to be treated as legitimate nationals when applying for visas."

"Elias, I would be in and out of Sudan in about seventy-two hours, and I wouldn't do anything that would raise the slightest objection. I would do nothing more than observe and listen. I wouldn't write anything until I was back here."

Elias Khoudri began, once again, to tap on his desktop as he considered her request. Then, after what seemed like an eternity to Alexandra, he turned his gaze to her and slowly nodded. "I would apply in the name of Sabirah Najat just in case there is some record of the Salaman family leaving in 1948," he said.

"We can do that?"

"Look, Alexandra, this entire travel application will be a bit of a farce—a harmless farce but a farce nonetheless. I don't see why it would make any difference whether you applied as Alexandra Salaman or Sabirah Najat. The application will be issued as a courtesy to me. There might be a small chance that there's a record of Alexandra Salaman leaving with her family twenty years ago. We know there will be no record of Sabirah Najat."

"And the process can be expedited?"

"Theoretically, yes."

"How?"

"By having someone who is respected walk the application through the bureaucracy."

"Someone like you?"

"Heaven help me," he whispered aloud. "Yes, someone like me."

And, indeed, one week later Elias Khourdri was handed official travel documents authorizing Sabirah Najat to travel to Sudan as an assistant to Dany Haddad, a freelance correspondent. They would fly to Cyprus and then continue on for the 1,300-mile flight south to Khartoum. He arranged for two sets of round-trip tickets—one from Tel Aviv to Nicosia and back and one from Nicosia to Khartoum and back.

Alexandra, having found a way to get to Khartoum to cover what she believed could be the biggest story of her career now faced a much more stressful dilemma—how to tell Noah and Amos what she intended to do. Noah would be beside himself. There would be no reasoning with him. Amos, she was certain, would forbid her to go and more than likely have her visa revoked, forcing her to immediately return to the United States. Frank Markazie would express serious reservations but, after all was said and done, accede to her judgment. Then again, she thought, why tell them at all? She and Dany could arrange to arrive in Khartoum on Tuesday, August 29, and be on their way back to Nicosia sometime Friday, September 1. She would write nothing to offend the Sudanese while she was in Khartoum, and she had authentic travel documents issued by the Arab authorities approving her presence at the summit.

It seemed so simple. Cyprus was temporarily stable following the coup that brought Greek colonel George Papadopoulos to power three months earlier. A brief three- or four-day respite in Cypress would raise no objections, and, immediately following a brief detour to Khartoum, she could return safely to Tel Aviv having upset no one.

Noah, fully preoccupied with planning the Potomac Center IPO, had become acquiescent to Alexandra's decision to remain in the Middle East until the Khartoum conference was concluded. He raised no objection when she told him she was going to travel to Cyprus for a two- or three-day respite during which she would begin writing her final column on the aftermath of the war. She promised she would return to Washington immediately following the conference and then take time off to accompany him on the road show.

Amos, no fan of Colonel Papadopoulos, thought there were better places to unwind but, like Noah, offered no objection. Alexandra's boss, Frank Markazie, approved her plan to travel to Khartoum after being assured that the diversion to the Sudanese capital was perfectly safe.

CHAPTER
TWENTY-EIGHT

By mid-August, Karen and Noah were together some part of every week. She typically would fly into Washington Monday afternoon, join Noah for dinner, and then spend the next three days with him reviewing financial progress, planning slides for the group presentations, and determining strategy for the one-on-one meetings Mid-America was arranging with prospective investors. He was fascinated as Karen handicapped the different analysts and money managers with whom they would be meeting during the road show. She knew just what financial and operational aspects of Potomac Center to emphasize with each of them. Noah enjoyed the time he was spending with Karen, and he eagerly looked forward to her arrival every Monday afternoon. Karen, not surprisingly, relished her return trips to Washington, and it was with growing reluctance that she returned to Chicago every Friday morning.

They tried to remind themselves that this was all strictly business. Perhaps it took too much self-reminding. There was, after all, a history. Noah, the young CEO of Potomac Center Properties, was, but a dozen years earlier, the guy with whom she had fallen in love when they were both freshmen at Stanford. And every so often, as he watched Karen skillfully and confidently project Potomac Center financial data into strong selling points for the IPO, his mind would drift to that night at

Stanford when they first made love to one another on the front seat of his roommate Rolly's car. Their years at Stanford, their engagement, their time together in Washington—it, indeed, took a lot of self-reminding that now this was all strictly business.

And from a strictly business perspective, the business at hand looked very good. The gigantic South Coast Plaza Mall in Costa Mesa, California, developed by the Segerstrom family was a sensation, and the King of Prussia Mall outside of Philadelphia was also booming. To add to the mall mania, Dominic Visconsi was proposing his huge Garfield Mall in Cuyahoga County, Ohio, and there were rumors that Edward DeBartolo from Youngstown was planning the world's largest shopping mall on the site of a racetrack in North Randall, Ohio. Noah's Potomac Center was the newest and certainly the most exciting urban-development project of its kind. The Street, as Karen referred to the investment community, would love it.

Noah was relieved that Alexandra had committed to return home following her report from Cyprus on the Khartoum summit in time to accompany him on the road show. There were too many memories of the years he had spent with Karen to pretend that there were no feelings. Traveling alone with Karen for two or three weeks, being together from morning until late in the evening and sharing a suite with her, even a two-bedroom suite, would, he knew, be asking for trouble.

***

At Elias Khoudri's suggestion, Alexandra purchased a hijab, a couple of long skirts, and plain, modest long-sleeve blouses to wear while in Khartoum. He advised her to maintain as low a profile as possible.

"You're quite beautiful, Alexandra. That's not necessarily an asset in Khartoum. Remain as inconspicuous as possible, and go nowhere without Dany," he cautioned. "Remember, Sudan is no longer a British colony. You'll be in an overwhelmingly Islamic country. They, more or less, still follow the old Indian or British legal codes, but things are changing there."

Their departure from Tel Aviv that last Tuesday in August was un-eventful. They handed their round-trip tickets to and from Nicosia to the passport-control officer and explained that they were going to spend two or three days in Cyprus and return to Tel Aviv before sun-down on Friday. The young Israeli passport officer took an extra min-ute or so studying Alexandra's American passport, lingering on the line that showed Jaffa as her place of birth. He looked into her eyes, smiled, and waved them on.

Alexandra and Dany made their way through the international airport in Lakatamia, a suburb of Nicosia, where they transferred to a BOAC 707 and continued on, flying south over the Mediterranean toward North Africa. Alexandra was riveted to the sight unfolding far below as the flight approached the coastline of Egypt. The mighty Nile Delta formed a huge fan where the river poured into the sea. She had never seen anything like it. The mouth of the river yawned so wide it seemed to spread from horizon to horizon, all the way west toward Alexandria and east toward Port Said.

The flight continued south into Egypt, flying over the Nile for another thousand miles as the river coursed north, making its way through the Sahara from its confluence with the Blue and White Nile tributaries at Khartoum. The landscape to the east and west beyond the narrow fertile ribbon along the banks of the river was desolate des-ert. It could have been Mars, she thought.

As they approached their destination flying low from the north, she gazed down at the landmass between the two tributaries that merged to form the Nile— the White Nile from the southwest out of the highlands of Uganda and the Blue Nile from the southeast out of the mountains of Ethiopia. And then she saw it—Khartoum, the land squeezed between the two tributaries to form the elephant's trunk that gave the city its name.

"I wonder why they selected Khartoum," Alexandra asked, curi-ously, as they both peered through the window at their seats. The city, or at least what they could see of it descending to the airport's single runway, seemed a gaggle of nondescript, low-lying dwellings and other structures spread out on a carpet of harsh brown, almost orange sand. There seemed to be no paved streets in Khartoum. There was simply sand everywhere.

CHAPTER
TWENTY-NINE

A rush of hot, humid, sand-laced air assaulted them as soon as they stepped from the Boeing 707 onto the metal stairway to the tarmac. Alexandra made her way down the steps holding in place the hijab she had put on as the plane landed, fearing the gusty wind might blow it askance. The metal handrail was hot from the afternoon sun, and she could feel the grit of sand under the soles of her sandals.

The poorly ventilated arrival hall was crowded, the air foul and stifling, and the din deafening. Alexandra mused that most of Sudan's one hundred languages and five hundred accents were represented among the arriving passengers. They made their way through the airport's passport-control station without incident. The black Sudanese officer seemed familiar with the travel document that identified Alexandra as a Palestinian refugee.

"Why you come to Sudan?" he asked.

"I am Mr. Haddad's assistant," she answered, glancing to Dany. "We are here to report on the Arab League conference."

"Ah yes," the passport officer replied. "Many, many people come because of conference." He then waved them both through after a cursory glance at Dany's Lebanese passport.

"Hey, mister...lady," a tall, thin black man yelled, running toward them as soon as they exited the arrival hall with their bags. "Hey, you!

You need drive hotel. You come wid me. No wait for taxi. You be here forever. You come. I take hotel."

Alexandra and Dany looked at the crowd bunched together at the curb waving and yelling for taxis and nodded to the driver as he approached them.

"Where you go?" the man asked as he effortlessly took their bags from them.

"Grand Hotel," Dany answered. The man was taller than Dany by two or three inches. His hair was almost white and close-cropped, and three linear scars on both of his cheeks caught Dany's eye.

"OK, you go best hotel," the driver replied.

The car, an old black Land Rover, was parked nearby, caked in sand dust from the haboob, or sandstorm, that had swept through the area weeks before. The driver opened the rear door for them, hurried to the rear of the car, and placed their luggage in the trunk. The car's upholstery was threadbare, and the springs groaned and pushed back against their weight as they settled into the rear seat.

"We take Africa Street north to Nile Street. Nile Street very beautiful," the driver said, proudly. Alexandra pulled her hijab from her head and leaned back, exhausted, against the seat. The dusty, hot air rushing in through the open windows was suffocating.

"Whew," she whispered. "It's like a steam bath."

"Air very wet today," the driver said.

"Yes, air very wet," she replied.

"Are you OK?" Dany asked.

"I'll be fine," she whispered. "I just hope there's a fan in my room."

"Many rooms in Grand have fans," the driver said. "Grand best hotel Khartoum."

"What is your name?" Dany asked.

"I'm Daoud," the driver answered.

"I'm Dany Haddad, and this is my assistant, Miss Sabirah Najat. Can you drive for us while we're in Khartoum?"

"What time you want me to pick you up at hotel?"

"I'm not sure yet, but let's plan on nine o'clock tomorrow. Then we'll take it from there."

"You will have best driver in Khartoum," the man said, grinning widely.

"You're Nubian, Daoud?"

"Yeah, I'm Nubian," the driver replied proudly. "You tell from scars on my face?"

"That and your name. I'm a history professor. Daoud Abdul-Latif was the first mayor of Khartoum."

"Yes, I call myself Daoud to honor Daoud Abdul Latif."

As they turned west onto Nile Street, the route magically transformed from dull and tired anonymity to Old World splendor. Alexandra sat upright to take in the view of central Khartoum's beautiful north shore. Gone were the low drab buildings, unsurfaced dirt streets, and endless sand-strewn landscape through which they had been driving. Nile Street was paved and adorned with shade trees. The Blue Nile rushed by the embankment on the north side of the street on its journey to join the White Nile where the two rivers met just a short distance ahead. Government ministries housed in picturesque colonial buildings, remnants of the strong British influence in Khartoum, lined the south side of Nile Street. Public and private buildings alike were festooned with huge pictures of Sudan's Ismail al-Azhari, Egypt's Nasser, Jordan's Hussein, and other Arab League leaders, and flags of the league's member countries were hanging everywhere. Their route took them past the University of Khartoum and the president's palace, where, for better or worse, history was about to be made.

Dany and Alexandra were among the last journalists to arrive at the nearly hundred-year-old Grand, a vestige from Khartoum's early colonial history. It wasn't grand like Washington's Shoreham Hotel or the Mayflower, or the newer Phoenicia in Beirut, but it was better than they expected. All of the guests, it seemed, were there for the summit. The foreign ministers from the respective Arab League countries had arrived in Khartoum earlier and hammered out an agenda for the summit. Alexandra and Dany met in the restaurant after checking into their rooms. Their accommodations were small but adequate, and there was, indeed, a ceiling fan in their rooms just as their driver had promised.

The bar was crowded, but Alexandra recognized a considerable smattering of English among the journalists who had gathered at the Grand. The summit agenda dominated conversation at the hotel that afternoon. Alexandra wasn't sure whether the agenda was released to the press by the league's public-relations people or simply leaked as the preliminary sessions drew to a close. From what she and Dany could determine, the summit would focus on three main objectives. First, the league was determined to erase every vestige of what they called the impacts of Israeli aggression. Alexandra observed to Dany that that could mean anything—further military action, economic co-operation, or diplomacy.

"Who among the Arabs will be the first to publicly begin talking to the Israelis?" Dany asked. "I don't see it happening."

According to the unofficial agenda strewn about at the bar that night, the second-highest priority was the removal of foreign bases from the area. But the real news to many of the journalists was a ru-mor floating around that Saudi king Faisal Bin Abdel Aziz was exert-ing pressure on Nasser to get out of Yemen. The king was apparently insisting that Nasser withdraw his sixty thousand troops from Yemen. King Faisal knew Egypt was going to ask for massive financial help from Saudi Arabia, and the king was in no mood to tolerate Egyptian troops on the Arabian Peninsula any longer.

Alexandra and Dany, both tired from their hours of travel, were eager to grab a fast dinner and call it a night. They made a quick stop at a buffet table and helped themselves to a serving of *aseeda*, a Sudanese dish consisting of wheat flour, oil, and honey. It was served with an orange sauce mixed with peanuts, onions, yogurt, and minced beef. They were about to make their way to a table when a man working his way through the buffet line just in front of Alexandra turned and gestured to her with a broad friendly smile. "You haven't tried the *ko-rasa*. You must. I promise you'll like it," he said. "It's simply fried and chewy bread severed with *takleya* paste on top."

"*Takleya* paste?" she answered, hesitantly.

"Yes, yes, it's delicious. It's made with ground okra mashed with onions, tomato sauce, and minced beef. It's absolutely delicious," he promised.

"Well, thank you very much," Dany chimed in to make sure the stranger knew Alexandra was accompanying him. "I'm Dany Haddad, and this is—"

"Sabirah Najat," the stranger interrupted, with a wholehearted laugh. "I recognized you as soon as you entered the room."

Dany, momentarily lost for words, was about to correct the stranger when Alexandra broke in.

"And where do you know my work from?" she asked, smiling broadly, her heart racing wildly.

"Let me introduce myself, Sabirah. I am Hamid Abdula Hashimi. I am the executive director of the Trans-Arabic Alliance, and I publish a newsletter called *Cultural Jihad*. I have been copying all of your columns from the *Washington Evening Star*. They've only run your picture once, but I recognized you as soon as you entered the bar. Yours is not an easy face to forget. You are an Arabian beauty. Why in the world don't they run your picture over every column?" he asked. His voice was jovial enough, though his stare less so, Alexandra thought.

"I'm here assisting Mr. Haddad," she answered.

"Of course, of course. You certainly wouldn't be here working for the *Washington Evening Star*," he replied with a forced laugh.

"Well, I'm sure we'll see more of you during the next few days. Thank you for recommending the *korasa*," Dany said, extending his hand to Hamid Hashimi.

Dany and Alexandra helped themselves to a portion of the *korasa* and headed to an empty table, leaving the stranger standing there.

"This is not good," he whispered as they took their seats.

"Let's not jump to any conclusions," she replied. "So he recognized me as Sabirah Najat, and he has read my work. What's threatening about that?"

"He has read your work, and he republishes your work every week. He knows you write for the *Evening Star*, a newspaper that is not credentialed here, and that you're from America, with whom Sudan has broken off diplomatic relations, and that you've been writing from Israel, with which Sudan is technically at war. Furthermore, he publishes some rag called *Cultural Jihad*, for God's sake. I don't like it at all."

"Well, there's not much we can do about it now. Look, he's here covering the summit just as we are. Let's just go about our business for the next couple of days, and we'll be gone with all the other journalists by Friday afternoon."

They quickly finished their dinner and left the restaurant to return to their rooms. Midway through the lobby, Alexandra suddenly grabbed Dany's arm. Startled, he looked at her as she cocked her head toward the hotel telephone room. There, through the door window, they saw Hamid Abdula Hashimi gesturing excitedly as he spoke to someone on the telephone. Alexandra and Dany looked at one another, and after a momentary pause, they continued through the lobby of the Grand Hotel.

They decided they really had no choice other than to do what they had come to Khartoum to do. Trying to change their flight reservations in order to leave right away would be complicated and, quite probably, arouse more attention than would be wise. After all, they reasoned, they were there to do what four hundred other journalists were doing in Khartoum: covering an historic summit meeting. And so, they met their Nubian driver, Daoud, as planned at nine o'clock the following morning. Their concern about Hamid Abdula Hashimi was eased somewhat when he greeted them at breakfast that morning. He simply smiled cordially and said he hoped they had a good day. There was nothing menacing in the brief exchange.

Daoud drove them the short distance to the parliament building just over the White Nile Bridge in the sprawling Omdurman section of Khartoum. Their route took them west on Nile Street. To the north, across the Blue Nile, they could see Toti Island, three square miles of green grassland at the very heart of the otherwise sandy palette of Khartoum. Tori seemed an island of tranquility, surrounded by the Blue and the White Niles to the east, west, and south and, just beyond the rushing waterways, the hustle and bustle of central Khartoum, Omdurman, and Khartoum North. To the north of Toti Island, the mighty Nile emerged from the confluence of the Blue and White. As they approached the White Nile Bridge leading to Omdurman, the Blue Nile veered north to their right, and to their left, the White Nile came roaring toward them, passing under the bridge as though giving chase to the Blue Nile.

***

Alexandra and Dany were directed to the press area in the parliament building. No one seemed to know what was going on. The press was being informed more by rumor and supposition than by formal briefings by league officials. They arrived in time to see the procession of well-waxed, shiny black limousines roll in delivering King Faisal of Saudi Arabia, President Nasser of Egypt, Abdullah Sallal of Yemen, Sheikh Ahmad Sabah of Kuwait, Abdul Rahman Arif of Iraq, and Jordan's king Hussein.

Ahmad Shukeiri, chairman of the Palestinian Liberation Organization, arrived a few minutes later. Two kings, five presidents, and one emir had already arrived. Shukeiri made no pretense of cordiality. "He's not very happy to be here," Alexandra said in a low voice.

"He has no interest in diplomacy at all," Dany replied in a whisper. "Diplomacy implies accommodation, and Shukeiri is vehemently opposed to any accommodation whatsoever with Israel."

"Do you think any of these heads of state are interested in accommodating Israel?"

"Well, you've heard the same rumors I've heard about Jordan and Egypt wanting to ratchet down war as the only alternative," he answered.

"Israel isn't going to leave the West Bank anytime soon," Alexandra replied. "There's too much dissension in their ranks to do that. How could Egypt and Jordan entertain any accommodation that left Israel on the West Bank?"

"It looks like Algeria and Syria are not going to be represented here, at least not by anyone who can make a decision," Dany said.

"There's no more chance of a consensus emerging here than there is in Israel," she answered.

"Well, who knows?" Dany replied with a shrug. "Supposedly President Bourguiba and King Hassan would support some kind of accommodation."

"That's may be true, but if Syria and Algeria want a continuation of conflict, and Shukeiri and his PLO are insistent on who knows what, how can anything constructive come out of this?"

Alexandra's question was more perceptive than she knew. Inside the meeting room where the conference was actually taking place, Nasser and Shukeiri were exchanging heated words. Nasser, attempting to find a middle ground between constant war and actual recognition of Israel, argued that the blockade of the Straits of Tiran would have to be lifted anyway, and as long as Israel agreed not to fly its flag, there would be little lost in looking the other way as Israeli ships passed through. He reminded the conferees that Egypt had shouldered the lion's share of every war since the nakbah, including the 1956 Suez War and the most recent conflict.

King Hussein was supportive, suggesting that he would be willing to allow a path to the Western Wall and perhaps one or two other sites that the Jews considered sacred. He, too, argued that such a move would not entail recognition of the Jewish state. Israel would simply be expected to vacate the rest of the West Bank—their Judea and Samaria. Everyone knew that Bourguiba of Tunisia and Hassan of Morocco were sympathetic to the Egyptian and Jordanian positions.

PLO chairman Ahmed Shukeiri, however, was livid. He would have none of it. He and several other Arab leaders were openly scornful of Nasser during the meeting, and by the time the shouting was over, only Jordan's Hussein remained at Nasser's side.

Shukeiri reminded the delegates of the Egyptian president's pledge on the eve of the Six-Day War. "D-day is approaching. The Arabs have waited nineteen years for this and will not flinch from the war of liberation. This is a fight for the homeland—it is either us or the Israelis. There is no middle road," Nasser had said. And now, after getting their faces slapped on the field of battle by the Israelis, they sat in Khartoum grasping for the very middle road they had all renounced such a short time ago.

Ahmed Shukeiri reminded the kings and emirs and the Arab presidents gathered around the table that Nasser himself had proclaimed that their aim was the full restoration of the rights of the Palestinian people. "You said our immediate aim was the perfection of Arab military might and that our national aim was the eradication of Israel," Shukeiri shouted, pointing an angry finger at the Egyptian president.

"And you!" Shukeiri continued, turning to the Hashemite king of Jordan. "Did you not tell the entire Arab nation that all their armies surrounded Israel? Did you not say to the world that the peoples of the United Arab Republic, Iraq, Syria, Jordan, Yemen, Lebanon, Algeria, Sudan, and Kuwait were all ready for battle—that there is no difference between one Arab people and another?"

"And you!" he continued, pointing to President Abdul Rahman Aref of Iraq. "You sounded so self-assured when you told the world that the existence of Israel is an error that must be rectified. This is our opportunity, you said, to wipe out the ignominy that has been with us since 1948."

"You were very specific," he ranted, pointing again at President Nasser. "You said to your people our goal is clear—to wipe Israel off the map. You promised we would all meet in Tel Aviv and Haifa."

Nasser sat quietly, silently enraged. His country had suffered half of all the Arab losses in their repeated wars with Israel.

"We Arabs have waited nineteen years for this war of liberation, and we must not flinch. This is a fight for the homeland—the Palestinian homeland. It is either the Israelis or us. There is no middle road," Shukeiri shouted, and then he paused to let his familiar words take effect. "Those were my words on the eve of the battle last June, and those are my words today," he bellowed. "Any accommodation you make with the Zionists will be at the expense of the Palestinian people. You have no right to do that. The struggle must go on. The rights of the Palestinians must not be compromised."

Nasser continued to hold his tongue, but he was seething. Who did Shukieri think he was, moralizing to the president of Egypt, the nation that had already sacrificed well over twenty-five thousand men to the Palestinian cause?

There was really no official hard news released during the conference, but there was no scarcity of rumor. Word spread among the journalists that there was discord in the conference room and that Shukeiri was the cause. Alexandra and Dany speculated what that might mean. Perhaps the Tito plan was being seriously considered.

"You want driving tour of city?" Daoud asked as they began the drive back to the hotel.

"Sure, why not?" Dany replied. The temperature had hovered near one hundred degrees all day, and the air rushing in through the Land Rover's windows would be a welcome respite from the hot, dusty air that permeated everything in Khartoum. Dany and Alexandra were taking no chances traipsing around Khartoum and planned to confine their time in the city to the hotel and parliament. Touring the city on foot would be pushing their luck. While Dany's credentials were solid, they both knew Alexandra's travel documents wouldn't stand much scrutiny if there were a problem. A driving tour was the safest way to see Khartoum.

They headed north from parliament on Al Mawrada Street past the Al Mawrada Market and on to the tomb of Muhammad Ahmad bin Abd Allah, who, eighty-six years earlier, had proclaimed himself to be the Mahdi, or the messianic redeemer of the Islamic faith, in Sudan. Next to the Mahdi tomb stood the house of his successor, Abdallahi ibn Muhammad, who called himself the Khalifa. The Mahdi and the Khalifa both waged war against the British, who, along with the Ottoman-controlled Egyptians, had continuously ruled northern Sudan. The Egyptians considered northern Sudan to be little more than a military outpost—territory they coveted in order to safeguard the Nile, which sprang from the landmass shaped like an elephant trunk known as the Khartoum. The British finally quelled the endless uprisings of the Mahdi and Khalifa at the end of the nineteenth century and promptly destroyed the Mahdi tomb. It wasn't until the middle of the twentieth century, shortly before the British granted Sudan independence, that the British allowed the Sudanese to rebuild the tomb.

"This is the number-one place visitors come," Daoud explained. They drove on to the Hamed-al-Nil Mosque, a favorite tourist attraction. Daoud urged them to return Friday afternoon in order to see the Sufi twirling ritual the dervishes practiced in order to attain their ecstatic trance. "They do this by twirling faster and faster. Everyone comes to see the twirling dervishes," Daoud said.

"Well, I'm afraid we'll have to miss them," Dany replied. "We're on an early-morning flight Friday."

"Ah, you want to be back in Israel before sundown," Daoud responded, with a laugh.

Dany and Alexandra looked at one another, startled. "What makes you think we've come from Israel?" she asked.

"You arrived from Cyprus. No tourists in Cyprus now, but Israel nearby. You Palestinian. Daoud loves Palestine."

"Why does Daoud love Palestine?" Alexandra asked.

"Many Nubians still live in Jordan Valley, near Jericho. Thousands of Nubians once lived in Judean caves. Daoud feel close ties to Land of Israel—to Palestine," he said, quickly correcting himself.

"Are you Muslim, Daoud?" Alexandra asked.

"Yes, Daoud Muslim. Long, long, time ago Nubians were Christian. Then Islam came and Nubians have been Muslim ever since."

Alexandra nodded but didn't pursue the matter. "I'm sorry we'll have to miss the twirling dervishes," she said.

"Are you married, Daoud?" Dany asked, curious to know more about their affable driver.

"No. No longer married," Daoud answered. "My wife, my dear Cena—she die last year."

"Oh, I'm sorry," Dany responded.

"That's terrible, Daoud," Alexandra said. "I'm so sorry."

"My Cena—she die from fly. From trypan."

"Trypan?" Alexandra asked softly and sympathetically.

"Yes, Daoud means trypanosomiasis. It's the horrible disease caused by the tsetse fly. It's prevalent in sub-Saharan Africa."

"Oh my. How horrible," Alexandra said.

"Yes, very horrible," Daoud answered. "My dear Cena very sick from fly. She lay in coma for a long time before she die. Many people die from fly here. People also die from mosquito here, from malaria. People die from typhus here too. Water bad. Much sickness in Sudan. Much sickness all over Africa everywhere below the big desert."

"I'm so sorry for your loss, Daoud," Alexandra said, reaching forward and gently touching the driver's shoulder.

Moved by her compassionate gesture, Daoud looked up at Alexandra through the rearview mirror. There were tears in his eyes.

"You very kind woman, Miss Sabirah."

She smiled, caringly, at his reflection in the mirror. He saw there were tears in her eyes too.

As they headed east toward the bridge that would take them across the Nile to Khartoum North, they passed a walled compound. The wall surrounded an ugly structure, ugly even for Khartoum, consisting of a couple of stark, ominous clay-colored multistory hulks. There were bars on many of the windows.

"Now that's what I call ugly architecture," Alexandra said as they drove by.

"Very bad place," Daoud replied. "Very bad."

"It's a prison, isn't it?" she asked.

"Yes, Miss Sabirah. Omdurman Prison. Very bad place," he answered, somberly.

They crossed over into Khartoum North and passed the beautiful Al Sayed Ali Mosque and, only a short time later, the disgusting Kober Prison before heading south over the Blue Nile Bridge and turning west into the sun toward the Grand Hotel. Khartoum seemed languid, more lethargic than repressed. It was a huge city that seemed to exude none of the energy of Cairo or Beirut or Washington, or any of the world's major cities.

The dining room at the Grand that evening was abuzz with rumors that PLO chairman Ahmed Shukeiri had threatened to quit the summit. Shukeiri was furious that the conference had devolved into a discussion of what each nation had to do to protect its honor rather than focusing on the plight of the Palestinians. The conference, it seemed, was more about how to deal, or not deal, with the Israelis than it was about how to destroy them. Dany wondered how Shukeiri, as chairman of the PLO, could afford to alienate these Arab potentates on whose largess he depended.

Alexandra spotted Hamid Abdulla Hashimi and smiled to greet him as they approached one another in the crowded dining room. He returned the smile, halfheartedly, she thought. Hashimi paused just enough to half bow and continued walking past her, barely altering his stride.

"What do you make of that?" she asked Dany.

"I don't know. Maybe we'll have to wait until the next issue of *Cultural Jihad* to find out."

***

Alexandra and Dany arrived at parliament in time to see the parade of black limousines pull up once again to deliver the most powerful men in the Arab world. The limousines were waxed spotless, and blinding bursts of white-hot sun reflected off of the automobiles' flashy chrome trims as the cars turned into the driveway. The potentates barely acknowledged the many journalists who were gathered as they exited their cars and hurried into the parliament building. Alexandra found it impossible to read anything into their expressionless faces.

The tension inside the conference room was palpable, and tempers quickly flared. A first draft of the formal statement the league planned to release to the press had been distributed, and Ahmed Shukieri bristled as he read the proposed statement.

"This is a travesty," he shouted, holding up the draft. "This concedes the Zionist entity's foothold on Arab land."

"It does no such thing," one of the emirs replied. "It is a strong rejection of Israel."

"The word *Palestine* is only mentioned one time, and it is a vague, weak mention at that," Shukieri snapped. "Palestine is the issue. It is the only issue."

"No, there are other issues!" the emir of Kuwait insisted. "We must have a unified position on oil production. Our brethren who were attacked in the June war depend on Arab oil money from their Arab brothers to rebuild."

"This proposed resolution says no three times about what the Arab nation will not do regarding the Zionist entity, but it says nothing about not compromising any Palestinian rights," Shukieri loudly complained.

"These are three very powerful no's," King Hussein replied. "No peace, no recognition, and no negotiation."

"Then there must be a fourth no," Shukieri insisted. "No compromise of any Palestinian rights."

"We think that is clearly implied in the resolution," the king replied, evenly.

"We all feel that way," the emir of Kuwait said.

Ahmed Shukieri looked around the table and, seeing no support for a stronger stand, stormed from the room.

***

That evening a draft of the Arab League's resolution, which was to be formally released to the world the next day, was made available to the journalists in Khartoum. While the formal statement was nearly five hundred words long, for all practical purposes, it could be reduced to six words—no peace, no recognition, no negotiation. Alexandra and Dany, and over four hundred other journalists from around the world, studied the single-page resolution and pondered its meaning and the impact it would have on the course of history.

RESOLUTION OF THE ARAB LEAGUE SUMMIT, KHARTOUM, SUDAN. SEPTEMBER 31, 1967

The conference has affirmed the unity of Arab states, the unity of joint action and the need for coordination and for the elimination of all differences. The Kings, Presidents and representatives of the other Arab Heads of State at the conference have affirmed their countries' stand by an implementation of the Arab Solidarity Charter, which was signed at the third Arab summit conference in Casablanca.

The conference has agreed on the need to consolidate all efforts to eliminate the effects of the aggression on the basis that the occupied lands are Arab lands and that the burden of regaining these lands falls on all the Arab States.

The Arab Heads of State have agreed to unite their political efforts at the international and diplomatic level to eliminate the effects of the aggression and to ensure the withdrawal of the aggressive Israeli forces from the Arab lands, which have been occupied since the aggression of June 5. This will be done within the framework of the main principles by which the Arab States abide, namely, no peace with Israel, no recognition of Israel, no negotiations with it, and insistence on the rights of the Palestinian people in their own country.

The conference of Arab Ministers of Finance, Economy and Oil recommended that suspension of oil pumping be used as a weapon in the battle. However, after thoroughly studying the matter, the summit conference has come to the conclusion that the oil pumping can itself be used as a positive weapon, since oil is an Arab resource which can be used to strengthen the economy of the Arab States directly affected by the aggression, so that these States will be able to stand firm in the battle. The conference has, therefore, decided to resume the pumping of oil, since oil is a positive Arab resource that can be used in the service of Arab goals. It can contribute to the efforts to enable those Arab States which were exposed to the aggression and thereby lost economic resources to stand firm and eliminate the effects of the aggression. The oil-producing States have, in fact, participated in the efforts to enable the States affected by the aggression to stand firm in the face of any economic pressure.

The participants in the conference have approved the plan proposed by Kuwait to set up an Arab Economic and Social Development Fund on the basis of the recommendation of the Baghdad conference of Arab Ministers of Finance, Economy and Oil.

The participants have agreed on the need to adopt the necessary measures to strengthen military preparation to face all eventualities.

The conference has decided to expedite the elimination of foreign bases in the Arab States.

The chatter started slowly as the newsmen read the document and increased in intensity and volume as more and more of the assembled journalists finished perusing the statement. Soon the din filled the dining room. It seemed that everyone suddenly and simultaneously had something to say.

"Well, who would have guessed it? They're going to start pumping oil again," Dany opined sarcastically, after reading the resolution.

"This isn't funny, Dany. I can't believe it has so precious little to say about the Palestinians," Alexandra said. "I can see why Shukieri was so infuriated."

"You think Shukieri was angry; just wait until the Israelis see this. I think they all believed the war would ultimately produce face-to-face talks. That's what usually happens after wars are fought. This amounts to another rejection of Israel's right to exist."

"This will give the hard-liners, the old Jabotinsky faction, just what they need to dig in their heels, and, as usual, the Palestinians will be left out in the cold," she replied. Alexandra scanned the room and watched as everyone discussed and debated what it all meant. It was history in the making, and, she thought, it was more depressing than illuminating.

They decided to turn in and pack for their morning flight back to Nicosia, where they would transfer to their return trip to Tel Aviv. It was going to be a long day. Daoud was meeting them at seven o'clock in the morning to take them to the airport. They met in the dining room the next morning at six thirty and quickly made their way through the breakfast buffet line. There were only a few other journalists in the room at that hour as most flights left at night because of the daytime heat. They each selected a small bowl of porridge, which the locals call *asida*, and a dish of flatbread, or *kisra* as it is called in Sudan.

Alexandra and Dany finished breakfast and went immediately to the reception desk to settle their accounts. Daoud, waiting by the entrance to the hotel lobby, waved to them. It was already uncomfortably hot in Khartoum. The desk clerk stared at them as they approached. He was expressionless. Gone was the broad smile with which he usually greeted everyone.

"Haddad and Najat checking out," Dany said as he approached the front desk.

"They have your papers," the clerk said, nervously pointing to four men standing off to the side, dressed in the powder-blue uniforms of the Sudanese police. Alexandra's heart began to pound as she turned to the officers.

"What's the meaning of this?" Dany asked. "We have a plane to catch."

"Not today you don't," the officer who appeared to be in charge replied. "You come with us."

"There must be some mistake," Dany objected. "We're journalists. We've been here covering the Arab League summit."

"You come with me now," the officer said, taking Dany by the arm.

"You!" one of the other officers called out, gesturing to Alexandra. "You come with us. He go with them; you come with us." Alexandra turned to Daoud. The driver moved toward them.

"You stay there!" one of the officers yelled to Daoud.

"I'm their driver, sir. I can vouch. They here to attend conference. I drive them to parliament building every day."

"You stay there!" the officer insisted. With that, two of the officers led Dany away, and the remaining two officers each took Alexandra by an arm.

"You come with us now," they commanded.

The few people who were in the hotel lobby watched as they were led away. No one objected. No one interfered. Alexandra turned and looked to them, hoping against hope that someone would intervene and explain that they were journalists who were in Khartoum just doing their job. And then she spotted the one familiar face among the onlookers. Hamid Abdulla Hashimi stood impassively watching as they were led away.

Dany was ordered into one of two police cars that were parked in the driveway. The motors were idling and the lights flashing. He was ordered to the rear seat, and the two officers with him took places on either side of him. Alexandra was led to the second car, and the two officers who had escorted her from the hotel had her sit between them in the rear. Alexandra saw the car in which Dany had been placed take a right turn out of the hotel driveway. The car in which she was placed turned in the opposite direction toward the bridge to Omdurman. She twisted in her seat to look back through the rear window. She saw the other police car, siren wailing, speeding away toward the east. Then she spotted Daoud's Land Rover speed out of the Grand Hotel's driveway following the car taking her away.

CHAPTER THIRTY

Alexandra knew it would be futile to say anything to either of the officers between whom she was squeezed in the backseat of the police car. She was too frightened to speak anyway. It was already almost one hundred degrees in Khartoum, and even hotter in the back of the car. She struggled to remain calm, as she grew ever more light-headed. Her heart pounded, and perspiration glazed her face and ran in rivulets down her torso and spine. She trembled as the pressure of the officers' arms and thighs pushed against her from either side. What had gone wrong? What could have happened?

Then she saw it: the tight cluster of sorrowful buildings surrounded by the dreadful wall, the compound Daoud had called Omdurman Prison. "Very bad place," he had said. Alexandra felt her knees shake as the police car pulled up to the entrance. The driver exchanged a few words with the guard at the gate. The guard peered through the open window and focused intently on Alexandra. There was terror in her eyes. The guard just stared for what seemed an eternity. His eyes slowly roamed over her body as she sat pinned between the two police officers, her olive complexion pale by comparison. He grinned and nodded. "Welcome to Omdurman," he said, ominously drawing out the words.

Daoud's Land Rover pulled up just as the guard began to lift the barrier to the entrance of the prison compound. Daoud jumped from his car and ran to the police car. "Miss, I bring you food and water. Eat or drink nothing here. Wait for Daoud to bring food. Here, food and water make you sick."

"Daoud!" she screamed. "Find help!"

"I bring you food," he yelled, as the police car pulled away and drove into the compound. The two policemen took Alexandra by each arm and walked with her into the wretched, foreboding building. An acrid stench hung in the air as they ushered her down a dimly lit corridor. As they moved into the bowels of the building, she heard the sound of high-pitched voices jabbering simultaneously, alien, unintelligible, and frightening sounds, a chorus of language echoing off the walls, meaningless and threatening to her. She tried to calm herself, to quiet the heartbeat banging in her ears, to conquer the trembling she felt throughout her body. They finally came to a room toward the far end of the corridor. The door was closed, the green paint peeling from the wood.

"You wait here with officer," one of the policemen commanded, as he opened the door and entered the room. Alexandra stood there staring at the door. She stared straight ahead, as though in a trance, afraid to look around, afraid to look farther down the corridor, afraid of what she might see.

CHAPTER
THIRTY-ONE

The door opened, and the policeman beckoned her to enter. She walked into the room as the policeman left. An older, somewhat overweight, olive-skinned, balding man, perhaps fifty years old, dressed in Western beige slacks and a white shirt, sat behind an old metal desk perusing a document, apparently about Alexandra. He looked up at her; his eyes were dark, as were the puffy circles upon which they rested. Alexandra noticed a cheap plastic nameplate at the front of the desk imprinted with Arab script and English lettering. It identified the man as Inspector Muhammad Faizel. There was one metal chair in front of the desk. The room was otherwise bare except for a large color photograph of Sudanese president Ismail al-Azhari hanging on the wall and a bucket and mop propped in one corner. A dirty ceiling fan groaned as it rotated slowly above the man's desk. Inspector Faizel didn't invite her to sit down, so she stood there as he returned his attention to the document he had been reading. He was not a tall man—no more than five and a half feet. Finally, after several minutes he lifted his eyes to her.

"Sabirah Najat?" he asked.

"That's the name I sometimes write under. My name is Alexandra Salaman," she answered, trying to maintain as much composure as she could.

"Your conference registration papers say you are Sabirah Najat. It is a crime to use a false name on an official document."

"I'm Alexandra Salaman," she said, wiping away with the back of her hand the tears she felt welling up in her eyes.

"Give me!" he demanded, pointing to the handbag slung over her shoulder.

She nodded and promptly handed it to the man.

He opened it and held it upside down, letting the contents tumble to the desktop.

Alexandra's heart raced faster as she saw the two flight envelopes land on the desk, each with the remainder of a round-trip ticket, one to Nicosia from Khartoum and the other to Tel Aviv from Nicosia. Her American passport was lying there next to her Arab League travel document and the two tickets. A folded copy of the Arab League resolution, which had not yet been made available to the general public, along with tissue, several Sudanese pounds and piastres, her unmarked room key from the Dan Hotel, and a package of Wrigley's spearmint gum were scattered on the desk.

The man methodically placed the two airline-ticket envelopes next to one another. Then he placed, side by side, the American passport issued to Alexandra Salaman and the Arab League's travel document issued in the name of Sabirah Najat. He picked up the hotel room key and examined it closely.

"Hotel room key?" he asked.

"Yes," she answered, weakly.

"Your hotel key?"

Alexandra nodded. "Yes," she whispered.

"From Grand Hotel?"

Oh God, she thought. "No. Not from Grand."

"Where from?"

Her mouth, quivering ever so faintly, turned dry.

"Where from?" Muhammad Faizel asked again, raising his eyes to hers.

"It's from the Dan Hotel," she answered.

"From what city?"

Her heart pounded, and she could feel her chest heaving faster as her breathing increased. She knew she dared not lie. "It's from the Dan in Tel Aviv," she said, softly.

Inspector Faizel glared at her as he tossed the key back onto the desktop. He reached over and picked up the two ticket envelopes. "Why didn't you book one ticket from Tel Aviv to Nicosia with a connecting flight to Khartoum and a return from Khartoum to Nicosia with a connecting flight to Tel Aviv? Why did you book two separate round-trips?"

"It seemed less complicated," she answered, weakly.

"You mean it seemed easier to fool us when you landed in Khartoum?" he replied angrily.

"Just less complicated," she said, barely above a whisper.

Inspector Faizel tossed the tickets down and scooped up the American passport and Arab League travel document. He studied the documents for several minutes. Then he raised his eyes to meet hers. "Which document is fake?" he demanded, slowly drawing out the words.

"Neither is fake," she answered. "They were both issued by the proper authorities." Alexandra saw the veins at Inspector Faizel's temples pulsate as his anger rose.

"You think we are stupid?"

"No, no—of course not. I spoke the truth," she answered.

"The American passport is issued to Alexandra Salaman," he said, his voice rising as he held up the passport. "The Arab League travel document is issued to Sabirah Najat. Which is fake?"

"I explained I'm a journalist and sometimes I write under the name Sabirah Najat," she said, tearfully, making no attempt to hide the terror in her voice.

"I didn't ask you what you do; I asked you which document is fake. What other papers do you have? Do you have any other papers in your clothes?"

"No, I gave you everything," she answered.

"Take off your clothes," he demanded.

"What?"

"Your clothes. Take off your clothes. I want to examine anything you might be hiding in your pockets or in your undergarments."

"No…no, I'm not hiding anything," she pleaded.

"Take off your clothes, now!" he shouted. "Hand me each item of clothing. We will see if you are hiding any other documents."

Alexandra froze. She shook her head, frantically. "I'm not hiding anything. I swear. I'm not hiding anything," she pleaded.

"Your blouse. Hand me your blouse," he demanded. She stood there. There was dead silence in the room except for the whirring ceiling fan above them. Inspector Faizel rose from his chair and held out his hand. "Your blouse!" he demanded again. Alexandra took a deep breath. She bit down on her lip to try to maintain her composure. Her hand trembled as she awkwardly began to unbutton her blouse. She removed the garment and handed it to him. He snatched it from her and ran his hands through the blouse. Finding nothing, he dropped it to the top of his desk.

"The skirt," he demanded, his hand outstretched.

Alexandra was breathing heavily now. She unsnapped the fastener of her skirt and bent down and stepped from it. Her hands shaking, she handed him the skirt. Without taking his eyes from her, he jammed his hand into each of the side pockets of her skirt. He then turned it inside out and ran the bottom hem through his fingers.

"Undergarments," he demanded.

She knew it would be futile to protest. She unhooked her bra and handed it to him, quickly crossing her arms over her breasts. He examined the bra quickly and tossed it onto the desktop with the other garments. Then he held out his hand for the one remaining item of underclothing. Alexandra fought back her tears as she slipped out of her panties and handed the last of her clothing to Inspector Faizel. Without taking his eyes from her, he ran the garment through his hands.

"Your sandals," he demanded coldly, dropping her panties to the desk-top. She bent down and removed each sandal and handed them to him. He examined them, turning each sandal over to make sure the soles were entirely intact. They stood there facing one another. Naked, Alexandra surprisingly felt less fear than she had experienced moments earlier when she was forced to undress in front of him. Disrobing was humiliating—standing and confronting him less so. The tears subsided. "May I have my clothes back?" she asked, surprised at her own composure. "I would also like to be directed to a restroom—a toilet. I need to use a toilet."

"Use the bucket in the corner," he replied. "The prisoner areas have what you call a toilet, but I'm not through with this interview. The bucket is a luxury compared with the hole in the ground you'll use while you're with the other prisoners. I will leave you alone in the office for five minutes. Use the bucket as necessary and get dressed." He walked from the room, closing the door behind him.

Alexandra, as though in a trance, walked over to the corner of the room and removed the mop from the bucket. She braced her back against the corner walls and slowly lowered herself over the bucket. She fought the paralyzing fear and the feeling of hopelessness that descended upon her. Think, think, think, she kept telling herself. After relieving herself, she went to the desk to retrieve her clothes and quickly dressed. She was determined to face Inspector Faizel as a professional journalist who was in Khartoum along with over four hundred other journalists doing her job, meaning no harm to the government of Sudan. Her need for sub-terfuge was regrettable but harmless. She was a member of the press and was in Sudan for no other reason than to report on the summit. Making an international incident over the matter served no one's interest.

Muhammad Faizel returned to the office in exactly five minutes as he said he would.

"What are we to do with you?"

"Allowing Dany Haddad and me to return to our jobs would make the most sense," she answered. "We have no ill feelings toward your country."

"You have no idea how much trouble you are in, do you?"

"I've done nothing wrong. I came here the only way I could. The travel documents I received from the Arab League are not forged. They're authentic. I've been working out of Tel Aviv like hundreds of other journalists because I'm not able to work out of Sudan or Egypt under the current circumstances. I'm a reporter. That's all."

"Is it?" he asked, tauntingly.

"Yes," she answered defiantly.

"We don't even know who you are. You hide your identity."

"I am Alexandra Salaman. I am a Palestinian Christian whose family lost their home in the nakbah. We had to leave in 1948. I write for the *Washington Evening Star* in Washington, DC."

"I think you are a Muslim named Sabirah Najat who abandoned Islam. That, Miss Najat, is a very serious matter here."

"Look at my passport. That's my picture, and that's my name, Alexandra Salaman. I was born in Jaffa."

"How do we know that this is an official passport? You have two different documents with two different names. You admitted the Arab League travel document is authentic, did you not? One is legitimate, and one clearly isn't. Which one are we to believe?"

"The one with my picture. You can see that I'm Alexandra Salaman."

"I can also see that you are Sabirah Najat," he replied as he opened his desk drawer. "Here is another document with your picture." He pulled the latest issue of *Cultural Jihad* from the drawer and tossed it onto the desk.

Alexandra gasped. There in front of her was the issue of *Cultural Jihad* with the reprint of her column from the *Washington Evening Star* with her picture over the name Sabirah Najat. Muhammad Faizel sat there tapping his fingers together, his eyes fixed on hers, searching for her reaction.

"You see, here you are Sabirah Najat. That's how you came into our country. That's whom the only travel documents that we recognize say you are. That's whom this newsletter says you are. There is your picture, and there is your name."

"I'm Alexandra Salaman," she replied, barely above a whisper. The strong resolve evident only moments earlier now faltered. "I want to see your superiors," she finally said.

"No, you really don't, Miss Najat. In fact, you can't imagine how lucky you are. It is sheer luck that you are here standing in front of me, instead of some official in central Khartoum. You see, Hamid Abdullah Hamishi called me, because I belong to the Trans-Arabic Alliance and I subscribe to *Cultural Jihad*. I'm the only member the Alliance has in sub-Saharan Africa. Mr. Hamishi knew you wrote for the *Washington Evening Star* and had been writing from the Zionist entity in Tel Aviv because he reprints all of your columns."

"That doesn't contradict anything I've told you. Sabirah Najat is merely a pseudonym I use."

"But Sabirah Najat is a safer name for you here than is Alexandra Salaman," he replied.

"I don't understand," she said, fear evident once again in her voice.

"Sabirah Najat isn't responsible for the martyrdom of Ali Abdul Shoukri. That would be Alexandra Salaman."

She was speechless. Her heart, once again, began racing. She could feel her chin quiver, revealing her fear to Muhammad Faizel.

"You see, Sabirah, and we will call you Sabirah here, a Palestinian colleague who reads *Cultural Jihad* was very close to Ali Abdul Shoukri. The Palestinian saw your picture in the newsletter and communicated with Hamid Abdullah Hamishi, the publisher. The Palestinian's name is—"

"Omar Samir," she interrupted, weakly.

"Yes, Sabirah, Omar Samir. He is the mastermind of your current dilemma. When Hamishi learned from Samir whom you were, he called me. I'm his only contact in Sudan. Had he called our Justice Ministry, I think you would, indeed, disappear off the face of the earth.

Omar Samir assumes you now have, or soon will, disappear off the face of the earth."

"Are you saying the Sudanese government doesn't know I've been detained—that I'm here?"

Inspector Faizel smiled sinisterly. "They would hang you, Sabirah. They would hang you within twenty-four hours. You are here illegally. You came from a country with which we are at war, and you live and work in a country with which we have no diplomatic relations. And by the way, did I mention that Mr. Samir told Hamid Abdullah Hamishi that you, a former Muslim, consort with a Jew in America?"

"I have never been a Muslim."

"Sabirah Najat, not a Muslim? Who would believe that?"

"Am I a prisoner of Sudan?"

The inspector leaned forward, glaring into her eyes. "No, Sabirah, you are not a prisoner of Sudan. You are a prisoner of Muhammad Faizel," he replied. "You are *my* prisoner," he said, emphasizing the word *my*. "The government of Sudan doesn't even know you are here. You should be thankful. For a prisoner of Sudan, the punishment for a Muslim who abandons Islam is death."

"I've never been a Muslim," she protested, futilely.

"Of course Sabirah Najat was a Muslim," he retorted.

"I was never Sabirah Najat."

"You are now."

"What are you going to do with me?" she asked, her voice shaking, her confidence gone.

Inspector Muhammad Faizel looked at her, menacingly. "Whatever I want," he replied. "That's what I am going to do with you, Sabirah Najat—whatever I want." He drew out the words to drive home the hopelessness of her position. "But for now, you will be taken to your new quarters. You'll have some cellmates. I'm afraid the accommodations won't be quite up to what you are used to with the Jews at the Dan Hotel in Tel Aviv."

"You can't do this," she cried.

Muhammad Faizel began to laugh as though she had just made a joke. He rose from his chair and leaned forward on his desk. "Look around, Sabirah. Look where you are. What do you mean I can't do this? Don't you see I've done it?"

"You can't make me your personal prisoner. This is insane," she pleaded.

"Here, Sabirah, I am your salvation. None of the guards here will lay a hand on you because they know you are my prisoner. They can do as they wish with the other women. It is like what Americans call a perk, you know, a benefit, but you they won't touch because they know you are my prisoner." With that, he walked to the door, opened it, and disappeared for several minutes. Finally, he reappeared with another man in a khaki uniform, a guard, she assumed. He was taller than Alexandra by several inches, and his head was clean-shaven. His eyes were impassive, expressionless, and his skin black. He did not speak. He immediately took Alexandra firmly by the arm, turned, and walked from Inspector Faizel's office, pulling Alexandra as he went.

They continued down the same corridor through which Alexandra was brought to Inspector Faizel's office. The air in the dark passageway got hotter and heavier as they continued into the interior of the prison. Then they passed a cell, a large pen, lit only by the small barred window high on the far wall. They passed by too quickly for Alexandra to count how many women were in the stone room, but she saw that there were many, perhaps twelve or fifteen. An elderly woman squatting over an opening in the floor looked up at her. A strong, pungent, ammonia-like odor permeated the air. Alexandra tried to stifle the cry that rose in her throat. She began to feel light-headed and tried to pause long enough to brace herself against the damp stone wall that lined the corridor. The guard tugged at her arm and kept walking. She followed, half-stumbling, determined not to fall. They passed several other cells, large pens, some of which opened into walled, outdoor holding areas. All were crowded with women. Some held sheets over their heads as protection from the scorching sun. As they continued down the corridor, another guard and prisoner came walking toward them. The woman looked to be no more than twenty years old. She grimaced with each step, and while she wasn't crying, Alexandra saw that her face was streaked where tears had fallen. As they passed one another, Alexandra turned and quickly focused on the red stain on the back of the woman's dress. And then they came to the end of the corridor.

The cell was smaller than the others they had passed. There were also fewer women in it—only six. The guard took a key attached to his belt and opened the door to the cell. With a slight push, more a nudge than a shove, he directed her into the cell and, after locking the cell door, turned and left without uttering a word. The women, hunched on the floor, their backs against the sidewall, eyed her curiously but did not speak.

Alexandra moved to a corner of the cell opposite the other prisoners, turned, and faced the women. She absently folded her arms across her torso as though to comfort herself. She slowly surveyed the cell. There was no furniture, no stools, no bed. Patches of fabric, remnants of blankets, and an old garment lay out on the ground, revealing where the women slept. She looked up through the single barred window and saw the clear sky over Khartoum. Then, near the back wall, she saw the soiled hole in the floor. "The bucket is a luxury compared with the hole in the ground you'll use while you're with the other prisoners," Muhammad Faizel had taunted her. The filthy hole in the floor, the loss of dignity, the hopelessness of it all was overwhelming. She had no idea where they had taken Dany, and Noah thought she was in Cyprus enjoying a respite before returning home. Alexandra finally buried her face in her hands and wept uncontrollably.

CHAPTER
THIRTY-TWO

"Hi, Barb, has Alexandra called?" Noah asked as he entered the Potomac Center reception room. "I thought I would hear from her Saturday evening or sometime yesterday when she returned from Cyprus."

"Nope. No calls this morning. When was she due back in Tel Aviv?"

"I'm not sure. I assumed sometime before sundown Friday."

"Is that when she said she would return?"

"She didn't say, exactly. She just said she was going to get away for a few days to Cyprus while she finished her last column from the Middle East."

"Well, she probably stayed the weekend. You'll probably hear from her tonight or tomorrow morning."

"Yeah, you're probably right. I called the Dan earlier, and they said she hadn't returned yet."

"I wouldn't worry. Alexandra is one girl who can take care of herself. She's probably traveling back to Tel Aviv today. I bet you'll hear from her a little later or sometime tomorrow."

"Yeah, I'm sure you're right," he replied. "Have you heard from Karen this morning?"

"Karen is on her way in from the airport. She took the early-morning flight and called just before you arrived. She should be here any minute."

Karen was spending the weekend in Washington so she and Noah could rehearse and make any last-minute changes to the IPO presentation, which would commence the following week, right after Labor Day. They planned to take the Eastern Shuttle to New York Sunday evening, check into the Plaza Hotel, spend Labor Day in the city, and begin their first round of presentations the following day. The road show would officially commence with a large luncheon with nearly one hundred analysts and money managers at the Plaza Hotel. Karen had lined up private, one-on-one lunch and dinner meetings with interested investors on Monday evening and for lunch on Tuesday and Wednesday. They planned to remain in New York through Thursday before flying up to Hartford. If all went according to plan, Alexandra would join them sometime in New York and continue on with them for the remainder of the road show.

Noah was unnerved when he still hadn't heard from Alexandra by the time he and Karen were boarding the shuttle to LaGuardia late Sunday afternoon. Karen reminded him that everything ground to a halt in Israel between sundown Friday and sundown Saturday. Alexandra could very well be in the air flying from Nicosia to Tel Aviv on a red-eye at the very time they would be flying to New York, or, more likely, Alexandra was planning to return to Israel after the weekend, sometime Monday. She urged Noah to stay focused on the road show. "Alexandra will catch up with us, if not in New York, then in Harford or Boston," she assured him.

"This has been the longest period of time during which we've had no contact with one another since she returned from the Middle East nearly four years ago," he said.

"Noah, she's wrapping up the biggest assignment she's ever had or may ever have. You have to cut her some slack," Karen replied.

"Yeah, you're probably right," he conceded. "But still, I just wish she would call."

CHAPTER THIRTY-THREE

It was around nine o'clock that first night before Daoud returned to Omdurman with food, water, a thin mattress, and a sheet. She was hunched over in a corner, her head resting on her arms, when a guard escorted the Nubian to her cell.

"You give her food and bedding, and then you must leave. No visit," the guard instructed Daoud.

Alexandra sprang to her feet when she saw him. "Daoud, you came," she cried. The guard opened the cell door and admonished Daoud to move quickly. Alexandra ran to Daoud and threw her arms around him as soon as he entered the cell.

"Daoud, listen carefully—Amos Ben-Chaiyim, Mossad. Say it," she whispered in his ear frantically.

"Amooz Ben Kaiyum Mossad," he repeated as he hugged her.

"Call, find him…Mossad, Israel," she whispered, desperately clinging to him.

"Amooz Ben Kaiyum Mossad," he whispered back to her, again.

"They're going to kill me," she cried frantically as the guard separated them.

"I come back tomorrow with food and water for you. No eat anything here."

"Call…Call…Call Amos," she repeated as the guard took Daoud by the arm and led him from the cell. Daoud went back to the Land Rover and sat there for several minutes concentrating on what Alexandra had said. He reached up to the visor and pulled a pad of paper and a pencil from the rubber band that held them in place. "Amooz Ben Kaiyum M——" he wrote, deciding it best not to have anything with the full name Mossad written on it. Then he sat back and contemplated what to do next.

There was no way to connect to Israel by phone from Sudan, and he knew it would be dangerous to try. Both Chad to the west and Uganda to the south had diplomatic relations with Israel and, therefore, telephone service as well, but he knew it would be dangerous driving his Land Rover through southern Sudan to get to Uganda or through Darfur to the west to get to Chad. Gondar in Ethiopia was probably the closest place where he might be able to try calling Israel and the person who went by the strange name Alexandra had whispered to him. Daoud knew there was no time to apply for visas, so flying to Gondar was out of the question. Bus travel, he knew, would involve hours of delay at the border. Overland border crossings were generally only for tourists. He possibly could bribe his way across the border if he drove, maybe by pleading it was to visit a dying mother. It would be a long and treacherous drive, nearly four hundred miles, all of it over rough terrain and mountainous dirt roads. It had not rained for the past few days, so the roads might be passable. If it rained before he got to Ethiopia, he knew his mission would be doomed.

He sped away from Omdurman prison to stop at his one-room shanty to get his hands on all of the money he had saved from years of chauffeuring visitors in Khartoum. He also thought of several trinkets that might be tradable at the border. Then he snatched from a drawer a ring he took from his beloved Cena's finger the day she died.

He purchased four containers of petrol to make sure he had enough fuel for the trip. The drive was horrible. As he drove as fast as he dared from the desert flatlands of Sudan eastward toward the highlands of Ethiopia, Alexandra's last desperate words to him kept ringing in his ears. "They are going to kill me," she had said. He drove through the night determined to get to the Sudanese border at Gallabat and cross over to Metemma in Ethiopia by the time the crossing opened in the morning. Whenever his eyes grew heavy with fatigue, Alexandra's words urged him on—"They are going to kill me." The Land Rover groaned and bounced its way through the night. He prayed the tires would hold up, the radiator wouldn't overheat, and the engine wouldn't break down. Several buses were already lined up at the border crossing when he finally reached Gallabat. He slowly crept forward as each bus was allowed to pass. A border guard approached him warily.

"*Ummi* dying," Daoud cried. "I drive all night to see Mama before she die," he pleaded.

"You have permission to leave Sudan?"

"No time. Ummi dying. Need to see my ummi before she die," Daoud answered, tears rolling down his cheeks. "Please help me see my ummi before she die."

The border guard waved him to the side of the road. "You stay!" he commanded Daoud and walked back to the crossing station. A few moments later, the guard returned with another uniformed man who appeared to be his superior.

"You have no papers?" the supervisor asked.

Again Daoud began to sob. "My ummi dying. Please permission me for one day. I give you all my money to hold. If I don't come back within twenty-four hours, you keep money. If I'm one minute late, you keep money. I just want to see Ummi before she die."

The two guards talked for a moment at the side of the road and then returned to the Land Rover. "You come with me," the more senior officer said. "Open trunk, and then you come with me."

Daoud did as he was told. As the border guard began to rummage through the rags and other junk in the Land Rover's trunk, the supervisor led Daoud to the crossing station.

"You know you can't just drive across the border with no papers. You know that, don't you?"

"Ummi be dead before I can receive papers. You know that, don't you?" Daoud answered.

"You fool. You stupid," the man barked at Daoud. "To cross border, you need to stop at National Security station, you need to go to customs, and you need to stop at immigration, all here in Sudan, and then you have to go to immigration on other side in Ethiopia and to Ethiopia customs, and you have no papers to show anybody? What they gonna say across the border right there in Metemma?" the man asked, pointing through the window to the pathetic little town on the other side of the barrier.

"You give me emergency permission and come with me to border and explain to guard standing there in Metemma. My ummi dying while we stand here talking."

"You know penalty for lying about emergency?"

Alexandra's words rang in his ears: "They're going to kill me."

"You come with me to my ummi in Gondar. If you think she not dying, you shoot me," Daoud replied, as he broke down and began sobbing.

The Sudanese crossing officer studied Daoud as he stood there, tears falling from his eyes. He hesitated for a moment and then turned to a filing cabinet and pulled a file from the drawer. After rifling through a sheaf of papers, he pulled a form from the file. He scribbled on the form and then walked to a desk and selected a stamp from a drawer. He looked at Daoud one more time and then slammed the stamp down onto the document.

"This has no meaning over there," he said, jabbing his thumb toward the barrier separating Gallabat from Metemma. "Come, I'll talk to the Ethiopians, and we'll see what they say."

As they walked toward the barrier, the officer made a gesture with his arm, and the barrier on the Gallabat side of the border was raised. They stopped midway across a short no-man's-land. A guard from the Metemma side walked to the halfway point to meet the Sudanese officer and Daoud. The Sudanese officer explained the nature of Daoud's emergency and showed him the form he had just completed. The

Ethiopian guard told them to wait while he went into the crossing station on the Ethiopian side of the border. Around a half hour later, the guard returned with a superior at his side. The Sudanese officer explained the nature of Daoud's emergency and handed the Ethiopian officer the form he had filled out and stamped. The Ethiopian shrugged and explained that no one had called to alert them that an emergency case would be coming through.

"No time to make arrangements. I learned my ummi, my mama, had a stroke and is going to die within twenty-four hours. I drive all night to try to see my ummi, my mama, before she die. We not see one another for twenty years. Please help me see my dying ummi… Please!" The Ethiopian removed his cap and scratched his head.

"Where your car?" he asked. They turned, and Daoud pointed to the Land Rover on the Sudanese side of the border. Daoud saw that the trunk and doors were open and that the seats had been pulled out during the search of the car.

"You not back in twenty-four hours, you go to jail for very, very long time. Wait here. I give you paper for your windshield—permission to be in Ethiopia for twenty-four hours."

"I be back, sir. I be back," Daoud said, shaking the Ethiopian's hand. He ran back to his car and helped the guard reinstall the front seat and backseat. Then, he slowly moved the Land Rover forward and waved appreciatively to the guards as the car glided under the raised barriers and on into Ethiopia. It took another four hours to travel the 120 miles from Metemma to Gondar. He traveled east, passing through the hamlets of Maganan, Aykel, and Azezo, where traffic crawled as pedestrians, goats, and dogs clogged the dirt roadway. At a couple of points along the way, he noticed small grass huts with what appeared to be Stars of David atop the thatched roofs. This was the Falasha area about which he had heard, but he couldn't believe he was passing through villages in which black Jews actually lived. Finally, a few miles north of Azezo, the road arched north and rambled on into the outskirts of Gondar.

CHAPTER
THIRTY-FOUR

Noah was at his best at the Plaza presentation. He reviewed the Potomac Center business model, the urban focus, and the rebirth of America's major cities, which he predicted would be in full swing during the course of the next generation. The visuals of the project were well received. The idea that Potomac Center could be a model for many major metropolitan areas struck a responsive chord with the analysts, and the center's first-year financial progress dazzled them. Karen was impressed with how well he handled questions, and, it seemed, the analysts were too. Just as the meeting was about to draw to a close, an analyst sitting in the middle of the room raised his hand to ask a question.

"Yes," Noah said, pointing to the man.

"I'm George Markanos from Deutschland Trust. First, congratulations on an excellent presentation," he began.

"Thank you," Noah answered, recognizing the notorious short seller about whom Karen had warned.

"Noah, your project has impressed a lot of people, including me. Am I correct, though, that your vision is very much an urban vision? You are more focused on the major metropolitan areas than you are on rural America."

"Yes, I think that's a fair statement, George," Noah replied.

"You know many people are referring to this summer as the summer of rage. You're planning major capital investments in major cities, but aren't you concerned about what is happening in our major cities? Since the King assassination, there have been huge race protests, even riots, in Atlanta, Boston, Cincinnati, Detroit, Chicago, Milwaukee, Minneapolis, Newark, and just last month your home city, Washington, DC. Isn't this concept of yours extremely vulnerable to urban unrest?"

"Sure," Noah answered. "But projects like Potomac Center can also be the salvation of our major cities. Just look at how well Potomac Center is doing. The construction of these projects will provide construction employment and new capital formation in our cities, and when the projects are up and running, they will provide new opportunities for people to find jobs in sales, service, maintenance, transportation, and so on. We believe the pluses far outweigh the negatives."

"Good answer," the short seller conceded. "Time will tell, of course."

The analysts were uniformly complimentary as they shook hands with Noah following the meeting. Karen was ecstatic.

"Noah, you hit the ball out of the park. I think they loved it," she said.

Noah nodded. "Thanks, Karen. I know we have a couple of one-on-ones this afternoon, but I want to run up to the suite and call Barb to see if she has heard anything from Alexandra," he replied.

"Sure. I know how concerned you are, Noah. I'll come up too. It's only nine thirty in Tel Aviv. If Barb hasn't heard anything, I'll call Amos. I have his apartment number," she replied. "He may have some ideas. He'll know how best to track her down."

They went up to the suite, and Karen watched as Noah placed the call to his secretary in Washington. Noah asked Barb if she had heard from Alexandra and, a moment later, shook his head, signaling to Karen that there had been no calls. Karen went into her adjoining bedroom and had the hotel operator place a call to Amos in Tel Aviv while Noah continued to talk. Luckily, he was in and promptly answered the phone. He listened as she explained that they hadn't heard from Alexandra. Amos wasn't particularly surprised that she had been out of touch, explaining that if she was visiting some of the hamlets in Cyprus, telephone communication might be hard to access.

"I'll make some inquiries and call you back at the Plaza regardless of whether I learn anything or not. But tell Noah not to worry. I'm sure she's fine. Alexandra is street-smart, and things are pretty quiet in Cyprus right now. I can't imagine she would have run into any trouble there."

Their concern temporarily assuaged, Noah and Karen continued with their meetings in New York.

***

"Mr. Haddad, we're sorry to have inconvenienced you this way. Your credentials are in order, and I'm sure you'll be able to leave soon. Inspector Faizel has some questions for you, and he's been detained," the assistant warden at Kober Prison explained.

"This is outrageous," Dany protested. "You're detaining me for no reason."

"That is regrettable, but we have assigned you our most private space here at Kober."

"You are detaining me in a prison hellhole. I don't care how private my cell is; you have no reason to detain me here. I'm an accredited journalist."

"Well, that isn't exactly true, you know. You are traveling with someone whose credentials are very questionable. Inspector Faizel is trying to get to the bottom of this. Meanwhile, you are being housed in a private room and not a typical cell, and we're bringing you food from the outside. We are doing everything we can to accommodate you as comfortably as possible."

Dany knew he had to be very careful. He had no way of knowing what Alexandra was telling them, nor did he know what name she was claiming as her own. He also knew that if she had admitted she was Alexandra Salaman, she could be in serious trouble, and if she was insisting that she was Sabirah Najat, that could be equally dangerous, given that there was no such person. He knew he could only protest so much without more information. What Dany didn't know, of course, was that Inspector Faizel had no intention of allowing him to leave Sudan alive.

***

Noah and Karen were preparing to leave Hartford for the drive to Boston when she received Amos's call.

"Karen, I haven't been able to find out much yet, but what I have learned is interesting."

"What have you learned?" she asked.

"Are you in a place where you can talk?"

"Yes, I'm in my room. Noah is on the other side of the suite in his room. What have you learned?"

"Karen, did Noah say anything to you about Alexandra traveling with Dany Haddad?"

"What!"

"Karen, this might not mean anything, but here's what I've learned so far. Alexandra and Dany left Tel Aviv last Tuesday on a flight to Nicosia. Alexandra told me she wanted to get away for a few days, but she didn't say anything about wanting to get away with Dany Haddad."

"Holy shit, are you telling me she and Dany are traveling somewhere together?"

"All I know is that she and Dany left Tel Aviv together. They were on the same flight, and they were seated next to one another."

"Whew…I don't know what to make of that," Karen said.

"Karen, I know Alexandra. It's not what it seems. I'm positive of that."

"What do you think it means?"

"I think they're working on something together."

"Like what?"

"I have a hunch that it has to do with the recent conference in Khartoum, but I don't want to guess. I'll know more in a day or two. Has Noah said anything at all about what she would be doing?"

"No. Just that she wanted to get away for a few days to write her last column from the Middle East. But she thought she would be back in time for the IPO road show we're doing for Potomac Center. It didn't sound like she was traveling to do anything more than finish her last column and get some rest. Nothing about any other work—more like she wanted a brief break from work."

"So, she thought she would be back in the States by now?"

"Well, not necessarily. The road show will go on for most of the month."

"Let me do a little more digging. I'll get back to you as soon as I can. I don't think I'd say anything to Noah about Alexandra and Dany traveling together just yet. It sounds like he has enough on his mind, and I really don't think we should jump to any conclusions."

"I agree. I won't say anything." They ended their conversation, and Karen sat at the desk contemplating what she had learned.

"You won't say anything about what?" Noah asked from the doorway to the living room.

"How long have you been standing in the doorway?" she asked.

"Long enough to know Amos didn't want you to tell me something."

"Oh shit," Karen whispered.

"What the hell is that all about?"

"Amos needs a little more time."

"What didn't he want you to discuss with me, Karen?" Noah asked, his tone more insistent.

Karen knew there wasn't any way she could avoid answering his question.

"Noah, Amos learned that Alexandra and Dany Haddad are traveling together," she replied.

"What!"

"Alexandra and Dany are together, I guess in Cyprus. Amos thinks it has to do with their work, and he wants to dig a little more. He didn't want you to be worried. That's why he asked me not to say anything. Noah, I agree with Amos; I'm sure there's a very logical explanation."

"Why wouldn't she say anything?"

"Probably because she knew you would flip out if she told you she was traveling with Dany."

"She said she wanted to get away for a few days. She didn't say she and Dany wanted to get away for a few days."

"Noah, don't be a jerk. She knew what your reaction would be had she told you that. Amos feels certain it's work related."

"Then why hasn't she called? She's been gone for over a week."

"You know, telephone service can be pretty bad in some places. Noah, I'm sure she's fine and you'll hear from her soon," Karen said, with more certainty than she really felt.

"What if she's in some sort of trouble?"

"Noah, I don't think we have any reason to think that Alexandra is in trouble. Let's not jump to conclusions."

CHAPTER THIRTY-FIVE

"You, lady! Come with me!" the guard yelled as he opened the cell door and pointed to Alexandra. She got to her feet, steadying herself against the stone wall.

"You come," the guard called again.

Alexandra walked from the cell and faced the guard. He took her by the arm and began walking briskly back toward Muhammad Faizel's office. Alexandra tried to calm her nerves as fear tugged at her gut. She was breathing heavily, and she could feel her jaw trembling. The door to Inspector Faizel's office was ajar, and he waved them in as soon as he saw them standing there. The guard brought Alexandra to the front of his desk.

"Close the door, and I don't want to be disturbed until I call for you," he said, waving the guard away. Alexandra knew she couldn't conceal her fear as he sat there staring at her, his face expressionless. The only sound in the room was the whirring of the ceiling fan and the sound of her heavy breathing.

"So your driver, your black friend, brought you food and a blanket," Inspector Faizel finally said, breaking the silence.

"Yes," she answered, softly.

"And you embraced him?"

"What?" she murmured.

"You ran to him and embraced him?"

"I—I was happy to see him. He brought me food and—"

"And you embraced him?"

She nodded. "Yes—I hugged him because I was happy to see him."

"It is forbidden to have any contact with visitors."

"I didn't know. No one told me that."

"Do you know why it is forbidden?"

"No, please. There's no need for this. It was just a hug because I was so happy to see someone I knew—someone who brought me food and a blanket."

"Do you know why it is forbidden?" he shouted.

Alexandra shook her head. "No," she whispered, lowering her head into her hand.

"Put your hand down. I'm talking to you," he commanded her.

"I won't hug him again," she answered.

"Do you know why it is forbidden?" he yelled more loudly than before.

Alexandra shook her head. "No. No, I don't know why, but it won't happen again."

"It is forbidden because he could have given you a knife or a gun or drugs."

"Yes, yes. I understand now. I won't let it happen again."

"How do I know he didn't give you anything?"

"He didn't. I won't let it happen again."

"Are you hiding anything that he gave you, Sabirah?"

"My name is Alexandra," she answered, crying as she spoke.

"Why are you changing the subject?"

"I swear, he didn't give me anything," she cried.

"We'll have to see, won't we, Sabirah?"

"Please, I beg you. Don't do this."

"Take off your clothes, Sabirah. There is no other way for me to know you are not concealing anything the black man gave you."

"I'm not. I swear, I'm not concealing anything."

"Take off your clothes—now!" he commanded her.

Slowly, making no effort to protest further, she began disrobing. She dropped her blouse and skirt on his desk and paused. He rose, glaring at her. She stared back, pleadingly. He stared back, menacingly. She tried to control her fear as she removed her bra and panties. She dropped them on his desk, stooped down, and unfastened her sandals. She placed them on his desk and stood facing him, crossing one arm across her breasts and dropping the other arm down across her pelvis.

"Raise your arms so that I can see that you are not concealing anything," he demanded. Alexandra complied. Inspector Faizel peered at her for what seemed an eternity.

"My God, you are a beauty," he whispered as he slowly walked from his desk and circled behind her. "Do I have to search further, Sabirah?"

"No," she answered, sobbing, pleading. "Please don't do this to me." He stepped closer to her. She could feel his breath on the nape of her neck.

"How can I be sure you are not concealing what the black man may have brought you?" he whispered into her ear. "You know I can search further, don't you, Sabirah?"

Alexandra tried to control her breathing, as she gasped for air. Her hands, still raised above her shoulders, were trembling rapidly. "Plea… Please…don't do this to me," she cried.

"You know I can search further, don't you, Sabirah?"

She nodded frantically. "Yes, I know," she said.

"You know what?" he demanded.

"I know you can search further," she replied.

"Is there any place on your body I can't search, Sabirah?"

"No," she answered, shaking her head.

"No what?"

"No, there is no place on my body you can't search."

"You can bring your arms to your sides," he finally said, returning to his chair.

"Can I get dressed?" she pleaded.

"Soon. First, I want to have a chat with you." Alexandra felt nauseous. She was breathing heavily, and tears blurred her vision.

"Can I please sit down?" she asked. "I'm getting sick."

"In a moment, in a moment," he answered. "First, we will chat."

"I'm going to be sick," she said.

"Go get the bucket. Keep it in front of you in case you get sick." She stared at him in disbelief. "Go on. The bucket is in the same corner as it was when you last used it. Go get the bucket before you get sick and soil my office." Alexandra turned, walked across the office, and picked up the bucket. She brought it back, placed it in front of the chair, and sat down without asking his permission. He smiled at her feeble act of defiance.

"I didn't invite you to sit down, Sabirah."

"I'll faint if I have to stand any longer," she answered. Inspector Faizel nodded.

"Then you may sit, Sabirah. I'm a compassionate man," he replied.

"What do you want of me?" she asked.

"You see, Sabirah, under our custom, as you know, when a Muslim apostate comes back to Islam, we are very compassionate, very considerate."

"I'm not a Muslim. I've never been a Muslim."

"And when a Muslim woman returns to Islam to marry a Muslim man, we can be very forgiving of her transgressions."

"What are you talking about?" she asked, incredulously.

"I will tell my wife that I am divorcing her, and I will take you as my wife, and all of this can be over," he answered.

Alexandra sat there, naked, trying to absorb what Muhammad Faizel was proposing. She was speechless.

"I am Alexandra Salaman. I am a Palestinian American. I am a Christian. I was born in Jaffa and immigrated with my family to America twenty years ago. I have never been a Muslim."

"You see, I can divorce my wife in one day if I choose. I can tell her three times I am divorcing her, and it is done. I can declare our marriage over and take you as my wife as soon as you come back to Islam," he replied, utterly ignoring what she had just said. "It would be better for you to live in my house than to live here."

"You mean it would be better for me to be a prisoner in your house than a prisoner here at Omdurman."

"You would be an Islamic wife rather than an apostate prisoner."

"You are mad," she said. "You can't be serious."

"Oh, I am very serious, Sabirah. I can't have you unless I divorce my wife and marry you, or else I would be committing adultery. That would be a very serious offense in Islam. Whom would you rather be with? Me or the guards here?"

"What are you saying?"

"I will give you one week to think about what I have proposed, Sabirah. Right now the guards know you are my prisoner. They won't touch you. In one week, Sabirah, I will tell them you are no longer my prisoner. I will tell them you are their prisoner. Sabirah, do you know what will happen to you?"

"You are mad," she answered.

"We have twenty guards here, Sabirah: fifteen during the day and five at night. They will line up for you, Sabirah. How long do you think you will last? How long do you think you will be as beautiful as you are now? How long do you think you will live?"

"May I get dressed?" she asked, defiantly.

"Of course," he answered, pushing her clothes over the top of his desk and onto the floor.

"Get dressed, Sabirah, and think about what I have offered. I don't know what I would enjoy most—having you to myself or watching them have you," he said, gesturing to the door, where the guard waited.

***

"I'm really worried about her, Karen," Noah said, as they picked at their dinner that night at the Hilton in Hartford.

"Noah, Alexandra and Dany are both journalists, and they obviously must be working on a major story together. Maybe it has taken longer than she thought it would, and maybe they're not where they can just pick up a phone and call, but I'm sure they're safe and that we'll hear from them very soon."

"It's just not like Alexandra to be out of touch this way," he replied.

"Look, we're used to having a telephone wherever we are. It's not like that everyplace in the world, especially that part of the world."

"I know. So how do you think we're doing so far?" he asked, changing the subject.

"The road show is going great. I checked with the office. We've received several calls from portfolio managers already asking for pieces of the offering. I think you could sell more than half the company. That's how strong I think demand for the shares will be."

"You know, I'm worth more than I ever dreamed I would be, and I couldn't care less."

"You're very distracted right now, and you have every right to be, Noah. But you and Alexandra are going to have a wonderful life because of this offering and because of what you have built with Potomac Center."

"I just wish she would call. I'm worried, Karen. It's just not like Alexandra to drop out of contact with me like this."

"Noah, it's barely been a week. If there had been an accident, we would have heard something by now."

"Karen, we have more to be concerned about than an accident. We know there are people over there who despise her, and me too, for that matter." Karen reached over and took Noah's hand.

"Let's not go there, Noah. We have no reason to think that Alexandra is the victim of foul play. And remember, she's not alone. She and Dany Haddad appear to be working on something together. I think she's all right, and I think we'll hear from her very soon."

Karen and Noah decided to drive the one hundred miles to Boston following their meetings in Hartford with Aetna and the Hartford, two of the nation's insurance giants. Karen thought the portfolio managers at both companies seemed well-disposed toward Noah and Potomac Center.

"They took a lot of notes," she said as they headed northeast toward Boston. "And I thought you really got their attention with the sales-per-square-foot data you shared with them for store after store. You knew how the center was performing at every level. They like that."

"Karen, if we haven't heard from Alexandra or Amos by the time we're through in Boston, I don't know what I'm going to do. I'm worried sick."

"You haven't heard a word I've said, have you?" she asked, reaching over and squeezing his arm affectionately.

"I just know something is wrong, Karen. I just know it. I don't know how I'm going to go on with this road show with this on my mind."

"Noah, right now, all you know is that your fiancée is traveling and hasn't been in touch for a few days. You can't walk away from a business event of this magnitude because you haven't heard from your fiancée for a few days. Hundreds of people are now involved and focused on Potomac Center. Most of them are expecting to meet with you over the next several days. Staying focused on Potomac Center is probably the best thing you could be doing right now." He nodded but didn't respond.

"Noah, it's going to be all right. I just know it is."

"I don't know how long I can stay focused," he finally said. "I can't bear the thought of Alexandra in any kind of distress."

"I can't either, Noah. I mean that. But right now we don't know that she's in any kind of distress."

There was a message awaiting Karen when they checked into their rooms at Copley Square upon arriving in Boston. "Call me—Amos" was all it said. Noah stood, nervously, by Karen's side as she asked the hotel operator to place the call to Tel Aviv.

"I hope I'm not calling too late, Amos. I know it's midnight there," she said as soon as she heard his voice.

"No, no, it's fine. Are you alone?" he asked.

"No, I'm with Noah. He's right here," she replied. "You can speak candidly."

"Hi, Noah," Amos said.

"Hi, Amos. What do we have?" Noah replied.

"Well, it's not much, but it's not good either."

"What do you mean it's not good?" Noah answered, his heart pounding. "What's happened?"

"We don't know if anything has happened. What we do know is that Alexandra and Dany Haddad apparently traveled from Nicosia to Khartoum."

"To Khartoum!" Noah cried.

"It looks that way. Dany received press credentials to cover the Khartoum summit. It appears that Alexandra accompanied him under the name Sabirah Najat. Somehow, she was able to get authentic travel documents issued in the name of Sabirah Najat through the Arab League. We don't know for sure that anything went wrong. We just know she left Israel for Nicosia with Dany Haddad, and now we've learned that he was on his way to Khartoum. Noah, I think it's a safe bet that Alexandra accompanied him there."

"And we don't know what, if anything, may have happened to them there?" Noah asked.

"*Desert Song* hasn't heard from Dany. They're concerned, but to answer your question, no, they haven't heard that there were any problems. They just haven't heard from him. They're in the dark, just as we are."

"What do you make of it, Amos?" Noah asked, his voice faltering—betraying the dread he felt.

"I don't know what to make of it. There have been no announcements from Sudan of any allegations involving journalists who were in Khartoum for the summit. If they ran into any trouble with the Sudanese government, we'll hear from them. *Desert Song* has made an official inquiry to the Sudanese about Dany and Alexandra. If the Sudanese are holding them for any reason, we'll know very shortly."

"Would the Sudanese have any reason to hold them?"

"Well, they wouldn't have had any reason to hold Dany."

"What is that supposed to mean?" Noah asked.

"While Alexandra had authentic travel documents, they were issued in a phony name. That wasn't the smartest thing to do when traveling to a place like Sudan. On the other hand, she would not have been doing anything that would have been of concern to the Sudanese. I don't think they would have discovered the name discrepancy. I'd be surprised if there's any issue with the government there."

"So what do we do now?"

"We'll check with the hotel to see if they checked out when they were scheduled to. Dany was reserved at the Grand in Khartoum. I presume Alexandra was too."

"Yeah, I guess she was," Noah replied, sadly.

"Don't jump to any conclusions, Noah. We know they didn't make their plane back to Nicosia last Friday. If they checked out of the hotel Friday morning as planned, they're either still in Khartoum or traveling around in the area. There's a lot going on in southern Sudan and in Darfur that could keep a couple of journalists like Alexandra and Dany very busy, and, for what it's worth, phone service would be practically nonexistent in those regions."

"So, do you think they're all right?"

"I think the odds are just as good they are as they aren't. Let's not guess. Noah, I'll call you as soon as we have any additional information. Karen gave me your itinerary, so I'll know where to find you."

"OK. Thanks, Amos."

Noah turned to Karen and shrugged. "I don't know if I should feel better or worse after hearing from Amos. I hadn't thought of it before, but it would be like Alexandra to look into the situation in Darfur or southern Sudan while she was in Sudan. I just don't understand why she didn't tell me where she was going or why she wouldn't have called by now."

"She knew you would worry, and she's probably not within a hundred miles of a telephone. I think Amos is right. It makes sense. They're probably in Darfur or southern Sudan preparing to win a Pulitzer. Did she say anything about traveling under an assumed name?"

"No. She didn't mention that," he replied.

"I think Amos has it right. It makes perfect sense that they would want to get as much done as they could, being so close to those other news spots."

"Yeah, I guess so," Noah agreed. "If there was something else to cover in the area, Alexandra would find that very tempting."

"Hungry?" she asked, changing the subject.

"No, but let's grab something to eat anyway."

"We can order room service and have something sent up to the suite."

"That sounds like a great idea. I really don't feel like running out," he said.

Noah and Karen chatted over a prime-rib dinner and a bottle of cabernet sauvignon. They discussed the meetings that were planned for the following day. Karen said she expected around seventy-five analysts and portfolio managers at the hotel luncheon, and she also lined up a breakfast meeting and a dinner meeting, after which they were scheduled to fly out to Chicago to begin the Midwest leg of the road show the following Monday.

A hotel attendant came to roll the room-service table from the suite around nine o'clock. They were both relaxed, having enjoyed a generous meal and most of the cabernet. There was nothing more to discuss about the meetings planned for the next day. Karen could see that Noah was deep in thought, and she had little doubt about what or on whom he was focused. She got up, walked over to the clock radio on the desk, and turned it on. Slowly turning the dial, she stopped just as sound of the Casinos singing "Then You Can Tell Me Goodbye" began to drift from the speakers.

"Come on, Noah, let's dance," she said, reaching down to remove her shoes. "We need a change of pace."

He looked up at her and smiled. "The wine and the music do go well together," he said as he got to his feet.

They began to sway in each other's arms to the music.

"Kiss me each morning for a million years. Hold me each evening by your side."

Karen laid her head on his shoulder and lightly draped her arm around him.

"Tell me you'll love me for a million years. Then if it don't work out, then if it don't work out, then you can tell me good-bye."

Noah gently tightened his grasp around Karen's waist.

"Sweeten my coffee with a morning kiss. Soften my dreams with your sighs. Tell me you'll love me for a million years. Then if it don't work out, then if it don't work out, then you can tell me good-bye."

Karen slowly moved her hand to the back of Noah's neck.

"If you must go, oh no, I won't grieve. If you wait a lifetime before you leave."

They slowed, barely moving at all, swaying ever so slightly.

"Then if you must go, mmm, I won't tell you no. Just so that we can say we tried. Tell me you'll love me for a million years. Then if it don't work out, then if it don't work out, then you can tell me good-bye."

They held on to one another for several moments, the separation between their bodies gone. He pulled back enough to look down at her. Her eyes glistened with tears. Noah gently pulled her up and embraced her, her toes barely touching the floor. They stood clinging to one another for several seconds.

"I'm sorry, Karen. I shouldn't have done that," he said, easing her down. "The stress…the music…the wine…you…I just…"

"Go," she whispered. "I don't want you or me to have anything to regret."

He nodded and smiled. "Get some rest," he said, as he turned to go to his room.

"Yeah, you too," she replied.

Moments later, Karen slowly sank down into the sudsy, warm water in the oversize bathtub in the Copley's marble-cladded and mirrored bathroom. The lights were dimmed, and she closed her eyes to savor those few moments in Noah's arms.

CHAPTER THIRTY-SIX

Six thousand miles to the east, Alexandra stifled her cry as she lifted herself from the soiled hole over which she had squatted to relieve herself. The other women ignored her as she returned to the flimsy mattress Daoud had brought her. He hadn't come that evening to bring her food and water. The other women in the cell each gave her some of the food that had been brought to them from the outside as they had been doing for several days, but food was the last thing on her mind. Muhammad Faizel's threat was all she could think of. "They will line up for you. Sabirah. How long do you think you will be as beautiful as you are now? How long do you think you will live?" Soon it would be daybreak. Soon Muhammad Faizel would return.

Amos awakened to the sound of the phone on the nightstand next to his bed. It was six o'clock in the morning.

"Yeah?" he answered.

"Amos, you have to get here right away," the voice said.

"What's going on?"

"We don't know, but there's some guy calling from Gondar, Ethiopia, crying into the phone. We think he's calling for you. He's hard to understand, but it sounds like he's pleading for you."

"What does he want?"

THE EDEN LEGACY

"He won't say. He keeps crying, 'Miss Sabirah going to die if Mr. Ben Kaiyim don't come.' We don't know what he's talking about, but it sounds like he's trying to say your name."

Amos bolted from bed and threw on clothes as he rushed to his car. Ten minutes later he was at Mossad headquarters, where several colleagues were gathered around the speaker next to the phone on his desk. It was 6:20 in the morning.

"Amos Ben-Chaiyim, here," he yelled into the phone.

"You Amooz Bin Kaiyim?"

"Yes, yes. Who is this?"

"I'm Daoud. I drive Miss Sabirah and Mr. Dany in Khartoum."

"Where are they now? We're looking for them," Amos yelled into the phone.

"Oh, Mr. Amooz, something terrible, something terrible."

"What! What has happened?"

"Miss Sabirah in Omdurman."

"Omdurman section of Khartoum?" Amos asked, dumbfounded.

"In Omdurman Prison, Mr. Amooz. She in Omdurman Prison. Omdurman so bad, Mr. Amooz. Omdurman terrible place. Miss Sabirah say they…they going to kill her," Daoud replied, crying almost uncontrollably as he spoke.

"Are you in Gondar? In Ethiopia? I don't understand."

"I drive all night from Khartoum. Can no call Tel Aviv from Sudan."

"How did you know to call me here?"

"Miss Sabirah say call Amooz Bin Kaiyim at Mossad. She make me repeat name."

"When did you last see Miss Sabirah?"

"I bring her food and water and blankets. Food at Omdurman no good. Very bad. I bring her food and water. You come get her. Guards at Omdurman very bad. They will hurt Miss Sabirah. They will do terrible things," Daoud said as he cried into the phone. "You must come get Miss Sabirah."

"Do you know why they arrested her?" he asked.

"No. She not do anything wrong. I drive Miss Sabirah and Mr. Dany every day to summit conference. They not do anything wrong, Mr. Amooz. They arrest them when they get ready to leave hotel to come home. I see them get arrested. I was in hotel lobby to take them to airport."

"Did they take Mr. Dany with Miss Sabirah?"

"No, they take him another place."

"Where did they take Mr. Dany?

"Daoud not know. Probably Kober Prison. They drive Mr. Dany in that direction."

Amos turned to one of his colleagues gathered around the phone. "Call M16. Ask the Brits to find out why Sudan arrested Alexandra Salaman and Dany Haddad. Make sure they understand that Alexandra may have been using the name Sabirah Najat. Tell them it's extremely urgent—that a life may hang in the balance. Tell them Alexandra was taken to Omdurman Prison and that we think Dany Haddad was taken to Kober." He spoke into the phone, "Daoud, you said you drove all night. When can you return to Khartoum?"

"I try to go back right away. I go as soon as I can cross border. I have to bring Miss Sabirah food and water. She must not eat Omdurman Prison food. She die from that food and water."

"Tell her you found me."

"I try. They not let me talk to Miss Sabirah—only bring food and water, but I try."

"What you did was wonderful, Daoud."

"Please, Mr. Amooz, don't let them kill Miss Sabirah," Daoud begged.

"No. No, we won't let them do that, Daoud." Amos replied.

It took about an hour for the Brits to confirm that the Sudanese Ministry of Justice had no reports of arrests of any foreign nationals. No foreigner would be arrested, except for street crime, without orders from the central government.

"What do you make of that?" Amos asked.

"Assuming Alexandra Salaman and Dany Haddad are not pick-pockets, it sounds like it could be a rogue operation of some kind," one of the other Mossad agents replied. "There's no way a foreign national could be in Omdurman or Kober without the central government having sent them there, and we know from the Brits that that didn't happen. The Brits say those prisons are for petty criminals. They also confirm what the caller said. They're awful places. Amos, you should know the Brits say the guards at Omdurman commonly rape female prisoners. Maybe that's why they picked them up. Alexandra Salaman is one beautiful woman."

Amos winced. "Regardless of why they picked them up, someone there probably knows by now that Alexandra was traveling under a pseudonym on her travel documents. That's a serious offense. We have to get them out fast."

"That won't be so easy, Amos. The Sudanese government may not have arrested them, but they are the only people who can release them. They're technically at war with us and have very strained relations with the United States. Besides, Sudan is a bureaucratic nightmare. I don't know how we resolve this quickly," one of the agents said.

"We could ask the Swiss to look into it for us," someone suggested.

"No," Amos quickly replied. "Any government-to-government inquiry will kick off a process that will take days, maybe weeks, to navigate. We have to get Alexandra and Dany out of there fast."

"We certainly can't send any of our people into Omdurman to rescue Alexandra, and we're not even sure where they're holding Dany Haddad."

"I have an idea," Amos replied. "It's a long shot, but we don't have time to study a lot of different alternatives. I need to make some calls. Somebody call Benjamin Bar-Levy. Get him here as soon as possible. I'll need him to sign off on what I have in mind."

Amos looked up at the clock on the wall. It was seven o'clock in the morning in Tel Aviv. He hurried down the corridor to his office and grabbed the phone on his desk.

"Get me Noah Greenspan at the Copley Plaza Hotel in Boston," he instructed the switchboard attendant.

"It's midnight there," the voice said.

"I know what time it is there. Please call now."

The phone rang in the living room separating Noah's and Karen's rooms.

Noah jumped out of bed and hurried to the phone. Karen hurried from her room, fastening the tie on her robe as she rushed to the phone.

"Noah, it's Amos; we have some news."

"Is she all right?" Noah asked, afraid of what he was about to hear.

"We think so, but she's in real danger and in a bad place."

Noah tilted the phone away from his ear so that Karen could hear what was being said too. "I have Karen here by the phone too, Amos. What the hell has happened?"

"Alexandra and this Haddad fellow are in Khartoum. They're in prison."

"What! What in the hell are they still doing in Khartoum? How did they wind up in prison? What did they do?"

"It doesn't appear they did anything wrong, other than Alexandra traveling with a questionable travel document. Noah, we were able to get British intelligence to make some inquiries for us. The Sudanese government did not arrest them. They know nothing about them being arrested."

"I don't understand; you said they were in prison."

"They are. The city police, though, not the central government, apparently arrested them. Assuming they didn't commit some street crime, we think it could be a rogue police operation."

"But why? Why would they arrest them for no reason?"

"We don't know. What we do know is that she is in a terrible place right now, called Omdurman Prison, and we think they are holding her without having charged her with anything."

"Why would local cops do that?"

"We don't even want to think about that, Noah."

"Oh my God," Noah groaned. "Can we protest to the government of Sudan?"

"That's pretty problematic, Noah. First, we certainly can't, and your government has no diplomatic relations with Sudan. It would take weeks, even months, to go through normal diplomatic channels. And, don't forget, Alexandra is traveling with really questionable papers. It could be years to get her out if we protest to the Sudanese government."

"Are you saying there is nothing we can do about this?"

"Not through normal channels, Noah. We have to get her out of Omdurman fast. It's a horrible place, staffed by horrible people.

"Do you have a plan?"

"I think so, but it is going to take a good bit of money."

"What do you have in mind? Money is no object. I'll come up with whatever you need."

"I think it works to our advantage that the Sudanese government hasn't charged her with anything—at least not yet."

"What do you mean not yet?"

"Well, they could charge Alexandra with entering Sudan illegally—from Israel, no less. They haven't, because they don't officially know that she has been arrested or that she is in one of their prisons."

"So what are you suggesting?"

"That we arrange to ransom her and Dany."

"What!"

"I think I may be able to find an intermediary, someone they would recognize, who could call a very high-ranking Sudanese official and say he has learned that his fiancée or mistress has been apprehended on trumped-up charges by low-level Khartoum police and that he would be willing to pay to have her quietly released into his custody. He could say he believes the local police have arrested her simply because she is a foreigner and very beautiful and that he thinks they are mistreating her, maybe abusing her. Because there is no record of her having been arrested, they might go for it. He would send his private jet to whisk her out of Sudan before it becomes a scandal."

"Amos, that sounds pretty far-fetched. I mean the part about arresting her because she's so beautiful and, you know, abusing her."

"That's why it might work, Noah. And by the way, I'm not sure it's so far-fetched."

"Are you serious?"

"I'm very serious, Noah."

"How much money do you think it will take?"

"We would need to pay for a plane and dangle enough money in front of the right official to get the deal done quickly."

"How much?"

"Could you arrange to transfer a million dollars?"

"My God, you *are* serious."

"Can you do that?"

"Yeah, I can arrange to do that."

"Where am I supposed to transfer the money to?"

"I don't know yet. I'll have to get back to you, but I need to know we have the means to make a deal like this if I suggest it."

"Whom are you going to recruit to offer this bribe?"

"I'll have to get back to you with that answer."

"What are the chances of this working?"

"I have no idea. I'm hoping it's outrageous enough to work."

"How did you find out all of this?"

"Noah, Alexandra and Dany hired a driver in Khartoum, who, at a huge risk, drove all the way to Gondar in Ethiopia to call me. It is a miracle he was ever able to reach me. Alexandra told him to find me. He couldn't call from Sudan, so he drove all night to get to Gondar. He could have been jailed himself for trying to cross the border between Sudan and Ethiopia. He may be jailed yet trying to cross back into Sudan. He's bringing her food and water at Omdurman. If this works, it's because an incredible, poor Sudanese man risked his life for Alexandra."

"See if you can work out the details. I'll come up with the money," Noah said.

∗∗∗

Benjamin Bar-Levy rushed into the office as Amos sat there contemplating his next move.

"So our friend has gotten herself arrested in Khartoum. What the hell was she doing in Khartoum?" he asked.

"She was with four hundred other journalists covering the Arab summit."

"Why was she arrested?"

"We don't know. She obviously wasn't breaking any laws."

"For Christ's sake, Amos, she was breaking the law just being there."

"Benjamin, the Sudanese government doesn't even know she's there. They didn't have her arrested."

"She's in that hellhole in Omdurman, and the Sudanese government doesn't know she's there? Is that what you are saying?"

Amos looked up at Bar-Levy and just nodded.

"How long has she been in Omdurman?"

"Over a week."

"Who in the hell is holding her there?"

Amos shrugged. "We don't know."

"Someone has her imprisoned in Omdurman, and you're telling me the government is unaware that she's there?"

"Yes, that's what I'm telling you."

"My God, I can't imagine what she's been through. What do you propose doing?"

"Getting Alexandra and Dany Haddad out of there."

"How do you plan to do that?"

"Close the door, Benjamin."

CHAPTER
THIRTY-SEVEN

The front-desk clerk at the Palmer House in Chicago handed Noah a message as soon as he checked in, just before noon. It was marked urgent. Noah tore open the envelope as he walked to the elevator. The message simply read, "Call me as soon as you receive this message. Amos." Amos's office telephone number and his apartment telephone number were both typed under the message.

Noah called the office number first, assuming Amos would be working late.

"Ben-Chaiyim," the now-familiar voice answered.

"Amos, it's Noah."

"OK, Noah, here's what you need to do. I'm going to give you very specific instructions and very few details. We are not going to discuss any other details over the phone. Just do as I say and don't ask a lot of questions. Do you understand?"

"I understand," Noah replied.

"I need you to have your bank telegraph one million dollars to Piraeus Bank in Athens, Greece, with instructions to further transfer the funds to account number five-eight-three-zero-three-three-eight-seven-three-seven-nine, which is an account held in the Athens headquarters of Piraeus."

"Whose account is that?" Noah asked as he jotted down the name of the bank and the account number.

"I can't divulge that at this time."

"OK," Noah finally answered after a brief pause.

"Unfortunately, today is Saturday, and no funds will be transferred until Monday, but you should personally call whomever you deal with at your bank as soon as we hang up. Make sure the funds are transferred at the earliest possible moment. If all goes according to plan, we can have Alexandra and Dany Haddad out of Sudan within eight hours after Piraeus Bank receives a guarantee of funds."

"Does Alexandra know we're working on this to get her out?"

"No, Noah. Nothing will happen and nothing will be communicated until Piraeus opens Monday."

"Can I ask into whose accounts these funds are being transferred?"

"No, you cannot. I'm sorry, but this is all I can discuss with you at this time. We've arranged for an offer, a ransom of sorts, to be made for Alexandra and Dany's release. We won't know until that offer is made and is accepted whether this will work."

"Do you think this is going to work?"

"Stranger things have happened."

"That's not an answer."

"I don't have an answer, Noah."

"So the offer hasn't been made yet?"

"No. We can't make an offer without the funds in hand. If an offer were made and the funds turned out not to be available, it could be disastrous for Alexandra and Dany."

"Can we be sure that the funds will be returned if the offer is rejected?"

"I think so," Amos replied.

"You think so?"

"Yes."

"But you're not positive?"

"No. Once the transfer is initiated, Noah, we all have to hold our breath. We have to pray that our story is believed, that the offer is accepted, and…"

"And what?"

"That Alexandra and Dany are alive and in any condition to travel. They've been in custody a week now."

Noah's hands began to shake, and, for a moment, words stuck in his throat. "I'll…track down my banker," he finally said, his voice choked with emotion.

The plan was audacious. Following the war in June, a small team of Israeli intelligence officers, including Amos, began meeting with a group of Greek intelligence personnel assembled by Colonel George Papadopoulos. Papadopoulos, two months earlier, on April 21, had led a successful coup against the government of King Constantine. Colonel Papadopoulos and his Aprilianoi, as the other members of the junta were known, were eager to cooperate and pool intelligence with the Israelis. Amos became quite friendly with one of the senior members of the Greek intelligence team, Georgios Paulamarios, who was known to be very close to Papadopoulos.

Amos called Paulamarios in Athens immediately after he discussed his plan with Benjamin Bar-Levy. Bar-Levy thought Amos's plan was an extreme long shot, which was probably why he approved it. He liked the audacity of it. Amos explained to Paulamarios that Israeli intelligence believed that rogue prison personnel at Omdurman and, possibly, Kober Prison were holding Alexandra Salaman and Dany Haddad prisoner and that the Sudanese government was unaware of their imprisonment.

"Why would these rogue officers arrest Alexandra and Dany Haddad without their government's approval?" Paulamarios asked.

"We're not sure," Amos replied. "We know there is a terrorist cell that has targeted Alexandra, because she informed us of a terrorist plot she learned of several years ago when she was a student in Beirut. She was in Khartoum last week to cover the Arab summit for the *Washington Evening Star*, where she works as a reporter and columnist. What is strange is that we've confirmed that the Sudanese government does not know of her arrest. We're guessing someone involved with the prison nabbed them for the terrorists and never informed the government. In other words, they're using the prison to hold them—maybe kill them—but Sudan doesn't know it."

"What is Dany Haddad's role in all of this?" Paulamarios asked.

"He had no role. We think they grabbed him because he was traveling with Alexandra."

"What is your interest in this?"

"Well, first, Alexandra Salaman helped us avert a massacre."

"There's more?"

"Yes, there is. I, personally, have a very strong attachment to this woman. She is incredibly beautiful, and I'm very worried about what they have done, or might yet do, to her in that hellhole of Omdurman."

"What do you want us to do?"

"Ransom them. It's risky, but here's what we think might work," Amos answered.

***

"You, come!" the guard commanded, as he unlocked the cell door. Alexandra got to her feet and walked to the guard. He was a huge man. He took her by the arm and, after locking the cell door, began walking down the corridor toward Muhammad Faizel's office, pulling Alexandra along with him. She had trouble keeping up, and as she lagged, the guard tightened his grip and yanked at her arm. Her lips were parched, her belly ached, and she couldn't bear facing another session with Muhammad Faizel.

"Ah, Sabirah, come in. Sit down," Inspector Faizel said as she entered his office.

"Here, have some water," he said, pouring into a glass from a pitcher on his desk. "It's OK. It's clean, not like the piss in there," he said, cocking his head back toward the cells. Alexandra took the glass and gulped down the warm water.

"Would you like something to eat?"

She shook her head. "No, can I have more water?"

He stood as he poured more water into her glass. "You see, things can be more pleasant, Sabirah."

She drank the second glass of water without taking her eyes from his.

"So, I have important news for you. Sit down, Sabirah." She sat down, warily, opposite him. "I have twice told my wife I am divorcing her. Tomorrow I will tell her for the third time, and then I will be free to have you," he said. She sat there for a moment weighing his words, not knowing how to respond. She shook her head as if to say no. "I will take you to my house tomorrow as soon as the cow I am married to leaves," he said.

"No, you won't. I will not come to your house."

"Oh, you'll come, Sabirah. You'll come."

"Never!" she answered.

Muhammad started to laugh. "Of course you'll come. Mustafa!" he yelled. With that, the guard who brought her to him entered the office.

"Stand up, Sabirah," Muhammad Faizel commanded. Alexandra rose to her feet, her heart pounding.

"Come here, Mustafa." Muhammad Faizel walked around his desk, took Alexandra by the arm, and pulled her toward the guard until she was facing him, their bodies almost touching. Alexandra's chest heaved with every breath. Muhammad put his hand on the small of her back and nudged her even closer to Mustafa. They were standing face-to-face, their clothes touching as they breathed. Muhammad Faizel walked back around his desk and sat down again. Alexandra turned to face him.

"Turn back to Mustafa," Muhammad Faizel yelled. "Look at him. Look into his eyes and don't look anywhere else." Alexandra and the guard stood facing one another, their bodies almost touching. She thought she detected fear on his face. Muhammad Faizel sat there watching them, waiting in anticipation. Alexandra gasped, and her body trembled as the guard became aroused and she felt him against her. Mustafa's breathing increased. His face turned grim.

"So, Sabirah," Muhammad Faizel began. "Would you like to come home with me tomorrow or stay here with Mustafa today? From what

I can see, Mustafa can take good care of you. Shall we have Mustafa take care of you?" Alexandra was breathing too rapidly to answer. She felt Mustafa pressing against her, his expression more of agony than anticipation. And then she collapsed onto the floor.

Meanwhile, not thirty minutes away, just over the White Nile Bridge in central Khartoum, Ali Ahmed Hussein, Sudanese minister of foreign trade, was getting an earful from Petros Kourtras, chairman of Aegean Marine Group, one of the world's largest shipping lines and the largest shipping line servicing Port Sudan. The shipping magnate was screaming into the phone. "My fiancée, Alexandra Salaman, was picked up by goons from Omdurman Prison and has been held there for a week without having done anything wrong or broken any law. I've checked with the Ministry of Justice, and they have no record of anyone ordering her arrest. If there is a hair harmed on her head, no ship of the Aegean Group will ever enter Port Sudan again, and I can assure you no other Greek ship will ever see your port again either," Kourtras yelled into the phone. "Your damn cotton and sesame seeds can rot on the dock."

"There...There must be some mistake," the minister of trade stammered.

"There's no damned mistake," Kourtras screamed back. "She was in Khartoum for the summit. I was going to call Ismail al-Azhari himself, but you and I have been friends for a long time, so I'm calling you, but so help me, I'll call al-Azhari if I have to. Some of your damn police have kidnapped my fiancée, and I believe they are abusing her. They're holding her colleague, Dany Haddad, too. It's an outrage. It's a scandal, Hussein!"

"Why would they do that?"

"Because they don't know who she is—that's why. She was there with Dany Haddad, a journalist, who was covering the summit. She's a prominent writer herself in the United States, a Palestinian American for heaven's sake. She writes under the pseudonym Sabirah Najat. I think they grabbed her because she's the most beautiful woman that's ever stepped foot in Khartoum, and they thought she was theirs for the taking. Well, they picked on the wrong woman. I'll make Port Sudan a pariah port. I've got a plane in the air right now that will land in Khartoum in five hours. My chief of staff, Amos Andropolis, is coming to get them, and they had better be ready at the airport when he arrives."

"Petros, we have procedures. I'll see to this as quickly as possible, but we must go through the proper channels. This is all highly irregular. It could take a few days."

"I'll tell you what is irregular, Ali. Kidnapping a woman and imprisoning her and, I think, abusing her because some goons think they can get away with it. That's what's irregular. I have already checked with your Ministry of Justice. They know nothing of her arrest. It's a rogue operation, Ali. My fiancée is the victim, and I won't stand for it."

"What do you want me to do?"

"Mr. Andropolis will have five hundred thousand American dollars with him when he arrives. He'll give that to you for your trouble. In return you deliver Miss Salaman and Mr. Haddad to him. You get that done, or I'm telling you, no Greek ship will ever enter Port Sudan again."

Ninety minutes passed before Alexandra was fully conscious, having wafted in and out of consciousness several times after collapsing on the floor in Muhammad Faizel's office. She opened her eyes, squinting against the light shining down from the ceiling fixture. She tried to fathom what was happening. Dany was standing there, bending down over her. An oscillating portable electric fan was positioned on the floor next to her, sending breezes of warm but welcomed air over her body.

"Dany?"

"Yes, Alexandra, it's me. This is Ahmed Kareem. He is a deputy to the Sudanese minister of foreign trade," Dany replied, motioning toward a man in a full-length, flowing white dishdasha.

Alexandra reached out for Dany's hand. "Help me up, Dany. Help me to the chair." Dany and the Sudanese official each assisted Alexandra to her feet. "What's happened?" she asked as she sat down in the chair.

"Miss Salaman, you and Mr. Haddad here have been the victims of a terrible miscarriage of justice, a serious crime, actually. I can assure you those responsible will be severely punished. Your fiancé, Petros Kourtras, has sent a plane for you. His chief of staff, Amos Andropolis, is personally coming to escort you and Mr. Haddad back to Athens," the man said. "Please accept our deepest apologies. The people of Sudan would never condone what has happened to you."

Alexandra tried to concentrate on what she had been told. Petros Kourtras, her fiancé? The name meant nothing to her. And then the name Amos Andropolis, the name Amos Ben-Chaiyim had used when he first contacted her when she was a student in Beirut. She glanced over to Dany. He smiled, nodding ever so slightly. "My fiancé has sent a plane for us?" she asked.

"Yes, he learned what had happened. Someone, thankfully, got word to him. We will take you to the airport to meet the plane as soon as you feel well enough to make the drive. Mr. Andropolis is going to escort you back to Athens."

"Mr. Andropolis? Amos Andropolis?"

"Yes, Mr. Amos Andropolis. He is Mr. Koutras's chief of staff. I thought you would know him."

Alexandra smiled and nodded. "Yes, of course. Amos Andropolis." Alexandra decided not to ask any more questions. Amos was, somehow, involved in the rescue scheme that was in progress. She was, of course, totally confused about the involvement of Petros Kourtras, the name of her supposed fiancé, and a name totally unknown to her. "Let's go," she said. "I'm ready."

She and Dany were escorted out of Omdurman Prison and to a waiting Bentley T1 black sedan. The government official from the Foreign Trade Ministry followed behind them for the thirty-minute drive to the airport. They were driven to a hangar not far from the main passenger terminal. They waited on the tarmac for about a half hour at a spot shaded by the hangar. Then, the deputy foreign trade minister pointed to a sleek white Learjet 24 that was about to touch down on the airport's sole runway. "That would be your fiancé's plane," he said.

"Yeah, it sure looks like it," she replied, smiling.

A few minutes later, the Learjet taxied to the hanger. Alexandra studied the plane curiously. It had wingtip auxiliary fuel tanks on each wing. The letters *AMG* were painted on the tail, and *Aegean Marine Group* was emblazoned in blue script along the entire length of the fuselage. The plane was still whining loudly as it pulled up close to where they were standing before coming to a stop. The engine noise decreased rapidly, but the pilot kept the engine running. The stairway unfolded from the side of the plane, and Amos Ben-Chaiyim, dressed in a business suit, appeared at the top of the stairs. Alexandra stifled a cry and the urge to yell his name. Dany watched, dumbfounded, as Amos hurriedly descended the stairs carrying a briefcase. He walked past Alexandra and up to Ahmed Kareem. "You are Ahmed Kareem?" he asked.

"I am," the deputy foreign trade minister replied.

"May I see some identification?"

Ahmed Kareem reached into a leather shoulder bag and extracted a Sudanese identification card. Amos studied the card carefully for a moment and then returned it and handed the man the briefcase. Just as the Sudanese deputy trade minister turned to leave, another car came speeding through the open gate to the tarmac. It was a black Land Rover.

"Daoud!" Alexandra screamed.

"You know who this is?" Ahmed Kareem asked, startled.

"Yes, he's a friend who has come to say good-bye. He brought me food at Omdurman. Someone must have told him we had come to the airport."

"Very well, then," Ahmed Kareem said. "I will bid you farewell. Have a pleasant journey, Miss Salaman, and please accept our apologies." Ahmed Kareem turned and walked back toward his car, nodding at Daoud as he passed him.

"I came to Omdurman with food and water for you, Miss Sabirah, and they told me at Omdurman you had gone to airport. I come to say good-bye."

"You are Daoud who called me in Tel Aviv?" Amos asked.

"You Mr. Amooz?"

"Yes," Amos replied. "I'm Mr. Amooz."

"Daoud, what are you going to do now?" Alexandra asked.

Daoud shrugged. "I drive people in Khartoum," he answered, as tears welled up in his eyes.

"You can't stay here in Khartoum, Daoud. They will put you away when they realize what has happened."

"What can I do, Miss Sabirah? Khartoum only place I know."

"Daoud, come with us. Come with me to America. You'll have political asylum in America."

"What I do in America, Miss Sabirah?"

"You'll be with me and my family and my fiancé. You'll be safe."

"We have to go," Amos interrupted. "We're really pushing our luck standing here like this."

Deputy Minister Kareem stopped at the fence and turned to observe the curious spectacle unfolding on the tarmac.

Alexandra grabbed Daoud's arm. "Please, Daoud. Please come with us. It will be good. It will be much better, much safer for you in America," she pleaded.

"Daoud, listen to Miss Alexandra—Miss Sabirah. It will be an entirely new life for you," Dany said.

"We have to go now," Amos said, urgently, as the deputy minister, sensing that something was wrong, began to slowly walk back toward them.

Alexandra tugged at Daoud's arm. "Please, please, come with us, Daoud." He paused for a moment, tears streaming down his face.

"OK! OK, I come to America," he finally said.

"Board quickly," Amos said. "We have to get out of here."

As soon as they were on board, the copilot retracted the stairs and locked the door shut. The Learjet turned and began rolling across the tarmac, even before they were seated, and headed onto the airport's single long asphalt runway and raced north, full throttle, without waiting for clearance from the control tower.

"Amos!" Alexandra screamed joyously. "What just happened?"

"What just happened is that Daoud here saved your lives," he answered. He then explained the audacious scheme he and the Mossad worked out with Greek intelligence. "We recruited Petros Kourtras, who is chairman of Aegean Marine Group, to intervene on your behalf."

"My fiancé, Petros Kourtras?" she asked, more a statement than a question.

"It's a very long story. You can't imagine the risk Daoud here took to free you. Alexandra, he drove all the way to Gondar Ethiopia, talked his way across the border to call me, and then made his way back to Khartoum."

"I was quite certain we were going to die back there," Dany said.

"My fate would have been worse than death," Alexandra murmured. "You can't imagine what I've been through." Then, almost as an afterthought, Alexandra looked at Amos, quizzically. "Amos, what was in the briefcase you handed to the man from the Foreign Trade Ministry?" she asked.

Amos smiled. "Your ransom," he answered.

"No, really. What was in the briefcase?"

"Five hundred thousand American dollars," he replied.

"Are you serious?" she asked, wide-eyed with astonishment.

Amos nodded.

"Where did you get that kind of money?"

He smiled. "Noah Greenspan loves you very much. You can be absolutely sure of that."

"Noah," she said in a whisper as she fell back in her seat.

"I went by the Dan and grabbed a change of clothes for you from your closet and dresser," Amos said. "When we reach cruising altitude, you'll find fresh things in the head to change into."

"Thank you, Amos. You always did think of everything. I'd like to burn what I'm wearing. I never want to see any of this clothing again."

"We'll have to take Daoud shopping for a new wardrobe too," Amos replied.

"Amos, will we have any trouble clearing Daoud into Israel and then into the United States?" she asked.

"Kind of late to ask that question," he replied, laughing.

"Really, Amos. Daoud couldn't remain in Sudan."

"I think I'll be able to walk him though immigration at Tel Aviv. Getting him through Immigration in the States is going to be a bit more challenging."

"Surely, he'll qualify for political asylum," she replied.

"Of course he will, but there's a complicated process for securing political asylum. You can't just show up and have it handed to you. You have to apply for it—petition for it."

"Can the Israeli government help?"

"Of course. Daoud is a very special case. He saved an American citizen, a journalist, from torture and certain death. Ordinarily we would talk directly with Secretary of State Rusk, but he's not too happy with us right now. In fact, he's furious about the *Liberty* fiasco—the American ship your people attacked."

"I remember," she said, nodding.

"What a fuckup," he replied.

"So what should we do?"

"I'll talk to Bar-Levy. He'll know whom to call—maybe Rusk's deputy, Cyrus Vance. The circumstances are so compelling that I'm sure we'll get it worked out. Fortunately, the government of Israel owns El Al. It would be impossible to clear Daoud to fly commercially without a passport. We'll have to arrange for someone from the States to meet your El Al flight when it arrives at JFK and walk Daoud through immigration," he said. "He'll be in your charge, Alexandra."

Alexandra sat there contemplating everything that had happened in the past few hours. She turned and looked out as the Learjet flew over Port Sudan, heading toward the Red Sea. The plane banked north and raced between Sudan and Saudi Arabia, its course set for Tel Aviv. She smiled as the moon rose far in the distance over the curvature of the earth.

CHAPTER THIRTY-EIGHT

Noah and Karen were meeting in the suite, going over the details for the luncheon that would begin shortly in one of the Palmer House banquet rooms, when they were interrupted by the chime of the doorbell. As soon as he opened the door, a bellman handed Noah an envelope marked urgent. He tipped the bellman and tore open the envelope. Karen watched as he suddenly burst into tears, shaking with emotion. She jumped up and ran to him.

"What is it, Noah?" she cried, fearing the worst.

He handed her the message.

From: Aviation Depart: Aegean Marine Group, Athens, Greece
        "Wheels up at Khartoum—everyone safe."

It was four o'clock that afternoon before the call finally came through from Tel Aviv. "Alexan…" he cried, before breaking down, too emotionally wrought to finish even saying her name.

"Noah, I'm OK, I'm OK. I'm back at the Dan in Tel Aviv. I'm exhausted, but I'm OK. Noah, I love you!" she cried into the phone.

"Oh God, I love you too, Alexandra. I was so worried about, you."

"I've been to hell and back, Noah. You can't imagine what happened to me, but I'm OK, and I'm safe."

"I can't wait to see you, Alexandra."

"I'm flying home tomorrow, Noah. The El Al flight leaves Tel Aviv at four o'clock in the afternoon—that's nine in the morning your time—and arrives at JFK at nine o'clock tomorrow night."

"I'll cancel the rest of my meetings this week and meet your flight."

"You'll do no such thing. Continue what you're doing. I'll spend Wednesday with my folks, square away some things at the *Star*, and fly to wherever you'll be Friday. Call them and call Yusuf and tell them I'm all right."

"Of course," he answered. "They'll be so relieved. They've been worried sick."

"Where should I come to meet you?" she asked.

"We'll be in Los Angeles. We finish up in Dallas this week, and we're flying to LA Friday afternoon to begin the West Coast leg of the tour. We'll be staying at the Beverly Hills Hotel. Let me know your flight information when you have it squared away, and we'll plan to meet your flight."

"I can't wait to see you," she said.

"You're OK, Alexandra?"

"I'm fine now, Noah. It was horrible. I…I don't want to talk about it now."

"But you're OK."

"I'm OK. I think I'll have nightmares about what happened for a long time, but, yes, I'm OK."

"Amos has been incredible," Noah said.

"Noah, you don't know the half of it. He actually flew into Khartoum pretending to be the chief of staff of the Greek shipping magnate who got Dany and me out of Sudan. Oh, and, Noah, he told me about the ransom—the five hundred thousand dollars you paid."

Noah laughed. "I wonder if that means I'm getting back change."

"You are!" she answered, laughing. "Amos told me the bank in Greece is wiring back the unspent money. And, Noah, our Sudanese driver, Daoud, risked his life to get word to Amos. He actually drove through the night to Gondar, Ethiopia, to call Amos. He had to talk his way out of Sudan and into Ethiopia. None of this would have worked had it not been for Daoud. Noah, you can't imagine what would have happened to me if I had been forced to remain there one more day. Daoud is coming back to the States with me, and we have to get him political asylum in America. The Israelis are working with people in the State Department so that Daoud can fly back with me."

"I'll have our corporate attorneys talk to their firm's immigration lawyers," Noah replied. "We'll have to find a place for him to stay."

"I already have."

"Really? Where?"

"With you."

"With me!"

"Yeah, you have plenty of room, and Amos said we'd need an address for Daoud in America. I think you should hire Daoud at Potomac Center. Maybe, once he learns his way around Washington, he can be your driver."

"I don't need a driver," Noah replied, laughing.

"Well, maybe Potomac Center should have a driver," she replied.

"You're serious, aren't you?"

"He saved my life, Noah."

"He actually got word to Amos that you were in danger?"

"Noah, there is so much to tell you. But yes, Daoud and Amos, and my Greek fiancé, absolutely saved our lives."

"Your Greek fiancé?"

"Yes, seems I'm engaged to one of the biggest shipping magnates in the world. He paid the bribe—well, you actually did—and he sent his company plane to come get us. By the way, Amos is flying back with us too. He has meetings with the FBI about the Shoukri terrorist cell."

"Were they involved in this?"

"It's a long story. I'll fill you in on what I know when I see you. Tell Karen Amos will be with me when we get back to the States."

"I will. See if he can fly out to the coast with you.

"I'll mention that to him. I don't know what his schedule will be once he gets to Washington."

***

"She got away?" Omar Samir asked, in disbelief. "How in the world could she have gotten away? I thought we had her in a bottomless pit and that no one other than your Alliance member even knew she was being held."

"That's true, Omar. She was in Omdurman, and the Haddad fellow was in Kober Prison. No one in the Sudanese government knew we had them. I told my contact there that he could do with her as he pleased, as long as no one else in the government knew she was there. Those prisons are bottomless pits," Hamid Abdullah Hamishi replied.

"So how did she get out?"

"All I know is that her fiancé, some big Greek shipping executive, learned she was in Omdurman, and he apparently bribed someone to get them both out. I heard he sent a private plane for them."

"That is crazy. She's not engaged to a Greek businessman. She's engaged to some Jew in America."

"That's all I know, Omar. That's what I've been told."

"You think she's in Greece?"

"I don't know what to think. All I know is that she slipped away."

"OK, Hamid, OK. Thank you for trying to help us. I think she'll be back in Washington very soon. I'm not through with her yet."

***

KHARTOUM AND THE THREE NO'S—PLUS ONE OTHER
By Alexandra Salaman

Perhaps the rest of the world can add a fourth no to the three no's embraced by the kings, emirs, and presidents who met at the Arab League summit in Khartoum, Sudan, two weeks ago. They pledged that there would be no negotiation, no recognition, and no peace with Israel. It now seems safe to add a fourth no—no hope for the region.

Wiser minds did not prevail at Khartoum, although they were there. This reporter watched with other journalists who were there to cover this historic meeting as a parade of sleek new limousines delivered the Arab heads of state to the Khartoum summit for their deliberations during the two-and-a-half-day conference. While the official statement released in Khartoum implied solidarity and a united front among the defeated Arabs, those of us who were there know better. Bitter disputes raged behind closed doors, but word invariably leaked to those of us who were on the other side of those closed doors.

The not-so-secret secret plan offered by Yugoslavia's Marshall Tito for Egypt and Jordan to begin to disentangle from perpetual belligerency without any formal recognition of Israel was roundly rejected. King Hussein is rumored to have proposed allowing a narrow path for the Jews to travel to the Western Wall in return for Israel vacating the West Bank, including the Old City of Jerusalem, and the league also rejected that idea. No doubt the Israelis would have too.

President Nasser, who has lost the most in lives, treasure, and territory in the ongoing fighting with Israel, was apparently prepared to reopen the Straits of Tiran to Israeli ships as long as those ships didn't openly fly the Israeli flag. While it is doubtful that the Israelis would have accepted these morsels from King Hussein or President Nasser (why would they, given their hard-won gains on the West Bank, Sinai, Golan, and entire Gulf of Aqaba), it may have signaled a beginning. A beginning of a process that is probably inevitable, sooner or later anyway. Reliable sources have indicated that Israel was prepared to give back to Egypt all of the Sinai in return for a peace agreement ending the state of belligerency between the two countries. That, too, was rejected. Alas, it seems as if the Arab League is ready, willing, and eager to fight Israel to the last Egyptian soldier.

Perhaps the most interesting but least reported aspect of the summit was the fury hurled at the participants by Ahmed Shukeiri, the lawyer who chairs the executive committee of the Palestine National Council, which is the legislative body of the Palestine Liberation Organization (PLO). He reportedly fumed at the manner in which the participants gave short shrift to the priorities of the Palestinian people. In a pique of anger, Shukeiri stormed from the meeting and didn't return. Given his close ties to the largely discredited Egyptian president, Abdul Gamel Nasser, his days at the helm of the PLO may well be limited. Standing in the wings to replace him are Yahya Hammuda, yet another lawyer, and Yasser Arafat, a firebrand who heads a faction of the PLO known as al-Fatah. Arafat wants to lead a Palestinian armed struggle against Israel, something he has advocated since his days as a student at Cairo University, where he was president of the Union of Palestinian Students.

If there were voices of moderation at the summit, it would seem they were too quiet to influence the outcome. Meanwhile, Israeli officials are publicly wringing their hands over the Arab League's three no's as tantamount to Arab rejection of the Jewish nation's right to exist. Privately, however, some of these handwringers are breathing a sigh of relief. Rather than wringing their hands in worry, they are rubbing their hands together in anticipation. They see the three no's of Khartoum as a green light to begin aggressively settling the West Bank—land they view as ancient Judea and Samaria given to them by God Almighty. It is almost as though Ze'ev Jabotinsky's vision is being fulfilled. All that is missing is the East Bank.

CHAPTER
THIRTY-NINE

Noah and Karen waited at the gate at LAX for the flight from Dulles. It was the middle of September, and Noah hadn't seen Alexandra since the Six-Day War in early June. While they had spoken at least once a day since her return, he felt like she had been gone for years. Noah waited impatiently as the passengers began disembarking from the United McDonnell Douglas DC-10. They came through the Jetway door in groups, clusters of men and women, a few at a time. And then she appeared, a little thinner, he thought, but beautiful as ever. She paused to quickly survey the crowd who had come to greet friends and relatives as they exited the airplane.

"Alexandra!" Noah called to her. She spotted him and ran, half laughing and half crying, into his waiting arms. He hugged her tightly as she clung to him, neither wanting to let go of the other.

"I don't ever want to be away from you again," she cried as she pulled away from him. "Oh, Noah, I thought I was never going to see you again."

"Let me look at you," he replied, holding her at arm's length for a moment before clutching her tightly in his embrace again.

Amos and Daoud followed behind Alexandra. Daoud stood by, speechlessly, as Karen embraced Amos.

"So, you're the Noah I've heard so much about over the years," Amos said as he turned and shook Noah's hand.

"Amos!" Noah replied, somewhat emotionally. "Amos, I'm forever indebted to you. I don't know all of the details, but I do know you somehow managed to pull off an incredible rescue to free Alexandra."

"Here's the man who gets all of the credit, Noah," Amos replied, gently pulling Daoud over to meet Noah. "I arranged a scheme to free Alexandra. Daoud here really risked his life to get to me so that I could do that. What he pulled off was a real miracle, and it is a miracle that Daoud is alive and here in America today."

Noah turned to Daoud. The tall, lanky Nubian from Sudan stood there, unsure how to respond, a bit overwhelmed by the crowds exiting and entering Jetways all around them. Noah extended his hand, and Daoud clasped Noah's hand in both of his.

"I'm so happy, Miss Sabirah—I mean Miss Alexandra—safe," he finally managed to say, tears in his eyes.

"Welcome to America, Daoud. I can never thank you enough for what you have done for Alexandra, and for me."

"No, no, Mr. Noah. Daoud in America. Imagine that. Daoud is forever indebted to you," he responded.

The limousine Noah had hired was waiting at the curb as they exited the terminal. Daoud chuckled as he climbed into the sleek Lincoln Continental. "I waited my whole life to be a passenger—to ride in the backseat," he said as they headed out toward Beverly Hills. The evening traffic crawled slowly north on the San Diego Freeway, stopping frequently as cars jockeyed to change lanes.

"Daoud never see so many cars. Looks like every car in America on this road," he said.

"Not even every car in Los Angeles is on this road, Daoud. This city has freeways like this everywhere, and they're all busy like this."

"What kind of car did you drive in Khartoum?" Karen asked.

"Land Rover. Old Land Rover probably still sitting at airplane hangar in Khartoum," he said, laughing at the thought.

Noah had already registered Amos and Daoud at the hotel and saw to it that they both had comfortable accommodations. After dropping off their luggage, they all gathered for snacks and drinks in the suite Karen had arranged for herself and Alexandra and Noah, as she had in every city in which they had been traveling. The living room and bar area, positioned between the two bedrooms, was generously sized and well furnished and featured large bay windows that looked out over the grounds and Sunset Boulevard beyond.

They talked at great length about the audacious rescue of Alexandra and Dany and, in greater detail, about Daoud's harrowing drive to get to a telephone from which he could reach Tel Aviv.

While Alexandra discussed the horrible conditions at Omdurman, she chose not to discuss her personal encounters with Muhammad Faizel, other than to say that she didn't think she would be alive or would have wanted to be alive had she had to remain there for another day.

Noah looked at her as she spoke and simply shook his head in disbelief, contemplating how close he came to losing her.

"So, Amos," Karen interrupted during a pause in the conversation, "you're here to meet with the FBI?"

He nodded. "Yes, we're quite concerned about a particular terrorist cell. It's called the Ali Abdul Shoukri Liberation Front. We think they were probably responsible for Alexandra's arrest in Khartoum, and we have reason to believe they may be planning something in the United States."

"That's the group that—"

"Yes, it's the group named for the man—a student whom I met in Beirut," Alexandra said, interrupting Karen's question. "He was planning a massacre and was using the timing of my stories in the *Evening Star* to send messages to his accomplices in Israel."

"And you think this group had something to do with Alexandra's imprisonment in Khartoum?" Noah asked.

"We don't know for sure, but it looks that way."

"What makes you think so?"

"Well, you remember that *Evening Star* story that ran Alexandra's picture over the name Sabirah Najat."

"I'll never forget it," Noah replied.

"Well, Alexandra's jailer, this Muhammad Faizel, had a copy of a newsletter published by an anti-Israel group called the Trans-Arab Alliance. The newsletter, called *Cultural Jihad*, reprinted that column with Alexandra's picture. In fact, we've learned that they ran all of Alexandra's columns from Israel."

"That's true. He took the newsletter out of his desk drawer when he was interrogating me."

"What does that have to do with Alexandra's arrest?" Karen asked.

"We asked ourselves that question too, Karen. We were able to obtain the list of all the credentialed journalists who were covering the Khartoum conference. One of them was Hamid Abdulla Hashimi. Hashimi is the executive director of the Trans-Arab Alliance. He publishes the newsletter that ran Alexandra's picture over the name Sabirah Najat."

"And we ran into Hashimi at the Grand Hotel in Khartoum," Alexandra said.

"What does that prove?" Noah asked.

"Maybe nothing. But we think Muhammad Faizel must have been a member of the Alliance. That's the only reason he would have had a copy of *Cultural Jihad* in his desk drawer. So, bear with me. Hamid Abdulla Hashimi runs into Alexandra and recognizes her. Now suppose this anti-Israel Alliance has members who were cohorts of Ali Abdul Shoukri and one of them recognized Alexandra's picture in *Cultural Jihad* and knew she wasn't anyone named Sabirah Najat. Suppose they knew she was really Alexandra Salaman, the journalist who was responsible for the martyrdom of Shoukri, and suppose they contacted Hashimi and told him that the picture he ran in *Cultural Jihad* was not Sabirah Najat but Alexandra Salaman."

"Connect the dots for me, Amos," Noah replied.

"Hashimi knows the Alliance has a member in Khartoum who happens to be an official at Omdurman Prison, Muhammad Faizel. I think it's plausible that Hashimi knew there was a price on Alexandra's head and he knew that Faizel could pick her up and imprison her at Omdurman and no one would ever hear from her again. The Sudanese government wouldn't even know she was being held there. In fact, we confirmed that they didn't know she was there. Why would a jailer have Alexandra arrested without being ordered to by his government and hold her there without any charges being filed against her? She was, essentially, his private prisoner."

"Unbelievable," Noah said.

"I think Amos is right, "Alexandra interjected. "Faizel did wave that damned *Cultural Jihad* rag in front of me, and he insisted the first time he questioned me that I was really Sabirah Najat and not Alexandra Salaman. It was awful. He had my American passport identifying me as Alexandra Salaman and my Arab League travel documents that identified me as Sabirah Najat. He said the *Cultural Jihad* newsletter, which ran my picture over the name Sabirah Najat, proved whom I really was. He also said, in no uncertain terms, that I was his prisoner and not the Sudanese government's prisoner. I asked him what he was going to do with me, and he answered, 'Anything I want.'"

"So, we have a very bizarre, illegal arrest and ask ourselves why," Amos continued. "The one thing that seems to tie Muhammad Faizel to anything at all outside of his world at Omdurman Prison is that damned *Cultural Jihad* newsletter. It ties Faizel to Hashimi, and we're betting Hashimi has ties to the Ali Abdul Shoukri Liberation Front. Imprisoning Alexandra at Omdurman as Faizel's private prisoner would have been the Shoukri Front's grand retribution for her perceived treachery."

"You can't imagine what he made me do and what he was about to do to me," Alexandra said. "Another twenty-four hours and—"

"Let's not talk about it," Noah said, putting his arm around her.

"I wouldn't be here if it were not for you, Daoud. You brought me food and water at Omdurman, and you risked your life to reach Amos."

"Daoud, you'll stay with me in Washington," Noah said. "And after Alexandra and I are married, you'll live with us. We have plenty of room, and you'll have plenty of privacy. Meanwhile, I'll have some-one show you around Washington and familiarize you with our crazy street grid so that once we get your status resolved and get you a driv-er's license, you can drive for Potomac Center."

"Washington streets must be much more complicated than in Khartoum," Daoud replied, laughing.

"If you found your way to Gondar, Ethiopia, you'll find your way around Washington just fine," Noah answered.

It was midnight before they broke up. Daoud returned to his room, and Alexandra and Noah left Karen and Amos in the living room and retired to their bedroom. Noah carefully closed and turned the latch on the two back-to-back doors separating their bedroom from the rest of the suite. He walked over to Alexandra and took her in his arms. "I want to set a date for our wedding," he said, as he kissed her. "I've never missed anyone so much or worried about anyone as I've worried about you."

"There was a time back there in Sudan when I couldn't imagine ever seeing you again," she said, as tears filed her eyes. "Noah, it was so horrible. I was in a primitive dungeon, the prisoner of a madman, and no one knew I was there."

"Except Daoud," Noah replied.

"Except Daoud," she said.

"Well, now you're ten thousand miles from that sick part of the world, and you're here in America and in my arms."

Moments later, lying in bed together, he pulled her naked body close. "I love you so much," he said.

She looked into his eyes and smiled. "I love you too, Noah."

"My beautiful Alexandra," he whispered.

And, suddenly, she heard the voice of Muhammad Faizel. "My God, you are a beauty," he had taunted her, as she stood before him, naked. Alexandra's body shook as she began to relive that moment.

"Alexandra, what is it?" Noah asked, startled by the tremor he felt in her body and the fear he saw on Alexandra's face.

"Hold me tight, Noah. Hold me," she cried.

Noah held her as tightly as he dared. She embraced him, clinging to him as her breathing slowly returned to normal.

"I was reminded of something that happened to me at Omdurman," she said.

"Did something I said remind you of Omdurman?" he asked.

She nodded. "Faizel said, 'My God, you are a beauty.'"

"And you were..."

"Naked," she answered.

Noah pulled her even closer, as she buried her head in his shoulder and wept. They lay there, silently, in each other's arms for nearly an hour, their breathing the only sound in the room. He softly kissed her closed eyes and stroked her head tenderly as she clung to him. She reached up and kissed him. Noah reciprocated, slowly and then more urgently, and as he became aroused, he felt Alexandra begin to tremble. He pulled back enough to look into her eyes and smile reassuringly. She saw only the guard, Mustafa, staring into her eyes, and it was Mustafa she felt pressing against her.

"Oh my God," she moaned.

"It's OK, Alexandra. You're safe," he whispered. "No one is going to hurt you—not ever." Noah continued to hold her as she regained her composure and slowly drifted off to sleep. He held her through the night, heartsick at the thought of the horror she had experienced.

***

Karen and Amos sat together on the couch in the adjoining living room reminiscing about all that had transpired since they had first met in Israel earlier that summer. She told Amos she had been in love with Noah when they were students at Stanford, which was about the time Amos and Alexandra were crossing paths in Beirut. Amos, of course, knew that Karen and Noah had been engaged to one another during the years he and Alexandra were together in Israel.

"Amazing, isn't it?" she said. "I was engaged to, and madly in love with, Noah at the very time you were probably the most important person in Alexandra's life."

He nodded. "Yeah, I've thought about that too," he replied smiling. "And here we are, and there they are," he said, tilting his head toward the bedroom.

"Any regrets?" she asked.

"No, not anymore," he replied. "Alexandra belongs here in America, and with Noah Greenspan. I know that now. You know what Alexandra did for my country and for me was beyond heroic. She certainly had no love for Israel, given her family's history and her people's history. But she knew that she alone could prevent a senseless massacre of innocents, although at terrible risk to herself, and she did the right thing. The risk was enormous, but she knew what she had to do, and she did it."

"I first met Alexandra when Noah and I were freshmen at Stanford," Karen said. "My family and I were passing through Washington during the Christmas holidays. I spent a day with Noah and Alexandra gallivanting around Washington."

"Interesting," he replied. "What did you think of her?"

"At first, I thought there was no way I could compete with her. Amos, she was such a beautiful teenager and very sure of herself. I mean very comfortable in her own skin. It wasn't until she told me she was about to go away to school in Beirut that I believed I had any chance with Noah."

"How did you feel when you ran into her this summer at the Dan Hotel in Tel Aviv?"

"You know, I felt like I had run across an old friend. I was truly happy—thrilled—to see her there. We've both moved on with our lives. I'm doing really well in my career, and she is obviously doing extremely well as a journalist in Washington. I don't feel there is any lingering baggage to carry around. Alexandra, as you know as well as anyone, is pretty special, and I've come to really like her."

"I admire all of you," he said. "You amaze me."

"And look at the role you played in saving her life—in actually bringing her back from God only knows what and back to Noah. And that was at a huge risk to your own safety. That was an outrageously audacious, even reckless, plan you pulled off."

"There was no conventional way to get Alexandra and Dany Haddad out of there."

"You put your life on the line for her."

He shrugged. "And here you and I are," he replied.

"So when will I ever get to see you again?" she asked.

"I'll be making a trip or two back to the States because of this AASLF business."

"To Washington?" she asked. He nodded. "Do you really think Potomac Center or Noah and Alexandra are in danger?"

He paused for a moment to contemplate his reply before nodding. "Yes, Karen. I do. We know Omar Samir, a known terrorist, was in the States trying to get his hands on the architecture plans for Potomac Center. I would bet anything the same Omar Samir was behind Alexandra's ordeal in Khartoum. They intended to kill, or worse, at Omdurman. So yes, I think they're both in danger. These people don't give up easily, Karen."

"Are you confident you can stop them?"

"We're good at what we do, Karen, and if we can keep Samir and his gang looking over their shoulders, there's a good chance they'll find other mischief with which to keep themselves busy. Right now they still don't know that we're onto their plans or that we believe they had anything to do with Alexandra's arrest. If the FBI or we can get them in our crosshairs, we'll stop them. That has to be our objective."

"I hate to think that this awful business is the only thing that might bring us together from time to time."

"Is that important to you, our getting together from time to time?"

Karen looked up at him and tried to gauge the seriousness of his question. She nodded. "Yes, Amos. I think it has become very important to me. I've come to like having you in my life," she replied, reaching over and taking his hand.

"You know, we have a consulate in Chicago," he said, his eyes fixed on hers.

"And?"

"And I could probably swing an assignment there or, more likely, at our embassy in Washington."

"Would you really consider that, or are you teasing me?"

"I'm not teasing you, Karen. I'm pretty sure I'll be working with our American counterparts for the foreseeable future because of the potential of this Palestinian terrorist threat directed at Americans on American soil. I can make the case that I should be assigned here until this issue is resolved."

"And you're considering doing that?"

"I would if—"

"You're telling me you would consider a transfer to the States to be near me?" she asked, anxiously.

"If it was important to you. If it meant we could, you know, be together, yes, I would," he answered.

Karen sat there looking at him for several moments and then moved to him. "Please don't tease me about this, Amos," she said, her voice appealing for candor. Amos returned her gaze for a moment or two and then turned her in his arms so that she was looking up at him. Her heart raced. He leaned down, holding her firmly in his arms, and kissed her. "I'm not teasing you, Karen," Amos said. "If I transfer to America, it will be to be near you."

***

Neither Noah nor Alexandra discussed what happened that first night they were together in Los Angeles. Alexandra knew she needed time to adjust to normalcy, and she knew Noah understood that too. The nights that followed were filled with affection and caring, but, for the time being, that was the extent of their intimacy. They traveled north to San Francisco, Portland, and Seattle. Alexandra savored the time with Noah, although she was, of course, still burdened by the intrusions into her consciousness of Inspector Faizel and the guard Mustafa.

Traveling with Noah during the remainder of the road show provided a much-needed diversion from the haunting memories of Sudan.

She marveled at Noah's grasp of the minutest details of the operations of Potomac Center. Watching Noah at the podium reminded her of the very first time she saw him addressing a large demanding crowd. It was seventeen years earlier. The place was the Ohev Shalom Congregation, an old inner-city Orthodox synagogue in Washington. The occasion was his bar mitzvah. She was only twelve years old.

The road show was progressing quite well. Investor interest in the IPO was building across the country with each presentation Noah delivered. Karen was certain that, barring some unforeseen shock to the financial system, the price of Potomac Center shares would close well above the anticipated initial offering price. It should have been an exhilarating time for Noah. Alexandra was safely home, investors were clamoring for a piece of the Potomac Center public offering, and his net worth was soaring with every passing day. He could only hope that time would soon banish the lingering trauma that haunted Alexandra.

"Let's get married on the first anniversary of the opening of Potomac Center," he said as he and Alexandra waited to board their flight back to Washington. "We're going to have a huge celebration at the center, and as soon as it's over, we could have our family and friends remain for our wedding."

"Are you serious?" she asked, laughing.

"Why not?" he replied. "It's a beautiful venue, it has special meaning for us, and it avoids any religious issues about where to have a wedding ceremony. We can select from two or three great restaurants at Potomac Center."

"So we're going to get married in a mall?"

"Not just any mall," he answered.

"Our mall," she quipped.

"Ours and, in a few days, a few thousand other owners."

"I'm warming up to the idea," she replied.

CHAPTER FORTY

Noah and Alexandra gathered with Yusuf and the Salamans, Ed Scallion, Daoud, and Hy and Esther Greenspan that Sunday afternoon for a cookout at Noah's Georgetown town house. It was the first time they were all together since the Six-Day War. They flew on to New York that Monday evening in order to be on the floor of the American Stock Exchange the next morning for the opening bell when Potomac Center would trade as a publicly owned company.

So, at half past nine the morning of October 7, 1968, Noah, standing between Alexandra Salaman and Karen Rothschild, on a balcony overlooking the exchange's trading floor, slammed down the gavel to commence the first day's trading of Potomac Center Properties of America.

Instantly, the lit ticker symbol PCPA began crawling across the Lectrascan electronic display high above the trading floor.

"PCPA 32…PCPA 32…PCPA 32½…PCPA 32¾…PCPA 33… PCPA 36¼…XTMM 12…SWVA 22½…PCPA 40…PCPA 40½… PCPA 45."

Noah watched as his already considerable net worth increased by over $32 million during the first few minutes of the opening bell.

"Does that mean what I think it means?" Alexandra asked as the ticker kept crawling across the electronic display.

"It does, Alexandra, but those prices for the stock can turn around and run in the opposite direction just as fast."

"What a great launch, though," Karen said. "It's been a great initial public offering.

"My God, Noah, look what's happening," Alexandra cried, tugging at the sleeve of his suit.

"PCPA46...PCPA46½...PCPA48...PCPA50."

"Noah, you've become forty-five million dollars richer," Alexandra said, making no effort to hide her excitement.

"Only if I sell right now," he answered, laughing.

Noah and his coterie were not the only people on the floor of the American Stock Exchange watching the steady rise of Potomac Center's share price. George Markanos, the short-sell analyst from Deutschland Trust, watched the ticker with growing interest. Potomac Center looked to him like a short seller's dream. Noah had acquitted himself well during the road show leading up to the IPO. He had spoken to hundreds of analysts and portfolio managers as he toured the country, and they were uniformly impressed with Noah and with Potomac Center. George Markanos was impressed with Noah too. Potomac Center's SEC registration statement was impressive, and his presentations during the road show were straightforward and free of hype. Noah knew his business like the back of his hand, and his enthusiasm for the role projects like Potomac Center could play in the future of urban renewal was convincing. Most of all, Noah engendered trust. With the market well on its way to recording, for the first time ever, two billion-share trading days, George Markanos knew that many of the new IPOs would enjoy very impressive but short-lived debuts. He found nothing with which to quibble in the company's financial statements or Noah's remarks to analysts in city after city. He also knew, however, that it would take very little to spook investors who were, initially, eager to participate in Potomac Center's success story. He had seen it all before. Retail investors and nervous institutions that made a lot of money very fast were always quick to sell at the first inkling of trouble in order to lock in their gains. The short-sell analyst looked up once again at the electronic ticker board. "PCPA56...PCPA56½...PCPA 58...PCPA58¾...PCPA60..."

Markanos wistfully envisioned a short sale of one hundred thousand shares that pared the share price back to the opening bid of $32. That would yield Deutschland Trust a cool $2,800,000 and a very handsome bonus for him. The only problem, Markanos thought, was that there was nothing about which to be critical—at least not yet. The financials, the fundamentals, and the management all looked solid. Give me an excuse to write a short-sale recommendation, Mr. Greenspan, he mused. Any legitimate excuse will do.

***

"So you're really worth one hundred and fifty million dollars?" Alexandra asked, snuggling up to Noah in their bed at the Plaza.

"For the time being," he answered.

"You could be worth even more tomorrow," she teased.

"Or a whole lot less," he replied.

"You're really not that impressed with all of this, are you?"

"It tells me I've succeeded at something really big, Alexandra. And yes, that's very reassuring. But, frankly, I don't like it being the definition of my worth. It could go as fast as it came—even faster. In that respect, worth, or at least the financial definition of it, can be very fleeting. It's simply a calculation of the value others place on what I have or what I've done. There are other things that are far more important and far more valuable."

"Such as?"

"You," he answered without hesitating.

She smiled and squeezed closer to him. "You really mean that, don't you?"

"Do you know what was really exciting about being up there this morning ringing the opening bell?"

"Tell me," she asked in a whisper, her lips brushing his ear.

"Having you there next to me. So help me, for a second, I saw you as that eleven-year-old girl standing next to Yusuf on the steps of N. P. Gage elementary school that day we first met."

"What do you remember most about me when we first met?" she asked, playfully.

"Your green eyes," he answered, without hesitation. "Your beautiful, enchanting, green eyes. They're exactly the same now." She smiled blissfully and, for the first time since her return, contentedly, as they held each other.

"And what do you see, Alexandra?" he asked.

Her smile slowly widened as she contemplated his question. "My Noah," she answered. "My Noah…just you…just my Noah."

And with that, they embraced one another anew. They kissed, tenderly at first, and then frantically. Alexandra held Noah tightly, as she rolled onto her back to receive him. It was the first, but not the last, time they made joyous and satiating love to one another that night. The ghosts of Omdurman were receding.

CHAPTER
FORTY-ONE

Noah and Alexandra returned to Washington happier than they had been for a long time. She was now recognized as one of the *Evening Star*'s premier writers, and Noah was basking in the glow of Potomac Center's success. They were widely viewed as one of Washington's most admired couples. Noah, indeed, had much about which to be happy. The last vacant space in the Potomac Center office building had been leased during the past week, as had the last two spaces in the retail mall. He had mixed feelings about the new RadioShack lease, given how close to bankruptcy the chain had been five years earlier. Nonetheless, he approved the lease. The chain had downsized its stores dramatically so there was really little risk to the Potomac Center Mall. Noah was quite pleased with the lease for the last retail space available at Potomac Center. It was with an independent local florist, Chesapeake Floral Designs. While Noah didn't know the company, he liked the idea of having some local retailers in the mall, and, besides, they paid the entire first-year's rent in advance.

He was also delighted with the lease for the last remaining space in Potomac Center Office Plaza. He knew Questex-Irvine quite well as the firm had bid on the engineering for Potomac Center. They didn't get the job because their bid was too high, but Noah had been very impressed with the sophisticated proposal the firm had submitted.

Apparently, a division of the firm, Questex-Irvine Materials Testing, needed Washington offices, and Noah was delighted the division had selected Potomac Center to be its home.

Noah had just begun to review the center's third-quarter financials when he heard the two familiar names mentioned on the small television set on his credenza. He had made it a habit to tune in to re-broadcasts of *Washington Week in Review* on WETA-TV, Washington's public-education television station, broadcasting from its new studio at Howard University. He hadn't been paying much attention until he heard the voices of FBI agents Lawrence Hogan and Mike Atkins. They were the two agents who had met with him right after the Six-Day War to discuss the possible threat to him and Potomac Center posed by the Ali Abdul Shoukri Liberation Front. Noah swiveled around in his chair to watch the program. Peter Lisagor was interviewing the two men.

"We don't usually have the opportunity to interview FBI agents," Lisagor said.

"The bureau doesn't usually do interviews," Agent Hogan replied. "We've been made available by the bureau because Agent Atkins and I have been tasked to assess the threat of terrorist attacks against American citizens and American institutions."

"Here in the United States?" Lisagor asked.

"Yes," replied Agent Atkins.

"Is it the bureau's view that there are such threats against American interests?"

"We really don't know for sure," Agent Hogan replied. "But we take any and all threats very seriously."

"And there have been such threats?" Lisagor pressed.

"No, not specifically. However, there are groups abroad that are advocating armed conflict, and as I said earlier, we take all threats very seriously."

"Groups advocating armed conflict with the United States?"

"We have no direct reports of threats against Americans or American property; however, since the recent fighting in the Middle

East, we are observing the formation of groups that are advocating armed struggle, possibly on a worldwide scale."

"Can you be more specific?"

"Well, there's the ANM," Agent Atkins replied.

"The ANM?"

"The Arab Nationalist Movement, which was founded by a Palestinian doctor, George Habash, has embraced what Dr. Habash calls the Guevara view of the revolutionary human being. Guevara, as we know, sees the United States as the world's great oppressor. So a movement that advocates armed conflict and embraces Guevara's worldview is a movement we would want to watch very carefully."

"By the Guevara view, you mean Che Guevara?"

"Yes."

"And you are specifically concerned about this Arab Nationalist Movement?"

"We're watching them and other splinter groups that have formed."

"Can you be specific?"

"Well, the Arab Nationalist Movement, along with a group that calls itself the Palestinian Liberation Army, established a faction called the abtal al-Aduah, or the Heroes of the Return," Agent Atkins explained. "This group has since merged with two other groups, Youth for Revenge and a Syrian-backed group called the Palestine Liberation Front. They now operate under the umbrella of the Popular Front for the Liberation of Palestine, which Dr. Habash leads. We've also recently learned of a group known as the AASLF, which does seem to have designs on targets outside of the Middle East."

"AASLF? I presume that means something."

"It stands for the Ali Abdul Shoukri Liberation Front," Agent Atkins answered. "Ali Abdul Shoukri was a very militant Palestinian who was killed by the Israeli army a few years ago."

"And has this group threatened any Americans or American interests?"

"We don't discuss any details of ongoing investigations, but we take any and all threats seriously."

"So there have been threats?"

"We didn't say that. We're just very proactive about any possible threat."

"And you're participating in this discussion to be proactive?"

"Exactly."

"How are you being proactive?"

"Well, we're advising large public venues simply to be alert to anything out of the ordinary."

"What kinds of venues?"

"Any kind of large public venue."

"Such as?"

"Well, just to give an example, there have been very large projects like the King of Prussia Mall near Philadelphia and, all the way over on the West Coast, the new Costa Mesa Mall. We want people to be alert to anything suspicious or unusual."

"And what about the new Potomac Center Mall here in the nation's capital?" Lisagor asked.

"Of course, but we're not pinpointing any one project or venue. We're just advising the management of large public venues to be a little more alert. A little more vigilant."

Noah swiveled back to his desk and sat there thinking about what he had just heard. He opened his desk drawer and shuffled through some papers until he found the business card Agent Hogan had handed him shortly after the Six-Day War. He leaned back in his chair as he dialed the number on the card.

"Agent Hogan" the voice answered.

"Agent Hogan, this is Noah Greenspan."

"Good morning, Mr. Greenspan. How can I help you?" Agent Hogan responded.

"I just caught the rebroadcast of the WETA interview you did with Peter Lisagor earlier this week. Has there been some new development regarding this AASLF terrorist group?"

"Nothing specific, Mr. Greenspan. We were really only planning to urge all Americans to be more alert as they go about their daily business in what has become a more turbulent world. Frankly, my young colleague, Agent Atkins, went a little overboard with all of that specific discussion about the various Palestinian groups that have formed in recent years."

"So we don't know anything more specific about the Shoukri group?"

"We really don't. I think you know everything we know, Mr. Greenspan. I'm sure it was unsettling to hear Agent Atkins refer to them in the Lisagor interview, but we haven't heard anything more about them."

"You'll let me know if you do, right?"

"Of course. As I said, Agent Atkins went a bit overboard. We've learned nothing new regarding that group."

"OK, thanks," Noah responded. "You'll let me know if anything new develops, right?"

"Absolutely," Agent Hogan answered.

"Damn, I hope Alexandra didn't hear that broadcast," Noah whispered to himself. All she has to do is hear that someone on television was talking about the Shoukri group and Potomac Center. The buzz of the telephone intercom quickly interrupted his thoughts.

"Noah, there's a George Markanos on the phone for you. He says he's with Deutschland Trust," Barb said.

"Greenspan," Noah answered.

"Hi, Noah. George Markanos here."

"Hi, George. How can I help you?"

"How's the quarter looking?"

"Damn good," Noah answered, with a faint chuckle.

"Nice public offering you had."

"Thanks, George. We were really delighted with how it went."

"So, do you ever watch *Washington Week in Review*?" Markanos asked, abruptly changing the subject.

Noah, caught off guard, was momentarily lost for words.

"Noah?"

"Yeah, yeah, I heard you, George. Yes, I watch the program from time to time."

"Did you watch it this week?"

"The last one I saw was with Peter Lisagor interviewing two FBI agents."

"Yeah, that's this week's. You know they mentioned Potomac Center."

"Yes, along with other malls and public venues."

"What do you think of that?"

"Well, I think I'm glad the FBI is alert to those things."

"What things?"

"You know, what they talked about—the possibility of terrorist attacks against Americans and American property."

"Do you think they have any knowledge about an impending attack somewhere in the United States?"

"You would have to ask them that," Noah replied, unsure of how to handle the short seller's questions.

"Don't you think it's interesting that they specifically mentioned malls as possible targets?"

"There are thousands of large public venues in the United States, George. I think they just mentioned shopping malls as an example."

"Don't you think it's interesting that they specifically mentioned King of Prussia, Costa Mesa, and Potomac Center?"

"Actually, as I recall, they didn't mention Potomac Center. Peter Lisagor threw that in."

"But they agreed."

"I think they would have agreed with any mall he may have mentioned anywhere in the United States."

"I'm thinking they must have some current information about a possible attack here in the United States," Markanos said. "Why else would they be on television telling everyone to be vigilant?"

"George, I spoke with one of the FBI agents. I asked Agent Hogan if the bureau had any specific current information about a threat against malls in the United States. He said they didn't. He said they just went on the TV program to urge people to be alert, given all the turmoil in the world."

"You called one of the FBI agents?"

Noah cringed at his own clumsiness. "Of course I did. Potomac Center was specifically mentioned during that interview. I wanted to know if they knew something I didn't know."

"And what did he say?"

"I'm not sure I should be quoting FBI agents, George. I can tell you that I was satisfied that they had no specific information about plans to attack any mall in the United States. They just wanted people to be alert at all large public venues. That's all."

"You had Agent Hogan's telephone number?"

"Anyone can call the FBI and ask for an employee, George."

"Is that what you did? I mean, did you call the FBI switchboard in Washington and simply ask for Agent Hogan?"

"George, what difference does it make how I reached Agent Hogan? I'm telling you what he said to me."

"Yeah, you're right. It doesn't make any difference how you reached him."

"He told me that they appeared on the program to urge people to be alert and to report anything they thought might be suspicious."

"Just being cautious, huh?"

"Essentially, yes."

"Say, Noah, I'm just curious about something."

"What's that, George?"

"Had you ever spoken to Agent Hogan before?"

Oh shit, Noah thought. "What difference would that make?" he answered.

"Had you?" Markanos asked again, somewhat more insistently. "I mean it sounds like you were on the phone with him within minutes, maybe even seconds, of the time the program aired."

"George, I told you what Agent Hogan told me. They did not go on that program because of any specific threat they knew of. They simply wanted to urge people to be observant and to be vigilant."

"You know, Noah, I can't figure out why you're evading my last question. I mean it's really a simple question. A yes or no answer would do. Had you ever spoken to Agent Hogan before?"

"Suppose I had, George. What difference would it make? Agent Hogan told me that they did not go on that program because of any specific threat. All the bureau was doing was urging people—"

"Yeah, yeah, I know," George Markanos interrupted. "They were just urging people to be cautious."

"That's absolutely right, George."

"You know, Noah, I spend most of my time asking questions to executives like you. I often have people dodge tough questions. But I asked you a simple question, and you're dodging it. Do you know what that tells me, Noah? It tells me my simple question is, for some reason, really a complicated question."

Noah knew he couldn't admit to George Markanos that Agent Hogan and Agent Atkins had called on him months earlier without opening the conversation to progressively more troublesome questions.

"I'm sorry you feel that way, George. I've told you Agent Hogan said that their appearance on television did not relate to any specific threat. It was only to urge caution."

"Yeah, I hear you, Noah. But maybe that's what I should do."

"What's that?"

"Urge caution," Markanos replied. "Anyway, thanks for taking my call. I know you're a very busy man, so I'll let you get back to work."

Noah sat there for several minutes going over the conversation he had just finished with George Markanos. Well, that couldn't have gone worse, he thought.

"Barb!" he called into the intercom. "Get Karen Rothschild for me."

Noah discussed Peter Lisagor's interview with the two FBI agents with Karen. He explained that he told Markanos exactly what Agent Hogan had told him—that the two agents appeared on the program to urge Americans to be vigilant and that they were not on the program because of any specific threat.

"So what's the problem?" Karen asked.

"Markanos was irritated that I wouldn't give him a straight answer about whether or not I had ever spoken to Agent Hogan before today."

"Why wouldn't you give him a straight answer, Noah?"

"Because I couldn't tell him that those agents had met with me. First, it wouldn't be appropriate to discuss a meeting with the FBI, and besides, that meeting had nothing to do with their appearance on *Washington Week in Review*. The FBI was just urging people to be vigilant because of all the turmoil in the world."

"The FBI met with you?" Karen asked, surprised by Noah's comments.

"I must have mentioned that to you, Karen. It was when we learned that Omar Samir and that AASLF group were Middle Eastern terrorists."

"The first I heard about that group was after Alexandra got rescued from that prison in Khartoum," she replied.

"So, do you think we have a problem?"

"That depends on what Markanos does now."

"What the hell can he do? I have no obligation to discuss a meeting I may have had with FBI agents four months ago. It wasn't as though they were investigating Potomac Center or me. They were just being very cautious and giving me a heads-up that—"

"You or Potomac Center might be the target of terrorists?" Karen said, finishing his sentence for him.

"Karen, Agent Hogan assured me that the bureau was just urging caution and vigilance because of the world situation and that it had nothing to do with the meeting he previously had with me. They would have been on the *Washington Week in Review* program if that business with the AASLF group or that Samir character had never taken place. It's the world situation that they're concerned about, not me or Potomac Center," he argued, unconvincingly.

"Noah, George Markanos couldn't care less what motivated the FBI to go on television to urge the American public to be vigilant. He sees Potomac Center as a company whose shares are selling at a one hundred percent premium to the average price-to-earnings ratio today. If he can make a case that there's too much risk in the price PCPA is commanding in the market, he will short the stock, and he'll make a lot of money at the same time."

"That would be a shitty thing to do," Noah replied.

"Grow up, Noah. This isn't penny-ante stuff. The Street is full of jackals looking for a fast score. You haven't done a damn thing wrong, but the rapid run-up in the price of Potomac Center shares makes the stock very vulnerable to even a suggestion of trouble."

"What do you think is going to happen, Karen?"

"Markanos might short you," she replied. "If he thinks he can make a case, he probably will. He's kind of sitting pretty. If he shorts the stock, he and his clients will make a bundle on the way down, and they would probably buy more stock after they cover their short position and ride the stock back up."

"I don't have time to worry about this kind of crap," Noah answered, irritably.

"You shouldn't worry about it, Noah. If it happens, your net worth and that of a lot of other investors in Potomac Center will take a temporary haircut, but the stock will recover faster than you think. Markanos isn't going after the fundamentals. He's going after something that hasn't happened and that will probably never happen. The pygmies might run and affect the stock for a day or two, but the big boys will see a flimsy short sale as a buying opportunity. Remember, an ill-advised short sale can actually become very bullish."

"How in the world can something like that be bullish?"

"Noah, those short positions are taken by a short seller selling borrowed shares that the short seller is confident are going to crater. That's stock he doesn't own. He's borrowed the shares from a broker and sold them confident the price is going to plummet. He pockets the money from the sale and hopes to buy back the same number of shares at a much cheaper price when the stock falls. He'll pocket the difference and return the lower-priced shares to the broker he originally bor-rowed them from, and everybody is happy. But if the stock goes up instead of down, those shares he borrowed still have to be returned to the broker. A short seller sitting with a short position when the stock is rising rather than falling has to jump in and buy shares to replace the shares he borrowed, or else he stands to lose a fortune as the price of those shares continues to go up instead of down."

"So you don't think this is that big a deal?"

"Look, in my opinion, if Markanos recommends shorting the stock, we may see a dip for a day or two, but when the stock turns around, and it will, his short sellers will be running to buy shares to cover their short position."

"So you do think we'll take a hit if he shorts the stock?"

"Of course we will, but it will be very temporary. When a stock is hyped, you may or may not see any movement in the share price, but when potentially negative things are reported about a stock, you get an almost instantaneous downward price correction. That's just life on the Street, Noah. But that downward pressure can turn around like a boo-merang if the market decides it was unjustified, as it will if Potomac Center is shorted. That's why a lot of ill-advised short sales can turn very bullish. A short sale isn't ever pleasant, but it's a pretty effective way of separating the pygmies from the serious investors. Don't sweat it. I'll have our people begin drafting a response to a short-sell recom-mendation, just in case Markanos takes a shot at us."

"When do you think it might happen?"

"When was the program aired?"

"I'm not sure. I watched a rerun this morning."

"If he's going to recommend going short on the stock, he'll do it very quickly," she answered. "Your phone will be ringing off the hook. You should talk to your CFO, and you should both be prepared to take a lot of calls. Just tell any callers what you told me—that the FBI did not go on television because of any threat against Potomac Center or any other mall. They're urging Americans to be very vigilant because of the world condition, and they only used shopping malls as an example of large public venues where people should be alert to anything suspicious," she said. "Don't deviate from that message."

"Thanks, Karen. This has been very helpful," he replied.

***

It was late afternoon when George Markanos looked out from his small, cramped, and dimly lit office at Deutschland Trust's fifty-first-floor office in the Commerce Building on William Street. He was just around the concrete-canyon corner from the Federal Reserve and a couple of short blocks from the New York Stock Exchange. He hated the gray narrow streets of the sun-starved cityscape known as the Wall Street district. It's as cold as a lot of the people who work down there, he thought.

George Markanos would release his short-sell recommendation on Potomac Center Properties of America before he left for the night. The shame was that he really liked Noah Greenspan and the business he had put together. But he knew his job wasn't to extoll the virtues of solid companies. His job was to ferret out instances where stock prices may be too heady relative to risks, whether chronic or short-lived, real or imagined. He knew, better than most aficionados, that retail investors—especially new investors—typically run from a stock that has been targeted by a respected short seller.

People would read about his short-sell recommendation in the morning papers or get a call from their broker, and a predictable flurry of activity would ripple through the Financial District below. Weak-kneed investors would get spooked at the thought of taking a hit, no matter how temporary, and would race to dump a stock they had enthusiastically embraced days before. Seasoned and well-informed investors would shrug off many short sales, knowing that a solid performance would catch the short sellers when the shares turned around, and would confront those short sellers with unlimited losses until the short sellers covered their short-sell positions. *What a shitty way to make money,* he thought.

Alexandra knew, before Noah, the news about Deutschland Trust's short-sale recommendation on Potomac Center Properties of America. She pulled Deutschland's press release off of the Business Teletype and hurried over to her desk at the *Evening Star* to call Noah.

"Noah, it's Alexandra. George Markanos did write a short-sell recommendation," she said as soon as he answered his phone.

"How do you know?" he asked.

"I pulled it off the Business Wire. Noah, it will be on every financial page by the end of the day."

"Can you read it to me?"

"Yeah, sure. Honey, you're not going to like it."

"Alexandra, that's like saying you're not going to like your root canal. Of course I'm not going to like it, but, trust me, it will all turn out OK."

"OK, here goes," she answered and began reading the Business Wire story.

...*October 11, 1967—Deutschland Trust's Markanos Recommends Short Sale of Potomac Center Properties of America (PCPA): Cites Terrorist Threat.*

We are recommending going short on Potomac Center Properties of America (PCPA), a developer, based in Washington, DC, of very large mixed-use properties that integrate big-box anchor malls, office buildings, and residential multifamily housing into an urban envirocomplex.

Two FBI agents appeared on public television's Washington Week in Review *this week to urge Americans to be extra vigilant when congregating or passing through high-traffic public venues such as shopping*

malls, performance arenas, airports, and railroad stations.
Washington Week in Review *moderator Peter Lisagor
asked the agents if they could give specific examples of venues of concern. They cited large malls in Pennsylvania and
California. Lisagor asked about the new Potomac Center
complex in Washington, DC, and the agents acknowledged
that Potomac Center would be in the same category as other
high-traffic public venues where caution would be merited.*

We discussed the Washington Week in Review *interview with Noah Greenspan, developer and CEO of
Potomac Center Properties of America. We were led to believe by Mr. Greenspan that the FBI might have information about a specific threat to Potomac Center. While Mr.
Greenspan did not acknowledge that the FBI had actually
warned him about such a threat, he was elusive and refused
to comment when we asked whether he had been visited by
the FBI regarding any threat to Potomac Center.*

*We also note that Mr. Greenspan's fiancée, Miss
Alexandra Salaman, is a reporter for the* Washington
Evening Star *and recently spent several months in the
Middle East reporting on the situation there under the
name Sabirah Najat. Several years ago, Miss Salaman was
involved in a major international incident involving a
terrorist group while she was a student in Beirut. She was
credited with foiling a planned massacre of Israelis and fled
Beirut for Israel, where she spent some years thereafter.*

*While we have been impressed with the operations of
Potomac Center and with Mr. Greenspan as its founder
and chief executive officer, we are troubled by his refusal to
acknowledge or to deny that he has been contacted by the
FBI regarding a possible terrorist threat to Potomac Center.*

*Shares of Potomac Center, which were listed on the
American Stock Exchange on October 2, 1967, opened at*

*$32.00 and soared into the stratosphere, closing at $64.00
by the end of the day. Yesterday, the stock closed at $79.50
after trading briefly at $80.00 per share. We think Potomac
Center is a fine company, run by exceptional management,
but given the unquantifiable risk of terrorism that may be
directed at the site, we believe the company's PE at two and
a half times the average multiple of publicly listed companies cannot be justified, and we have, therefore, taken a
short-sell position in the stock.*

George Markanos, CFA

"Jesus Christ, Markanos brought you into the damn piece."

"I'm so sorry, Noah. I'm sick over all the trouble I've caused."

"This isn't about you, Alexandra. There's no reason for you to be
stressed over this. Karen says it will all blow over in a matter of days."

"So, do you know where Potomac Center is trading now?"

"Actually I don't, but I can see that our lines are ringing off the
hook, so I think I'll know as soon as we hang up."

"I can tell you now. I was just handed the ticker. PCPA is trading
at thirty-eight dollars a share. You're down about forty dollars a share
on a volume of two hundred and fifty thousand shares traded so far.
Noah, you've lost a fortune."

"Alexandra, I haven't lost anything. I'm not selling. It's going to
be a roller coaster for a day or two, but the shares will recover. Mid-
America is issuing a rebuttal today."

"Why would Deutschland Trust do something like this?"

"To make a lot of money, Alexandra. They went short by selling
borrowed shares at seventy-eight dollars a share. If they step in and
buy Potomac Center at these low prices and replace the stock they borrowed, they and their clients will pocket a small fortune."

"Do you really think it will all be OK?"

"Karen does."

"Do you?"

"Alexandra, honestly, I haven't the slightest idea. Karen seems to know all about this crap, and she says the stock will bounce back. She said this just washes out the nervous money."

"I hope the day gets better for you, Noah. I'm sorry you're having this aggravation, and I hope Karen is right. I hope it turns around fast."

"Any other news going on in the world, Alexandra?"

"Actually, there is. AP has just reported that Che Guevara was caught last night in Bolivia, and they executed him this morning."

"Really?"

"Yeah, really."

"Well, it shows there are a lot more significant things happening in the world than Deutschland Trust shorting our stock."

"I love you, Noah."

"Now, that's the best thing I've heard all day. I love you too, Alexandra."

Within minutes of Deutschland Trust's short-sell recommendation reaching the nation's brokerage houses and newsrooms, Mid-America's response was on Business Wire.

OCTOBER 11, 1967—SHORTING PCPA ILL-ADVISED, SAYS MID-AMERICA

Mid-America Ventures urged its clients to hold firm and to take advantage of any weakness in the share price of Potomac Center (PCPA), following a short-sell recommendation by Deutschland Trust's George Markanos. While the FBI does not comment on active investigations, the bureau did confirm to Potomac Center that the appearance of two of its agents on the Sunday public-affairs television program Washington Week in Review *did not pertain to any known threat against targets in America. "Our agents were on the program to urge Americans to be cautious and vigilant, given the high level of turmoil in the world. Any inference that the bureau knows of any specific, impending attack on American property is unfounded," said Cal Remos, a spokesperson in the Bureau's public affairs office.*

Mid-America Ventures believes that any weakness in the shares of PCPA resulting from today's short-sell recommendation represents an attractive opportunity for investors to increase their holdings in the company.

Mid-America Ventures is the investment banker of record for Potomac Center Properties of America and was the manager of Potomac Center's recent initial public offering.

Karen's predictions turned out to be right on the money. By the time the market closed that afternoon, shares of Potomac Center had recouped all of the value that was lost earlier in the day because of the Markanos short-sell recommendation. Noah eagerly grabbed the phone when Karen called to say the stock had closed at eighty dollars a share. It had been a turbulent day, but the price of the stock was at its high when the closing bell sounded.

"Karen, you were amazing. You predicted exactly what would happen today. We got clobbered when Markanos's short-sell recommendation hit the news, and we bounced back as soon as Mid-America's response was on the wire."

"Short selling can be a dangerous game, Noah. You know, when you buy a stock, all you can lose is what you invested, but when you short a stock and it keeps going up, you keep losing until you stop your losses by buying shares to cover your short position. Theoretically, a short seller's losses can be unlimited."

"Well, I hope a lot of short sellers lost their shirts," Noah replied.

"Nah, you really don't. I would have preferred that Potomac Center had never been associated with a short sale. It leaves a bitter taste in one's mouth."

"But look at all the people who made money because of Markanos's bad recommendation. People were able to buy PCPA at IPO prices for a while today."

"Yes, and Deutschland Trust was probably among them. They probably bought twice as many cheap shares at the bottom as they sold on the short sale. I would guess they made money on the way down and on the way up, but some people who had bought shares this week at a premium and then sold this morning could have taken a real beating. That's never a good thing. People really get pissed," she said.

"Well, I want you to know how impressed I've been ever since you first suggested I go public. You're very good at what you do, Karen. Your advice has been superb."

"Yeah, then again, I was the one who advised against selecting the architect whose design made Potomac Center the hottest project in the country." Noah was, momentarily, silent as recollections of Karen begging him not to select Yusuf Salaman's proposed design for Potomac Center ran through his mind.

"Your advice back then was sound, Karen. Fortunately, it all worked out, but your concern was well-founded."

"You made the right call, Noah. You stuck to your guns when very few others would have," she said.

"Well, I hope you got a nice bonus from Mid-America as a result of the IPO."

"I did. In fact, I just took a new apartment with the bonus. The building isn't quite finished, but it's right on the lake. It's called Lake Point Tower, and, Noah, it's a Mies van der Rohe–designed project, just like Potomac Center. It's the tallest apartment building in the world."

"Wow! That's what I call moving up in the world," he laughed.

"Well, I couldn't have done it without you and Potomac Center," she replied.

"And there would be no Potomac Center without you, Karen," he answered.

"You know, it all turned out all right in the end, didn't it, Noah?"

"Yeah, Karen, it really did. You must have a lot of happy associates at Mid-America."

"Yes, I think I do, and you have a lot of happy shareholders at Potomac Center, Noah."

As Noah and Karen were happily conversing between Washington and Chicago about how well things had turned out, Saul Kronheim, the class-action lawyer who almost sank Potomac Center four years earlier, was taking a call from Gunnar Kjarski, a tough, hardworking immigrant who had made a small fortune building low-cost inner-city housing in the City of Brotherly Love. Gunnar Kjarski had just lost a bundle as a result of the Deutschland Trust short-sell recommendation.

***

Noah and Alexandra settled down to a quiet Chinese takeout dinner at his town house that Friday night after a tumultuous week. They talked about Deutschland Trust's short sale and how it backfired as soon as Mid-America's rebuttal hit the wire.

"You find it all exciting, don't you, Noah?" Alexandra asked as they moved to the couch, each with a freshly poured glass of Inglenook cabernet sauvignon.

"I would have preferred that Markanos leave us alone—but, yes, I'm pretty happy about the way it turned out. They attacked us, and we won. They gave themselves the black eye they intended for us."

"Were you worried when the stock initially crashed the way it did?"

"Not too much. Karen kept her cool. She warned me that the stock would get clobbered and then bounce back, and that's exactly what happened. She was terrific," he replied. Alexandra nodded thoughtfully but didn't immediately respond.

"Karen has been quite the heroine," she finally said.

"You're not upset with Karen, are you?"

"No, I'm really not. We've become good friends, Noah. You know that. Actually, I like her—and I admire her."

"But something's bothering you," he replied.

Alexandra leaned over and laid her head on his shoulder. "I'm kind of discombobulated," she answered. "I feel like I'm always making a mess of things. I'm not thirty years old, and I've been involved in these awful controversies involving really bad people. I've come close to getting myself killed on more than one occasion, and you can't imagine what they were doing to do to me in Khartoum if Amos hadn't gotten me out of there. I just feel like I'm a living, walking burden to people I love and who I know love me." Noah draped one arm around Alexandra's shoulder, reached over with his free hand, and tilted her chin so that she was looking up at him.

"Alexandra, you're a treasure to the people who love you. I don't think I could face the day that anything ever happened to you. The *Evening Star* considers you one of their very finest journalists. Amos risked his life to protect you. No one considers you a burden, Alexandra—no one. I think you are one of the most admired women in this city."

She smiled. "Thank you for saying that, Noah. It's just that I sometimes feel that you and Karen would have had an easier life together— that someday you'll wake up and question your own judgment about whom you wanted to spend the rest of your life with."

"No, Alexandra, I made that decision a long time ago. Don't you think I asked myself that question more than once? I simply knew I would be happiest with the only woman I love more than myself. Please don't ever wonder where my head is on that question."

She snuggled closer to him. "You're one of a kind, Noah. I've always known that." They luxuriated in each other's company, finishing second glasses of wine. Noah was lying on his back, his head on Alexandra's lap. They were listening to music, and the conversation had turned to ideas for the wedding they were planning on the first anniversary of Potomac Center when the phone rang.

"Who in the hell could that be?" he said, as he swung his legs over the edge of the couch and moved to the bar to take the call. Alexandra, also concerned about someone calling so late on a Friday night, followed Noah to the phone.

"Mr. Greenspan?" a familiar voice asked.

"Yes, this is Noah Greenspan. Who's calling?"

"It's Mark Caztaneo from the *New York Times*, Mr. Greenspan. I'm really sorry to be calling so late on a Friday night, but I'm trying to put a story to bed for the Sunday *Times*, and I needed to talk to you."

"No problem, Mark. It's been a long time. I don't think we've spoken since the class-action suit with the architects four years ago. How can I help you?" Noah turned to Alexandra and shrugged, mouthing the name of the paper.

"It's about the suit, Mr. Greenspan. I gotta ask you, did the FBI call or meet with you to warn you that Potomac Center might be the target of a terrorist attack?"

"What suit?" Noah asked. "I have no idea what you're talking about."

"Really?" the reporter replied. "You don't know that you've been sued?"

"Sued! Who in the hell is suing me?"

"I'm sorry, Mr. Greenspan. I hate to be the first to tell you, but you and Potomac Center have had a shareholder class-action suit filed against you. Your old friend Saul Kronheim has filed suit on behalf of some shareholder by the name of Gunnar Kjarski and, I guess, everyone who lost money when your stock tanked after the Deutschland Trust short sale."

"That's crazy," Noah replied. "The stock recovered as soon as Mid-America set the story straight. The stock was back at its all-time high within a few hours."

"Yeah, you guys got on top of it right away. Those short sellers in the morning were probably buyers by afternoon trying to cover their short positions before the day was out. You really turned around the stock fast."

"So who's suing me?"

"Well, I guess some of the people who bought the stock at or near its high on the day you had your IPO, sold when Deutschland Trust issued its sell recommendation, and probably unloaded the stock for a lot less than it cost them when they bought during the IPO. I mean, some investors who bought the stock when it was selling at over sixty dollars a share were getting less than forty dollars a share when they sold after Deutschland Trust sandbagged you."

"So, had they waited an hour or two, their shares would have been in the black. We ended the day at an all-time high."

"Yeah, I see what you're saying, Mr. Greenspan, but they didn't wait. They sold because Deutschland Trust went short on the stock. That's why I gotta ask you if what Deutschland Trust was saying is true."

"Mark, if I'm being sued, I'm not going to discuss anything or answer any questions except through my attorney."

"And who would that be, Mr. Greenspan?"

"I don't know yet. This is the first I've heard about a suit. How much are they suing me for?"

"Eighty million dollars, Mr. Greenspan."

"What!"

"Yeah, you're being sued for eighty million dollars. It seems the stock traded nearly seven hundred thousand shares on Deutschland Trust's sell recommendation, and most of those shares hit the market when the stock broke forty dollars a share. So you had a lot of shareholders taking a hit of thirty to forty dollars a share because of that sell recommendation. They're claiming a direct loss of twenty million dollars, and they're asking for punitive damages of triple their losses, or an additional sixty million. That's how they got to eighty million dollars, Mr. Greenspan. The triple damages are because they're claiming fraud."

"Fraud?"

"Yeah, they're alleging you defrauded them by not divulging that you had been warned by the FBI that your project was a target. They apparently took a huge hit before the stock turned around."

"Well, I guess that's their problem then—off the record, of course."

"Yeah, I understand what you're saying, but Kronheim is alleging, on behalf of Mr. Kjarski and the other sellers, that you had been warned by the FBI that Potomac Center was the target of a planned terrorist attack and that you went ahead anyway with your public offering without divulging that information in your SEC registration statement or during any of your meetings with analysts in the run-up to the IPO. You see what I'm saying? That's why I wanted to give you the chance to deny that the FBI ever told you any such thing. I would think you would want me to quote you saying that—assuming the FBI never told you any such thing." Noah was, momentarily, speechless. "Mr. Greenspan?"

"I'm sorry, Mark. I'm not commenting on these allegations."

"You know I'm going to have to write that you had no comment about the allegation that the FBI had met with you to warn you about a possible terrorist attack."

"That's exactly right. You can say I had no comment."

"OK, got it. Sorry to have been the one to break the news to you, Mr. Greenspan. I'm sure we'll be talking again. Have a nice weekend."

"Yeah, you too, Mark." Noah turned to Alexandra and simply shook his head. "Can you believe this? Can you fucking believe this?"

"I'm so sorry, Noah. And no, I can't believe this is happening."

"They're suing me for eighty million dollars. They're alleging I withheld information in our registration statement about having been warned by the FBI that Potomac Center was the target of a planned terrorist attack."

"Oh my God," she answered. "Would you have been required to disclose that the FBI had met with you?"

Noah shrugged. "Who the hell knows?" he answered in a whisper.

"This is my fault too, Noah. It's all because of that mess with Shoukri," she said, her eyes filling with tears. "God, I've caused you nothing but grief." Noah reached out and pulled her into his arms.

"Alexandra, the only time I've known grief has been when you weren't near me. This is not grief, Alexandra. It may be a pain in the ass, but it's not grief."

"But what are you going to do, Noah?"

"Right now, I'm going to take you to bed and show you how much I love you," he answered. "Tomorrow, I'm going to call my attorney. First things first, Alexandra."

CHAPTER
FORTY-TWO

Noah's attempts to reach any of the attorneys he knew at Higgins and Harper that weekend were unsuccessful. He left a message with the law firm's answering service that he needed to see Stanford Sherman, the lawyer who represented him four years earlier when the losing architects who competed for the Potomac Center commission sued him. Noah spread out the Sunday *Times* on the kitchen table so that he and Alexandra could read the story together. Mark Caztaneo's feature on the suit was prominently displayed above the fold on page 1 of the business section. "Oh my God," Alexandra murmured as she began reading.

"NO COMMENT!" CEO'S RESPONSE TO SUIT ALLEGING HE WITHHELD KNOWLEDGE OF POSSIBLE TERRORIST ATTACK
By Mark Caztaneo, NY Times staff reporter

October 13, 1967—Noah Greenspan, CEO of Potomac Center Properties of America (PCPA), has refused to comment on the allegation in a shareholder class-action suit filed Friday that the FBI had warned him that a Middle Eastern terrorist group has targeted his high-profile urban-development project, Potomac Center. The project is a huge highly successful mixed-use complex on the banks of the Anacostia River, a branch of the Potomac River. It comprises a large shopping mall, an upscale office building, residential units, and a marina with approximately one hundred boat slips.

According to a suit filed in the US District Court, Eastern District of Pennsylvania, by prominent plaintiff's attorney Saul Kronheim, the FBI had warned Mr. Greenspan several months ago that the bureau had reason to believe that a Palestinian terrorist group had targeted Potomac Center. The suit further alleges that Mr. Greenspan went ahead with an initial public offering while withholding information that the FBI had warned Potomac Center (PCPA) that the project was in danger of being attacked.

According to the suit, Mr. Greenspan is engaged to Alexandra Salaman, who is a Palestinian American whose family immigrated to America in 1948 during the Israeli War of Independence. Miss Salaman, who is a reporter for the Washington Evening Star, *was a target of terrorists when she was a university student in Beirut and, subsequently, fled to Israel, where she finished her education and worked as a journalist for several years. Miss Salaman recently returned to Washington after several months in Israel, where she was on assignment for the* Evening Star, *covering the war last year in the Middle East. The suit alleges that Miss Salaman's relationship with Mr. Greenspan is the reason Potomac Center has been targeted by terrorists.*

Potomac Center is not new to controversy. Four years ago, Mr. Greenspan was sued by a group of architects who had unsuccessfully competed for the Potomac Center commission after he selected Miss Salaman's brother, Yusuf Salaman, to be the architect for the project. Mr. Kronheim was also the attorney who represented the plaintiffs in that suit, which was unsuccessful.

PCPA shares soared from $32.00 to $64.00 when the company had its initial public offering on October 7 and was trading at $79.50 when Deutschland Trust analyst George Markanos recommended selling the stock after two FBI agents appeared on Washington Week in Review, an educational television program broadcast on WETA-TV, to urge Americans to be vigilant in large public venues such as shopping malls. Potomac Center was among those malls mentioned.

The suit, which was brought on behalf on Mr. Gunnar Kjarski and other investors who suffered losses following the Deutschland Trust sell recommendation, alleges that Mr. Greenspan had an obligation to divulge that the FBI had specifically warned him that they had knowledge that Potomac Center was being targeted. The suit further alleges that failure to provide this information to unsuspecting investors constituted fraud.

The plaintiffs are seeking a judgment of $80 million, which includes $20 million of direct losses and $60 million in punitive damages. The FBI has stated that their agents were simply urging people to be vigilant because of international tensions and that they were not referring to any particular threat. When asked if they had contacted Mr. Greenspan prior to the Potomac Center initial public offering to warn him of a possible attack on Potomac Center, the bureau responded that they do not comment on specific investigations.

Shares of PCPA closed at $81.00 Friday.

Noah finished reading the story, put his arm around Alexandra, and pulled her close. He saw there were tears in her eyes. "It's nothing, Alexandra. It's a fishing expedition by investors who want to recoup their losses at my expense. Please don't be stressed over this—I'm not," he lied.

Alexandra knew, of course, that Noah was stressed. Hadn't she been the cause of constant stress in his life? Her father and brother had warned her when she and Noah were teenagers that no good could come of their growing attachment to one another. It was at her initiative that they had made love to one another in Rock Creek Park shortly before he left for Stanford. And it was her decision to go to the university in Beirut that had so upset him and almost destroyed their relationship. She could only imagine how he must have felt when news broke in America about her apparent involvement with Palestinian terrorists. And then there were those years when she was with Amos Ben-Chaiyim in Israel. Was it any wonder that Noah and Karen Rothschild became engaged while she was making such a mess of things? And then she returned to America, destroying Noah's relationship with Karen. He had begged her not to take the assignment in Israel after the fighting in June. And what of her tryst with Dany Haddad? What Noah must have gone through when she was in prison in Khartoum, she thought. It had cost him a half million dollars to free her. And now this—she was at the heart of an $80 million suit filed against Noah. How could she have been so naive? How could she have thought of her and Noah as the "Heirs of Eden" when she wrote that feature as a high-school intern writing for the *Evening Star*? More like the "Curses of Eden," she thought.

***

Stanford Sherman finished reading the *Times* article, peered at Noah over the top of his reading glasses, and tossed the newspaper onto his desk.

"How the hell do you keep getting into these messes, Noah?"

"That's not the response I expected from my attorney," Noah replied. "Is this going to be a problem, Stan?"

"Maybe yes, maybe no," the attorney replied.

"For that, I'm paying you four hundred dollars an hour?"

"It could have been worse. I could have simply answered yes."

"So what do you really think, Stan?"

"This is a class-action suit, Noah, just like the last case with the architects, which means a judge has to certify the class. If the class is certified, it could go either way. I could see a jury looking at all of the facts Kronheim would try to bring in and deciding you should have either divulged your meeting with the FBI or delayed the public offering until whatever threat the FBI was warning you about had passed. Then again, a jury could conclude that there was no clear, unquestionable threat and that you had no obligation to divulge anything about your meeting with the FBI."

"And what do you think a jury would decide?"

"Hard to predict what juries will do."

"I understand that, but what do you think?"

"I think a reasonable person could easily make an unreasonable decision given what the plaintiffs will present."

"You think I could lose?"

"Yeah, I do. I think you would win on appeal, but you could lose in the lower court."

"Shit!" Noah muttered under his breath.

"So, we fight certification of the class," Stanford Sherman replied. "We'll argue that this class should not be certified—that the plaintiffs have no standing to sue."

"What are our odds of prevailing?" Noah asked.

Sherman shrugged his shoulders. "Who the hell knows?" he answered. "A lazy judge will certify the class. He'll say, we'll let the jury decide the case. That saves him the trouble of crafting a well-thought-out opinion on whether the case meets the requirements of constituting a proper class action."

"And what if we get a really good judge?"

"We should win. I don't think you meeting with the FBI constituted a disclosable event."

"So what's the next step?" Noah asked.

"I'll file a motion for dismissal—sort of a summary judgment that the case should be thrown out. There will be a hearing, and if the court refuses to certify the class, we're done."

"And if the class is certified?"

"We'll begin settlement discussions. We won't want to risk an eighty-million-dollar verdict."

"Do you think a jury could hammer me for eighty million dollars?"

Stan Sherman leaned back in his chair, folded his hands behind his head, and stared up at the ceiling while he considered his response.

"Jesus Christ, Stan, I didn't ask you to recite the Constitution."

The attorney smiled and glanced over to Noah. "That might be easier, Noah. But to answer your question, if this went to a jury, yes, I think a jury could hammer you for eighty million dollars. Think about it. You're rich. Kronheim would show panoramic pictures of Potomac Center, maybe some big aerial shots too, and he would point to you and say, 'He owns it all...except for the interest he sold to unsuspecting victims for tens of millions of dollars, knowing full well that the entire project was being targeted by terrorists.' He would tell the jury that your victims collectively paid much more to buy less than half of the project than you had invested in all of Potomac Center. He would tell them, 'After an attack, Noah Greenspan would have the money, and the unsuspecting investors would have the rubble.'"

Noah sat there, speechless.

"So, Noah, we fight to keep the class from being certified," Sherman said.

Noah, still stunned by the attorney's hypothetical jury summation, nodded. "Go fight the fucking certification, Stan."

CHAPTER
FORTY-THREE

Omar Samir liked the café in Cairo's Windsor Hotel. It still had the feel of a British officers' club, which it had been during the First World War. A perfect place to ruminate over the plot he had hatched against Potomac Center. He smiled as he reread the AP story in the *International Herald Tribune* about the class-action suit against Potomac Center. *They have no idea,* he thought as he sipped his coffee.

"The story doesn't worry you, Omar?" Khaled Kassab asked.

"Not a bit. The Americans have probably figured out that AASLF is not an investment group and that there is no project called Palestinia. So what? They may know Potomac Center is, or was, probably a target, but they don't when, where, or how. Nothing is going to happen for many months. Demolishia is only shipping seventeen and a half kilos of plastique a month to Questex-Irvine Materials Testing in Washington, so it will be many months before we are ready. The Americans will have decided that there was no plot or that whatever plot there was has been abandoned. No one from America has made any inquiries to Demolishia. Meanwhile, the entire world knows that the FBI is scratching their heads trying to figure out what is going on. They have no idea. "

"But they know something is going on, Omar."

"They know I called on the Salaman woman's brother many months ago to inquire about the architecture. They know nothing else. They have no idea where to even begin to look."

"Why would the FBI have visited Potomac Center?"

"We don't know for sure that they did. All that we know for sure is that they warned Americans to be cautious. I'm telling you they have no idea what to do other than to tell Americans to be cautious."

"When do you think we will be ready, Omar?"

"We should have the one hundred and forty kilos we'll need by next June. June will be a good month. The weather should be pleasant in America, schools will have closed for the summer, and American tourists will be flooding into Washington. Potomac Center will be very crowded in June. It will be wonderful."

"I can't believe we're shipping the plastique right into Potomac Center," Khaled said.

"I'm telling you, it's perfect," Omar replied, slapping the tabletop. "We opened Questex-Irvine Materials Testing in the Potomac Center office complex last month without a hitch. Our friends provided the attorney to sign the lease, as well as the money for the rent, and they will continue to see to it that the rent is paid on the first of the month, every month, right on time."

"Unbelievable," Khaled replied. "It is unbelievable."

"The plastique will arrive in a small package every month and will be stored in a locked closet until we are ready. It's a perfect plan, and it's already working. We have a base right in the heart of Potomac Center."

"It's the last place the FBI would think of looking," Khaled agreed.

***

Agent Hogan sat at his desk looking at the oversize aerial view of Potomac Center he had pinned to the large bulletin board on the wall behind his desk. "Why did they want the architectural plans for this project?" he asked. "What the hell are they planning?"

"Maybe nothing," Agent Atkins replied. "All we know is that five months ago Omar Samir was trying to get the plans to the center. As far as we know, he never got them."

"Mike, he did get the tenants' manual, and that gives a pretty complete overview of Potomac Center."

"And that's all we have to go on, Larry. A Palestinian has the tenants' manual for Potomac Center. What are we supposed to do with that?"

"Why did they want it?" Agent Hogan replied.

"It could be anything. Curiosity. Maybe they have no plan at all."

"Let's think this through. We know they hate Noah Greenspan's fiancée. Alexandra Salaman exposed them to the Israelis years ago when she was in Beirut, and the IDF took out their leader, Ali Abdul Shoukri. They probably hate Noah Greenspan too."

"Right, and that's virtually everything we know," Agent Atkins replied. "What the hell are we supposed to do with that?"

"If they wanted to attack Potomac Center, what kind of an assault would require architectural plans?"

"Maybe none would *require* architectural plans, but the plans could come in handy for almost any kind of an attack," Agent Atkins replied. "If they just wanted to shoot up the place, they might want to know where all the entrances are. If they wanted to gas the place, they might want to know where the ventilation system was located. It's kind of far-fetched, but if they wanted to bomb the place, they might want to know more about the structural design of Potomac Center."

"The Shoukri gang didn't bomb anything. They weren't into explosives. They were shooters."

"So where does that leave us?" Agent Atkins asked.

"It could be anything, Mike. Thousands of shoppers go through that place every day. On holiday weekends or during the summer, tens of thousands will go through Potomac Center. We know a group of terrorists have, or had, a keen interest in Potomac Center—enough of an interest to have traveled all the way to Baltimore from the Middle East to get their hands on those plans. I don't think they would do that just to shoot up the place."

"You're probably right, Larry, and some kind of gas or biological attack would seem way too sophisticated for these guys. That leaves some kind of bomb attack, but I have to tell you that seems really far-fetched."

"Yeah, it does. I don't know where we would even start to look. We can't search everyone who enters the mall or search the thousands of cars that park there every day."

"And think of all the packages that are shipped into Potomac Center. Every store in the place receives parcels and mail every morning, and there are delivery trucks at the receiving dock all day long," Agent Atkins said.

"Let's assume they're planning to bomb the place," Agent Hogan replied.

"Why would we assume that?"

"I don't know; it just makes more sense to me, given their interest in the architecture. Look, we have to start somewhere. Let's just concentrate, for now, on the assumption that they plan to bomb the place."

"OK, so where do we go from here with that assumption?"

"Where would they get the explosives, and how would they get them here?"

"We could start checking for unusual sales of explosive material like dynamite."

"Or reported thefts of explosives," Agent Hogan said.

"You're assuming they would get the explosives here in the States."

"It doesn't seem likely that they would try to enter the United States with that crap—does it?" Agent Hogan asked.

"I'll ask our army friends at Aberdeen Proving Ground what the most likely explosive materials would be and where the stuff is most likely to be available."

"Well, it's a start," Agent Hogan" replied.

***

"You OK, Alexandra?" Markazie asked.

"What—yes. I'm fine," she answered.

"You sure?"

"I'm sure. Why are you asking?"

"Because I've been watching you stare at the wall for the last fifteen minutes, Alexandra. And it's not the first time I've watched you do that since you've been back."

"I'm fine, Frank."

"Come into my office for a minute, Alexandra. We should talk."

"I'm really fine, Frank," she insisted as she followed him into his office.

"No, you're not fine, Alexandra," he replied, as he sat down behind his desk. "You're a mess. Sit down, please." Alexandra started to object but instead sat down, silently, opposite him. "I don't have to tell you how responsible I feel for what you went through, Alexandra."

"Are you dissatisfied with my work since I got back, Frank?"

"Hell no. You can turn out more good copy in your sleep than half the people I've got working here. This isn't about your work, Alexandra. It's about your head."

Alexandra looked at him for a moment and then brought her hands to her face. "I am a mess, Frank. I don't know what to do. During the day all I can think about is what I'm putting Noah through, and at night I dream about Omdurman and what they did to me and what they were going to do to me. I can't fall asleep without Muhammad Faizel waking me up."

"I understand, Alexandra."

"No, Frank, you really don't. Faizel forced me to stand in front of him naked. He gave me a choice of letting him rape me or having the guards rape me. I was twenty-four hours away from that, Frank. It's almost surreal that I'm here now looking back on all of that as though it were a dream. I'd be dead by now if Daoud hadn't risked his life for me and if Amos Ben-Chaiyim hadn't come for me when he did and if Noah hadn't wired a half million dollars for my ransom. I was that close to absolute hell," she said, holding her thumb and forefinger an inch apart.

Markazie nodded his understanding while he considered how best to reply. *How in the hell do you respond to that?* he thought to himself.

"That's yesterday's news, Alexandra," he finally said. "You're only twenty-nine years old, and you have a huge future in front of you. You've been through hell, but it's over. You're engaged to a wonderful guy. You have a great career in front of you, and you have the support of this entire organization. You have some things to work through, and I understand that. You'll get all the help you need from your colleagues here. I'm behind you one hundred percent. Hell, everybody is, but you have to stop torturing yourself. Khartoum is over. Omdurman is behind you."

"I know," she said, nodding. "I just need some time."

"Take all the time you need, Alexandra. Why don't you and Noah take a few days or a week or whatever time you need? You can drive over to Ocean City while the weather is still pretty nice and stay at my town house on the beach at Ocean Colony. Everyone has left the shore, so you two could have some quiet time together. Take long walks on the beach at sunset. Get your feet wet in the sandy muck and let the sea breeze mess up your hair. It'll do you good." She smiled across the desk at him.

"That's very nice, Frank. Maybe we will," she said, as her composure returned.

"You know, Alexandra, a dozen years or so ago, I said you were the best intern I ever hired. I'll update that assessment. You're among the best journalists I've ever hired. You just came back from hell, Alexandra. You've seen a slice of life very few people in this country have ever seen. In time, when the trauma of it all has receded, you'll be a better journalist because of it. You know why? Because you really know that that slice of life exists—not because you've read about it but because you've lived it. As rotten as you feel right now, you have an insight that very few people have into life as it really exists for most people on this damn planet. Few writers in this damn profession can touch you, Alexandra."

She sat there for a moment while his words sank in. Alexandra rose, walked over to her boss, leaned down, and kissed him on the cheek. "Thanks, Frank. I appreciate that," she said as she turned and walked from his office. "Really, more than you know."

CHAPTER
FORTY-FOUR

Ocean City, just north of Assateague Island on Maryland's Eastern Shore and only a two-hour drive over the Chesapeake Bay Bridge from Washington, was, in many respects, an ideal diversion for Noah and Alexandra, even if only for a long weekend. Frank Markazie's Ocean Colony town house was among a cluster of a couple dozen identical multistory beach houses built a few years earlier on the Atlantic coast about a mile south of the Mason-Dixon Line. Most of the houses on the shore were deserted as autumn moved inexorably toward winter. The temperature, cool during the day, turned brisk in the late afternoon as the sun descended toward the western horizon. The clear blue skies of summer had already begun to transform into a skyscape of elongated steel-gray clouds.

While Noah and Alexandra both brought some work with them, they both knew they were there, primarily, to draw solace from one another and to heal from the stresses that dogged them. It was to be a restorative respite from the nearly catastrophic summer and those old uncertainties that challenged their bond with one another.

They spent that first afternoon reading the material they had brought with them. Logs crackled in the pot-bellied fireplace. Noah sprawled comfortably on the thick carpet of the living room reading the plaintiffs' brief Saul Kronheim had penned for the shareholder suit against him. Alexandra, seated on a timeworn but comfortable leather couch, edited copy she was preparing about the first Israeli settlements being established on the West Bank near the Judean Mountains south of Jerusalem.

Stan Sherman had appended a note to the copy of the suit. "News—maybe good, maybe not. Judge Maurice Golden, who tried the last case Kronheim brought against you, has been selected to hear this one too." Noah was worried. Everything hinged on whether or not Judge Golden would certify the class. Noah's concern, at least at that moment, wasn't whether he would win or lose the case. He was far more concerned about Alexandra. Stan Sherman had warned him that if the class was certified, Alexandra would be called and examined as a witness. Kronheim had plastered her all over the plaintiffs' brief. Yusuf would be called too, but it was Alexandra about whom Noah was worried. She would be fair game, given her involvement with Shoukri, Sherman had warned. Kronheim's plaintiffs' brief proved him right.

Alexandra, according to the brief, had consorted with known terrorists when she was a student at Phoenicia University in Beirut, a known hotbed of radical rhetoric. Alexandra's press reports, according to the plaintiffs' brief, were used to tip off Arab conspirators in Israel of shipments of arms caches to be used in a planned massacre of civilians. The brief, regurgitating old press clippings, described Alexandra as the cause of Ali Abdul Shoukri's death at the hands of the Israelis after she fled to Israel. The brief suggested that she was the link between Noah and those terrorists who wanted to destroy him and his Potomac Center project. Noah Greenspan, the brief charged, knew of this danger and chose not to divulge it to prospective investors such as the plaintiffs, who suffered great financial loss as a result. Stanford Sherman had warned Noah that plaintiffs are often prone to throw everything they can think of into plaintiffs' briefs, including the proverbial kitchen sink.

Noah knew Alexandra was already emotionally stretched thin, and being questioned in public and under oath about her relationship with Shoukri, and maybe even about Khartoum and Omdurman, would be a disaster for her. Noah hadn't yet mentioned to her the prospect that she could be called as a witness. He looked over to Alexandra sitting there on the couch. She had her legs tucked comfortably under her as she read. She was beautifully serene, more relaxed than he had seen her in weeks. The beige turtleneck of the sweater she wore seemed almost a pedestal on which rested the head and face he so adored. His every instinct was to protect her. *I'll never let this go to trial,* he thought to himself. *I'll pay the entire $80 million before I let them put her through that. I'll sell the entire mall first.* "Want to go for a walk along the beach?" he asked.

"Sounds great," she answered, putting down the draft of the feature story she had been editing. "Let's walk in the brine. Markazie said it would do me good to get my feet wet in the sandy muck along the water's edge."

"Come on. It will do us both good," he replied, getting to his feet.

Noah and Alexandra donned jackets and began strolling south hand in hand along the beach, ankle deep in the watery brine of spent waves flowing back into the Atlantic. The sun was making its daily descent toward the western horizon over Assawoman Bay, the stretch of water that separated Ocean City from the mainland, and the resulting chill in the air was invigorating. A deserted boardwalk amusement park loomed ahead. A few weeks earlier, it was teeming with people and engulfed in the sounds of carousels, shooting galleries, arcade barkers, banter, laughter, and the sporadic but predictable wailing of children temporarily separated from their parents. Now, however, the abandoned amusement park had lost any semblance of amusement. It looked sad and pathetic, boarded up for the coming winter. Other than a few children flying kites fifty yards or so ahead and a couple of golden retrievers running along the water's edge, they had the huge beach to themselves. The rhythmic sound of the waves crashing on the beach and the cries of ever-hungry American herring seagulls swooping about overhead in search of any scraps or morsels they could spot accentuated the rare solitude they were enjoying at that moment.

"Look," Alexandra said, smiling and pointing down to her bare feet.

"Prettiest feet I ever saw," Noah replied.

"Look at the muck squishing up between my toes."

"Yep, that's muck all right," he replied with a laugh.

"It feels good, Noah. Don't you feel it? Markazie says it's like therapy."

"Is it? Therapeutic, I mean?"

"Yeah, kind of. It's sort of primordial—me and nature," she said, as she reached down, scooped up some of the muck, and squeezed it through her fingers. "I think I know what Markazie meant. You know, a thousand years ago if someone were walking right here on this spot, this is the same feeling they would have felt between their toes. They would look out and see the same ocean and probably see and hear the same seagulls. It sort of brings you back to earth. It says forget all the shit that goes on every day that can make you so miserable. When all is said and done, this is all any of us are—creatures making footprints in the sand that disappear each time a wave rolls back out to sea."

Yeah, he thought to himself. *I only wish that plaintiffs' brief would disappear as quickly.* They continued walking until they reached the amusement park before turning around to start back.

"What do you say we stop and pick up some hard-shell crabs and beer at Phillips Crab House on the way back? We can eat out on the deck and watch the waves roll in."

"I like that," she said. "And I like that too," she continued, pointing up at the bright full moon that had risen over the ocean, its reflection stretching across the water as far as the eye could see. Noah stopped dead in his tracks and looked up at the star-studded sky. How many times over the years, miles apart, had they both peered into the same night sky, their eyes fixated on that same moon, their minds fixated on one another? She stood there facing him, smiling tenderly, joyful tears in her eyes, her hair blowing about in the strong ocean breeze. Noah pulled her into his arms and kissed her.

"My God, I love you, Alexandra," he said, "It's overwhelming how much I love you."

"We're going to be all right, aren't we, Noah?" she asked, anxiously, as she embraced him.

"Going to be?" he asked, pulling away just enough to look into her eyes. "Alexandra, we *are* all right. We've always been all right. Do you doubt that? Do you doubt that, even for a minute?"

"No, Noah, I don't doubt the strength of our love for one another. I just have this nagging fear of something ominous always lurking around the next corner."

"We've been around a lot of corners, Alexandra, but here we are. I've never loved you more than I do right now—and you know what? I am absolutely positive I'll feel the same way tomorrow. Do you want to know why I'm so certain of that? I'll tell you why," he said without waiting for her to answer. "Because I've experienced this exact same feeling ever since that first time I knew I loved you."

"We were just kids," she replied, as she reached up to kiss him.

"My point exactly," he said. "I've been more in love with you each day ever since."

"Let's skip the hard-shells," she murmured into his ear as they embraced. "Take me back to Markazie's and make love to me."

***

Alexandra came down to the kitchen early the next morning to brew a fresh pot of coffee. The town house, with its eastern exposure and large sliding glass doors at every level, was flooded in sunlight as the sun rose over the horizon, its intensity magnified by the glistening ocean surface. Alexandra poured some coffee into a mug and sat at one of the kitchen barstools while she waited for Noah to come downstairs. They had planned to drive north along Ocean Highway a short distance to Libby's, a favorite of locals, for pancakes, waffles, and generous omelets. It was blissfully quiet with only the hungry cries of seagulls whizzing to and fro in search of their own morning meal. Alexandra looked around, approvingly. Frank Markazie had created a delightful getaway here on the water's edge. As she scanned the room, her gaze settled on the papers Noah had left on the floor in front of the fireplace. She got up from the barstool and walked over to the reading material he had left in a neat pile the night before. She bent down low enough to read the top page.

US District Court, Eastern District of Pennsylvania
Gunnar Kjarski on behalf of himself and all others similarly situated,
Plaintiffs,
v.
Noah Greenspan and Potomac Center Properties of America,
Defendants.
Court File No. 11-25631 Shareholder Class Action
Complaint in Class Action

Alexandra picked up the document, walked back to the barstool, and sat down to begin reading. Her chest tightened and her hand shook nervously as she turned the page.

***

Noah came down into the kitchen and immediately noticed the copy of Kronheim's class-action suit spread out on the counter. He called for Alexandra and, when she didn't respond, ran out onto the deck to see if she was on the beach. He spotted her walking alone along the water's edge about a hundred yards to the north. He yelled for her, but if she heard, she didn't acknowledge it. Noah bolted from the beach house and began running toward Alexandra.

"Alexandra!" he yelled as he ran to catch up to her.

She stopped and turned as he approached her. Alexandra smiled, perfunctorily, her face otherwise expressionless.

"Hey, what's up?" Noah asked, doing his best to appear unconcerned.

"'What's up?' I read the suit—that's what's up. The whole damn thing is about me. I've already cost you a half million dollars, and now I might cost you everything. Can you imagine how much they will want to get me on the stand? This is a nightmare, Noah. I'm a nightmare—your nightmare."

"Alexandra, no one is going to get you on the stand, and once we get this stupid suit thrown out, it will all be over."

"Of course they'll get me on the stand. The whole goddamned suit is about me. And you know what? I think they have a good case. If I were the judge, I'd throw the book at you."

"Alexandra, I promise you you'll never have to testify, and you're wrong about the suit. It's a lousy suit. It's a fishing expedition. There was no specific threat against Potomac Center, and, besides, I was told by the FBI not to discuss the meeting they had with me with anyone."

"Did Stan Sherman tell you it was a lousy suit and that they wouldn't get the class certified?"

"He said that would be the winning strategy."

"Goddammit, Noah. That's not what I asked you. Stop treating me like a child, damn it. What did he really say?"

"He said our strategy will be to fight certification of the class," Noah answered.

"Because he knows Kronheim probably has a damn compelling case."

"Alexandra, you always fight certification in a class-action suit. If the class isn't certified, the whole damn thing goes away."

"And if the case is certified?"

"I'll settle."

"Why would you do that, Noah? You just said there was no specific threat and that you were told by the FBI not to discuss their meeting with you with anyone, and certainly not with huge audiences. Why would you settle?"

"Suits are messy and time-consuming. It's always best to settle a suit like this," he replied.

"You'd settle to protect me," she yelled. "That's the only reason you would settle. That's why you said, with such certainty, that I would never have to testify."

"So what, Alexandra? Yes, it's true. I would settle before I let them so much as ask you your name. Why is that so damn upsetting to you?"

"You know, Noah, being a burden is an awful burden. Can you understand that? I don't want to go through life being your burden."

"You're talking nonsense, Alexandra."

"Am I? Think about it, Noah. Think of all times I've been a burden to you. My father, who really loves you like a son, couldn't stand to think of us even dating when we were kids. My brother, your best friend, hated the thought of you and me being together. Then I made the decision to go off to school in Beirut, and then there was the entire Shoukri mess. I stayed away for nearly five years, Noah, and now this. And you know what else, Noah? This Palestinian-Jewish issue will never go away either. Who are we kidding? Read that damn suit. It's all about Alexandra the Palestinian refugee and her fiancé, Noah Greenspan, the Jew."

"It doesn't say that," he replied, quietly and unconvincingly.

"Let's go back to the city," she answered, abruptly. "This deserted beach town is giving me the creeps." With that, Alexandra turned and started back toward the house. Noah grabbed her by the arm and spun her around so that they were facing one another.

"No!" he yelled. "No, goddammit, we're not going back to the city. Yesterday having the entire beach to ourselves was wonderful, and today it's giving you the creeps. Does that make any sense, Alexandra? The damn lawsuit is what is giving you the creeps Alexandra, and that's exactly what Kronheim wants it to do. The suit is creepy. Kronheim is creepy. The shareholders who rushed to dump the stock and then got burned when the stock recovered so quickly are creeps. You and I are fine, Alexandra."

"Noah, you could have your pick of any woman you wanted. Why don't you step back and think about that?"

"I have, Alexandra," he replied, taking hold of her arms. "I have thought about that. I have the only woman I want. She's right here, standing barefoot with me in this wet muck. I have her. I'm holding her right now. You, Alexandra Salaman, are the only woman I want. You're so much more important to me than that stupid lawsuit. Don't make that fucking lawsuit into some crisis in our lives. It's a pain in the ass, but it's not that important. It really isn't."

Her expression softened as she looked into his eyes. She smiled and laid her head on his shoulder. He squeezed her gently in his arms. A solitary seagull flying overhead seemed to trumpet its approval as it swooped by.

"Let's go to Libby's and get some pancakes," he said, as they turned back to return to the beach house.

"I don't want you to settle," she replied, slipping her arm around his waist. "I'll be fine."

CHAPTER
FORTY-FIVE

"So, Mike, what have we learned?" Agent Hogan asked.

"Larry, we're searching for the proverbial needle in a haystack," his colleague replied. "Aberdeen provided a list of every domestic producer of demolition explosives. It's endless. What's worse, our people don't think AASLF would use an American supplier. If their mode of attack is going to entail explosives, they'll more than likely obtain the stuff abroad and smuggle it into the States."

"Seems pretty risky to be transporting explosives halfway around the world."

"There is plenty of new explosive material on the commercial market that's quite stable. So-called plastic explosives used to be available only for munitions, but now you can buy this stuff abroad on the commercial market. Mark my words: it's going to be a problem. It's only a matter of time. Transporting it wouldn't be very difficult either," Agent Atkins replied.

"They would probably find sources for explosives in Europe rather than trying to deal here with du Pont de Nemours or Hercules or Atlas or any of hundreds of smaller domestic producers," Agent Hogan agreed. "Did Aberdeen have any thoughts about whom likely foreign suppliers might be?"

"Yeah, we contacted Imperial Chemical Industries in Britain; they're huge but couldn't offer much help. There's also a Czech outfit called Demolishia that began manufacturing plastic explosives three years ago for civil-engineering projects, mostly in Czechoslovakia. We contacted them to see if they've sold and shipped any plastic explosives to the United States or to the Middle East."

"Any luck?" Agent Hogan asked.

"Nah, it doesn't look like it. They've sold a lot of the stuff to North Vietnam, though. The only American customer they've ever shipped to is Questex-Irvine Materials Testing. Questex-Irvine is a huge and very responsible outfit. In fact, they do a lot of work for the US government. Other than that, no one in the United States is using this plastique stuff. We Americans apparently like dynamite and TNT."

"Let's see if we can find out if the Czech outfit has shipped anything to anyone in the Middle East."

"We asked them that," Agent Atkins replied. "Questex-Irvine in Egypt is a customer. They're working on that big dam in Aswân, Egypt, so that makes perfect sense. I don't think we have to worry about the Questex-Irvines of the world."

"Yeah, you're probably right. That probably also explains why Questex-Irvine Materials Testing is a customer. They probably analyze all the new material they use."

"Well, let's contact our counterparts in Europe and see if they have any thoughts about where we might inquire. It's going to be a slog, though. For all we know, somebody could be cooking up this stuff in some basement in Mozambique" Agent Atkins said.

***

Alexandra spent almost all of her weekends with Noah, frequently spending the night with him at his town house. She slept peacefully when he was next to her. He had become her sentry, keeping Muhammad Faizel from intruding into her dreams. They spent hours together talking about their work. Potomac Center was preparing for its first Christmas season, and the excitement among retailers in the mall was almost palpable. Alexandra continued to grind out stories about the Middle East and was widely recognized in the city as one of the leading specialists writing about the Israel-Palestine conflict. She was generally receptive to Noah's comments about the stories she was writing and appreciative that he rarely debated the opinions she expressed, even when she knew he didn't agree. She watched him with particular interest one night early in December. He had been reading a draft of Stan Sherman's motion for dismissal of the class-action suit. Noah had put aside Sherman's motion and picked up a draft of a story she had written for the Sunday edition of the *Star*, which she had given to him to read. She could tell that he wasn't pleased with what she had written. Noah had a habit of punctuating his displeasure with a sigh of annoyance. She also knew he wouldn't offer a comment unless she invited him to. These past few months since her return from Sudan, he was simply loath to upset her. He glanced up at her and smiled.

"What?" she asked.

He shrugged. "I didn't say anything."

"But you were thinking that you would like to. Is there something about the story that bothers you?"

"I haven't finished reading it," he replied.

"I would appreciate your thoughts, Noah. Honestly, I would," she said.

"OK." He nodded as he turned his attention back to her story.

ISRAELIS REESTABLISH JUDEAN HILLS SETTLEMENT ON WEST BANK
By Alexandra Salaman

The question of whether Israel will begin to claim and settle land on the West Bank, which has been controlled by Israel since the Six-Day War, has been answered. The Israeli settlement of Kfar Etzion is now an established fact of history. It would, perhaps, be better described as a reestablished fact of history, because it sits on land legally purchased from Arab landowners nearly a half century ago. It was part of a group of similar settlements known as the Etzion Bloc, also purchased and settled by Jews.

Jordan's Arab Legion attacked the settlements in 1948 following the establishment of the State of Israel by the United Nations. The inhabitants of Kfar Etzion were cut off from the defending Israeli forces, captured, and massacred. That, sadly, is also an established fact of history.

It would defy logic to assume that Kfar Etzion will be the first and last Israeli settlement on the West Bank. The die is now cast. Jews will, once again, dwell in the land they call Judea and Samira.

Following the recently concluded Six-Day War, Israel finds itself in control of the entire former Etzion Bloc. Hanan Porat, whose parents were forced to flee twenty years ago, leads an activist group that petitioned Israeli prime minister Levi Eshkol to allow the reestablishment of Kfar Etzion, and, after considerable hand-wringing, the prime minister has agreed. While Eshkol is known to have had reservations about civilian settlements on the West Bank, the Etzion Bloc resonates deeply in Jewish consciousness, and the reestablishment of this Jewish settlement was strongly endorsed by Ra'anan Weitz, head of the Settlement Department in the powerful Jewish Agency; Haim-Moshe Shapira, the minister of internal affairs; and Michael Hazani, a leader in the National Religious movement.

The establishment of the Kfar Etzion settlement is also consistent with the plan Israeli minister Yigal Allon has proposed to partition the West Bank between Israel and Jordan, create a Druze state in the Israeli-occupied Golan Heights, and return most of the Sinai Peninsula to Egypt.

The only problem with these elaborate plans is that they have been uniformly rejected by all of the Arab belligerents in the recent war that would have to agree to them. Having recently returned from the Arab League conference in Khartoum, this reporter believes that any Israeli dream of Egypt, Syria, or Jordan buying into such a plan is, in fact, a pipe dream. Israel's Arab neighbors—indeed virtually all Arab countries—are committed to the now-famous three no's of Khartoum: no recognition, no negotiation, and no peace.

Furthermore, the recent emergence of the very militant Palestine Liberation Organization, which is committed to armed struggle against Israel, makes any agreement between Israel and any of the Arab nations, or even the Palestinian population on the West Bank, virtually impossible.

Israel, of course, understands this perfectly well. Nonetheless, the Jewish state has moved forward with the establishment of Kfar Etzion. This settlement, which has a history that tugs at the heartstrings of every Israeli, is the first of what is certain to be many settlements to follow.

Noah finished reading Alexandra's column and looked over to her. Her eyes were already fixed on him as she awaited his comments.

"It's good, Alexandra. It provides news, perspective, and, I guess, some real insight into what the reestablishment of Kfar Etzion portends for the future. Settlements are certain to be a huge emerging issue."

"But?"

"No buts. I have no criticism of the column at all. Frankly, I don't see how anyone could take issue with what you have written."

"Yet you seem displeased," she replied.

"You know, Judge Golden will soon be deciding whether or not to certify the class in the Kronheim suit against me and the company."

"And my column about Kfar Etzion could influence his decision? Is that what you are thinking?"

"No, not your column about Kfar Etzion, but I do worry that any of your columns that focus on the Israel-Palestine issue could influence his judgment."

"Why do you feel that way? I don't understand."

"Kronheim is going to argue that you are a thorn in the side of certain Palestinians and that they are targeting me and Potomac Center as a way to strike at you. The more you are in the press writing on the very issues that Kronheim says has inflamed the terrorists, the greater the odds that Judge Golden may decide that it is a reasonable case to turn over to a jury to decide. Judge Golden isn't going to decide the merits of the case at this time. He's only going to decide whether to allow the case to move forward."

"And you think my columns might just tip the scales in that direction?"

"They might," he replied.

"So you want me to stop writing about the Israel-Palestine issue until Judge Golden makes his decision? And if Judge Golden decides to certify the class, I guess I should stop writing on the subject while some jury is then hearing the case and making its decision."

"Stan Sherman would probably be happier if you did."

"I'm not asking Stan Sherman. I'm asking you."

Noah took his time to consider Alexandra's question. For several moments there was only silence as they looked at one another.

"No, honey," Noah finally responded. "You keep writing. Ali Abdul Shoukri didn't silence you five years ago, and Omar Samir hasn't silenced you either. We're sure as hell not going to allow Saul Kronheim and Gunnar Kjarski, whoever he is, to silence you now."

"Thank you, Noah. I don't know what I would have done if I had to stop writing because of all of this," she said.

***

It was purely coincidental that Amos Ben-Chaiyim and Dany Haddad met at Paris's Orly Airport on the way to New York, just before Christmas. Amos had stopped in Paris for meetings with representatives of the Service de Documentation Extérieure et de Contre-Espionnage, better known in Israel and the United States simply as SDECE, the French equivalent of the Mossad or the CIA. Amos was on his way to Washington for meetings at the Israeli embassy regarding the AASLF matter. Israeli and American intelligence teams were convinced that a major terrorist plot was under way, and Amos had, at his request, been assigned to work with the joint American-Israeli effort to stop it.

Amos hadn't seen Dany since their hurried departure from Khartoum. Dany explained that he was connecting in Paris on his way to New York—that he had been asked by the Israeli Foreign Ministry to travel to New York as an observer at meetings pertaining to a new UN protocol that had just been approved. The new 1967 protocol extended the 1951 United Nations Convention Relating to the Status of Refugees to cover those deemed to have become refugees subsequent to the 1951 convention—specifically, those Palestinians claiming refugee status as a result of the Six-Day War.

"I had heard that the ministry was going to ask you to take this UN assignment on," Amos said as they took their seats on the Pan Am flight to JFK.

"I gave it a lot of thought," Dany replied. "I may be the first Palestinian to go to the United Nations representing Israel."

"How do you feel about that?" Amos asked.

"Look, I think we have to search for common ground. The one certainty in our region is that Palestinians and Jews are destined to live side by side. That's the future. We have to choose how we're going to live side by side. I have no intention of living as a refugee for the rest of my life. I would prefer to live as an Israeli citizen than as a refugee or as a stateless person living in limbo between Jordan and Israel. I may not agree with every Israeli policy, but I know there is only one democracy in the Middle East, and it's Israel."

"I suspect you'll get a pretty cold shoulder from virtually all of the Arabs you'll be sitting with," Amos said. "I really admire you, Dany. I really do."

"After Khartoum, a cold shoulder in New York will be nothing," Dany replied.

"What's taking you to the States?" he asked.

"We're pretty sure the Shoukri cell is up to something. We've put a team together with the Americans to try to stop it."

"And you're part of the team?"

"Yeah," Amos answered. "I'm part of the team."

"Do you think Alexandra and Noah are really in danger?"

Amos nodded. "Yes, Dany, I really do."

"Do you have any idea what they might be up to?"

"Nothing concrete. I'm pretty sure if they try something, though, it's going to be big. They didn't need the drawings of Potomac Center if they only wanted to harm Noah or Alexandra."

"How can you protect something as huge as I understand this Potomac Center is?"

"You can't," Amos replied, "You have to figure out what they are up to and stop them in their tracks, ideally before they get anywhere near Noah or Alexandra or Potomac Center."

"Do you think you'll be able to do that?"

"I have no idea, Dany. If they make a mistake or we get very lucky, maybe."

"After what you pulled off in Khartoum, I'll bet on whatever team you're on."

"That was audacious and very risky but not very complicated. They were either going to fall for our ruse or they weren't. Fortunately for all of us, they fell for it."

"And I'm living testimony to that," Dany said. "You really risked your life to get us out of there. I'll never forget that."

"You know, that was relatively easy—dangerous but easy. When you have almost no options, as was the case in Khartoum, it really focuses your thinking. But with Potomac Center, well, that's an entirely different story. First, there are thousands of people there at any given time, and the Shoukri people have the luxury of picking their time. Once their scheme is in play, there's almost nothing you can do. They can either shoot up the place or bomb the place. You don't want to have to react after guns are going off or bombs are exploding. That's certain carnage."

They fastened their seat belts as the stewardess pointed out the emergency exits, demonstrated how to don the life preservers, and explained what to do if the oxygen masks were activated during the flight. The Boeing 707-320C lifted off with a full load of passengers, baggage, and cargo containers filled with small packages and mail. Amid the freight was an innocuous package, transferred from Czech Airlines, weighing seventeen and a half kilos, addressed to Questex-Irvine Materials Testing, Potomac Center Office Complex, 1500 M Street, SE, Washington, DC.

CHAPTER FORTY-SIX

Stanford Sherman handed Noah the response he had prepared to the plaintiffs' brief Saul Kronheim had filed against him and Potomac Center Properties of America.

"Want some coffee, while you read our response?"

"Sure, it's freezing out there," Noah replied, as he took off his jacket and draped it over a vacant chair at the small conference table in Stan Sherman's office. Sherman poured Noah a cup of coffee from the carafe on his credenza.

"Can I make notes on the draft?" Noah asked as he uncapped his pen.

"Yes, of course, but you'll find it pretty cut-and-dried."

Noah leaned back in his chair and began to read.

United States District Court,
Eastern District of Pennsylvania
Gunnar Kjarski on behalf of himself and all others similarly situated,
Plaintiffs,
v.
Noah Greenspan and Potomac Center Properties of America,
Defendants.

Court File No. 11-25631 Shareholder Class Action
Defendants' response to plaintiffs' pretrial
proposed findings of fact and conclusions of law

Defendants respectfully submit the following response to plaintiffs' rep-
resentations and proposed findings of fact and conclusions of law.

Noah read his attorney's response to the suit, which consisted of a sentence or a brief paragraph for each and every allegation made in the $80-million-dollar complaint, explaining why the defendants disagreed. He tossed the draft of the response down on the conference table and leaned back in his chair. "So that's it?"

"What do you mean?" the attorney replied.

"That's our defense? Agree, disagree, or deny along with a couple of sentences each justifying why we agree, disagree, or deny?"

"Essentially, yes," Sherman replied. "Of course, we'll make a much more detailed case at the hearing, but this response simply lays out where we are in disagreement with the plaintiffs. It's standard procedure, Noah."

"When is the hearing, Stan?"

"We're not sure. Judge Golden is tied up with a major case right now, so he hasn't scheduled our hearing yet. I would guess it would be another thirty days or so."

***

"Khaled, I received this message at the front desk this morning," Omar Samir said, making no effort to conceal his excitement. "It's working. The entire world will be shocked by what we will have accomplished."

Khaled Kassab took the note from Omar and unfolded it.

"My God, we've done it," he whispered, astonished. Khaled looked around the café to see if they were being observed by any of the other guests at the Windsor. He leaned over the table excitedly and embraced Omar Samir. "You are a genius, Omar. No one else could have done this," he cried. His hands shook as he read the words carefully. "Second shipment arrived at Q-I Materials Testing safely this afternoon."

"You see, Khaled, we now have thirty-five kilos at the target. We have twenty-five percent of all the plastique we'll need right there sitting in a closet at Potomac Center."

"It's unbelievable, Omar. It's so simple. The plastique is there. We shipped right under their noses," Khaled replied, barely able to control his excitement.

"Our friends at Demolishia ship seventeen and a half kilos a month on Czechoslovakia Airlines to Paris, where it's transferred to an Air France flight to New York. A cargo forwarder then drives it to Washington with other parcels being sent to the capital of America from Kennedy Airport. It's so simple it's undetectable."

"Omar, we'll be ready by summer," Khaled cried, joyfully.

"What a birthday party this Potomac Center will have."

"No one will ever forget it," Khaled replied, slapping the tabletop.

"When the time is right, Ahmed will go to America and prepare the charges. He will supervise our plan for placing the charges exactly where he has specified. The entire complex will be turned into a pile of rubble in an instant."

"How will he do that? How will he be able to place the charges throughout this Potomac Center?"

Omar Samir grinned from ear to ear. "Ah, my friend, I told you I had a plan, did I not?"

"Yes, Omar. You said you had a plan."

Omar simply nodded. "A pile of rubble. That's all that will remain," he said, wagging his finger.

***

Stan Sherman was surprised when his secretary told him Judge Golden was calling.

"He's on the phone? Judge Golden is holding on the phone?" Sherman asked, incredulously.

"That's what the man said. He asked to speak to you and said to tell you it was Judge Golden calling from Philadelphia," the secretary replied.

"This is Stanford Sherman," the lawyer said as he picked up the phone.

"Well, it's been a long time, Counselor. I didn't expect to see you and your client, Mr. Greenspan, back in my courtroom, but here we are."

"Well, we know we'll have a fine judge hearing the case," Sherman replied.

"Counselor, that's why I'm calling. I've read your answer to the plaintiffs' complaint. Of course, I've read the plaintiffs' brief as well. I would like to suggest that you and your client along with Mr. Kronheim and his client consider meeting with me in my chambers for a strictly informal pre-certification-hearing conference. This would, of course, be entirely voluntary, and nothing discussed at the conference I'm suggesting would in any way be prejudicial to either side. I just think it might be worth everyone's time to consider an amicable settlement before we all get committed to a process that might possibly be extremely costly and very time-consuming. I've discussed this with the opposing counsel, and he is willing to consider this if you and your client are."

"I'll certainly discuss this with my client, Judge. It is unusual, though. I'm sure he'll want to know what this implies."

"It doesn't imply a damn thing, Counselor. Tell your client it implies that Judge Golden thinks it would be a good idea."

"Yes, sir, Your Honor."

"Tell your client I would like to invite him and opposing counsel to meet with me in my chambers on March fifteenth at nine o'clock in the morning."

"I'll tell him, Your Honor."

"Oh, and one other thing. I'd like to invite Miss Salaman and her brother, the architect, to come along as well. I emphasize the word *invite*, Counselor. I think if I can have the key parties to this case in the room at the same time, it might be very helpful, but no one has to feel obligated to come. This is not a subpoena. It's an invitation to an informal conference."

"I understand, and I'll convey that," Stan Sherman replied.

"See you March fifteenth then," Judge Golden said and hung up the phone.

Stan Sherman immediately called Noah following his conversation with Judge Golden. "I've just had the strangest telephone conversation with Judge Golden," Sherman said as soon as Noah picked up the phone.

"What now?" Noah asked.

"He wants to have a conference in his chambers with you and me and Kronheim and his client as well. He says it's strictly voluntary and nothing discussed during the conference by anyone will be prejudicial to either side."

"Is that all he said to you?"

"Actually, no. He said he would also like Alexandra and Yusuf to be there if at all possible."

"What—he wants Alexandra and Yusuf to be there? What do you think this is all about?"

"He obviously wants to discuss some kind of settlement."

"Is that good?"

"Noah, I really don't know. It sure is unusual. Especially his inviting Alexandra and Yusuf to be there."

"What do you think we should do?"

"Noah, if the judge invites you to a conference in his chambers, you go."

"Why do you think he would like to have Alexandra and Yusuf there?"

"I guess he wants to ask them some questions."

"Do you think he's going to pressure us to settle?"

"I would guess he's going to pressure both sides to settle."

"Well, like you said, when the judge calls, you answer."

"I'll tell him we'll be there on the fifteenth," Sherman replied.

***

Saul Kronheim and his client, Gunnar Kjarski, were already there when Judge Golden's clerk showed Noah, Yusuf, Alexandra, and Stanford Sherman into the judge's chambers.

"Good morning, gentlemen and Miss Salaman," Judge Golden said, standing to greet them as they entered. "I hope you had a pleasant journey up from Washington."

"We did, indeed, Judge," Stan Sherman replied.

"It's good to see you again, Mr. Greenspan, Mr. Salaman. You too, Counselor," Judge Golden said, nodding to Stan Sherman. "And you, I presume, are Alexandra Salaman," he continued, extending his hand to her.

"Yes, I'm Alexandra Salaman," she replied, shaking his hand.

"So, make yourselves comfortable," Judge Golden said as he moved to his chair. "Please, find a comfortable place to sit." Everyone quickly took a seat in one of the leather chairs that had been placed in a semi-circle in front of Judge Golden's desk.

"Miss Salaman, I've read all of the columns you wrote last summer from the Middle East. I want you to know what a pleasure it was to read perspective that wasn't trying to sell a point of view. You're certainly a fine writer."

"Thank you, Your Honor," she replied, surprised he had gone to the trouble to read her work.

"And, Mr. Salaman, I haven't visited Potomac Center yet, but I hear it's a grand project. I'm glad it worked out so well."

"Thank you, sir…I mean, Your Honor," Yusuf answered.

"So, let me tell you why I've invited you all to this rather unorthodox conference. In a nutshell, I think it is always wise to settle a case like this, if possible, without all of the expense and time of hearings or a trial. Just so all of you understand, this is an off-the-record discussion. My staff will take no notes. Furthermore, none of you will be bound by anything you say here. If you want to change anything you say or retract anything you say, that's fine. Nothing you say here will prejudice your case. This is a common type of preliminary conference over in England, and, in some cases, I think it works well here too. So you can look at this as a friendly little chat we're having while we can all still be friends. Any further gatherings we might have will be burdened by strict rules of procedure, which sometimes can be a real pain in the ass, if you'll pardon my language, Miss Salaman."

"You should hear the language in a newsroom, Judge," Alexandra replied, smiling.

"Are you comfortable with our having this chat, Mr. Sherman?"

"We are, Your Honor," Stan Sherman replied.

"How about you, Saul?"

"Perfectly comfortable, although we do think ours is an open-and-shut case, pure and simple, Judge."

"Saul, let me quote Oscar Wilde to you: 'The truth is rarely pure and never simple,'" Judge Golden replied, impatiently. "So, let me address some thoughts to you for a moment, Mr. Greenspan. You know, there are very conflicting views about whether or not the court should consider defense motions for summary judgments to dismiss a class-action suit such as this prior to deciding whether or not the class should be certified at all. There's one school of thought that I should be precluded from considering the merits of the case Saul here has brought against you on behalf of Mr. Kjarski and others until I determine whether or not the class should be certified. On the other hand, as I'm sure Mr. Sherman here has advised you, if a class is certified, the pressure on the defendant to settle is always enormous. Frankly, I think a lot of these cases become nothing more than legalized extortion. On the other hand, many people believe that the common person is no match for a corporate giant and, therefore, class actions are a way of leveling the playing field. So, I have a bit of a dilemma at this stage of this suit. Do you know what I mean?"

"Your Honor, my client is one of the most scrupulous business—"

"Mr. Sherman, I was addressing my remarks to Mr. Greenspan," Judge Golden said, interrupting Stan Sherman. "Do you know what I mean, Mr. Greenspan?"

"Yes, Your Honor, I understand," Noah relied.

"You see, Mr. Greenspan, there are pretty rigid guidelines for determining whether or not a class should be certified. And there was a revision just last year to what we call the FRCP—that's short for Federal Rules of Civil Procedure—that says that everyone who qualifies to be in a class is considered a member of the plaintiff class unless he or she specifically chooses to opt out. That makes it very risky for a defendant like you. You know what I mean?"

"Yes, I think I understand. You're saying that if this class is certified, it could be very costly if we lose the case."

"Not 'could be,' Mr. Greenspan. 'Will be' would be more appropriate."

"I understand," Noah replied.

"So, what am I required to consider in deciding whether or not to certify this class Saul here has concocted? There are only four criteria. First, we have what we call *numerosity*. That's just a fancy way of saying it's a whole lot of people—you know, too many to name everyone individually. Then we have *commonality*. That means there has to be a common question of law that applies to everyone. Another somewhat similar criterion is known as *typicality*. That's a fancy way of saying that the beef all these plaintiffs have with you is pretty similar or typical. Finally, we have something called *adequacy*. Adequacy just means that Mr. Kjarski here is representing the interests of the other members of the class who aren't going to be present in my courtroom."

Noah nodded. "I think I understand," he said.

"So while I haven't made up my mind yet, at first blush, I think Saul has put together a class that might meet all of these criteria."

"Like I said, Judge, *pure and simple*," Kronheim chimed in.

"Like Mr. Wilde said, Saul, the truth is rarely pure and never simple," Judge Golden snapped. "Your case is no cakewalk."

"Your Honor, I have to object to that."

"Oh, Saul, stop it. What the hell are you objecting to? We're not in court. We're just having a friendly chat here in my chambers," Judge

Golden retorted, making no effort to hide his ire. "Personally, I thought Mr. Sherman's response to your complaint was pretty compelling."

"We have great confidence in our case, Judge," Kronheim replied.

"I've seen a lot Philadelphia Eagles games lost because of overconfidence, Saul," Judge Golden fired back.

"Your Honor, I think we'll mount a very compelling defense should this come to trial," Stan Sherman interrupted.

"Yeah, I suspect you will, Counselor. But let me ask you something."

"Of course."

"What do you think the cost of your very compelling case will be to Mr. Greenspan—two hundred thousand dollars—three hundred thousand dollars? And Mr. Greenspan, how many days or weeks can you afford to be sitting up here in Philadelphia while this trial goes on? And what would you be willing to pay to just have all of this go away? And, Mr. Greenspan, how much will you have to spend to counteract the negative publicity this suit will bring to Potomac Center?"

"Your Honor, my clients lost millions of dollars because of the way Mr. Greenspan's stock dropped when news broke that Potomac Center was the possible target of a terrorist attack," Saul Kronheim said.

"Saul, your clients lost millions because they sold a very popular stock at the wrong time. The rest of the market didn't buy the story of the terrorist threat. It's that simple."

"We'll only know if Mr. Greenspan had been warned by the FBI if we go to trial," Saul Kronheim retorted.

"Well, I suspect that if the FBI met with Mr. Greenspan to discuss a possible terrorist threat, they would have asked him to keep the meeting confidential. That's what we would have done when I was an agent with the bureau right after I graduated from law school. The last thing we would have wanted would be for him to announce to the whole damn world that we were investigating a possible terrorist threat. And I'll tell you something else, Saul: there's a real public-policy issue here. I'd have to think long and hard about whether every business had an obligation to publicly disclose every threat someone made against his or her business. Think of it. The terrorists could have a field day just sending out warnings to businesses all over the country. They could shut down the whole damn country just sending out warnings."

"Well, Judge, just what are you suggesting?" Saul Kronheim asked.

"Saul, I'm suggesting that this case has some very complicated issues and may not lend itself to resolution through the courts. I would have to think long and hard about the public-policy implications of certifying a class in a case like this. On the other hand, Mr. Greenspan, if I decided that the tests of numerosity, commonality, typicality, and adequacy were compelling, Mr. Sherman here would have to defend you before a jury of twelve people essentially plucked off the streets of Philadelphia. They might see you as a megarich businessman who caused Mr. Kjarski, a hardworking immigrant to America, to lose all his money because you weren't being forthcoming in disclosing the risks of investing in Potomac Center."

"Therefore what, Your Honor?" Stan Sherman asked.

"Therefore, I'm suggesting that this case could go either way and that you, Counselor Sherman, and you, Counselor Kronheim, might best serve your clients' interests by reaching an amicable settlement."

"Judge, you're honestly telling me with a straight face that there is a chance you wouldn't certify my class?"

"Like I said, Saul, I'd have to give certification a long, hard look in a case like this. There are some very troubling public-policy issues with which I'd have to grapple. Certification is not a shoo-in for all the reasons I've discussed. And, Mr. Greenspan, I'm not sure I would want to bet on whom a jury would feel the most sorry for in a case like this." Judge Golden leaned forward on his elbows and looked slowly from Saul Kronheim to Stanford Sherman. "Rarely pure and never simple, gentlemen."

There was utter silence in the room. Saul Kronheim sat there tapping his fingers on the attaché case he held on his lap. Noah looked over to Stan Sherman, who simply shrugged his shoulders.

"Tell you what, gentlemen, I'm going to go have a cup of coffee. Saul, why don't you and Mr. Kjarski remain here, and, Mr. Sherman, why don't you and your entourage have a chat at one of the tables in my courtroom, which happens to be empty this morning. I would strongly urge you and Mr. Kronheim here to try to reach an amicable settlement and then go over to Bookbinder's and have a nice lunch."

Judge Golden returned about an hour later and reconvened both groups in his office. "So where are we?" he asked.

"Well, we would be willing to forego the fraud component and the sixty million dollars of treble damages that go with it," Kronheim said. "That just leaves the actual damages of twenty million dollars. We think that's very generous."

Judge Golden peered over the top of his glasses to Saul Kronheim. "Saul, there is no way the fraud count was going anywhere in my courtroom. I consider that the proverbial kitchen sink you plaintiffs' lawyers always throw into your plaintiffs' briefs. Nice try, but no gold ring." Judge Golden turned to Stanford Sherman.

"Counselor?"

"Two hundred and fifty thousand dollars. That's approximately what my trial costs would be."

Judge Golden nodded. "It's a start."

"Well, I'm not sure there's anything to discuss," Saul Kronheim said, getting to his feet.

"Oh, sit down, Saul. You know I don't go for theatrics."

"That's not a serious offer, Your Honor."

"Well, it had a pretty rational basis," Judge Golden replied, turning to Stan Sherman.

"Counselor, you based your settlement offer on the equivalent value of the hours you would otherwise spend trying this case. Is that right?"

"Yes, Your Honor, that is correct."

"Have you considered the cost of discovery? You're going to have to trace every trade the plaintiffs made on the day the short sale was announced and calculate the loss each one of them suffered. That's going to take a lot of man-hours. Someday you'll probably be able to push a button on one of those huge IBM 360s and have the machine just spit out the information, but there's no such shortcut available today. You'll have to get every brokerage statement from everyone in the class or get the specialist's book for the day."

Stan Sherman looked to Noah. His expression begged the question, what do you think?

"Your Honor, if Mr. Kronheim's clients will accept five hundred thousand dollars, I'll settle. Otherwise, we'll go to court," Noah said.

"A five-hundred-thousand-dollar settlement of an eighty-million-dollar suit is out of the question," Kronheim said. "Absolutely out of the question."

With that, Noah got to his feet. "Your Honor, I greatly appreciate your efforts this morning to resolve this dispute. I have very mixed emotions about what I have just offered to settle what I believe is a nuisance suit. I feel like I'm being taken to the cleaners for absolutely no reason. I really do appreciate all that you've done to resolve this. I really do. But if Mr. Kronheim here wants to do battle with me again, I'll see him in court, assuming you decide to certify this so-called class."

"You don't engage in theatrics, do you, Mr. Greenspan?"

"No, I don't, Your Honor. I'm not very good at it. And for the record, my offer is off the table when I'm out the door," Noah said as he turned to leave.

Judge Golden turned to Saul Kronheim. "I know a bluffer when I see one, Saul. Mr. Greenspan here—he's not one."

"OK, five hundred thousand dollars it is," Saul Kronheim said as Noah reached the door.

"And no disclosure of the amount," Stan Sherman said, getting to his feet.

***

By noon they had boarded the Congressional Limited Express at Philadelphia's Thirtieth Street Station for the return trip to Washington. Stan Sherman and Yusuf Salaman sat across the aisle from Noah and

Alexandra. Alexandra laid her head on Noah's shoulder and reached down and squeezed his hand.

"There goes another five hundred thousand dollars," she said, softly.

"I think our insurance will cover it," he replied. "Anyway, it's done."

"What would you have done if Kronheim had dug in his heels?"

"I would have walked. Once Judge Golden signaled that the fraud count wasn't going anywhere, I felt the risk of my digging in my heels was manageable."

"Do you think they would have put me on the stand if the case had gone to trial?"

"Stan Sherman says he could have limited the questions to Shoukri using the timing of your columns to alert his confederates in Israel."

"Sometimes I think those years in Beirut will haunt me for the rest of my life," she said.

"Alexandra, it was a miracle that you were in Beirut at that time. Just think of what would have happened if that cell hadn't picked you for their patsy. Do you realize how many innocent people would have been murdered if you hadn't made that decision to go to college in Beirut back when you were a seventeen-year-old high-school kid in LeDroit Park?"

"That decision came so close to destroying us—I mean you and me as a couple."

"But here we are, Alexandra," he replied, leaning down and kissing her softly on the side of her head. "Say, I have a great idea," he said, as though a lightbulb had just gone off in his head.

"I'm listening," she answered, looking up at him. "I know that when you say you have a great idea, it's never idle chatter."

"Let's ask Judge Golden to marry us. He wants to visit Potomac Center. I think he likes us, and we won't have to navigate a minefield trying to find clergy that will marry a Jew and a Palestinian Christian."

She thought for only a moment before responding. "He likes my writing," she said, smiling. "It was very nice of him to say what he did about my columns from Israel. I was surprised that he went to the trouble of finding what I had written and even more surprised that he was so complimentary. I don't have a problem with Judge Golden marrying us. I think I really like the idea. Do you think he would do it?"

Noah shrugged. "Only one way to find out."

"We're going to be all right, aren't we," she asked, though it was more a statement than a question.

"Think of all the obstacles we've already overcome," he replied.

"But here we are," she said drowsily, squeezing closer to him. Noah put his arm around her shoulder and whispered into her ear, "I love you." She smiled contentedly. By the time they crossed the Susquehanna River Bridge in Maryland, connecting Perryville to Havre de Grace, the clickity-clack monotony of the train's wheels rolling steadily south toward Washington had seduced Alexandra into a deep slumber.

CHAPTER FORTY-SEVEN

While Alexandra napped aboard the Congressional Limited, six thousand miles to the east, Omar Samir and Ahmed Hebraddi were enjoying coffee in the dining car as their train sped south along the Nile over the Imbaba Bridge toward Aswân.

"So, we have everything we need?" Omar asked.

Ahmed Hebraddi smiled and nodded. "Half the plastique is already at Potomac Center," he replied. "We're going to use electronic detonators. They're readily available in the States, and we've begun purchasing small quantities every month to avoid attracting attention. Everything is going as planned."

"Explain to me, again, how we will actually detonate them," Omar said.

"That's the easiest part, Omar. We're going to use standard two-way radios. They're cheap and even sold in retail stores in America. Anybody can buy them. The American company Motorola began selling a small, lightweight commercial walkie-talkie around five years ago. I purchased two of them. They call them the Handie-Talkie HT-200. I think they'll be perfect. They only weigh thirty-three ounces. They're the size of a brick. In fact, they've been nicknamed the brick. They're totally transistorized, very reliable."

"How do you call a bomb on a walkie-talkie?"

"That's exactly what you do, Omar," Ahmed answered, laughing. "You simply radio one walkie-talkie, the receiver, from another walkie-talkie, which is the transmitter."

"And who answers?" Omar asked, joining Ahmed in the laughter.

"The detonator answers," Ahmed replied, turning serious. He leaned forward, speaking barely above a whisper. "We simply disconnect the wires from the speaker in the receiving HT-200 and connect them to the lead wires in the detonator. There's a very thin wire between these lead wires, called a bridge wire. We set the volume on the HT-200 on high, which will assure that the current is much more than the bridge wire can handle. That current will be sufficient to vaporize—actually to create a miniature explosion of sorts in the bridge wire between the two lead wires. That tiny pop will set off the small charge in the detonator, which in turn will provide the quick surge of heat and shock to start a chain reaction of unimaginable force in the plastique."

"And that will be happening in twenty-eight different locations throughout Potomac Center?"

"Simultaneously, Omar. It will be like nothing the Americans have ever experienced."

"And Potomac Center?"

"Absolute rubble."

"And the thousands of people who will be shopping there?"

"All part of the rubble."

***

Amos had arrived in Washington by the time Noah and Alexandra returned from Philadelphia, and he left messages for them at both the *Evening Star* and Potomac Center. They called the Israeli embassy and asked the receptionist to leave word for Amos to join them for dinner that evening. Amos spent the afternoon meeting with the task force the Israelis and Americans had put together to evaluate the threat that AASLF represented in the United States. Amos met with FBI agents Hogan and Atkins in a small conference room at the bureau's headquarters on Pennsylvania Avenue.

"Other than this Omar Samir character snooping around trying to get his hands on the architect's drawings for Potomac Center, we haven't come across a shred of evidence that an attack is in the wind," Agent Hogan told the group at the outset of the meeting.

"But that's a huge shred," Amos interrupted.

"That may be true, but we have no indication of when such an attack might be planned or what it might be," Agent Atkins said.

"These people like to pick significant dates to make a statement. I would expect that your Fourth of July celebrations might be high on their list of attractive dates on which to strike," Amos answered.

"That doesn't help very much, Amos. Are we looking for shooters? Grenade tossers? Arsonists? Bombers? Are we looking for American anti-Semites or Arabs from the Middle East?" Agent Hogan asked. "We honestly don't know where to begin."

"I don't think we're looking for shooters, although that was the Shoukri group's specialty," Amos answered. "Shooting has only limited potential for these terrorists. I think if they strike, they'll want to do something spectacular. Remember, this attack, if it comes, will be a revenge attack. My hunch is that if they go after Potomac Center, they'll use explosives."

"Well, we've focused there too, Amos, but other than checking for suspicious sales or reported thefts of dynamite from construction sites, we have no obvious place to look. We don't think anyone is going to try to sneak dynamite into the United States."

"No, it wouldn't be dynamite. There's better explosive material being produced today."

"You mean this new plastic stuff?" Agent Atkins asked.

"Yeah, we're worried about that," Amos replied. "It's next to impossible to detect, and it travels well. It's very stable."

"We don't think that's likely here," Agent Hogan responded. "There are no industrial producers of plastic explosives here in the States."

"I know," Amos answered. "A Czech outfit started manufacturing plastic explosives about three years ago for civil demolition projects."

"Yes, we know. We've been in touch with them. The only American customer they have, though, is Questex-Irvine, and they're a first-rate outfit. In fact, they do a lot of work for the US government."

"Yeah, they're working all over the world—first-rate outfit," Amos agreed.

"If they were missing any explosive material, they would be on the phone with us within minutes," Agent Hogan said.

"I still have a hunch we're looking for bombers," Amos insisted.

"Well, it makes sense. We have seen a number of bombings in the past few years. Seems all the bad guys want to do is blow up things. Some antiwar types bombed US fighter jets sitting on the ground up in Edmonton a couple of years ago," Hogan said.

"And we had two bombs go off at our embassy in Gabon," Agent Atkins added.

"Yeah, and we had those bombings in Birmingham three or four years ago," Agent Hogan added. "They went after Martin Luther King's brother's house."

"The Palestinians haven't resorted to bombs yet, but with this new plastic explosive material available now, I think it's only a matter of time. You can move the stuff around with such ease," Amos said.

"Yeah, we've got our Ku Klux Klan. They're the ones that did the Birmingham bombing, but they like old-fashioned dynamite."

"Well, we have the Popular Front for the Liberation of Palestine and the Palestine Liberation Organization. So far they've been too busy fighting with one another to fight with us, but that won't last long. They're both gearing up for violent armed conflict against my country," Amos said. "The only group we're concentrating on right now is the Ali Abdul Shoukri Liberation Front. They have a real vendetta against Alexandra Salaman, and, I would guess, her fiancé, Noah Greenspan. And if they could, they'd really love to have a shot at me too—in fact, they did once."

"Yes, we've seen the file on Miss Salaman. You plucked her out of a real mess in Beirut, as I recall," Agent Hogan said.

"She saved a lot of Israeli lives," Amos replied, quietly.

***

Noah, Alexandra, and Amos met for dinner at the Golden Parrot, just north of Dupont Circle. The old mansion turned restaurant was a favorite of Noah and Alexandra's, especially when they had guests and wanted to talk over dinner. They knew, of course, Amos was in Washington to meet with the FBI agents who were working on the AASLF threat, so the conversation turned serious as soon as they were seated.

"I think something is in the works, something soon," he said.

"Why are you that certain, Amos?" Noah asked.

"Just a hunch," Amos replied. "We know they were here asking questions and trying to get the Potomac Center drawings last June, and we know they did get the tenants' manual, which probably provides all the detail they need."

"That's true, but they haven't done anything. Maybe they were just snooping around and have decided that it's too difficult or too dangerous," Alexandra suggested.

"You could be absolutely right, Alexandra, but we have no choice but to assume they are planning something until proven otherwise."

"Have you picked up on anything suspicious at all?" Noah asked.

"In an odd sort of way, yes. Noah, we haven't heard a word, not a hint, since last June."

"Maybe that's good," Noah answered.

"Definitely not good, Noah. They're quiet because this, or maybe something else, is the only thing they have in the works. Potomac Center is the only target we know they were planning to attack, so we have to assume that the center is the target."

"They're sure taking their time," Alexandra said.

"Yes, and that worries me too. It suggests a lot of planning or a lot of waiting for the right occasion."

"The right occasion?"

"Yes, an attack on a date that has some significance."

"Like the Fourth of July?"

"Funny you should say that. I suggested the same thing to the FBI agents this morning," Amos replied.

"Well, that would make a statement," Noah agreed.

"What about the first anniversary of the opening of Potomac Center?" Alexandra asked.

"Which is when exactly?"

"June fifth. That's the day Potomac Center opened," she replied.

"And the day the Six-Day War began," Amos answered, slapping his forehead. "That's it! That's the day they're planning to strike. I'd bet anything."

"Well, that barely gives you and the bureau two months to stop them," Noah said. "Our PR people are planning a big weeklong celebration at the center starting that day. Should we squelch that?"

"No, we'll just have to arrange a huge show of security around the anniversary celebration. They're not going to try anything if we have uniformed security all over the place. They'll assume we're onto something."

"So maybe we beat this thing, if we're right about the date," Noah said.

"It's not that easy, Noah. We may deter them for a while, but they'll bide their time and try to strike once we let our guard down. They may delay until the Fourth of July or maybe until your Labor Day, or maybe as soon as they think we've let our guard down."

"Well, we won't be able to maintain Potomac Center as an armed fortress indefinitely," Noah said.

"How secure is the receiving area for Potomac Center?" Amos asked.

Noah shrugged. "There's really no security to speak of. We just have a receiving-dock staff."

"That might be a place to focus on, Noah. There's a long history of parcel bombs and letter bombs being used to attack people. They've been used for two hundred years, sometimes pretty effectively. They're rather primitive but effective. They've even been sent to high government officials in Great Britain, and several were sent to President Truman back in the forties."

"But it doesn't seem like a letter bomb would be what they would use, assuming Potomac Center is the target," Noah replied.

"Probably not," Amos agreed. "But you probably should beef up security at your receiving area. It is the pathway into the center, other than someone just coming through the entrance doors."

Alexandra was becoming increasingly unnerved by all of the talk of the Shoukri cell and the continuing threat it represented to her and Noah and, maybe, hundreds of others.

"Have you heard from Karen, Amos?" Alexandra asked, changing the subject.

"Yes, we've stayed in touch," he replied, after a moment's hesitation. "In fact, I'm going to spend some time in Chicago before returning to Israel." Amos paused, awkwardly, before continuing. "I may be assigned to the States for a while. We're setting up a joint terrorism task force with the FBI over this Shoukri Front business. I'll probably be assigned to the team as our resident agent here."

"You'll be stationed here in Washington?" Noah asked.

"I will. Do you have any month-to-month vacancies at Potomac Center, Noah?" Amos replied, laughing.

"I wish we did. I think I'd feel safer with you nearby," Noah answered.

Alexandra listened as her fiancé and former lover engaged in friendly banter. *To think,* she mused to herself as Noah and Amos continued talking, *a madman, Ali Abdul Shoukri, is what brought the three of us together.*

"Amos, I have a question for you," Alexandra said, interrupting the conversation. "Noah and I were thinking of getting married at Potomac Center on the anniversary of its opening on June fifth. We would take over one of the restaurants on the top floor. Do you think that's smart, given the terrorist threat everyone is so worried about?"

Amos thought for a moment before answering. "You know, with all the security you're planning to have at the center on June fifth, it would probably be the safest place in the city."

CHAPTER
FORTY-EIGHT

Agent Hogan and his wife Ilona, enjoying a rare night out, decided to take in a late showing of *The Defiant Ones* at the Uptown Theater on Connecticut Avenue, just a five-minute drive from their modest Walbridge Place row house near Rock Creek Park. Ilona, still harboring the vestiges of a schoolgirl's crush on Tony Curtis, picked the ten-year-old movie.

Barking bloodhounds eagerly tracking Sidney Poitier and Tony Curtis, playing two shackled-together escaped convicts, as they ran through hostile, rain-soaked southern terrain reminded Agent Hogan of an article he had read in the *Washington Post* about a year earlier. The air force, as he recalled, had approved a dog-sentry program perfected by the District of Columbia's Metropolitan Police Canine Corps. Dogs trained by the police department had just been sent, along with their trainers, to Lackland Air Force Base to help establish the K9 sentry program for the air force. As Marge watched the Poitier and Curtis characters, Joker Jackson and Noah Cullen, slogging through the moonlit bayou, the yelping dogs hot on their heels, Agent Hogan scribbled on a pad in the darkened theater, "Can dogs sniff plastique?"

Two days later, Agent Hogan met with Metropolitan Police canine officer Nick Garfield, a senior handler, who had worked with the dogs that were now sentries at Lackland Air Force Base in San Antonio.

Nick Garfield was from Port Tobacco, Maryland, a ghost of a once-important port city that had, over the last one hundred years, withered on the vine as river silt and the routing of the railroads rendered the city irrelevant. Nick left Port Tobacco ten years earlier when he heard that the police department in Washington was establishing a special canine unit in which dogs would patrol the streets of the nation's capital with patrolmen handlers. The only work Nick had known as a teenager growing up in Charles County, Maryland, was topping and suckering tobacco plants in the fields. But he also knew that no one understood dogs the way he did, and if you could make a living working with dogs, well, that sure beat pampering tobacco.

"There's nothin' they can't sniff out," Nick answered with absolute certainty, when Agent Hogan asked whether dogs could be used to detect explosives. "Smell is as important to a dog as sight is to you and me. I think they even dream in smells the way we dream in images. A dog's nose and brain are equal parts of the greatest smelling machine God ever created."

"So you think if we wanted to, say, intercept a package with explosives in it, a well-trained dog could do that?"

"Gunpowder is puppy's play for a good dog. So are dynamite and TNT. All those explosives leave vapor trails. Some leave heavy vapor trails and are easy for them to sniff out, like fried chicken would be to you and me. Some of these newer explosives like what they call plastique don't leave so much of a vapor trail, but a good dog—yes, sir, a good dog will find plastique as long as it's been trained to recognize the stuff. It ain't easy, but give me enough time with good dogs and the explosive compound, and you can bet your ass they'll sniff out that shit."

"If we could supply the material we're worried about, how long would it take you to train dogs to detect the stuff?"

"You give me a month with the material, and I'll guarantee you my dogs will yank your arm off going after it," Nick answered.

***

It was a sunny but cool May morning when Daoud dropped Amos off at the Department of Justice to meet with Agents Hogan and Atkins. The building stood at Tenth Street, near the east end of Washington's Federal Triangle, just across from the National Archives. The apex of the Federal Triangle, formed by the convergence of Pennsylvania and Constitution Avenues, was, Amos thought, one of the most beautiful spots in the world. From there you could survey the two grand boulevards, which were anchored at the east end by the Capitol of the United States and about a mile to the west by the Treasury Department and, just beyond that, the west lawn of the White House. Many of the major agencies and museums of the nation were sprawled out along the Federal Triangle. The Smithsonian Institution stood like an old redbrick castle from another time and place just across the National Mall, which ran along the south side of the triangle, and far to the west stood the Washington Monument and beyond that the Lincoln Memorial. *Fantastic,* Amos thought as he turned to take in the view once again before entering the Department of Justice.

Agents Hogan and Atkins were waiting in the small conference room along with Dr. Grayson Talbot, a chemist from the bureau's crime laboratory.

"Good morning, Amos," Agent Hogan said as soon as he entered the room. "We asked Dr. Talbot to join us this morning. We've borrowed him from our crime lab."

Amos shook hands with Dr. Talbot and took a seat opposite him at the conference table.

"Amos, my colleagues here tell me you believe there might be a terrorist attack here in Washington and that you suspect it will be a bombing," Dr. Talbot said as soon as Amos was seated.

"Just a hunch," Amos replied. "Although we're not sure, we believe at least a year of planning that we know of has gone into this plot."

"And why does that suggest a bombing?" Dr. Talbot asked.

"We learned a year ago that the terrorists were trying to get their hands on the architectural drawings of Potomac Center, the new complex over on M Street, by the river."

"Oh, my wife and I know Potomac Center well. We live over near Capitol Hill and shop there just about every weekend."

"Once we knew that a terrorist cell was fixated on the drawings of Potomac Center, nothing else made much sense. It just wouldn't take that much detail or this much time if all they were planning was to shoot up the place."

"We told Grayson about the history. You know, about Mr. Greenspan and Miss Salaman," Agent Atkins said.

"Yes, it's quite a story," the chemist replied. "My wife and I read Miss Salaman's columns regularly in the *Star*. I know she's a Palestinian, and I presume Mr. Greenspan is Jewish."

"That's correct, but it's only a small piece of the story," Amos replied. "When she returned to the Middle East ten years ago to go to school, she became unwittingly involved with students there who were, in fact, terrorists. She discovered that they were using her in a plan to commit a massacre in Israel, and she ultimately alerted us. The plot was foiled, and the cell leader, a man named Ali Abdul Shoukri, was killed." Amos did not mention that it was he to whom Alexandra divulged the plot, he who spirited her away to Israel, and he who had fallen so in love with her.

"So the terror plot you're worried about is to avenge her betrayal?" the chemist asked.

"We think so."

"Well, then, I agree. A bomb plot seems most likely."

"The problem is we have no idea what they are going to do or when they are planning to do it," Agent Hogan said. "Our hunch is that they will try to use one of the new plastic explosives because of the ease with which they can move the stuff around, and we know it's now commercially available."

"But not in the United States," Dr. Talbot replied.

"True," Amos answered, "but Demolishia, a Czech company, is manufacturing the stuff. They call it plastique, and we know they've been selling it to the North Vietnamese."

"So you think if they're selling it to kill Americans over in Vietnam, they might be perfectly willing to sell it to terrorists to kill Americans right here in the United States."

Agent Atkins nodded affirmatively. "But the only American customer they have is Questex-Irvine, and they're a very true-blue company. Q-I is a major contractor to the United States government, and they have top security clearance. They're practically an arm of the government. It wouldn't be them."

"I agree," Talbot said. "They might be worth talking to though. They probably know as much as anyone about where the stuff is showing up."

"I've met with a dog trainer at the Metropolitan Police Department. They have a pretty effective canine unit, and one of their top trainers tells me if we could get some of this plastique, he could train the dogs to detect it," Agent Hogan said.

"That won't be difficult," Talbot replied.

"Well, we don't want the Czech company or, frankly, anyone else to know we're snooping around," Agent Atkins said.

"As I recall, the Czechs are using pentaerythritol tetranitrate to manufacture their particular brand of plastic explosive," Talbot replied. "We can get plenty of that right here in Washington."

"Where?" Agent Atkins asked, incredulously.

"Well, here, for beginners," Talbot answered, reaching into his jacket pocket and pulling out a small plastic prescription container from Dart Drugs. "Here, catch!"

Agent Atkins caught the container and looked curiously at the label. "'Peritrate'—it says 'Peritrate.' Twenty milligrams four times daily."

"Right," Talbot responded. "I take Peritrate for my angina. It's pure pentaerythritol tetranitrate. Petn for short."

"Which is?" Agent Atkins asked, somewhat puzzled.

"Probably the most explosive chemical compound in the world," Grayson Talbot answered. "It's the same stuff the Czechs use to produce their plastique."

"And you swallow this shit?"

"Four times a day," Talbot answered, with a chuckle. "I think Pfizer can supply you all the Petn you need to train your dogs."

"Isn't it dangerous?"

"For me to swallow?"

"Or for Pfizer to manufacture?"

"It takes a lot of heat and shock to set it off. That's why you need a detonator to weaponize the stuff into a bomb. Interestingly though, last year Hercules, a major American manufacturer of explosives, was granted a patent for a device that made it safer to press Petn into tablets like the ones you're holding in your hand right now."

"Holy shit," Agent Atkins whispered under his breath, as he looked at the little round green twenty-milligram Peritrate tablets he held in his hand. "This is plastique?"

"Essentially, yes," Talbot answered, laughing.

"He swallows the stuff four times a day," Agent Atkins murmured, incredulously.

***

It was a warm and sunny eighty degrees in Chicago when Amos landed at O'Hare to spend the weekend with Karen. They hadn't seen one another since they were together in Los Angeles during the IPO road show, and they eagerly embraced as soon as he disembarked from the plane.

"Look, you can see Big John," she said, pointing to the nearly completed John Hancock Center as they drove into the city from the airport. "That's over fifteen miles away."

"Incredible," he replied, truly impressed by the massive structure towering over the distant lakefront skyline.

"They just topped it off. Isn't it great?"

"Only in America," he said with admiration.

"Yeah, the poor developer went broke building it, but there it is—home to over seven hundred apartments and hundreds of offices. Wait till we get to my place. It's not the John Hancock, but Lake Point Tower really is the tallest apartment building in the world. It's right on the lakefront. Amos, I love it, and I can't wait for you to see it," she said, excitedly.

"It looks like Mid-America Ventures is treating you well," Amos said, patting the leather dashboard of Karen's new fire-engine-red Mercury Cougar.

"Actually, Potomac Center treated me well. That deal was a big feather in my cap. It made me the first female vice president of the firm."

"Well deserved and overdue, I'm sure," Amos replied.

Amos was, indeed, impressed when they entered Karen's apartment high atop Lake Point Tower. The blue glistening waters of Lake Michigan overwhelmed the eastern exposure, spreading as far as the eye could see to the east and north, and, far to the south. Amos could clearly make out Michigan City and Gary, Indiana, hugging the south rim of the lake. And, sure enough, as he looked north along the shoreline, there stood Big John towering like a mighty sentry over the Windy City.

The weekend was a welcome respite for both of them. Karen was riding high at Mid-America Ventures with the Potomac Center IPO under her belt. She had the wind to her back, and she had Amos all to herself, at least for a couple days. Amos also needed a break. He and his counterparts at the FBI were doing everything they could to stop what they were certain was going to be a devastating attack against Potomac Center, but he knew they weren't doing enough. No one had a clue where Omar Samir was, with whom he was working, and precisely what he and his cohorts were planning to do or when they were planning to do it. He was going to fly out to San Francisco from Chicago and join Agents Hogan and Atkins at Questex-Irvine headquarters for a brain-picking session. He did not harbor much hope that the Q-I people would be able to help, but the joint task force was at a dead end. Any additional insight might be helpful.

Karen curled up on the couch, her head resting on Amos's shoulder. Lake Michigan, which only a few weeks earlier was being whipped into a roiling frenzy by the last winds of winter, was now tamed and placid. It was, Amos thought, like a huge swath of aqua someone had splashed on an artist's canvas just for the two for them to gaze upon.

"Beautiful, isn't it?" she murmured as she snuggled closer.

He put his arm around her and smiled. "Reminds me of the Mediterranean," he answered. "It's very peaceful, like Tel Aviv."

"Tel Aviv is so far away," she replied. "I can't bear the thought of you leaving."

"Sometimes, I can't either, Karen. Like now, when I'm here with you."

"We could make a great life together here in America," she answered. "We really could, you know."

"It's a tempting thought, Karen, but I can't imagine ever leaving Israel."

"People make new beginnings in new places all the time," she said. "Couldn't you picture yourself doing that?"

"That's not the point," he replied. "Sure, I could leave, and I think I would do pretty well here, or almost anywhere."

"But?"

"I'm not as confident that Israel could do pretty well if people like me started to leave. Israel is thriving, Karen, but it is so vulnerable."

"It seems pretty secure to me," she replied.

"For the moment, yes," he agreed. "But don't be fooled by our military strength. Look, that lake we're looking at is actually longer than the length of my entire country, and it's wider too. Karen, I can run the width of Israel at its narrowest point in about two hours. You can fit all of Israel into the shoreline of Lake Michigan. That's what I mean when I say we're a very vulnerable country."

"You can't defend it by yourself, Amos," she replied.

"Sometimes I think I have," he said, smiling.

"Like when you and Alexandra stopped that terrorist attack a few years ago?"

He nodded. "Some Israeli, right now, while we're sitting here marveling at your beautiful Lake Michigan, is sitting in Israel working to stop the next attack against our people," he continued. "I guarantee it. Somewhere in Israel, someone like me has the task of discovering where some attack is being planned. How can I walk away from such responsibility?"

"I don't want you to walk away from me either," she answered in a whisper. He pulled her closer.

"I don't want to walk away from you, Karen. Maybe I can find a way to serve my country here in America for a while."

It was the most uninterrupted time Amos and Karen had ever spent together. That afternoon they strolled along the lakefront all the way from Lake Point Tower to Irving Parkway, five miles to the north. They paused about halfway, at Belmont Avenue, as they passed Temple Shalom, Chicago's largest Reform Jewish house of worship.

"That's where I belong now," Karen said.

"It's quite beautiful," Amos replied. "Sort of a mixture of Byzantine and Moorish architecture. You see a lot of that in my part of the world."

"It's a real landmark here in Chicago. It was actually designed as an assignment by three architecture students at the old Armour Institute."

"The Moorish era in Spain is often thought of as the golden age of Jewry. That's why Moorish architecture became so popular in the design of synagogues in central Europe, when Jews relocated there during, and after, the Inquisition," Amos replied.

"Ironic, but Jews thrived under Islamic rule in Spain."

"I guess, in a way, all of the Moorish-style synagogues are a tribute to a better time between Jews and Muslims," she said.

"Ironic but true," Amos answered.

It was close to sunset when they turned back after reaching Irving Parkway, and cooler air began riding in with the brisk breeze from the lake. Amos put his arm around Karen and pulled her closer. She laid her head against his shoulder and embraced him with both arms as they continued walking slowly back toward her apartment. They didn't speak. The only sounds were those of cars rushing along Lake Shore Drive and the waves gently rolling onto the beach from Lake Michigan.

"Do you like pizza?" Karen asked as they approached the end of the beach at Oak Street.

"Love it," Amos answered.

"Well, you're going to taste pizza as you've never tasted it before," she said, taking his hand and rushing across Michigan Avenue with him. They made their way west to Wabash and then headed south to Ohio, to Uno Pizzeria and Grill.

"You're right. I've never seen or tasted pizza like this," he said as he devoured a slice of Uno's original deep-dish pizza. Karen smiled as she gazed at Amos enjoying his first taste of Chicago-style pizza. Oh, if my colleagues at Mid-America Ventures could see me now enjoying pizza and wine with my Mossad agent from Tel Aviv, she thought. They sat there for about an hour following dinner and most of a bottle of chianti, holding hands and talking mostly about Karen's life in Chicago. "You know, I think this is the most time I've spent in months not worrying about what the Shoukri Liberation Front is up to," he said.

"Well, don't start worrying about it now," she replied with a mischievous smile. "We only have a weekend together."

He squeezed her hand, affectionately. "We'll have more than this weekend together, Karen. I promise."

She squeezed his hand, in return. "I hope you mean that, Amos Ben-Chaiyim, because I think I'm very much in love with you."

"I wouldn't have said it, Karen, if I didn't feel the same way," he replied. "When my brain allows me a reprieve from my work, my thoughts invariably turn to you."

"Do you mean that, Amos? Please don't say it if you don't really mean it."

"Do you think I've come all the way to Chicago to tease you, Karen? I know you know that I was in a relationship with Alexandra in Israel a few years ago. I will be honest with you—for a long time I couldn't get her out of my mind. You, Karen, changed all of that. It is you, Karen, whom I constantly think of now."

"Alexandra would be tough competition. I've lost to her once already," she said, pensively.

"You didn't lose to Alexandra, Karen. The bond between Noah and Alexandra was never really broken. Even when she and I were together in Israel, Noah constantly was on her mind. He came up in conversation all the time. They were sweethearts from adolescence on."

"I know," she replied, smiling. "She always came up in conversation when Noah and I were dating at Stanford. I never really felt secure when we were engaged, because I knew if she ever returned to the States, it would be more than Noah could have handled—or, maybe, it would have been much more than I could have handled."

"Alexandra and Noah belong together, Karen. They forged an incredible bond growing up in that black neighborhood in Washington, and it has been an amazingly strong bond. They're both very exceptional people. I admire their devotion to one another. A Jewish man and a Palestinian Arab woman totally devoted to one another. It's enough to give one hope."

"And is the Israeli from Tel Aviv and the girl from Chicago enough to give one hope too, Amos?" she asked, only half in jest.

"No need to hope, Karen. I have no interest, whatsoever, in any other woman, and once we figure out how to cope with the distance between Tel Aviv and Chicago, nothing would make me happier than to spend the rest of my life with you."

"So why are we still sitting here with cold deep-dish pizza and an empty chianti bottle between us?"

With that, Amos stood, threw down enough cash for dinner and tip, and took Karen's hand. "Come on," he said. "Let's get out of here."

Fifteen minutes later, they were back in Karen's apartment. The brilliantly lit skyline was breathtaking against the blackness into which Lake Michigan had now descended. "Look. You can see all of the high-rise apartment buildings on North Lake Shore Drive," she said, taking him by the hand to the large bay windows overlooking the lake and the northern shoreline. "And see those two buildings at the curve in Lake Shore Drive. Mies van der Rohe, the architect who inspired Yusuf's design of Potomac Center, designed them. And that beacon there, on top of the Palmolive Building shining out over the lake—that's to commemorate Lindbergh's solo flight across the Atlantic."

"Charles Lindbergh is the last person on my mind right now," he said, as he stood behind her and encircled her with his arms.

"I don't even want to think of you leaving in two days," she said. "I've never felt more content than I do right now. I wish this moment could last forever."

She leaned back against him as he moved his hands to her breasts. Their bodies slowly pressed together, as he gently tightened his touch. The slow, measured motion of her chest rising and falling with each breath she took heightened the serenity of the moment. He could feel her heart beating a steady rhythm under his hand and the urgent press of his body against the sacrum of her lower spine. She turned, almost breathless, in his arms as they kissed.

"I don't think I've shown you my bedroom yet," she murmured.

It was, for Karen, a blissful weekend. She had Amos all to herself. They explored Chicago, squeezing into the weekend as much as they could of what there was to see. Amos, with his arms wrapped around Karen, marveled at the city's architecture from the deck of the old Wendella riverboat. "Simply incredible," he remarked as the tour boat drifted by the sixty-five-story Marina Towers, the twin corncob buildings with apartments stacked over a dozen floors of parked automobiles and, at river level, dozens of boat slips. And later, after observing a dazzling array of architecture while cruising the Chicago River, they took Karen's Cougar and headed south on Lake Shore Drive. Karen drove through the campus-like cluster of buildings that included the nation's first planetarium and the world's largest indoor aquarium and then past the colonnaded neoclassical Field Museum and the Greco-Roman Soldier Field that reminded Amos of the Colosseum in Rome.

They wound up at the Midway Plaisance in Hyde Park, and he marveled at the neo-Gothic expanse of the University of Chicago.

"Chicago really is a world-class city," he said, as Karen drove back to Lake Point Tower. "We have nothing remotely like it. I can understand why it would be hard to leave."

"But easy to come back to—yes?" she replied.

"Chicago has all of this and Karen Rothschild too. Yes, very easy to come back to," he said, reaching over and squeezing her thigh affectionately. By day they thoroughly enjoyed the city. By night they thoroughly enjoyed one another.

Karen dropped Amos off at O'Hare early Monday morning. "I'll see you when I come in for Noah and Alexandra's wedding," she said, as he leaned in to kiss her one last time.

"I love you, Karen. Don't ever question that," he said as he kissed her good-bye.

She sat at the curb for an extra minute, watching Amos disappear into the terminal. "I love you too, Amos," she whispered tearfully, as she looked over her shoulder and eased the Cougar into the traffic lane for the drive back to Chicago's Loop.

CHAPTER
FORTY-NINE

Agents Atkins and Hogan were waiting at the gate when Amos disembarked in San Francisco. They picked up a Hertz rental car and drove to the Walnut Creek headquarters of Questex-Irvine International. The campus-like complex was immense, consisting of six separate large five-story red-roofed sandstone buildings, all of which were connected by walkways constructed with tinted see-though glass walls. The receptionist at Questex-Irvine's visitors' center directed them to a conference room just off the lobby on the ground floor.

Agent Hogan had not divulged anything specific when he called to arrange to meet with Dennis Baxter, Questex-Irvine's director of civil engineering. He merely told him the bureau wanted to discuss the threat of terrorism and the availability of new explosives on the world market. The two FBI agents and Amos waited in the plush conference room for several minutes before the Questex-Irvine people showed up. The room was designed to accommodate a meeting of up to a dozen people. An impressive display of contemporary art hung on rich mahogany walls, and an assortment of soft drinks, a tray of cut-glass tumblers, and a pitcher of ice water had been placed on a serving table at the rear of the room.

"Gentlemen, please pardon my tardiness," Dennis Baxter said as he burst into the room with a Questex-Irvine colleague. "I've asked Jim

Vinetti to join us. Jim is our explosives specialist. Whenever we want to blow things up, we always have Jim sign off on the demolition plan," Baxter said. They shook hands, and Agent Hogan thanked them for agreeing to meet on such short notice.

"Well, you certainly have stirred our curiosity," Baxter answered. "I presume it's not usual for the FBI and Israeli intelligence to be working together. How can we be helpful?"

"As I explained when we first spoke," Hogan began, "we're quite concerned that a terrorist attack is being planned against a target in Washington. While we're not sure, we think a bomb attack is being planned."

"Why a bomb?" Jim Vinetti asked.

"We know they tried to get a copy of the architectural drawings of the site, and they did succeed in getting a copy of the tenants' manual, which, in fact, does have pretty revealing schematics of the project."

"May I ask what the site is?" Baxter asked.

"It's called Potomac Center. It's a very large mixed-use development."

"I'm familiar with Potomac Center," Baxter answered. "We bid on the project several years ago. In fact, I'm sure we still retain the drawings with which we were supplied for bidding purposes. It's a very impressive project, and it's enjoyed many accolades in the trade press. I wish we had been selected."

"We're assuming terrorists want to blow up the place," Agent Atkins said.

"And you want to know how we think they would go about it?" Baxter asked.

"Yes, that's about right," Agent Hogan replied. "We're guessing they're planning to use this new plastic explosive that's available on the market now."

"Because it's easy to handle and transport?"

"Exactly."

"Well, as far as we know, it isn't available in the United States. It's only used in the military."

"But it is available abroad," Hogan replied.

Jim Vinetti nodded. "That's true. A Czech company is manufacturing plastic explosives for sale."

"Yes, the company is called Demolishia," Agent Atkins said.

"And you think the terrorists are going to try to sneak the stuff into the United States from Czechoslovakia?"

"That's our hunch," Hogan replied. "You know the Czechs are shipping this shit to North Vietnam."

"I don't think it's ever been used in this country," Vinetti said.

"Are you testing it for use abroad?" Amos asked.

"We're not testing it for use anywhere," Vinetti answered.

Amos and the two FBI agents glanced, curiously, at each other. "Several months ago Demolishia shipped some of their plastic explosive to Questex-Irvine Materials Testing. We've assumed you're considering using it in one of your projects," Amos replied.

"What the hell is Questex-Irvine Materials Testing?" Baxter asked.

"We assume it's your materials-testing division. It's registered with the General Services Administration," Hogan answered.

Dennis Baxter looked over to Jim Vinetti. "Do you know what the hell these gentlemen are talking about, Jim?"

"If we have a division called Questex-Irvine Materials Testing, I can sure as hell tell you it's news to me," Vinetti replied.

"You're telling us there is a company on the GSA Schedule of Contractors that calls itself Questex-Irvine Materials Testing?" Baxter asked, incredulously.

Agent Hogan reached into his pocket, removed a folded single sheet of paper, and slid it across the table to Baxter. It was a page from the GSA Schedule of Approved Contractors. And there, underlined in the middle of the page, he saw the line "BPA 871 Questex-Irvine Materials Testing."

"What the fuck?" Baxter whispered aloud. "Jim, look at this," he said.

"Where is this Questex-Irvin Materials Testing located?" Vinetti asked. "I can sure as hell tell you they're not here in Walnut Creek."

"Actually, we don't know," Hogan replied "We called last year to inquire about any sales in the United States. When they said they had only sold to Questex-Irvine Materials Testing, we didn't think any more about it. We just assumed you were analyzing the stuff here in Walnut Creek for your own use, and frankly, we breathed a sigh of relief. You're an iconic firm in America, and you do a ton of work for the government."

"Gentlemen, if we had a division called Questex-Irvine Materials Testing, I would sure as hell know about it. I'm telling you we don't have such a division, and we've never had such a division for as long as I've been here, and that's over twenty years," he said.

"Someone calling themselves Questex-Irvine Materials Testing has been importing plastique into the United States," Amos said. "We'll call Demolishia and determine where in the hell they're shipping their plastique. Let's see just where Questex-Irvine Materials Testing is located."

***

Finding an address or even a phone number for Questex-Irvine Materials Testing proved to be a daunting task. Calls to Demolishia were fruitless. Demolishia was adamant. Under no circumstances would the company divulge the address of any entity to which they shipped explosives. Ironically, such information was considered strictly confidential—in the interest of security, the company said. The US Customs Service was in the process of converting its paper records to microfilm and would need several weeks to search for import documents from Questex-Irvine Materials Testing. No address or phone numbers were to be found in any of the nation's AT&T information directories. The postmaster general's office was of no help either. Even more frustrating, the United States Department of State was reluctant to seek assistance from the Czech government. Political reform in Czechoslovakia had resulted in dangerous tension between the Czech government and the Soviet Union. The State Department feared the Soviets were planning to invade Czechoslovakia following the ousting of Czech hard-line Stalinist Antonín Novotný by liberal reformer Alexander Dubček. To avoid provoking Soviet action against Czechoslovakia, the State Department was pursuing a policy of non-involvement in the internal affairs of the Czech government. It would take the approval of no less than Dean Rusk at State to seek the assistance of the Dubček government, and there was just insufficient evidence of an impending attack to get the secretary of state involved.

***

Daoud dropped Amos off at the Justice Department to meet with Agents Hogan and Atkins before driving him across the river to National Airport to fly to Chicago, where he would spend another weekend with Karen. Amos was worried about the lack of progress. Nobody, it seemed, could find an address for Questex-Irvine Materials Testing.

"We've learned nothing since our meeting with Q-I three weeks ago," he said, pouring himself a cup of coffee.

"It's embarrassing," Hogan answered. "We believe the Czechs are sending plastique to an outfit here in America that calls itself Questex-Irvine Materials Testing, and we haven't a clue where they are. Demolishia won't cooperate with us. The State Department says we need more evidence before they'll intervene in a politically sensitive situation. The post office is of no help."

"We're the Federal fucking Bureau of Investigation, and we can't find a goddamned address," Atkins replied, crushing his empty Styrofoam coffee cup in his hand and tossing it into a wastepaper basket in the corner of the conference room.

"Look, let's assume Demolishia is air freighting their plastique to the United States," Amos said. "Your customs service tells us it can't provide any useful information if we can't tell them when shipments entered the United States. Assuming the plastique arrived at JFK, a freight forwarder would have probably cleared the package through customs and delivered it somewhere in this area. Can't your people canvass the freight forwarders at JFK? Some freight forwarder might recall a shipment or find the paperwork for a delivery to Questex-Irvine Materials Testing."

"That could be a problem," Agent Atkins replied. "The bureau thinks there may be mafia infiltration into some of the freight-forwarding businesses at JFK. While there's no official investigation yet, they know we're snooping around. Those outfits would freak out if we came calling."

"Maybe not," Hogan interjected after a moment's pause. "None of the freight forwarders are officially under investigation. Not yet, anyway. Maybe some of them would jump at the opportunity to cooperate with us. Maybe, just maybe, they would see it as an opportunity to earn some goodwill."

"It's worth a try," Amos said.

"We could have our New York field office responsible for JFK set up meetings for us with some of the freight forwarders operating out of the airport. If we can get a few to cooperate, the others might want to help too," Agent Hogan replied.

The deputy director of the bureau quickly approved the plan, and the following week Agents Hogan and Atkins began meeting with the freight forwarders in small groups of six to eight companies at a time. They did not divulge anything specific other than that they were seeking the delivery address of any parcels of any kind that had been forwarded to a company called Questex-Irvine Materials Testing. For the next two weeks, nothing came of the meetings with the freight forwarders. That all changed on the Friday before Memorial Day.

The telephone rang in the conference room at Justice, where Agents Hogan and Atkins were having their weekly progress-review meeting with Amos. Dr. Grayson Talbot, the chemist from the crime lab, joined them. It had started out as a discouraging meeting. Amos was certain that something was going to happen soon, but they were at a dead end. And that's when the call came through. The switchboard operator announced to Agent Hogan that a gentleman named Salvador Brusconi from East Bay Freight Forwarding was calling from

Jamaica, Long Island. Hogan looked to his two colleagues, engaged the speaker, and asked the operator to put the call through. The three men gathered around the telephone.

"This is Agent Hogan."

"Oh yeah, Agent Hogan. You met with me and some of the other freight forwarders out at JFK a couple of weeks ago. I think I might be able to help you."

Amos, Agent Atkins, and Dr. Talbot exchanged glances as they leaned in closer to the speaker in anticipation of what the caller had to say.

"Can you be more specific, Mr. Brusconi?"

"Yeah, sure. You were asking about deliveries to some outfit called Questex-Irvine Materials Testing."

"Yes, those are the shipments we were inquiring about," Hogan replied.

"Well, today's your lucky day" the voice on the speakerphone said.

"You handled a delivery to Questex-Irvine Materials Testing?"

"Several, to be exact."

"How many?" Hogan asked.

"Eight." The four men looked at one another again, their expressions a mixture of dread and astonishment.

"You said eight?"

"Yes, sir. There's been one parcel a month for the past eight months."

"Can you tell us where these shipments originated?"

"Yeah, I have the paperwork right here. Let's see. Yeah, here it is. Shipment originated in Czechoslovakia."

"Shit," Agent Atkins whispered.

"Does your paperwork show the weight of the parcels?" Hogan asked.

"Yeah. Seventeen and a half kilos in each shipment."

"Jesus Christ have mercy," Dr. Talbot whispered.

"You're saying you've delivered packages weighing a total of one hundred and forty kilos to Questex-Irvine Materials Testing?" Agent Hogan asked after hastily doing the multiplication on a memo pad.

"Uh, let's see. Yeah, it comes out to a total of one hundred and forty kilos."

Dr. Talbot shook his head in disbelief. "This could be catastrophic," he whispered.

"And what is the address to which you delivered these parcels?" Agent Hogan asked.

"How come you guys didn't just look up the address?"

"It's rather complicated," Hogan replied.

"Well, sure sounds like you really need the address."

Hogan rolled his eyes. "Of course we do. That's why we went to New York to talk to all of you."

"Well, you see, Agent Hogan, I need something too," Salvatore Brusconi said.

"What is it you need?"

"Immunity. You see, I don't know what's in those packages we been transporting. I'm guessing it's drugs. I don't want no trouble—you see my concern?"

"Certainly, I can assure you absolute immunity if any law was technically broken as a result of transporting these parcels."

"Well, my lawyer says I gotta be careful you don't charge me with some other offense after I cooperate with you now."

"Why would we do that?" Agent Hogan asked.

"Beats me, but you know how lawyers are."

"So what does your lawyer want from us?"

"Absolute immunity from prosecution for any crime you think I done in the past or for the next five years."

"Your lawyer knows we can't do that," Hogan answered.

"Actually, my lawyer says you can do anything you want."

"Well, that's an unreasonable immunity request."

"Why, you planning to charge me with somethin'?"

"Of course not."

"So what's the problem?"

"I don't have the authority to grant that kind of blanket immunity. I don't know if anyone does."

"Oh, OK. No problem. Call me if you change your mind, and I'll do my best to not let anything happen to these shipping papers. Stuff gets lost around here all the time, but I'll try to keep them from getting lost."

"Wait, are you saying you're not going to give us that address?"

"I sure want to help, but I gotta talk to my lawyer first."

"We need that information now," Agent Atkins interrupted.

Agent Hogan grimaced and stared at his colleague angrily.

"Who said that?" Salvatore Brusconi asked.

"One of my colleagues," Hogan said. "He's an impatient fellow."

"Yeah, I understand. My lawyer is the same way. Me, I got plenty of patience. Call me back here at East Bay Freight Forwarding when you have that—what did you call it—blanket immunity?"

"Can you tell us what city you forwarded the parcels to?"

"Nah. Let's talk as soon as you have that blanket immunity for me."

"I don't think I can do that."

"You know somethin'? I think you can. And I'll tell you somethin' else. I think you will."

"Mr. Brusconi—" Agent Hogan said, just as the line went dead.

"Let's get up there with a search warrant first thing tomorrow," Atkins said as soon as he realized Brusconi had hung up.

"We're blowing it, gentlemen," Amos interrupted. "You won't find a damn thing with a search warrant, and you'll silence the one person who can help us."

"If he has, in fact, delivered one hundred and forty kilos of plastique to a site, we'll have an unprecedented catastrophe on our hands," Dr. Talbot said. "That much pentaerythritol tetranitrate will damn near destroy an entire neighborhood."

"What the hell are we supposed to do?" Agent Hogan asked to no one in particular.

"Get him the goddamned immunity, get the address he's been shipping to, and then shoot the bastard if you have to," Amos replied. "Do whatever you have to do, but get him the goddamned immunity. Go to Robert Kennedy or Nicholas Katzenbach and get him that blanket immunity."

Agent Hogan glanced to Dr. Talbot, who simply nodded. "Larry, I wouldn't want to be responsible for what might happen because we couldn't come up with the immunity Mr. Brusconi is seeking."

By noon the following day the two agents and Amos were on their way to Long Island with the letter granting blanket transactional and testimonial immunity for a period of five years to Salvadore Brusconi. To Agent Hogan's surprise, Deputy Attorney General Katzenbach authorized the grant of immunity as soon as he and Dr. Talbot explained the circumstances and both the enormity and the immediacy of the threat. Agent Hogan drove into the Jamaica parking lot of East Bay Freight Forwarders as a Boeing 707 thundered overhead, ascending skyward from JFK. There were about twenty East Bay Freight Forwarding trucks lined up beyond the visitors' parking area. The building was newer and larger than Agent Hogan had imagined.

"You must be the people from Washington," the receptionist said as they entered the lobby area. "Mr. Brusconi has been expecting you. I'll let him know you're here."

"Welcome to East Bay Freight Forwarders," Salvatore Brusconi said as he stood to greet the three men. He was shorter than Hogan had imagined him to be—younger too—perhaps no more than forty. He was well-dressed, and, Agent Hogan noticed, his fingernails were freshly manicured.

"Your grant of immunity," Agent Hogan said, handing the document to the man.

"Would you mind giving it to my lawyer, Marty Hershman?"

The attorney, sitting on a couch against the wall behind them, rose to shake hands with the two FBI agents and Amos.

"Very pleased to meet you, gentlemen," the attorney said, extending his hand.

Agent Hogan decided he didn't like Marty Hershman as soon as the lawyer approached him. *Who wears a three-piece suit in Jamaica, New York, on a summer day?* The two men shook hands, and Hogan handed the man the grant of immunity. The lawyer walked back to the couch and sat down to read the document.

"Give the gentlemen the paperwork, Sal," Hershman said as soon as he finished reading the document from Justice.

The two FBI agents and Amos did not look at the shipping documents until they were back in the car. "Holy shit," Agent Atkins cried out. "Holy shit."

"What's the address?" Amos asked, anxiously. Hogan handed Amos the shipping papers. "Questex-Irvine Materials Handling, Potomac Center Office Plaza, suite 515, 1500 M Street Southeast, Washington, DC," Amos read the address aloud. "What the hell? Let's get to a pay phone. We have to talk to Noah."

"We should have him close down Potomac Center," Hogan answered.

"No, I wouldn't do that," Amos replied. "I think they're waiting for a significant occasion, perhaps the first anniversary of the opening of the center, which is tomorrow, or maybe July Fourth. In any event, if they have set the explosives, they're watching, and if they saw a mass exodus begin, they would immediately blow the center. The death and destruction would be catastrophic."

"What do you think we should do?"

"Let's contact Noah and see if the name Questex-Irvine Materials Testing means anything to him. Then I think we should have that dog trainer from the Metropolitan Police Department see if his dogs can detect any plastique anywhere in the Potomac Center Mall or in the office plaza."

They pulled into a diner on Jamaica Avenue, and Amos rushed inside to call Noah at his town house. The two FBI agents followed close behind.

"Noah, it's Amos calling from Jamaica, New York."

"What are you doing in Jamaica?" Noah asked.

"Never mind that right now. I have FBI agents Hogan and Atkins with me. We just met with a freight-forwarding company near JFK.

Noah, have you ever heard of a company called Questex-Irvine Materials Testing?"

"Sure, everyone knows Questex-Irvine. They're tenants in the office plaza at Potomac Center. Why? What's up?"

"How long have they been tenants, Noah?"

"They were one of the last tenants to sign a lease with us. That would have been last October, so they've been tenants for about eight months."

Amos closed his eyes, grimacing. Eight months corresponded precisely with the number of shipments East Bay Freight Forwarders had delivered to Questex-Irvine Materials Testing.

"Do you want me to run over to their office and check anything?" Noah asked.

"No. Don't do anything. Don't go there and don't call there. We're on our way back. We'll come to your place as soon as we return. We have some things to discuss."

"You sound worried. What's happened?"

"Noah, we'll talk as soon as we get back."

"Alexandra and I were going to go over to the mall for dinner. They're setting up for the opening anniversary celebration."

"When does the celebration begin?"

"Tonight at midnight. We're going to be open twenty-four hours a day for the next week."

"Wait for us at the town house. We'll get there as soon as possible."

"Amos, for Christ's sake, what's happening?"

"I can't talk from here. We'll see you in about five hours. Is Alexandra with you?"

"She's due here any minute."

"Stay there. Both of you stay there until we arrive," Amos said before hanging up.

Amos turned to the two FBI agents. "Questex-Irvine Materials Testing has been a tenant at Potomac Center Office Plaza for eight months. We never mentioned the Questex-Irvine connection to

Noah." It was the first time either of the FBI agents had ever detected fear in the Israeli's voice.

"There was no reason to, Amos. We all assumed Questex-Irvine Materials Testing was of no interest to us, and besides, we assumed they were in Walnut Creek with the rest of Q-I," Hogan answered.

"The first-anniversary celebration starts tomorrow. The mall is having a week of festivities and sales," Amos said.

"Amos, I have to call the director's office. This is much too big for us to be making decisions by ourselves."

"Of course. I understand, but I need to participate in that conversation. I know these people. My perspective will be important. See if we can meet with the bureau brass as soon as we get back to Washington. We don't know precisely when they plan to detonate, but if we make one wrong move and they think we're onto them, they'll blow Potomac Center in an instant. It's not just Potomac Center. We now know they have one hundred and forty kilos of plastique possibly ready to go off. The shock wave could even reach Capitol Hill. It's less than four miles away. We would have to evacuate the entire neighborhood, and we won't be able to do that without tipping off the terrorists."

"So what are we supposed to do?"

"We have to try to find where they've planted the plastique and disarm the device."

"Or devices," Agent Atkins interrupted.

"Larry, can you reach the dog guy at Metropolitan Police?"

"Yeah, Nick Garfield. He's the canine handler. I have his telephone number."

"Let's call and ask him if his dogs are ready. If they are, see if he can meet us at the Potomac Center Office Plaza tonight."

It was after six when they finally arrived at the Justice Department. Director Hoover had arranged for his trusted deputy Deke DeLoach to meet with the two agents and Amos. Hogan introduced Amos to the deputy director. It was his first encounter with a Mossad agent, and he studied Amos guardedly. Amos explained why the first priority should be finding and disarming the explosives. "If we try to evacuate Potomac Center, I believe they will detonate before anyone has any chance of getting a safe distance away. Potomac Center is remaining open twenty-four hours a day for the next week. It's scheduled to be one continuous celebratory sale. They're having entertainment and refreshments around the clock. There will be mobs of people there constantly. Trying to move them to safety will be more dangerous than trying to find the explosives."

"What is your best guess as to when they plan to detonate?" Deputy Director DeLoach asked.

"I think tomorrow is the target date. It's just a guess, but June fifth marks the first anniversary of the opening of Potomac Center, and it is also the one-year anniversary of the beginning of the Six-Day War. I also think July fourth could be the date, but if I had to guess, I'd say June fifth."

"So you're asking me to give you time to search for these explosives before they might be detonated in a crowded mall?"

"I think finding the explosives will be safer than trying to clear the mall," Amos answered.

"So, you think the explosives have already been placed?"

Amos nodded. "Again, it's only a guess, but every instinct tells me the explosives have, somehow, been put in place."

"How could they have done that without being noticed?"

"Well, workers have been preparing the mall for this week of celebration for several days now. They could have worked among the people doing the setup."

"How would you be able to disarm the explosives without being detected yourself?"

"We'll have to figure that out once we can physically see what we're dealing with." Amos replied.

"I'll call Aberdeen Proving Ground," the deputy director said. "Maybe we can arrange to have an army explosives specialist here by helicopter tonight. Aberdeen is only about fifty nautical miles away as the crow flies."

"I think we'll need someone who can remove a detonator from plastique," Amos said.

"What a nightmare…Twenty-four hours. You have twenty-four hours. Then we clear the entire area," Deputy Director DeLoach said, with absolute finality.

Amos rushed to Noah's Georgetown town house while the two FBI agents arranged to meet Nick Garfield and his Canine Corps partner "Trooper" at the Metropolitan Police Department's First Precinct. Trooper had been trained with crushed eighty-milligram tablets of Peritrate, the same medication Dr. Talbot used for his angina. Trooper could definitely detect Pfizer's crushed Peritrate. Whether the dog would be able to detect the same pentaerythritol tetranitrate packed into wads of plastique remained to be seen.

"So what's with all the intrigue about Questex-Irvine Materials Testing?" Noah asked, as soon as Amos walked into the town house.

"Yes, Amos. Why are you so concerned about them?" Alexandra asked.

"There's no such company," Amos answered.

"Amos, you're wrong. Questex-Irvine is known all over the world."

"Yes, but Questex-Irvine Materials Testing isn't."

"Amos, they're tenants of mine. They pay their rent like clockwork. I don't understand."

"Who signed the lease for them, Noah?"

"It was some lawyer. I don't recall his name. Why? What have they done?"

"They've taken delivery of one hundred and forty kilos of pentaerythritol tetranitrate at their Potomac Center office."

"What the hell is that?" Noah asked.

"Petn—plastique explosive, enough to reduce Potomac Center to a deep crater in the ground. Noah, Questex-Irvine Materials Testing is a front. There is no such company. The real Questex-Irvine engineering firm in Walnut Creek, California, has never heard of them."

"Oh my God, it's Omar Samir and the Shoukri Front," Alexandra cried.

"We think so, Alexandra," Amos replied.

"And you think they've planted this shit in Potomac Center?" Noah asked, incredulously.

"Yes, I do."

"Without anyone noticing? That's impossible."

"How many workers are on-site preparing for the weeklong first-anniversary celebration that begins tonight?" Amos asked.

Noah's jaw dropped as he considered his response. "I'm not sure. More than a hundred, I'd guess."

"So, do you really think you would notice if someone dressed like an electrician or a carpenter walked through the site with a toolbox filled with wads of plastique?"

"My God," Noah whispered. "What are you and your colleagues at the bureau going to do?"

"First, in about an hour, we're going to call on Questex-Irvine Materials Testing."

"Then what?"

"We don't know. We'll have to see what we find," Amos answered.

"I'm coming with you," Noah said.

"No, you're not, Noah. You would only be in the way. Please stay here with Alexandra. I'll call you as soon as we know something."

"I'm coming with you, Amos. It's my fucking mall, and it's me they're after. Besides, I know that mall like the back of my hand."

"I'm coming too, Amos," Alexandra insisted. "If Omar Samir is in the mall, I'm the only one who would recognize him."

"Do either of you realize how dangerous this could be?" Amos snapped.

"Let's go; we're wasting time," Noah said, walking past Amos toward the door.

CHAPTER FIFTY

Sam Muncile, the security director for Potomac Center, confirmed that the office plaza was empty for the weekend and that suite five fifteen was definitely dark. Amos met Agents Hogan and Atkins at the rear of the building. The bureau had also arranged for an ambulance from the Washington Hospital Center and two physicians, burn specialists, to meet them there as well. The ambulance was parked, inconspicuously, but close to the rear door. Officer Nick Garfield and his black Labrador retriever, Trooper, were waiting at the back of the building when they arrived. Sergeant Ray Cummings, an explosives specialist from Aberdeen, had arrived at National Airport by helicopter and was rushed to Potomac Center in an unmarked Metropolitan Police car.

"OK, here's what we're going to do," Hogan said to the men huddled at the rear door of the office plaza. "We know the building is empty, so we don't expect to run into anyone. We are here to determine if explosives are in suite five fifteen of this building or whether they have recently been in suite five fifteen. If we determine that the explosives are not here but that a vapor trail does exist, that means that the explosives are off-site being assembled or that they have already been assembled and are placed somewhere in Potomac Center. Officer Garfield and Trooper here will go in first. We'll follow behind them. If the dog picks up a vapor trail of pentaerythritol tetranitrate, which he's been trained to detect, he'll follow that trail to its source, perhaps a closet in suite five fifteen. Once Trooper thinks he's at the source, he'll simply sit down at that spot."

"Why don't we just turn Trooper loose in the mall and see where he goes?" one of the physicians asked.

"We assume the people we're after will be watching the mall closely once they have placed the explosives. If they see a dog and a handler searching the mall, we think they'll detonate on the spot. Right now, we believe they have no idea we're onto them."

"Let's get on with it," Agent Atkins said, and with that Sam Muncile pulled open the rear door to the Potomac Center Office Plaza.

Trooper charged into the building immediately, sniffing the floor as he moved. The dog looked back to see if Nick was there and began charging up the rear staircase as soon as he spotted his handler. Agents Hogan and Atkins, Amos, Noah, Alexandra, the two physicians, and the explosives specialist from Aberdeen followed closely behind.

Trooper charged up the stairs from the second-floor landing without pausing at the door to the corridor. "He's definitely onto something," Garfield yelled over his shoulder. The dog didn't pause at the third-floor landing and continued charging up the stairs, sniffing frantically as he ran. When they finally reached the top floor, Trooper was on his hind legs scratching at the door leading into the fifth-floor interior. Sam Muncile opened the door to the corridor, and Trooper rapidly sniffed his way past one office after another until he came to suite five fifteen, where he promptly sat down and waited for Nick Garfield and the others to catch up. Sam Muncile unlocked the door and turned on the lights to the suite. Trooper sprang to his feet and charged in. The dog ran through the small reception room and down a corridor to a double-door closet where, after sniffing at the bottom of the door, he again sat down with his back to the closet.

"That, gentlemen, is where the vapor trial takes us," Nick Garfield said. The men walked down the corridor to the closet door.

"Good boy, Trooper," Garfield said, stroking the dog while taking some cubes of food from his uniform pocket.

"Do you think the door might be booby-trapped?" Atkins asked.

"Your guess is as good as mine," Amos answered. "I'm opening the closet door," Amos volunteered. "If anyone wants to move away, this would be the time to do it." Everyone stood firm as Amos reached out and grasped the doorknob. He tightened his grip and slowly turned the handle. A light in the closet clicked on as Amos pulled the door open. Trooper charged into the closet and began barking frantically. The shelves were empty.

"It's pentaerythritol tetranitrate all right," Sergeant Cummings said as he looked into the empty closet.

"How can you be so sure?" Agent Hogan asked.

"No odor," the army explosives expert said. "None that we can detect anyway. If it were C-4, the place would smell like almonds. Petn is absolutely odorless to humans, but that dog—he smelled it all right. It's pentaerythritol tetranitrate, and that ain't good."

"We have to clear the mall," Agent Hogan said.

"Larry, I don't think we should do that," Amos replied.

"There are a few thousand people in there, Amos. How can we just keep quiet knowing they might be in mortal danger?"

"I'm telling you, I know these terrorists. If they think for a minute that we're evacuating the mall, they'll detonate."

"But maybe hundreds of people will get out first," Hogan argued.

"Do I understand that there might be one hundred and forty kilos of Petn planted throughout that mall?" Sergeant Cummings asked, interrupting the discussion between Amos and Agent Hogan.

"Yes, we have reason to believe that, during the last year, one hundred and forty kilos of plastique were delivered to this address...to this closet," Amos answered.

"Gentlemen, if it all blows at once, the odds are pretty good that no one will survive whether they are in the mall or in the parking lot running from the mall," the army explosives specialist said. "The roof will collapse, and everything in that mall, including every bit of construction material, every item of merchandise, every brick, and every shard of glass will become a projectile flying faster than the speed of sound. If anyone survived the shock wave, the collapsing roof and the flying fragments and debris would get them."

"Jesus Christ," Noah whispered as he took Alexandra's hand.

"This man is right," Sergeant Cummings said, pointing to Amos. "Our best bet is to try to find the explosive devices and disarm them."

"There's a million square feet of mall over there. How in the hell are we supposed to find a hundred and forty kilos of plastique spread throughout the place?" Agent Atkins asked.

"Not by standing here," Amos answered.

"Mike, call the bureau and ask the director's office or Deke's office to have every hospital in the area go on emergency disaster standby. Tell them to advise the hospitals that it's a drill but that the government takes it very seriously and that they will be graded on their readiness to act on short notice beginning midnight tonight," Agent Hogan said, taking command.

"Damn!" Army Specialist Cummings said as they entered the mall. "The place is mobbed. You'd think it's noon."

The mall was, indeed, pulsating with a deafening din. Music and chatter filled the air as hundreds of simultaneous conversations seemed to erupt as they walked through the doors. The cries of shoppers shouting out to one another, ambient laughter, and babies crying in the distance all comingled into an unintelligible roar. The aisles were crowded. People were walking in and out of stores, and lines had formed at the food court. Clowns on stilts made their way through the crowd, and jugglers entertained at the main intersections on each floor.

"It's the first night of the weeklong celebration of the first-year anniversary," Amos said. "Live music, free food, and everything on sale— it's a terrorist's dream."

"Where in the hell are we supposed to start looking?" Atkins asked. "Look at this place; it's huge. It's like standing downtown at the intersection of Twelfth and F Streets and looking in every direction trying to figure out where someone hid a small bomb. Don't you think we should get that explosive-sniffing dog in here? We're looking for a needle in a haystack without it."

"A cop with a dog is risky," Hogan said. "If the mall is being watched, that's probably exactly what the terrorists would be looking for."

"But maybe not a blind man with a Seeing Eye dog," Amos responded. "Look," he said, pointing to a kiosk where sunglasses were on display. Amos quickly turned to survey the stores nearby. "Larry, I'm going to buy a pair of sunglasses. See if you can get your hands on that Washington Senators windbreaker and baseball cap that mannequin is wearing," he said, pointing to the window display at the nearby Hecht's department store.

A short time later, a sunglasses-bespectacled Nick Garfield wearing the Washington Senators jacket and cap entered the mall tapping a five-foot-long white length of one-inch floor molding along the corridor in front of him as he walked holding on to Trooper's leash with his left hand. Amos, Ray Cummings, and the two FBI agents strolled inconspicuously behind. About halfway to the center of the mall, Trooper's behavior changed. He began pulling harder against the leash, and his tail began wagging higher and faster. The dog moved relentlessly past several of the vertical steel beams, weaved his way through the crowded aisles, and then, suddenly, stopped at the next steel column he came to, sniffed, and sat down with his back to the beam. They were about three-quarters of the way to the escalators at the center of the mall. A moment later Amos and Cummings and the two FBI agents caught up with Nick Garfield and Trooper. They walked to a rack of men's sport jackets adjacent to the steel beam at which Trooper had stopped.

"So what do you think?" Hogan asked, over his shoulder, to Nick, as he held up a sport jacket as though admiring it.

"It has to be the flower arrangements," Nick said, as he nonchalantly stooped to pet Trooper and slip him some treats. "Trooper stopped at this beam. Look, it has flower arrangements affixed about seven feet up from the floor. None of the other beams we passed have any flower arrangements hanging on them. It has to be the flower arrangements."

"Keep walking with Trooper, Nick," Hogan replied. "Circle back past one of the beams that doesn't have the flower arrangements and see if Trooper acts any differently. If he doesn't stop, go to the next aisle that has these steel beams and walk back toward the center of the mall and let's see if he stops at any other beam with flower arrangements hanging on it. We'll keep an eye on you."

Nick Garfield nodded, turned back toward the perimeter of the mall, and began following Trooper, tapping his makeshift cane as he moved along the aisle past one beam after another. He and Trooper made their way to the end of the aisle and then turned and walked parallel to the perimeter wall. They walked to the end of the south wall and turned along the west wall before coming to the next aisle along which steel support beams had been erected. Amos and the others stood breathlessly watching Nick make his way toward the center of the mall, past one beam after another. And then, just as he came to a beam with the same floral arrangements hanging on it, they saw him stop. They couldn't see Trooper, but they saw Nick bend down to give the dog another handful of treats.

"It's the fucking floral arrangements," Amos muttered to Noah. "Who put up those floral arrangements?"

"Chesapeake Floral put them up," Noah answered. "They're tenants. They asked me if it would be all right. They said they were thrilled to be part of Potomac Center and they wanted to contribute to the festivities."

"Where's their store?" Agent Hogan asked. "I'm guessing whoever planted the plastique somehow got them into Chesapeake Floral's baskets."

"They're the last retailer on the east side of the mall just before the service entrance. They're in one of the outlying aisles that feed into the center of the main floor."

"OK, let's go over to Chesapeake Floral," Hogan said. "Mike, you get Nick Garfield and Trooper and meet us there, and while you're at it, get an exact count on the beams with floral arrangements hanging on them."

"Let's spread out so that we're not so conspicuous moving through the mall. Noah, you and Alexandra lead the way," Amos said. "Just stroll over to Chesapeake Floral's store. We'll follow."

Noah knew something was wrong as soon as he and Alexandra turned into the long corridor on the east side of the mall. He saw that the Chesapeake Floral store at the very end of the aisle was dark. "They're closed," he said, as the rest of the group caught up to them.

"The place is empty," Ray Cummings observed as he peered into the storefront window. "It's absolutely bare."

"I don't understand this at all," Noah said. "Our tenants were asked to leave the lights on even if they couldn't be here. We specifically told all of our tenants that we didn't want any dark stores at night during the anniversary celebration."

"Who are these people?" Amos asked.

"Just a flower shop, Amos. They have a couple of locations over on the Eastern Shore, across the Chesapeake Bay Bridge. I liked the idea of a small local specialty store here. I can't understand why they're dark."

"Can they afford this kind of rent?"

"They paid a full year in advance when they signed the lease. I didn't give it any further thought."

"When was that?"

"It was nearly a year ago," he answered. Amos watched as Noah's jaw stiffened. "Oh shit," Noah whispered under his breath. "Amos, they signed their lease the same day Questex-Irvine Materials Testing signed. I remember because they were the last two leases we signed."

"Twenty-eight," Agent Atkins interrupted, as he, Nick Garfield, and Trooper approached the group. "Twenty-eight of the columns have flowers hanging on them."

"Bring Trooper over here by the door," Hogan called to Nick.

"He's picked up the vapors again," Nick replied. "He's straining at the leash."

"Let him go and let's see what he does," Amos said.

As soon as Nick released the leash, Trooper ran to the entrance of the empty Chesapeake Floral shop and began sniffing furiously at the edge of the door.

"I have a passkey to all the stores. Let's go in," Noah said.

Trooper moved quickly through the opened door and ran into the rear workroom used to assemble flower arrangements for customers. The black Labrador retriever jumped up so that his front paws were on the top edge of a long rectangular worktable as he sniffed the surface. Then he sat down with his back to the table.

"Good boy, Trooper. Good boy," Nick said, holding more treats in the palm of his hand. "Gentlemen, this is where they prepared their explosive devices," Trooper's handler said with absolute certainty.

"My God," Noah groaned. "They've run the entire operation right under our noses."

"Mike, you said there were twenty-eight beams with floral arrangements hanging on them. Is that right?" Amos asked, ignoring Noah's lament.

"Right. Twelve were in the center of the mall. They were hanging on six beams on each side of the escalators, and there were another sixteen beams, four on each of the main aisles running east and west and north and south away from the center."

"Ray, what would it take for pentaerythritol tetranitrate to cut through a steel beam the size of those holding up Potomac Center"?

The army explosives specialist considered Amos's question for a moment and shrugged. "I would say four, maybe five, kilos would do it," he answered.

"Oh my God," Agent Hogan murmured. "Five times twenty-eight equals one hundred and forty. Those flower arrangements contain all of the shit the freight forwarder delivered to Questex-Irvine Materials Handling during the past year."

"They know what they're doing," Ray Cummings said. "Nearly half of the Petn, sixty kilos, is hanging on those twelve beams, six on each side of the escalators right in the center of the mall. There are two baskets opposite each other on each beam. I'm guessing they have two and half kilos in each basket. That's five kilos on each beam. Mr. Greenspan, what's on the roof over those escalators?" Ray asked.

"Oh, Jesus...everything," Noah answered, his voice shaking. "Everything is up there. The air-conditioning compressors are on the roof over the escalators; the mechanical-system ductwork and fans are up there; cooling towers—everything. My God, there's tons of weight on the roof over those escalators."

"They blow out those twelve center beams, all of that weight will crash through. The beams on this floor are the only ones anchored into the ground. They collapse, and everything over them collapses. You'll have the weight of four floors plus the roof collapsing. That's probably enough to pull down the whole mall, but these bastards have another eighty kilos spread out on those other beams throughout the mall. This is unbelievable. If this blows, it's going to knock down a hell of a lot more than Potomac Center. The entire neighborhood around here is going to be severely damaged, if not destroyed."

"Ray, we have to know what we're dealing with. We have to see what's in those flower baskets hanging in the mall," Amos said.

"Well, we can't go back out into the center of the mall with a ladder and start climbing up to peek into one of those flower baskets," Atkins replied.

"Ray, have you ever walked on stilts?" Hogan asked.

"Yeah, when I was a kid," the explosives specialist answered. "What are you thinking?"

"I'm thinking we trade you for one of those clowns walking around the mall on stilts. You just walk around and peer down into those flower baskets as you pass by without stopping. Walk by enough of them until you get a clear picture of what they've got rigged up inside, but don't stop and stare into any of the baskets. Maybe we can figure out if there's any way of stopping this."

"I'm game," Ray replied. "It has to be a timer or a radio receiver of some kind. I'd bet it's a radio-receiving device. If we can determine exactly what kind of device they're using, we might be able to jam it without blowing up the place ourselves."

"OK, let's move," Agent Hogan said, taking charge. "Mike, pull one of those clowns off the floor. We'll need the stilts and any other clown garb he's wearing. Miss Salaman, would you please go over to the cosmetic department and find some kind of white face cream and bright-red lipstick for Sergeant Cummings?"

"Yeah, sure. I'll be back within ten minutes," she replied.

"No. I'll go," Noah said. "Alexandra, I want you out of here. Go back to my place and wait."

"Wait for what, Noah—for you to come home, or to hear that you're never coming home?"

"Alex—"

"No, Noah, I'm staying here with you. None of this would be happening but for my involvement years ago with Samir and Shoukri. As long as you're here, I'm staying here. There's no way I'm leaving Potomac Center as long as you're here. One way or another, we're spending the rest of our lives together." And with that, Alexandra turned and hurried into the mall.

Amos and Agent Hogan stood near the main door of the mall watching US Army explosives specialist Ray Cummings navigate on stilts, somewhat awkwardly, through the crowd. With his red and white polka-dotted smock, orange wig, bulbous red nosepiece, red lipstick, and white cold-cream-covered face, he looked pretty much like all of the other clowns wending through the crowd.

"Do you think he's slowing down too much when he passes those flower baskets?" Hogan asked.

"He's doing fine," Amos replied. "Every time he passes one of those beams with the flowers hanging on them, he's literally at the epicenter of what could be a catastrophe that could vaporize him in an instant. Where in the hell do we find men like that?"

"Yeah, I think my knees would shake me right off those stilts," Hogan answered.

It was just as they were about to leave the main floor of the mall and head back to the empty flower shop that another man standing near the center escalators caught Amos's attention. He, too, seemed transfixed on Ray Cummings's movements. Amos nudged Agent Hogan with his elbow. "That fellow standing opposite us—he's watching Ray very closely."

"Clowns wouldn't be clowns if people didn't watch them."

"I suppose, but there's something else about that fellow."

"What do you see?"

"He's from the Middle East."

"Are you sure?"

Amos nodded. "I'm sure. Egyptian, I would guess. Maybe Syrian."

"That's not much to go on," Agent Hogan replied.

"I know, but he's the only person watching Ray as closely as we are."

"Ray hasn't stopped to stare into any of those flower baskets. He's doing a great job."

"Let's see where he goes," Amos said, as Ahmed Hebraddi seemed to lose interest in Ray and headed to the entrance of the mall and directly toward them. They waited a moment or two after he passed and turned to follow him. Ahmed Hebraddi, who had been sent to Washington a few days earlier by Omar Samir to prepare the explosives, began walking through one of the many parking aisles toward the perimeter of the Potomac Center property. Amos and Agent Hogan followed at a distance of about thirty yards.

"I think he's our man, Larry," Amos said as they walked along behind Ahmed Hebraddi.

"Where in the hell do you think he's headed?"

"I guess to his car," Amos replied. "He's sure parked far from the mall. He's passed dozens of empty spaces."

"What the hell?" Hogan murmured as Ahmed Hebraddi walked off the property and across M Street.

Then they saw it: the white Chevrolet panel truck parked on the west side of the street. Hebraddi headed directly for the truck, pulled open the rear door, and climbed in.

"Holy shit, Amos. Look at the side panel of the truck," Agent Hogan said, grabbing Amos by the arm.

"Oh my God," Amos whispered. "Oh my God."

Emblazoned across the side panel of the truck over a painted rendering of the Chesapeake Bay Bridge were the words *Chesapeake Floral Designs*.

"What do you think we should do?" Agent Hogan asked.

"We can't do a damn thing until we know exactly what is in those fucking baskets," Amos replied. "All that bastard has to do is press a button if they're using detonators wired to radio receivers, and everything around us gets wiped out—including us."

"What if he drives away? I'll call and have a tail put on him."

"Our only chance of stopping whatever he's planning is to find a way to disarm whatever is in those baskets," Amos said. "And we can't do that until we know what the hell we're dealing with. Whatever we do, we can't alert whomever that is. All he has to do is press a goddamned button," Amos repeated.

"Come on, let's get back to the mall and see what Ray has discovered," Agent Hogan said. "I'll call for cars to keep that damned truck under surveillance."

They arrived back at the deserted flower shop just as Ray was making his way down the aisle from the center of the mall.

"Help me off these damn stilts," Ray said as soon as he reached the front of the shop. "Well, we've got one hell of a challenge on our hands, gentlemen," he said once they were all inside.

"Could you get a good look, Ray?" Noah asked, anxiously.

Ray nodded. "You're damn right I did. They've got a big wad of plastique—I'd say two, three, kilos—in each basket, and there are two baskets facing each other on opposite sides of each beam. That shit is pressed right up against the beam the basket is hanging on. That's five or six kilos on each beam."

"How are they going to set it off?" Amos asked.

"They've got a fucking Motorola Handie-Talkie wired to a blasting cap that's sticking right into the Petn. It's a Motorola HT-200. Those bastards bought a bunch of HT-200s and wired them to detonators. You can buy the damn things anywhere. I have a set at home. It's simple, but it'll do the job. Someone anywhere within two miles could bring this entire mall down. All he has to do is press the talk button on his unit, and his transmitting signal will go to the detonator wire instead of to the speaker in the receiving HT-200. They've just rewired the receiver wiring to the detonator instead of the receiver's speaker. They've got enough pentaerythritol tetranitrate in those twenty-eight flower baskets to make a mess of this entire neighborhood. Ain't nobody in or near this mall that's gonna walk away alive if they blow that plastique."

"What are our alternatives, Ray?" Agent Hogan asked, his voice somber.

"We have to find a way to jam the HT-200 frequencies and then cut the wires on those goddamned blasting caps and pull them from the plastique. That ain't easy 'cause those blasting caps can be dangerous as hell."

"How dangerous?" Noah asked.

"Well, it wouldn't take much to set one off. If that HT-200 transmitting signal somehow reached the wiring in the blasting cap while you were still holding it, it would detonate, and it could kill you, and it sure as hell would take off your hand and maybe your arm. I wouldn't want to drop one either. They ain't nearly as stable as C-4 or Petn."

"Walkie-fucking-talkies. Is that what I'm hearing?" Agent Atkins asked, incredulously. "Are you tell us that if someone out there pushes the transmitting button on a walkie-talkie—"

"We'd definitely be dead," Ray Cummings interrupted. "And so would everyone in that mall."

"Holy shit," Agent Atkins muttered under his breath. "Dear Mary, mother of Jesus," he moaned.

"Ray, what are our options?" Agent Hogan asked.

"Is there a RadioShack in the mall?" he answered.

"As a matter of fact, there is," Noah replied. "What can they do?"

"Well, for one thing, they can probably tell us what frequencies the Motorola HT-200s broadcast at. I could guess, but I'm not sure. They may or may not sell Motorola Handie-Talkies, but they'll know the frequencies even if they don't sell them."

"And then what do we do with that information?" Agent Atkins asked.

"We have to find a way to jam those HT-200s. How much time do you think we have?" Ray asked.

There was silence. "Amos, any thoughts? You know these people better than anyone," Agent Hogan answered.

"Not better than anyone," Amos answered. "Alexandra, what do you think?"

Alexandra glanced at her watch. "About an hour, I would guess," she replied, her voice shaking.

"What!" Agent Atkins cried out. "How in the hell did you come up with that?"

"She's probably right," Amos interrupted, nodding his agreement. "We attacked the Arabs at precisely seven forty-five in the morning exactly one year ago. It's eleven forty-five here in Washington. That's six forty-five in the morning in Israel and Egypt. If I had to pick a time these people planned to strike, I would say seven forty-five in the morning, Middle East time, which is an hour from now."

"My God, what in the hell can we do in an hour?" Noah asked.

"Ray, if you have any idea how to stop this, now is decision time," Hogan said.

"We can try to get our hands on a multifrequency jammer," Ray answered, unconvincingly.

"We have no time for that," Amos snapped, impatiently. "We have to get to three Washington radio stations right away and turn each of them into a frequency-jamming machine until we can disable those blasting caps."

"That would work," Ray agreed. "We would have to get each station to broadcast at very high amplitude at each of the three frequencies the HT-200 uses. The HTs have three channels, or three frequency ranges. If we could get three stations transmitting, each at one of these three frequencies, with a really powerful signal, we could jam all three channels."

"We don't have time to go to three stations. We'll have to call and convince them to cooperate," Hogan said.

"How in the hell are we going to do that on the phone?" Noah asked. "They'll think it's a prank."

"We have an hour to convince them otherwise," Amos replied.

"I'll try to reach Deke Deloach and see if he can get the president to make the call," Hogan said. "That's our only chance. We can try to have the White House reach the owners of the stations."

"That will take forever. I think there's a better way," Alexandra said. "The *Evening Star* owns WMAL here in Washington. We can try to get the *Star* to call WMAL and WTOP, and, I think, WAMU over at American University would be eager to cooperate. I can reach Frank Markazie right away. It would take hours to get the president involved. I'll tell Frank to tell the stations that it's a national emergency and that he's been asked to call the stations by the FBI. I'll put you on the line if he needs confirmation from the FBI," she said, looking to Agent Hogan.

"Well, declaring a national emergency is a bit over my pay grade, but what the hell?" Hogan answered.

CHAPTER
FIFTY-ONE

It took only a few minutes to obtain the frequencies for the HT-200s from the RadioShack general manager, and moments later Alexandra was dialing Frank Markazie at home.

"Markazie," Frank answered a bit irritably, having just fallen asleep.

"Frank, it's Alexandra. We have an emergency on our hands."

Markazie knew if Alexandra was calling at midnight about an emergency, it had to be serious. "You OK, kid?" he asked, as he swung his legs over the side of the bed and sat up.

"I am for the moment," she replied. "Listen carefully, Frank. Explosives are planted throughout the Potomac Center Mall, and we think they're going to be detonated in less than an hour. There are at least a thousand people in the mall for the all-night first-anniversary celebration, and an army explosives expert who is with us from Aberdeen Proving Ground say's he doubts anyone will survive if this stuff goes off."

"Jesus Christ, girl, what are you doing—calling in a story?"

"Listen, Frank. We have to get at least three radio stations to jam certain radio frequencies. Call WMAL first, then maybe WTOP, and then WAMU and get them to cooperate. Call every damn radio station in the area if you have to. It's the only way to stop this catastrophe from happening."

"How the hell am I supposed to do that, Alexandra?"

"Damn it, Frank, the *Star* owns WMAL. You have to call the station and get them to immediately broadcast at very high wattage on a specific frequency that I'll give you. Then you have to get WTOP and WAMU to do the same thing on separate frequencies that I have for you."

"You been drinking, kid?"

"Frank, this is no joke. You have to do this right away. If WTOP and WAMU both are told that WMAL is broadcasting a jamming signal to stop a national catastrophe, they'll cooperate too."

"Alexandra, can you get anyone from the government to OK this? I'm going to do it, but I'd be a lot more comfortable if I could say I was asked by the government to do this."

"Hold on, Frank, I have the FBI here with me," she answered, handing the phone to Agent Hogan.

"Mr. Markazie. This is Agent Lawrence Hogan of the Federal Bureau of Investigation. What Miss Salaman just told you is true. I'm here at the direction of deputy director of the bureau Deke Deloach. Please do what Miss Salaman has asked and please do it immediately. We have no time to waste."

"Deke Deloach knows about this? I know Deke."

"Yes, he does know about this. We are here at the deputy director's direction," Agent Hogan replied.

"Why haven't you cleared the mall?"

"We know they are watching the mall. If we start to evacuate the mall, they'll detonate. We're certain of that. Our only chance is to jam their transmission so that we can disable the detonators. We know what frequencies they have available. We can stop them, but we have to act immediately."

"Let me talk to Alexandra again."

"Yeah, Frank," she said, taking the phone from Agent Hogan.

"I'm on it, kid."

"Frank, here are the frequencies. Ask each station to take responsibility for jamming the frequency you designate. Emphasize that it's a national emergency."

"OK, I have a pen and paper. Shoot."

"Tell WMAL to broadcast between one hundred thirty-six and one hundred fifty point eight megahertz at full wattage. Tell WTOP to broadcast between one hundred fifty point eight and one hundred sixty-two megahertz and tell WAMU to broadcast between one hundred sixty-two and one hundred seventy-four megahertz. Tell them all to crank up the wattage, Frank. That should jam all three of the frequencies that the terrorists have available to them."

"How much time do we have?"

"We think they're planning to detonate at twelve forty-five, in about forty minutes. You have that much time to get all three stations to jam those frequencies, Frank. As soon as we're spotted disarming those detonators, the terrorists are going to start transmitting on one of those frequencies. They all have to be jammed, Frank, or a lot of Americans are going to die—including me."

"Why don't you get out of there right now?"

"Noah's not leaving, and I'm not leaving either."

"We'll stay here for the next half hour," Hogan said. "Let's give Mr. Markazie as much time as we can. We have cars watching the Chesapeake florists' truck. As soon as we know the frequencies are jammed, we'll grab whoever is camped out in that truck."

"What are you talking about?" Noah asked.

"Agent Hogan and I followed someone who was watching Ray very carefully while Ray was out there on stilts trying to determine what was in the hanging baskets. I'm certain this guy was from the Middle East—Egypt, I would guess. Anyway, we followed him. He's parked just off the property across M Street. He climbed into the back of a Chesapeake Floral panel truck. We're pretty sure that's where they're planning to transmit a signal from their HT-200."

"Alexandra, you should leave," Noah said. "There's no reason for you to be here."

"But there is, Noah. You're here."

***

Frank Markazie called WMAL first, as Alexandra suggested. She was right. If he could tell WTOP and WAMU that the *Star*'s station had already started jamming, the others might be more inclined to cooperate.

"WMAL," a man's voice answered.

"Let me speak to whoever's in charge. This is an emergency," Markazie barked, authoritatively.

"Who is this?" the voice asked.

"This is Frank Markazie, managing editor of the *Evening Star*. I need to speak to whoever is in charge right away. It's an emergency."

"Well, I guess that would be me at this hour."

"What is your name?"

"Phil Ricktor. I'm the night engineer."

"Thank goodness. Phil, we need to begin broadcasting at between one hundred thirty-six and one hundred fifty point eight megahertz with all the amplitude we've got."

"No fucking way I'm gonna to that. Who did you say you are?"

"I'm Frank Markazie, managing editor of the *Evening Star*. We own WMAL, and I'm telling you to begin transmitting between one hundred thirty-six and one hundred fifty point eight megahertz, and do it now and do it with a lot of extra wattage. Phil, we have to jam that frequency because a walkie-talkie that uses that frequency is wired to a bomb that's going to be set off in a matter of minutes."

"You'll have to call Andy Ockershausen. He's the general manager."

"Goddammit, Phil, I know who the general manager is. I go to the Senators' games with Andy every week. I don't have time to track down Andy. Thousands of people are going to die if you don't do as I tell you. This is a national emergency. I just spoke to the FBI, and we have to do this right away. I have two other stations I have to call in the next few minutes."

"Why you gotta call other stations?"

"Because the Motorola HT-200 has three frequencies it can transmit on, and we don't know which frequency these bastards are going to use."

"Yeah, I got a Handie-Talkie myself. You're right: one hundred thirty-six to one hundred fifty point eight is one of the frequency ranges. But I don't know. This could cost me my job it you ain't who you say you are."

"Listen to me carefully, Phil. If I'm not who I say I am, you could lose your job. But I *am* who I say I am, and if you don't do this, you sure as hell are going to lose your job, and over one thousand people are going to lose their lives. We believe they are going to transmit that signal in fifteen minutes. I have two other stations to call. We're wasting time. If I'm a prankster, you could lose your job. If I'm not, this city is going to experience the worst disaster in the history of the United States."

"Mr. Markazie, are you listed in the phone book?"

"Yes, what the hell difference does that make?"

"I'm looking up your number right now," the engineer replied. "I'll call you back in less than a minute. If you answer the phone, I'll do what you're asking. If you don't answer, you're one sick fuck," he said, slamming down the phone.

Phil Ricktor found Markazie's telephone number and nervously began dialing.

"Markazie here!" Frank answered. "Jam that goddamned frequency, Phil, and do it fast."

At 12:40 that morning, Noah turned Chesapeake Floral's Emerson radio to WMAL at 630 on the dial. Everyone gathered around to hear whether or not Frank Markazie had been successful.

"Oh shit," Ray Cummings said, as the mellow voice of WMAL's popular overnight host, Bill Mayhugh, came through loud and clear. "They're still broadcasting. This whole mall, all those people out there—everything—it's all going to blow any minute."

"Come on, Frank!" Alexandra pleaded out loud. Noah gently pulled her into his arms.

"I love you, Alexandra," he said softly. Agents Hogan and Atkins looked at Amos, who simply shook his head.

"We came so close," he whispered.

WMAL all-night disc jockey Bill Mayhugh, oblivious to the drama unfolding around him, continued his broadcast, reciting his favorite sonnet as he did every night, "The Potomac in the twilight is a river turned to flame, and the smell of cherry blossoms is like nothing you could name! That's why—" At that instant the broadcast was abruptly terminated, and nothing but static poured from the Emerson's speaker.

Alexandra brought her hands to her face. "Oh my God, Frank did it." Static filled the room when Noah, his hand shaking, tuned the dial to the remaining two stations. All three stations had abandoned their programming to blast high-amplitude signals into the frequencies as Markazie had instructed. Almost simultaneously, FBI agents and Metropolitan Police swarmed around the panel truck parked across from Potomac Center and overwhelmed Ahmed Hebraddi.

"Markazie came through for us," Mike Atkins cried out, excitedly.

"Alexandra came through for us," Amos replied. "Alexandra, you just saved over a thousand lives and headed off what would have been one of the biggest disasters in American history."

"I shudder to think what would have happened if we had pursued my idea of trying to reach the president," Agent Hogan said.

"Let's get on with cutting those detonator wires," Ray interrupted. "Who knows how long those radio stations will keep broadcasting at those frequencies. Somebody find a scale. Let's make sure those flower baskets are holding all one hundred and forty kilos of plastique that were shipped to Potomac Center."

Ray Cummings and the two FBI agents hurried from the floral shop. Amos lingered a moment before following them.

"You're amazing, Alexandra. You knew exactly what had the best chance of working. Anything else would have been a disaster," he said, as he turned to follow them. Alexandra tried to smile through her tears. She couldn't speak. She was shaking and just nodded. Noah took her into his arms. They were now alone in the deserted floral shop. Neither of them spoke for several moments. She laid her head on his shoulder as he affectionately brushed a kiss across her temple.

"They came so close to succeeding," she whispered.

"But they didn't, Alexandra. We…you succeeded."

"They came so close," she murmured. "This entire place, all of those people out there, us—it all almost came to such a violent end."

"But it didn't. It's over, Alexandra," he answered in a whisper.

"I don't think it will ever be over, Noah," she said, lifting her head from his shoulder as she looked into his eyes.

"Maybe not," he replied. "But you and I will never be over, either, Alexandra. We've survived it all, and you know what?" he said. "I love you more every day. When I think my love for you couldn't get any stronger, I'm proven wrong—every day."

"Ever the poet," she whispered, reaching up to kiss him.

They walked out into the mall, which had been cleared of shoppers. They had heard over the Potomac Center public address system that a fire alarm had malfunctioned and that a city-mandated fire drill had been ordered. Most of the shoppers patiently waited out in the parking lot while Ray Cummings methodically disarmed and removed the detonators and the plastique from the flower baskets hanging on the twenty-eight steel beams. Sure enough, the baskets contained precisely one hundred and forty kilos of pentaerythritol tetranitrate—all of the Petn that had been shipped from Czechoslovakia.

By two o'clock in the morning, the mall was reopened, and people began returning to the all-night celebration. Music filled the mall once again, and bargain hunters were soon clogging the aisles, meandering from store to store. Even the food court was busy providing free coffee and donuts.

CHAPTER
FIFTY-TWO

Noah and Alexandra slowly strolled, hand in hand, around the perimeter of the second level, stopping from time to time to look down at the shoppers scurrying about on the first floor. Life, once again, seemed full of promise. She laid her head against his shoulder as they walked along. He squeezed her hand affectionately as they stopped at the rail to look down.

"You would never guess it's almost three o'clock in the morning," he observed. "It must be the coffee we're dispensing down there."

"They have no idea how close they came to making the history books," she said, shaking her head.

And then, shortly after three o'clock that morning, the festiveness at the mall came to an abrupt end. They heard someone scream on the floor below. The music trailed off, and the shoppers suddenly stopped moving in the aisles below and started coalescing in small groups. One of the security guards spotted Noah and Alexandra at the rail looking down from the second level and waved frantically to get their attention.

"What's happened?" Noah yelled down to the guard.

"It's Senator Kennedy," the guard shouted. "He's been shot in Los Angeles."

"Oh my God," Alexandra cried. "Oh my God."

"It had to be some racist," Noah said, the murder of Martin Luther King, exactly two months earlier, still fresh in his mind. "Some of these people will never stop fighting the civil war."

"Let's run over to the *Star*," she replied. "Frank Markazie is probably already on his way there. We can see what all the news services are reporting, and I want to see whom he'll have covering this." As they hurried toward the main entrance of the mall, they stopped where a small group had gathered around a television set at the entrance to the RadioShack store. A CBS correspondent, Andrew West, was reporting from the banquet kitchen of the Ambassador Hotel in Los Angeles where the shooting had occurred a short time earlier. Everyone was watching and listening to the broadcast, not believing, grief-stricken. After a short pause, they continued on their way in silence.

Noah turned on the car radio as they pulled out of the Potomac Center garage to drive the short distance to the *Evening Star*. News of the shooting dominated every station. Noah reached to turn off the radio as they pulled into a parking space in front of the newspaper's Virginia Avenue headquarters. Then, they both sat there stunned as they listened to the report that Robert Kennedy had been shot by someone named Sirhan Sirhan, a Palestinian.

"Oh no," Alexandra cried. "No, no, no."

He pulled Alexandra into his arms to console her. "The world seems upside down," he said, embracing her. "John Kennedy, then Martin Luther King, and now this. When, in God's name, is it going to end?"

"It doesn't end," she whispered. "It never ends."

Nearly everyone in the newsroom was gathered around several television sets and wire-service Teletype machines. Most of the networks were repeating, over and over again, footage from the Ambassador Hotel's kitchen where Senator Kennedy had been shot less than an hour earlier. Noah and Alexandra lingered a moment behind a cluster of *Star* staff members watching the news on an RCA twenty-one-inch color television set that had been placed on one of the newsroom desks.

"Hi, Alexandra," one of the staffers said, looking back over his shoulder. "He's still alive. The ambulance just arrived at a hospital in

LA, but someone said they'll have to move him to another hospital that's better equipped to do brain surgery. It sounds pretty bad."

"Any more information about the man who shot him?" she asked.

"Some fucking Palestinian Arab," someone in the group answered. "That's all they know." Nausea swept through her body as the man's words sank in.

"Come on," Noah said, gently coaxing her away from the cluster of *Star* employees. "Let's find Markazie."

"Quite a night," Markazie said as they entered his office. "I rushed over here after I called the radio stations about jamming those frequencies, and now this horror in Los Angeles right on top of the near miss at Potomac Center."

"The country would have been learning about two disasters tonight if you hadn't gotten those radio stations to jam those signals, Frank," Noah said.

"You OK?" Markazie said, looking to Alexandra. "You look like hell."

"I feel like hell," she answered. "The close call at Potomac Center and now Robert Kennedy shot down in cold blood. This entire night has been a nightmare."

"It's been a horrible year," Markazie answered. "The war in the Middle East last year, Vietnam, the King assassination, all the riots in our cities, and now Senator Kennedy fighting for his life. It's like Toynbee said: history is just one goddamned thing after another."

"Do we know anything at all about the shooter?" Noah asked.

"I've got a couple of freelancers working on it in Los Angeles. All we know so far is that he was born in Jerusalem and immigrated here with his family when he was just a kid, around twelve years old. He comes from a Palestinian Christian family, and he went to high school and took some college credits in Pasadena. That's about it," Markazie said.

"He was a Palestinian Christian?" Noah asked, surprised.

"According to my freelancers I've got digging out there, yes, he comes from a Palestinian Christian family."

"Oh God," Alexandra whispered to herself, as she lowered her head into her hand.

"Strange name," Noah said. "Sirhan Sirhan."

"Not so strange," Alexandra replied, lifting her eyes to his. "*Sirhan*—it means *wolf* in Arabic. My God, could we have picked a worse week to be getting married?"

"Do you want to postpone the wedding?" Noah asked, anxiously.

"Why would you do that?" Markazie asked, before Alexandra could answer.

"Frank, it sounds like Senator Kennedy might not make it," Alexandra answered. "Sunday is not likely to be a very happy day, and maybe not the best day for a Palestinian girl to be marrying a prominent Jewish guy."

"Bullshit!" Markazie responded swiftly, a sharp edge to his voice. "Alexandra, if Senator Kennedy dies, do you know what we Catholics will do? We'll celebrate his life. And that's the way it should be. You and Noah—you two are something worth celebrating too—a faint spark, a tiny light in a very dark world and in a very dark time. You know what, Alexandra? If you let the reality of human suffering stop you, then there is no great time to get married. Awful—I mean just plain awful things are happening every day on every continent somewhere on this crazy planet. That's just the way it is. It's the way it's always been. But the world also needs good and hopeful things to happen, Alexandra. You and Noah getting married—that's good, and it's something to be hopeful about. You and Noah remind us that love also exists in a world that seems addicted to hate. Alexandra, you've seen our presses here. We run miles of newsprint through that web press every day at lightning speed, reporting one damn thing after another, and a lot of it is really bad news. You can stop the presses, but you can't stop the shit that becomes news. And you can defer your wedding, but every bad thing that is going to happen is going to happen anyway. Life goes on, Alexandra. It doesn't miss a beat. You shouldn't either."

"The killing. It never stops. It just never stops," she lamented.

"Of course it never stops," Markazie yelled impatiently, his voice booming. "For Christ's sake, Alexandra. Strife, deadly strife, has been humankind's enduring constant. But it's not life's only constant. People like you and Noah here—you're humankind's constant too. Without men and women like the two of you, there would be no hope. You two represent light over darkness, good over evil, hope over despair."

Alexandra managed a faint smile. "Thank you, Frank," she answered. She looked to Noah, who hadn't taken his eyes off of her from the moment Frank Markazie had begun talking. He smiled and nodded.

"So, Frank, whom are you going to have cover today's major news?" she asked after a long pause.

"I might write the news myself tonight, Alexandra. My best journalist is on wedding leave."

Alexandra managed a smile, and as she and Noah turned to leave Markazie's office, she paused a moment and then walked over to the editor and hugged him. "See you at the wedding," she said, reaching up to kiss him on the cheek.

"You bet, kid," he answered.

It was after four in the morning when Noah and Alexandra finally left the *Evening Star* that night. As they made their way through the newsroom, Noah draped his arm, affectionately, over Alexandra's shoulder as she leaned into him, her arm around his waist. They could hear and feel the muted roar and the intense vibration of the *Star*'s presses, now racing at sixty thousand copies an hour to print the morning edition. They walked into the cool summer air as the city awaited dawn. The Capitol, only a few blocks to the north, was brightly illuminated in stark contrast to the dark night. Noah and Alexandra drove west, along an eerily deserted Independence Avenue. Soon the sun would rise in Washington—exactly one year to the day since Dassault Mirage fighters and Super Mystères piloted by young Israeli airmen lifted off six thousand miles to the east flying low over the Mediterranean.

EPILOGUE

"Good evening, everyone," Judge Maurice Golden announced, welcoming the small gathering. The room grew still. Sharif and Samira Salaman stood directly behind Alexandra—and the Greenspans a step or two behind Noah. Yusuf was standing there too, off to the side nearest Noah, and Daoud stood off to the side closest to Alexandra. Close colleagues from the *Evening Star* and Potomac Center were seated in three rows that formed a semicircle around the small wedding party. Frank Markazie arrived a few minutes early and was seated at the center of the first row. Amos and Karen were seated on one side of him and Ed Scallion and Stan Sherman on the other. Everyone's attention was riveted to Judge Golden. "We're gathered here in this extraordinary place at an extraordinary time to witness and, in fact, to participate in the marriage of Noah Greenspan and Alexandra Salaman.

"Noah and Alexandra considered postponing their marriage because of the tragedy that took place in Los Angeles. It is hard to balance tragedy with joy. Yet it is important that we do—that we go on with life, that light supersedes dark, that positive conquers negative, that joy overcomes grief, and that love triumphs over hate.

"You know, this is a very special occasion for everyone here. For Noah and Alexandra—of course. For their families, friends, and colleagues—most definitely. And for me, it is a humbling honor. You see, nearly every marriage at which I have officiated has involved relatives of mine, or friends of relatives, and a few fine young men and women who have clerked for me or other federal judges with whom

I serve. Now, neither Noah nor Alexandra are relatives of mine—at least as far as I know. And they are not friends of any of my relatives, and neither Noah nor Alexandra has ever clerked for me or any of my fellow judges on the federal bench.

"Actually, I have never officiated at a wedding outside of Pennsylvania until tonight. So why this wedding? Why Noah and Alexandra? Well, I'll tell you why. Because, for me, it is a privilege. These two young people inspire me, as, indeed, they should inspire us all. They personify, to me, the enormous potential of our common humanity.

"I first met Noah around three years ago. Believe it or not, he was a defendant in my court. Don't worry; it was a civil case. Well, we met again this past spring. And you guessed it. He was a defendant again.

"It's a rather interesting way to meet someone. What I saw before me then, and what I see before me now, is, maybe, the most principled man I had, or have, ever met. I'm honored to be officiating this evening at his marriage to Alexandra.

"And, Alexandra, I feel I have known you for years because I have read almost everything you have written as a journalist. You are the personification of wisdom. You are a very special soul, Alexandra. You give meaning to Proverbs chapter three, verse fifteen. You are, indeed, more precious than rubies.

"You know, by all odds, Noah and Alexandra shouldn't be standing here in front of me this evening being joined in matrimony. History sadly suggests that they typically would be facing one another in acrimony—not matrimony.

"Alexandra is from a fine and warm Arab Palestinian family. Her parents, Sharif and Samira, whom I met only this afternoon, came to America twenty years ago with their two children, Alexandra and her brother, Yusuf. They were refugees from a conflict that seems to have had no beginning and seems to have no end. They became corner grocers here in Washington, DC. And who were their competitors? None other than Hy and Esther Greenspan, Noah's parents—two families facing off across both a competitive and a cultural divide.

"And when they finally met, it seemed as though a gear shifted somewhere in the universe that enabled these families to see all that could bring them together, rather than all that could tear them apart. Yusuf and Noah became the best of boyhood friends—a friendship that has remained strong and unshakable ever since. The Salamans and the Greenspans became close friends too, and they became business partners, building a highly successful chain of convenience stores they named, quite aptly, Milk and Honey. Yusuf and Noah became partners, of sorts, as well. Yusuf is the architect who designed Potomac Center, where we are all gathered this evening, and Noah built Potomac Center.

"Noah and Alexandra met at elementary school when they were kids. They tell me they fell in love with one another nearly twenty years ago. They really were just kids.

"I asked Noah what impressed him most about Alexandra when they first met. He told me it was her beautiful green eyes. Well, Noah, I'll let you in on a little secret. That's what impressed me too, when I first met Alexandra when she accompanied you to my chambers last March. Her eyes reminded me of jade, Noah, and that left a huge impression on me. Let me tell you why. You see, I collect jade. And when I looked into your bride-to-be's beautiful green eyes, I was immediately reminded of why I collect jade. Jade is believed to promote healing, stability, and relief from the anxiety of fear. It is said that jade protects people from negative influences and promotes a calming aura and a strong intellect. Call me a sentimentalist, but you know, that describes Alexandra perfectly.

"As I said, I've read Alexandra's work—everything from her first column, 'Heirs of Eden,' which she wrote when she was just an intern at the *Evening Star*, to all of her incredible reporting from the Middle East last year.

"Yes, they were just kids—kids who were determined to overcome every obstacle their respective cultures imposed and who, as adults, stand before us as testament to what can be when we are guided by reason and devotion to principle and by love.

"I have never agreed to officiate at a marriage when I have had real doubts about the durability of a proposed union. Marriage is, after all, a very early step in what is supposed to be a very long journey. Strong and happy, long-lasting marriages do not always come easily.

"Last year, 1967, there were one million nine hundred and twenty-seven thousand marriages in the United States, and the Bureau of Vital Statistics has informed me that this year we can expect about two million and seventy thousand marriages. Now, that's something to celebrate.

"Unfortunately, there were also five hundred and twenty-three thousand divorces in America last year, and we are expecting nearly six hundred thousand divorces this year in our country.

"I have performed many marriages during my service as a federal judge. As far as I know, most have endured and stood the test of time. I, however, take no credit for that. Every time I perform a marriage though, I wonder where the couple will be five, ten, fifteen, twenty years later. But I'm pretty certain about you, Noah, and you, Alexandra. Your continued love and devotion to one another will, I believe, long endure. It has inspired us all and it demonstrates what can be—and what should be. Love is, indeed, very powerful. Victor Hugo was so right. To love another person is to see the face of God."

Alexandra looked into Noah's eyes and smiled. He nodded ever so slightly.

"You know, you accomplished most of what it takes to be married when you obtained your marriage license here in the District of Columbia," Judge Golden continued. "I only need to ask you both a couple of questions in order to pronounce you husband and wife. But first, does Noah's best man have the groom's ring?"

"I do, Your Honor," Yusuf answered, handing a ring to Judge Golden.

"And does the man Alexandra described to me as her guardian angel have the bride's ring?"

"Yes, sir, Your Honor. I have the bride's ring," Daoud answered, handing the ring to Judge Golden.

"And, Daoud, would you share with our guests what you shared with me about this ring?"

"Yes, sir, Your Honor. This the ring I give to my dear Cena thirty years ago. She no longer here, but she be very, very happy knowing Miss Alexandra wearing her ring."

"And you carried this ring to the Sudanese-Ethiopian border to use it, if necessary, to barter your way into Ethiopia so that you could call for help to free Alexandra, who was being illegally imprisoned in Sudan."

"Yes, I give everything I have, if necessary, to free Miss Alexandra, he said handing Cena's ring to Judge Golden.

"Oh, Daoud," Alexandra whispered, tearfully.

"Alexandra, are you free to marry Noah, and do you wish to marry Noah Greenspan?"

"I am, and I do," Alexandra answered, her eyes glistening with tears.

"Then you may place the groom's ring on the ring finger of Noah's left hand," Judge Golden said, handing her one of the rings.

"And, Noah, are you free to marry Alexandra, and do you wish to marry Alexandra Salaman?"

"Oh God, do I ever," he answered.

"Then you may place this most special ring that Daoud brought with him from Sudan on the ring finger of Alexandra's left hand."

Noah and Alexandra looked into one another's eyes. She silently mouthed, "I love you."

"Now, while this is a civil wedding, there is a Jewish tradition that the groom shatter a glass at the very conclusion of the wedding ceremony," Judge Golden continued. "I'm going to place this wineglass, which as you can see is wrapped in tinfoil, on the floor in front of Noah. While there are endless explanations of how this custom came into being, the truth is that no one really knows why, or precisely when, or, with any certainty, what it symbolizes. While many believe it is to remind us of the destruction of the sacred Temple of Jerusalem, it actually really means whatever the bride and groom want it to mean. Some say it is a reminder of the fragile nature of life. It can symbolize the shattering of the old and the beginning of the new. It can mean letting go of the past while looking toward the future. Since this is a marriage ceremony that brings together two wonderful people from very different backgrounds, we are especially mindful of the barriers that peoples so often erect between one another. Yet, standing here together as participants in this wedding ceremony are truly extraordinary people from all three Abrahamic religions—Noah's family, Alexandra's family and Daoud, who risked his life to free Alexandra. I know that nothing would be more meaningful to Noah and Alexandra than for the breaking of this glass to symbolize the breaking down of barriers and the emergence of a world based on love, unity, peace, and understanding. May it be!"

And with that, Noah stamped his foot down, loudly shattering the glass.

"By the power vested in me by the United States of America, I now pronounce Noah and Alexandra husband and wife. You may kiss the—well, you've jumped the gun," Judge Golden said, as Noah pulled Alexandra into his embrace, practically pulling her off her feet as he kissed her.

At that moment Amos squeezed Karen's hand. "Judge Golden can marry me anytime," he said, looking into her eyes.

"Me too," she replied, squeezing his hand in return. "Anytime, Amos."

The End

59277185R00301

Made in the USA
Charleston, SC
31 July 2016